PRAISE FOR *ISN'T IT NICE WE BOTH*

'Moving, funny and original, this is both a character-driven comedy about who gets what after a couple splits – not just the assets, but the people – and a deep study of loneliness, grief and growth.'
—**Clare Fletcher**

'Relatable, witty and full of heart.'
—**Bridget Hustwaite**

'Heart-wrenching and beautifully observed, *Isn't It Nice We Both Hate the Same Things* is for anyone who's ever felt left behind while everyone else is surging ahead. Jessica Seaborn captures the disorientating loneliness and gritty hope of life after marriage with aching honesty and razor-sharp wit.'
—**Natalie Murray**

'A ridiculously relatable story of thirty-something friendship – fresh, funny and full of heart.'
—**Amy Lovat**

'An honest and heartfelt novel about the importance of surrounding yourself with people who bring out the best in you.'
—**Michelle Upton**

'A novel that explores the chaos, sadness and gravity of the most untold love story – friendship breakups – with laughter, empathy and a depth of emotion that will stay with you beyond the final page.'
—**Karina May**

JESSICA SEABORN

ISN'T IT NICE WE BOTH HATE THE SAME THINGS

This novel contains sensitive themes, including mentions of IVF, miscarriage and the death of a parent.

PENGUIN BOOKS

UK | USA | Canada | Ireland | Australia
India | New Zealand | South Africa | China

Penguin Books is part of the Penguin Random House group of companies whose addresses can be found at global.penguinrandomhouse.com

First published by Penguin Books in 2025

Copyright © Jessica Seaborn 2025

The moral right of the author has been asserted.

All rights reserved. No part of this publication may be reproduced, published, performed in public or communicated to the public in any form or by any means without prior written permission from Penguin Random House Australia Pty Ltd or its authorised licensees.

Penguin Random House values and supports copyright. Copyright fuels creativity, encourages diverse voices, promotes free speech and creates a vibrant culture. Thank you for buying an authorised edition of this book and for complying with copyright laws by not reproducing, scanning or distributing any parts of it in any form without permission. You are supporting writers and allowing Penguin Random House to continue to publish books for every reader. Please note that no part of this book may be used or reproduced in any manner for the purpose of training artificial intelligence technologies or systems.

Cover illustrations by Shutterstock, VK_art
Cover design by Nikki Townsend Design © Penguin Random House Australia Pty Ltd
Typeset in 12/17 pt Adobe Caslon Pro by Post Pre-press Group, Australia

Printed and bound in Australia by Griffin Press, an accredited
ISO AS/NZS 14001 Environmental Management Systems printer

 A catalogue record for this book is available from the National Library of Australia

ISBN 978 1 76134 010 9

We at Penguin Random House Australia acknowledge that Aboriginal and Torres Strait Islander peoples are the Traditional Custodians and the first storytellers of the lands on which we live and work. We honour Aboriginal and Torres Strait Islander peoples' continuous connection to Country, waters, skies and communities. We celebrate Aboriginal and Torres Strait Islander stories, traditions and living cultures; and we pay our respects to Elders past and present.

To friends – mine, yours, and those we have yet to meet.

7 MARCH

I haven't seen you in forever!
We should catch up.

                                                    8 MARCH

                Definitely!! Let's get dinner sometime.

                                                    29 JUNE

                Happy birthday gal!! Dinner soon?
                Miss you.

30 JUNE

Thank you!! And yes, of COURSE.
Let's plan something.

10 SEPTEMBER

Gah, it's been ages since I've seen your
face. When are you free to catch up?
It's been too long.

                                                12 SEPTEMBER

                I was literally *just* about to text you.
                Catch up sounds perfect! I don't mind
                where we go. What works best for you?

                                                25 DECEMBER

                Merry Christmas lady, congratulations
                on the engagement! So thrilled for you.
                Drinks soon to celebrate?

30 DECEMBER

Yes definitely!! Let's get cocktails
somewhere. Haven't seen you in ages,
we need to get together.

                          *Repeat until one of you dies.

PROLOGUE

On my wedding night, after the speeches have ended but before we've cut the cake, my best friend Genevieve scurries off. Rises from our table, grabs her purse, discards her soda water, and beelines through the crowd towards the bathroom. A frown is etched across her forehead.

Immediately, I follow.

I squeeze past the tables, worm my way through the dancefloor, navigate around the wishing well and down the corridor to the restrooms. I'm nipping at her heels, which *clack* loudly with each thunderous step.

Before she can close the bathroom door, I've stuck out my hand and forced my way through. Yanked on the train of my dress so it doesn't get caught. Shut the door behind me, the noise from the party softening.

Instantly, Genevieve insists I should leave. 'No, no,' she says, scrambling. Utterly frazzled. Hands tilting back and forth, outstretched. Her rich mahogany hair, blow-dried and wavy and perched on her collarbones, bounces. 'It's your wedding day. I can do this myself.'

It always amuses me when she tries to stand her ground. She's tiny. Wee and compact. One day I might just pick her up and put her in my pocket.

'I know you can,' I say. But I don't move. Defiant, feet rooted to the ground. 'But you shouldn't have to.'

'I'm fine, Charlie. Honestly.'

'Are you?'

As her lips purse and her eyebrows rise, I know she's contemplating fighting me on this. Telling me to get out, to go back to my wedding. She knows they'll be readying the cake, knows the photographer will be stationed near the bar where the lighting is best. Is aware that my friends will be looking for me on the dancefloor.

But ultimately, she also knows I'm right. She should not have to do this by herself.

'Sit down. It'll be over in five minutes.' I click my tongue against the roof of my mouth, hurrying her up.

She resists, but only for a moment.

Relenting, she sighs, pulls up her sheer ivory bridesmaid dress and plonks herself down on the toilet lid. 'Fine.' She hands me her suede purse. 'Thank you.' Her voice is so quiet I almost don't hear it.

I pluck the needle from inside her bag and undo the insulated packaging.

'IVF injections on a toilet lid. No one told me having a baby would be so romantic,' she says. Sighting the syringe, she winces and averts her gaze. 'One of your friends asked me why I wasn't drinking.'

'Was it Emmanuel?' I ask. 'He means well but he's nosy. Or Josie? She gets bold after her fifth champagne.'

'It was a man with five buttons undone.'

I let out a chuckle. 'Cinar.'

Her lips part; she's fascinated. 'Oh, *that's* Cinar,' she says, amused. 'The serial dater.'

'Correct.'

'The man who thinks chest hair attracts women?'

'Also correct.'

'I pictured him taller.'

'That's Emmanuel,' I clarify. 'Long neck, giant forehead. Cinar's the short one.'

But she's no longer listening. She's glancing down as I pinch a section of her torso, her mouth twitching. Her lip product is new – glossy and rose-coloured – but she cannot stop biting her bottom lip and it's all starting to rub off. I'd hoped discussion about the wedding might distract her, but she's grown quiet. I readjust my grip and she recoils.

'Bruce is drunk,' I say, hoping that diverting the conversation to her husband might help instead. 'He's gearing up for the dancefloor.'

'I know.' She smiles – tender, genuine. 'He's going to embarrass me, isn't he?'

'Probably.'

Laughing, she adds, 'Good. It means he's having fun.'

'And we aren't?' I ask, and she returns my smirk.

Usually, Bruce is the one who injects the needle. Calms her down, distracts her. Makes self-deprecating jokes to make her laugh. Reassures her when she's feeling like all of this is her fault. Tells her not to call herself harsh names like childless or empty. Since they started IVF, he's been home every night during a cycle. An IT consultant who used to be on call until seven o'clock, he now slips out of the office at five for a smaller pay cheque. Gone are the after-work drinks and the dinners with colleagues. Interstate conferences are timed around Genevieve's cycles, as are their holidays. Every evening, same time, his alarm goes off and Bruce knows he's needed. If one of his main tasks is something as simple as inserting a needle into his wife's abdomen, he'll ensure he's home for it.

Unless, of course, his wife gives him the night off. Forces him to forget about the needle and have fun. Drink. Dance.

Like tonight.

'Look at the size of this thing,' I say, holding it up in front of my face. In the mirror, it looks even larger. Longer than chin to forehead. 'Can't believe you have to do this every night.'

'Just wait until it's your turn. It's awful.'

I freeze, my body clenching. There's a silence while her words register, and then she crumples. Folds over, her upper body deflating. 'Fuck, I'm so sorry, I didn't mean it like that. I don't know why I said it.' She rests her head in her hands, looking at me between splayed fingers. 'You won't have to go through this, I bet.'

I pull her hands off her face. 'You're ruining your make-up.'

She grabs my wrist, gives it a squeeze and looks me in the eye. 'Thank you. For this.'

'This round is going to work.'

She's on the fourth, although I usually try not to say numbers. Any time she remembers how long it's been, how many years she and Bruce have been trying, she retreats into herself. Is devastated, all over again.

Genevieve glances down. 'It has to work,' she whispers. '*Has* to. Or I borrowed Mum's money for nothing.'

I force her to look at me again. She's paler than usual, and I know she's feeling defeated. 'You know she doesn't care about the money.'

Her parents would give her anything she asked for – anything she needed. She's the only child they could have, and they're not going to let her think, even for a second, that she's without their support. I know that on tough days, Genevieve wishes they didn't live so far away.

'It's about to go in.'

She glances down at the needle and jolts. 'A fairytale conception.'

Then, after a moment, she whispers, 'I'm barren, aren't I?'

'*Stop.*'

'Sorry,' she says, sullen. Her hair is starting to frizz now, as if compelled to return to its factory settings. 'I'm trying really hard not to say these things. It's just . . . It's been so long, Charlie.'

'I know.'

'And everyone around me is . . .' She trails off. 'It's hard to be happy for others, sometimes.'

'I know.'

'I think about teenagers getting knocked up in cars far too often. One and done, like *that*.' She snaps her fingers. 'Makes me livid.'

She closes her eyes. 'When people tell me they're pregnant, I'm happy for them, I really am, but I'm also sad, and then I'm so angry with myself for being sad. What a terrible person I am, for thinking like that.'

What about me? I want to say. *If I were pregnant, how would you feel?*

She clocks my expression, sees me avert my gaze. And in an instant, she's angled her face towards mine so I'm forced to look at her. 'If you were to fall before me, I'd be *so* happy for you. You know that, right?'

I gesture to the needle. 'I know you'd do the same for me.'

She smiles and nods, as if to say, *Yes, I would. I really would.*

The needle slides into her skin and she makes a pained squeak. 'I can't believe you're doing this for me on your wedding day.'

'Who cares that it's my wedding day?'

'*I* care,' she cries. 'This is the hottest you've ever looked and you're squatting next to a toilet for me.'

I smile.

'You should wear hair extensions more often,' she says, pointing to the sleek low bun at the base of my neck.

I touch it, delicately. I'm so used to my thin, wispy hair – ash blonde – that to feel such a large amount of hair on the back of my head throws me, every time.

She looks down at my dress. High-neck, intricate lace, fitted. It's vintage and elongates my body. She runs her fingertips over the sleeves. 'I still can't believe how stunning you look.'

I slide the needle out of her torso and stand. 'All done.'

Genevieve shimmies down her dress and rises from the toilet. 'I love you.' She pulls me in for a hug and I wrap an arm around her. Squeeze tight. 'The ceremony was beautiful.'

'Thank you.'

'*You* are beautiful.' She releases the hug. 'Did you see Dave's face? Poor man couldn't hold in the tears.'

Oh yes, I saw. A revelation for all of us. I'd never seen Dave cry before, and I'd be lying if I said it didn't unsettle me, give me pause before I continued down the aisle. Make me wonder what it meant, to have a husband you'd never seen be that openly vulnerable. The first time he's truly showing his emotions and it's the day we're vowing to be together forever.

'Is everything okay?' she asks, frowning.

'Yes, fine, why?'

She eyes me, a flicker of doubt. But I laugh off her concerns. Give her shoulder a reassuring nudge. 'I'm great.'

'Yeah?'

'Yes.'

'Good,' she says, relaxing. 'I can't believe you're *married*. I can't believe *I'm* married, sometimes.'

'Scary, isn't it?'

'A slippery slope,' she says, eyes widening. 'How fast I went from shots and clubs to checking budding tomatoes at eight in the morning.'

We laugh.

'And I can't believe I finally met your mum,' she cries. 'And your

sister. And Dave's vows were beautiful. And the speeches were—'
She kisses her fingers, then releases them. A moment later, she grabs my hands. 'You look happy.'
  'I am happy.'
  'Good. You and Dave are perfect.'
  Yes, we are. Perfect.

PART ONE

PART ONE

CHAPTER ONE

My marriage lasts two years.

Less, if we omit those final couple of weeks when everything imploded. When we stopped speaking to each other. When I discovered what he'd been hiding.

It's November, almost two months since I left him. The weather is crisp but bearable, and it's the first time I've worn make-up in six weeks. First time I've braved a social event. This is a momentous occasion, ready to be etched in stone. I'm wearing heels and I put volumising tonic in my hair, for Christ's sake. I plucked my eyebrows for this! I'm rising from the dead, I've decided.

'Are you sure that you're okay?'

Beside me, Genevieve cradles a bottle of champagne and her handbag. We're deep in the suburbs, Saturday evening. Minivans and station wagons line the street, with basketball hoops in driveways, chalk art adorning the footpaths, and tended flower patches in front of every home.

Outside Josie's house, balloons are tied to the letterbox.

Battling a rather ferocious wind, Genevieve gives her head a shake to try and keep her hair away from her face. It's longer now, cascading down her back. A section somehow slips into her mouth and with a graceless *puh puh puh* she spits it out. 'Jesus, this wind is not a vibe.'

I tuck the birthday gift under an arm and relieve her of the champagne.

'Do I look okay?' she asks, tucking hair behind her ears.

Lord, she looks matted. Absolutely psychotic. 'You look great.'

Her mouth flattens out; she knows I'm lying. Running a hand through her red hair, she attempts to tame it. Licks her fingers to calm down the flyaways. 'You didn't answer my question.'

'Am I sure I want to do this?' Pause. 'Yes, I'm sure.'

Time to live my life again. I've been stowed away in Genevieve and Bruce's apartment for six weeks and it's essential I move on. Get back out there, reconnect with friends, leave the house for something other than work, shower at least once a day, et cetera. If I am to believe all the lady websites, I am still a confident, successful woman who can achieve things!

'Because we can go home, if you'd prefer.'

To her two-bedroom apartment? Another night where the three of us squeeze together on the sofa and Genevieve asks me how I'm feeling every ten minutes while Bruce throws out ideas on how I could spend my time now that I'm separated from Dave? Nature stuff, sex with strangers (the younger the better), drinking (the more the better), facials, tattoos, training for marathons, signing up to dating apps. All suggestions provided by his colleagues who are divorced. It seems I've now entered some sort of club for the separated. The advice comes free.

No.

My first outing will be Josie's fortieth birthday party. No more feeling sorry for myself. A raucous, booze-fuelled celebration with my friends, without Dave, is exactly what I need. It's also important for me to profusely apologise that I have not contacted them in almost two months. Been busy processing the end of my ten-year relationship and all that.

'You look great,' Genevieve says.

'I think I'm wearing too much foundation.' Instinctively, I touch my face.

She slaps my hand away. 'No, you look good.'

'My hair is scraggly. It needs a trim.'

'It's been scraggly since birth.' She chuckles. 'No offence.'

We approach Josie's front door – tall, wooden with two brass handles carved into parrots rested on tree branches, their heads tipped down. The handles were plucked from the depths of a vintage store shelf, Josie once told me.

Genevieve hits the doorbell, and we wait. Josie's easily distracted and never on time, but she makes up for it with grand hand gestures and a soothing voice (and homemade body lotion that she gifts by the litre).

Genevieve rings the bell again, and then the door swings open with a great *oomph*. Josie's voice projects from within. 'Hello-h my god. *Charlie?*' Her arms fling out beside her, wide like the body of a tree.

'Happy birthday!' I chant.

She stands in the doorway, frozen. Her jaw lowered, hip popped to the side. I ogle her outfit for a moment. She's always dressed so ethereally. White, billowing dresses with ankle-high boots. Plaited hair. Tonight, she's wearing a tan, lacy dress. Black sandals with straps wrapped around her lower legs all the way up her calves. Birthday party tonight, off to fight the Romans tomorrow.

Behind her, a group of people are mid-conversation near the kitchen, and behind *them* more guests congregate by the hallway. And somewhere, maybe out in the yard, they've got music playing – folk, Josie's favourite.

'You're *here*,' she says, collecting herself and pulling me into a hug. 'You made it. Oh god, we've missed you.'

'I've been such a ghost, I'm sorry.'

'Don't apologise,' she says, releasing the hug. 'I was hoping you would come.' Then she whispers, 'When Dave told us he couldn't make it, I did wonder if that meant we'd see you.'

Well, yes, that did sway me. I wonder how long it'll be like this – Dave and me, alternating appearances. Dave and me, avoiding each other.

'I couldn't miss your big four-o.'

She winces on *big*.

I gesture beside me. 'You remember Genevieve, don't you?'

Josie's eyes squint while she works to place her. 'The school teacher?'

Genevieve frowns. Of all the ways someone could identify her, and Josie goes with *school teacher*. 'That's me.'

'We met at Charlie and Dave's wedding?' Josie says. Tone rising at the end, unsure.

Now we're all silent because Josie mentioned my wedding. She's looking at the floor like she wishes she could fall into it. Great stuff.

I divert, gesturing to Josie's dress. 'You look lovely.'

'Thank you.' She waves her hand to the side. 'Well, come in, come in.' Swinging the door wide, Genevieve steps through first.

Josie clocks the bottle of champagne in my arms. 'Oh, how lovely of you to bring that. Let me pop it in the kitchen.'

She plucks it from my hands and slips away, and I'm left alone at the threshold with Genevieve. And that's when I notice how pale she looks. How her body sways.

Suddenly, her face falls. Her mouth parts. She rests a hand on the wall next to her.

'Are you okay?' I ask.

She nods, but her eyes are unfocused, one hand over her mouth.

'You sure? Bathroom is down the corridor on your left—'

She slips away, darting through the living room and past some of the guests, her black and white cotton skirt flowing out behind her. Should I follow? Call Bruce? She seemed perfectly fine on the drive here, and outside.

When Josie returns, she does not notice Genevieve's absence. Simply brushes a piece of her pale chestnut-coloured hair out of her face and tells me that she's missed me.

'Sorry I haven't called,' I say. 'I haven't contacted anyone, really, except Genevieve and my family. And work, obviously. Took some time off to move in with G.'

'You're living with Genevieve now? We were all wondering.'

We were all wondering. She means the group – all six of them. Josie and Shaun, her husband, Cinar (interchangeable girlfriend not included), Emmanuel and his husband, Diego. Dave. I picture them together, huddled, dissecting what I did, what might've happened, where I've fled to.

Still standing at the threshold, I angle forward. Peek inside the home. Cast an eye over the wooden furnishings, the mandala rugs, the hanging ferns. All the natural light and high ceilings – I've been envious of this house since the first time I visited.

Then, I glance over the guests. No one I recognise.

'Shaun?' I enquire.

Josie waves her hand to the side, her wrist limp and face slack, as if to say *who cares about my husband*. 'He's here, somewhere.' Then she runs an eye over my rust-coloured, waist-hugging strapless dress. 'You look great.'

Her tone is genuine but she seems surprised. Like maybe I'm not expected to look good after leaving my husband.

I crane my neck around the corner and continue spying on the guests. 'Have the others arrived yet?'

The *others*. The rest of our group. Not sure what's going to become of it now that Dave and I have split. After ten years together, it's all going to be different, isn't it? The annual holiday to the mountains in May, the bi-yearly couples' game nights, all those cheese and wine tastings.

'Is that for me?' Josie points at the present I'm holding.

'Oh. Yes.' I hand it over. 'It's just something small. To say happy birthday.'

'This is very thoughtful. Thank you.'

Seeing her brings me a beautiful kind of comfort, and I feel instantly calm. I was nervous before, and now I'm not. Like a bucket of water poured over me, I'm reborn. Everything is in the past, and here we are, moving forward.

'I really have missed you,' I say, as her expression softens. 'How have you been?'

'Busy. *So* busy. Work, and the kids, and Shaun. And my *parents*. Wait until I tell you the conversation I had with them last week. It was unbelievable.'

Yes, please tell me. I'd love to be told that! I'll talk about anything! Anyone. I'll let you chew my ear off about lotion scents, if that's what you want.

But then she changes the subject. 'I'm sorry about you and Dave.'

'Oh.'

'I'll just say this quickly and then we can move on. I was *so* shocked when Shaun told me. We'd seen the two of you at Emmanuel's pot luck dinner and everything seemed fine. And then one week later, Dave tells us you've left him. Out of the blue, just like that.'

Silence. Then she adds, 'While he was in hospital with a broken hand.'

Jesus *Christ*, she's mentioned the hand. Somehow, in all the hoopla of leaving my husband, I'd completely forgotten about his broken hand! Dave was in a hospital bed when I left him, and I know I'm meant to feel guilty about that. But I don't. For once,

I don't have to mend him. For once, he is going to have to learn how to survive on his own.

She reaches out and grabs my forearm. 'You could've talked to me, you know, if you needed it. I wanted to make sure I said that, tonight. Made sure you knew. I would've been there. I know I've been friends with Dave for longer, but you're my family too.'

Without realising it, I'm teary. 'Thank you, that means a lot.'

And that's when I spot them: Cinar and Emmanuel. Emmanuel is wearing a sequined blazer with shoulder pads – oh, how he loves to show off new clothing purchases – and Cinar donning a woollen high-neck sweater, standing at the back of the living room sipping on mulled wine.

'He's been staying with his parents,' Josie says, and I realise we're back to talking about Dave. 'At their vineyard.'

'I know.' We've spoken a few times. Brief, and uncomfortable.

'He's a mess,' she says. 'Been wearing these deep V-neck T-shirts, two sizes too small. Lucky he's a wine salesman, because he's going to need plenty of it to get through the next few months, I suspect.'

Her sympathy isn't surprising, given their history, but I fear it's only facing in one direction and a teensy bit of jealousy slips through my body. And maybe some anger, too. What about how *I'm* going to get through the next few months? Do I get no empathy because I was the one who left?

'Has he seen anyone, while he's up there? Do you know?'

Her brow furrows. 'Seen anyone? What do you mean?'

'Nothing. Never mind.'

Dave and I agreed that we wouldn't tell anyone what triggered the downfall of our marriage. That we'd keep it to ourselves. But of course, I told Genevieve the second I could, and I've been wondering these past six weeks if maybe Dave did the same. If he chose someone to confide in. And if there's anyone in our group he would've told, it would've been Josie. Best friends since puberty, and all.

But I feel confident she's in the dark.

'Let's not dwell. It's my birthday after all,' she says, waving me further into the house. Through the kitchen, towards the back verandah. Out here, there's a garden of herbs and wildflowers, and two small vegetable patches. Wicker seating and string lights hung across the patio.

She flashes me a carefree smile. 'Gosh, you must have so much more time on your hands now. What have you been doing with yourself?'

What have I been doing with myself? Moving out. Putting all my stuff into a storage unit. Crying. Watching atrocious television. Crying some more. Convincing Mum not to fly across the country by telling her I'm doing very well (I can only do this when I'm not crying, though, so it's been difficult to achieve this more than once). Itemising all our belongings for our lawyers so we can work through our property settlement. We may not be able to divorce yet, but we can at least separate our assets.

'Oh, you know. The usual.'

'And how is Genevieve? I remember, at the wedding, she was—'

'Oh ... It didn't happen for them.'

Josie deflates, hand to her chest. 'Oh god, that's awful.'

'Their last round was a couple of months ago.'

She's visibly pained to hear this, shoulders lowering as if crushed under a great weight.

And then, suddenly, Shaun appears. Square face, bright blond hair split with a side part and held in place with a mountain of gel.

'Charlie, you came. How great to see you.' He pulls me into a hug, and I catch his strong scent. Like he's bathed in cologne – I sense cedarwood, with a tang of vanilla – and I know it's because Josie told him he had slight BO one day. Shaun never forgets a thing, and so now he stresses that he smells and no matter what Josie says, she can't stop him fretting. When she gets drunk, she lets slip that it's the one thing in her life she wishes she could change: 'Should've let him stink that day. Now he won't stop chewing gum and spraying his body with woodsy scents. It's like an addiction.'

Shaun turns to his wife. 'You didn't tell me she was coming.' He's got the widest grin of anyone I've met, and he's wearing crisp cream chinos so clean his lower body glows.

'Because I didn't know for sure that she was,' Josie replies, then smiles at me. 'It's a wonderful surprise.'

Her smile is unnerving.

And then, rather suddenly, Josie wraps an arm around Shaun's torso and abruptly kisses his cheek. Tells him he looks handsome.

I can see on Shaun's face that he's just as surprised by this as I am. Josie is not one for public displays of affection. Not sure I've ever seen her hold Shaun like this.

'Drink?' Shaun asks, pointing at me. 'We've stocked up on everything. Wine, bubbles, spirits. You name it.'

It's been a few minutes since I've seen Genevieve, and she's now at the forefront of my mind. Something is telling me – pleading with me – to check in with her.

'In a sec,' I say, holding up a finger. 'I'll be right back.'

I slip away, back inside and down the hallway, past some of the guests and the woven baskets with their towering indoor plants. Past the whimsical artworks on the walls and the macramé hangings.

Knocking twice on the bathroom door, I call out. 'G? You okay?'

After a brief moment, the door swings open. Genevieve stands there, face pale, hair in disarray, shallow breathing.

'You look like shit,' I say.

'I feel like shit.'

'What's wrong?'

'Nothing.'

She runs to the toilet to empty her stomach.

Darting over, I hold back her hair. 'You sure?'

'Must've eaten something funny.' Her voice is strained, her breath quickens.

'G, come on. It's me.' I crouch down beside her.

She stops vomiting, sitting down on the tiled floor. Her mouth spreads out in a smile. 'Surprise,' she says, her head tipping back. 'The twelfth round took.'

CHAPTER TWO

'You're pregnant?'

She vomits.

'Genevieve—'

I'm cut off by the guttural sound of her throwing up. And then she speaks (splutters, actually). 'Ugh, this could've been such a lovely moment but I've ruined it.'

'Are you okay?' I ask, rising and leaning against the vanity – made of reclaimed wood, nestled beneath a vintage, gold-trimmed mirror.

'Obviously *not*.' Then she laughs.

'Is there anything left in your body?'

'Not really.' She flushes the toilet and then sits down on the lid (the irony, I'm aware). The wall behind her is newly painted, I note – sage green.

Reaching forward, I grab at her hand. Give it a squeeze. 'You're pregnant?'

'Six weeks.'

'On the final round.'

She nods.

'My god, this is . . .' I'm still processing it. Letting her revelation sink in. Excitement builds – I feel it somewhere in my soul. After everything that's happened over the past few months, it feels like a light switching back on. 'Incredible.'

'I know,' she says, and then her face changes. A small smile, the hint of tears in her eyes. 'I'd gotten so used to seeing negative, I don't think I ever expected to see two lines.'

'But you told me it didn't—'

'We wanted to wait a little longer.' She clears her throat. 'In case it happened again.'

It. Miscarriage. The word hangs over us, haunting us.

'How have I not—'

'You're always at work.'

Well, yeah, that'd do it. As a breakfast radio producer, I'm out the door by four in the morning. Often not home until dinner. In bed not long after.

'But still,' I say, thinking back. 'I *am* home on weekends. And the apartment is small.'

She gives me a look.

'Sorry. Irrelevant.'

And then she's sliding off the toilet lid, yanking it open and vomiting again. Afterwards, she mutters, 'Women who go through IVF *twelve* times shouldn't get morning sickness. It needs to be a rule or something.'

'Maybe it's something you ate.'

'I haven't eaten in two days—'

Knock, knock.

Horror crosses Genevieve's face. 'Oh *god.*' She covers her mouth with her hand. 'I don't think I can move from here.'

Knock, knock.

I call out, 'Sorry, busy in here. Can you use another bathroom?'

Nothing for a moment, and then the *swish swish* sound of shoes shuffling away from the door.

'Thank you,' Genevieve mutters, sitting on the toilet lid again. At this point, she's just dry heaving. 'I feel disgusting.'

'You're glowing.'

She looks at me. 'Fuck off.'

She's vicious when she's sick.

'Jesus, G, why did you come?'

'Because you asked me to.'

'No, I didn't, you invited yourself,' I say, hands on hips. 'I told you I was fine coming alone, and you told me you didn't care.'

She dry heaves once more before replying. 'I thought it'd be fun.'

'A fortieth in the suburbs? With people you've met once?'

She looks for another excuse. Doesn't find one.

'Genevieve.'

She groans, relenting. 'Okay, fine. I thought it might be tough. After everything that's happened, I thought you might need a friend.'

I don't quite understand her logic. 'I've got friends here.'

'First time seeing them, though. Just thought . . . never mind.' She clutches her head. 'Any chance you've got painkillers in your handbag?'

'I didn't bring a handbag.'

'Shit.'

'Josie might have some.'

She waves it off. 'It'll pass, just give me a few minutes.' Then she relaxes a little, rolls her shoulders back. Runs her hands through her hair.

Pointing behind me, she smiles. 'She's got motivational posters all around the place, have you noticed?'

I turn, see the rustic watercolour artwork above the bathroom door. *Live Laugh Love*. 'Oh. Yeah. There's, like, six of those around the place.'

Genevieve's voice lowers to a whisper. 'I feel like, if you're over forty and you're hanging motivational quotes, then it's probably too late for you. Just a little forced, you know what I mean?'

I perch on the edge of the bathtub. 'She said Dave's been wearing V-neck T-shirts and then she made this face.' I jut out my chin and curl my lower lip over in an attempt to imitate it. 'Like she felt sorry for him. Like he's so depressed that I left him, he can't dress himself properly.'

'The man *can't* dress himself properly. He's got a broken hand.' And then she laughs.

When I don't reciprocate, she ceases. Wiggles closer to me. 'You want me to say it?'

'Yes, please.'

She clears her throat and recites, 'You're not a terrible person, you just left a terrible marriage.'

'Thank you.'

'And it's not your fault you ended it.'

'Thank you.'

It's become our mantra these past couple of months, whenever I feel overwhelmed about what I've done. About what Dave did. *You're not a terrible person, you just left a terrible marriage. And it's not your fault you ended it.*

Another knock on the door, this one quieter but there nonetheless.

'Can you use the other bathroom please?' I call out. 'We're busy.'

'*We?*' It's Josie. She may be softspoken, but I'd recognise that voice anywhere, even through a door.

I'm careful to open it a sliver, just large enough for me to slip out. Concern is etched across her face, the corners of her mouth pinched. When she sees me, she relaxes. 'Oh, Charlie, it's you. Is everything okay?'

Behind her, along the corridor, there's a line of three people. No one I recognise, but I realise just how much the party has grown since we've been in the bathroom. The living room and kitchen are much busier, the chatter louder. The music volume has been increased to compensate, someone switching it to a much more upbeat, contemporary playlist.

'Genevieve is unwell.'

'Oh no.' She lowers her voice. 'Has she drunk too much?'

In the twenty minutes we've been here? I'd laugh, if it were appropriate. 'No.'

Josie turns and shoos away the rest of her guests, directing them upstairs to the second bathroom. Then she turns back to face me. 'Is everything okay?' She checks no one is nearby to overhear before whispering, 'I'm sorry if I seemed . . . taken aback, when you arrived. I was surprised, but I *am* glad to see you.'

There's a pause, and she leans in a little closer. So close I can smell the alcohol on her breath. 'We've all missed you.'

Oh.

Oh.

She thinks I'm crying in the bathroom. Upset about being here, not yet ready for a party. Still struggling with what's happened between me and Dave. She thinks I'm hiding away, on the toilet, too scared to face the group.

Again, my instinct is to laugh, but I refrain. 'Genevieve really is unwell. Can you help keep people away from the bathroom?'

Realising her mistake, she straightens. 'I'll write a note for the door.'

'Thank you.'

'And you're sure . . . you're sure that you're okay? I imagine it must be hard coming here, after what's happened with Dave. You've always been a very brave person.'

Does she respect me or feel sorry for me? I cannot tell. It makes me feel a little sick, being this close to such a squished, sympathetic facial expression. When anyone looks at me like that, I want to reach out and poke their furrowed forehead and tell them I'm perfectly fine.

'Sorry, I've got to go.' I shut the door, locking it, and move back towards Genevieve.

'How are you doing?'

She's still sitting on the toilet lid, hunched over. 'Haven't vomited again, so that's a bonus.'

Fishing out my phone, I divert the conversation. 'I'm going to call Bruce and ask him to pick you up.'

'But then you'll be alone,' she says.

'G, I've been friends with these people for ten years.'

She nods.

'I'll be fine—'

Oh bugger, she's vomiting again. Clutching her head. Groaning, loudly. 'Okay, yeah, I might need those painkillers.'

CHAPTER THREE

Turns out, painkillers prove difficult to find. Nothing in the bathroom with Genevieve, and nothing in the cupboard under the kitchen sink. And no sign of Josie to ask where they might be housed.

'Everything okay?'

Swivelling on a heel, I find Emmanuel and Cinar standing behind me. Emmanuel, an auctioneer, with high cheekbones and a harsh jawline, and that deep olive skin tone. Leaning against the fridge, I realise he's a lot bulkier in the upper body since I last saw him.

And Cinar stands by the kitchen island, arms crossed. Rocking back and forth on the balls of his feet. He's got a beautiful face. Soft, gentle, with piercing blue eyes. So blue you can't look away. I've always wondered if he'd be as successful at pulling women if he'd been born with a different eye colour.

'I'm looking for painkillers. For Genevieve.'

Cinar clicks his fingers, lets out a relieved laugh. '*Genevieve*, that's her name. Been bothering me since you arrived.'

Emmanuel has an amused smile. 'The teacher.'

'The maid of honour at your wedding,' Cinar adds.

It's remarkable how quickly my wedding has been brought up at this party – not once, but twice. Like people cannot help but remind me that I did, indeed, marry their best friend.

We come together in a series of hugs – Cinar first, then Emmanuel – and exchange greetings. Emmanuel tells me Diego is sick and won't be attending, and after we've had a brief but mandatory discussion about how the flu is going around at the moment, I apologise that I haven't been in touch.

'It's been . . .' I trail off, trying to find the words. 'A time.'

Emmanuel nods, sympathetic. 'I can imagine. I'm sorry.'

It's genuine. And sincere. The silence between us tells me they're devastated the group is no longer what it once was.

And then we disband, rifling through the pantry. Checking, just in case the painkillers deceived me. We work our way through all the cupboards, one by one, talking as we search.

'So, the first of us to turn forty,' I say.

Emmanuel, who will be next, lets out a groan. He's always hated celebrating his birthday (acknowledging his age in any capacity tends to sour his mood). He's been telling his colleagues he's thirty-one for the past five years. The man couldn't pull off thirty-one even when he *was* that age.

Cinar muses, 'I think I'll organise a trip for mine, somewhere overseas. Haven't decided yet.'

Emmanuel is bitter. 'Well good thing you've got two years to figure it out.' Then he nods at me. 'And a whopping *eight* for you.'

Cinar looks at him. 'You haven't told us what you plan to do for yours—'

'Inject my forehead with botox, probably.'

'What about a toupee? Cover that bald spot you've got growing up there.'

'What do you mean *bald spot*?' he snaps, grabbing at his hair. He then clocks Cinar's smile. 'Oh, fuck you, I don't have a bald spot.'

'For now.'

Emmanuel turns towards me. 'Have you checked the bathroom? For painkillers.'

'I have.'

He puts his hands on his hips. 'Josie's handbag?' Then, without waiting for my input, he's gone and grabbed it from the counter. Shoves a hand in, copping a feel. 'Nope, nothing.'

While we move through the remaining cabinets, Cinar and Emmanuel update me on everything I've missed these past couple of months. Like a shopping list, ticking off each one.

'We're planning a holiday to Greece.'

'I'm seeing a new therapist.'

'Did I tell you I found a strange freckle on my back thigh?'

'I'm thinking of a career change.'

'I pulled my hamstring lifting the kids into a trolley the other morning.'

And then, finally, Cinar steps closer to me. 'Not sure if you'd heard, but I'm dating someone new.'

Of course you are. Serial dater, certified commitment-phobe. 'I hadn't heard, no. That's exciting.'

Emmanuel and I share a look. *Poor girl.*

'What's her name?' I ask.

'Quinn,' he replies, chest puffing out, proud. 'She's an artist. Like me.' He juts a thumb behind him. 'She's outside having a vape.'

Emmanuel and I share another look.

He's brought her to this party.

We have to meet another one.

We have to make an effort to make her feel welcome when he's going to dump her in three months anyway.

I sense the exhaustion across Emmanuel's face, and the tired way his shoulders fall forward. Honestly, same.

'It feels solid,' Cinar says, with an encouraging nod. 'I'm feeling good about it.'

Emmanuel tips his head back. 'Remind us how long it's been?'

'Two weeks.'

Emmanuel's expression remains neutral.

'I can see this one lasting.'

'You said that about the last two, and then you broke up with them.'

Cinar is sheepish, and embarrassed, so I jump in to console. 'I'm sorry it didn't work out with Alicia,' I say, then experience an instant panic. God, it *was* Alicia, wasn't it? Or was that the one before?

'Thank you.' He straightens. 'But Josie made me realise it wasn't working. I went to her for some advice, and she was like, "Cinar, the girl is fifteen years younger than you and doesn't know who Sean Penn is. Dump her." So I did. Turns out Josie's good at giving advice.'

One of Emmanuel's eyebrows – recently laminated and tinted – arches sharply, as if he's been practising. 'That's not advice, that's just . . . pointing out the obvious.'

'Well, you'll be pleased to know Quinn is only *one* year younger than me.'

'But does she know who Sean Penn is?' I ask.

He frowns, suddenly serious. 'You know, I haven't actually asked. Do you think I should?'

'I was joking.'

Emmanuel lets out a deep chuckle, and Cinar's face and neck grow red. He points at me rather aggressively. 'You wait until you're back out there, dating. It's rubbish, I'm telling you. Once you hit your late thirties all the good ones are gone.'

I avoid their eyes, and silence stretches between us. Somehow, I just *know* they're thinking about Dave.

Finally, Cinar speaks. 'Have you seen him? Since it happened?'

'No. Why? Have you?'

They nod.

Cinar says, 'We've driven up to see him some weekends. With his hand he can't really do much, so.'

'You've driven up? All of you?'

'He's not in a great way,' Emmanuel says. 'Although you seem to be doing well.'

Oh great, six weeks in hibernation and I've emerged looking *too* good. Not a problem I thought I'd have.

'That wasn't a dig,' he adds. 'You look good, is all I'm saying. Dave's beard is so big you can barely see his face.'

I swallow the guilt now lodged in my throat. Even after two months, and despite Dave's secrets, it hurts to be reminded of the pain I've caused. How different things are now. What his voice sounded like when I told him I couldn't do it anymore – strained beyond recognition.

Cinar adds, 'He's also been wearing the same pair of pants every weekend, have you noticed?' He turns to Emmanuel. 'Those khaki trousers? Would we call them khaki?'

'Who cares what colour they are, they're *fuggo*,' Emmanuel exclaims, face scrunched.

Laughing, Cinar segues. 'We'll go find Josie,' he says to me. 'Ask her for painkillers. You stay here.'

And then they're gone, leaving me here, in the kitchen, while they dart upstairs in search of help.

'Need these?'

A petite, bird-like woman with ear-length jet-black hair appears to my left. Posture straight, wearing polished loafer shoes and a burgundy jacket with shoulder pads, hands clasped together in front of her. Her perfume is intoxicating. Velvet. Vanilla. Musk.

In her outstretched hand, she holds a packet of paracetamol.

'Oh my *god*,' I say, grabbing and clutching them to my chest. 'Lifesaver. Can I take two?'

'You can have them all. I swiped them from Josie's handbag.'

'Really?'

'No,' she says. 'That was a joke.'

'Oh. Right.' I laugh. 'I'm Char—'

'I know who you are,' she says, offering a curt smile. 'I'm Quinn.'

'Cinar's girlfriend.'

This is not what I was picturing at all. For once, he's dating someone who was alive when the twin towers fell. Someone who probably uses an eye cream. Someone who wouldn't be mistaken for his daughter (only happened once, but Cinar has forbidden any of us to mention it).

'You're an artist too,' I note.

She nods. 'That's how we met.' Then she chuckles. 'Well, that's how he meets all of them, right?'

'All of who?'

'His women,' she says, sipping at her gin and tonic. 'His reputation precedes him.'

Okay, interesting – she's not clueless. It's a nice change. Refreshing.

'Well, I wouldn't describe them as *women*,' I say. 'More like—'

'Youth?' Quinn quips.

'I was going to say girls.'

She shrugs, as if to say that both descriptors would suffice. And in this moment, I decide that I approve of Quinn. Far too sensible for Cinar. Far too self-aware to be fooled by his antics. What a shame she'll be the next one voted off the island and he'll have a new girlfriend by February.

I catch her looking at my left hand. My *bare* left hand.

'It's awful, when they end.' She raises and wiggles her own left hand. 'I've been divorced six years now. Married a drummer after university and spent most of my twenties smoking weed and dressing like Frodo Baggins.'

We catch eyes and laugh. It makes me want to pull her in close. Here is someone who understands what I'm going through. Has stood where I am and come out the other side. I want to pick her brain. Take her to lunch. Ask her what happened, how it happened and how she feels about it now.

But then my phone erupts in my pocket – two text messages at the same time. I pluck it out, turn it over in my fingertips and read the notification.

Dave.

A knot forms in my stomach, seeing his name on my phone. It's been sporadic, our communication. Short, punchy text messages. Blunt phone calls. Mostly, we speak through our lawyers about dividing our assets (he's petitioning that he should get the porcelain dinner set because they were a wedding gift from *his* side of the family, but I didn't even know we *had* a porcelain dinner set).

At some point, Quinn slips away. Whether she sees my phone or just senses something has shifted, I do not know.

I open the messages, my thumb shaking a little. It feels like my ribs might just crack open.

> Charlotte, where is the engagement ring? You can't ignore me forever.

I touch my cheeks, hoping my cool fingertips dull the redness I'm certain is building across my face. *You're fine, Charlie. You're okay. And you absolutely* can *ignore him forever.* He's a slippery eel and it's *his* fault this marriage ended.

His fault.

His fault.

His fault.

The painkillers are still nestled inside my left hand, and I head back to the bathroom, Dave's messages playing over and over in my mind. It's the one thing he wants from me, to help finalise this settlement – the engagement ring. The one thing we have left to settle. The one thing still tying us together. I give him the ring, and it's over between us. For good. Finished. We never need to speak to each other again. He's keeping the apartment, and I'm living somewhere else. We've divided up all the other assets. There's nothing left to work through.

It's just this one, tiny thing left to give him, and then we're over for good.

I pass the staircase on the way to the bathroom, and I hear muted voices. A whispered conversation between Josie, Cinar and Emmanuel. They're on the landing, tucked away but not out of sight.

'She actually turned up,' Josie says. 'Can you believe it? Wait until I tell Dave. I'm in complete disbelief. How awkward. After everything she's put him through. *She* left *him*. And she turns up here?'

Beneath my feet, the floorboards creak. And they all turn. Josie, Emmanuel, Cinar. They see me, they recognise me, and then all three adorn a stricken facial expression.

So this is what they really think of me. My gut twists. My palms moisten.

And then, because the universe decides I have not taken nearly enough hits today, I get another message from Dave.

> I paid for that ring and I want it back.

CHAPTER FOUR

I've lost the ring, I'm afraid, and I was hoping he'd never ask for it back. Was really praying Dave would forget about the whole thing, maybe have some kind of memory loss incident.

But no.

He's remembered. Of course he's remembered.

It's the day after Josie's fortieth and Genevieve and I are hiking. Rocky, slopy inland terrain on a sticky, humid afternoon. We underestimated the fitness level required, and it feels like it's about to rain. Genevieve keeps pausing to catch her breath. My knees ache, my back is burning. We're navigating rocks, roots and gravel, and progress is slow. My hair is damp with sweat, and I've got horrendous blisters forming along my toes.

We wanted to connect with nature, but I feel like we're about to connect with the afterlife.

'This is lovely, isn't it?' she says, grasping her water bottle.

'Beautiful.'

'We should do this more often,' I say, and she nods in agreement, wiping the sweat off her forehead with the back of her hand.

When Dave and I split, Genevieve insisted we do everything I didn't get to do when he and I were together. And there are *so* many examples.

The man is allergic to strawberries. Deathly allergic. So I never had them in the apartment, never dared to eat one near him.

What have I done since ending the marriage? Buy just about every strawberry I could find and shove them straight into my mouth. Leave strawberries in the fridge and on the kitchen bench. Even bought strawberry-scented lip gloss.

The man works for his family's vineyard and refuses to buy wine that retails for less than twenty-five dollars. Won't have anything that cheap in his mouth, he'd say, and he would select an offensively expensive bottle whenever we went out for dinner.

The first wine I bought post-separation cost seven dollars and tasted like arse, but I drank the entire thing one afternoon and sent him a drunken text saying, *Guess who's got something cheap in their mouth.* (Did not go down well, would not recommend.)

And, of course, he hated hiking. Found it boring. Didn't like the impact on his knees. He ruined countless hikes complaining about the heat or the incline or how often we'd pass someone and they'd say 'Not long to go!' that it wasn't even worth it.

'Love the view,' Genevieve says, once we reach the top.

Clouds blanket the city, obstructing the entire skyline. 'So good.' Then I turn to her. 'How are you feeling?'

'Really good.' Her face is pale, her lips chapped.

'You're sure?'

'Promise.'

We find a spot to sit and rest our legs, taking a moment to recover before the descent back to the car. Without realising, I check the group chat on my phone. *Our* group chat – Josie, Shaun, Dave, Emmanuel, Diego, Cinar, me. Scroll through to see if I've heard from anyone last night. Look again to see if I've heard from Josie, after what she said. Genevieve clocks it straight away.

'Anything?' she asks, nodding at my phone.

I shake my head.

After everything she's put him through. And she turns up here?

Nothing can capture how much that gutted me – how awful it

feels, to hear your closest friends complaining about you as if you're a leech who needs to be surgically removed. *She turns up here?* Like I'm some stranger without an invitation. I RSVPed, bitch.

It's enough to keep me up at night, and I fear I will be thinking about this over and over in my head at 3 a.m. for the rest of my life.

Genevieve lets out a sympathetic sigh. 'I'm sorry.'

'I've been friends with them for so long.'

'But they knew Dave first,' she says. 'And now you're no longer together.'

They knew Dave first. I'd never thought of us like that. Never thought of them as *his* friends, but simply, *our* friends.

I don't respond immediately, because I don't want to admit the truth. Don't want to acknowledge, out loud, that I understand what she's trying to say. That something might be different now. That leaving Dave might have changed the group in a way I, perhaps foolishly, wasn't anticipating.

'I don't care that he knew them first.' They've been with me for a decade. They feel more like my family than my actual family, and I don't know what this would look like if they weren't there anymore. I think of them fading away and I feel this huge cloud settle over me. I will be alone. *Alone.* I'll have Genevieve, I'll have Bruce, and I'll have nobody else.

The thought makes me want to hurl.

Genevieve changes the subject. 'What are you going to do about the ring?'

The engagement ring. That beautiful, lost ring.

I know exactly where it is, I just can't get to it. It's lying at the bottom of the city's harbour after a waterside stroll ten months earlier. My fingers so swollen that my rings were rubbing my skin, I took them both off and the engagement ring slipped out of my hands and into the water. I was so distraught I threw up.

Dave never noticed the ring was missing, and I never told him. But *now* he remembers it exists.

'Honestly,' Genevieve continues. 'The gall of that man. You don't owe him anything.'

'He paid for the ring.'

'And he's paid for almost a thousand golf lessons and he's still *shit*, but is he going to ask for his money back? No.' Genevieve exhales rather dramatically.

I glance down at my left hand. 'I have no idea what I'm going to do. You got any ideas?'

'Plenty.' She starts counting with her fingers. 'Tell him you sold it. Tell him it's yours. Tell him he doesn't get to make demands. Tell him he's got knobby knuckles. Tell him you've regifted it. Tell him he's the reason the marriage didn't work out.'

Then she pauses, looking over at me. Her voice lowers. 'Or, you know, you could tell him the truth.'

'I think I'll just ignore him.'

'That works too.'

And then we rise, because the wind has picked up and we're getting chilly. Genevieve's phone *pings* and it's Bruce asking how the hike is going. Asking how she's feeling today, if she's eaten enough. She taps out a response and I wonder how much she's sugarcoating.

A moment later, I start to wonder if Dave would've been like that with me, if we'd decided to have kids. How concerned he'd be about me, on a hike, during peak sickness. And the fact I have to wonder at all tells me what I need to know – that we spent so much of the relationship focused on him, and his problems, that there was never a lot of time left for me.

'Bruce sent through a listing,' Genevieve says.

It's a regular thing we've been doing, Genevieve and I, while she and Bruce hunt for a home. Look over listings on weekends, compare prices, swipe through photos of bedrooms and gardens and kitchens and driveways. And then, when that property doesn't work out because someone outbid them or the auction price grew too high, we go back to the listing and moan about all the things that were *wrong* about the house – a lack of charm, too much wooden panelling, no secondary space for entertainment, no direct sunlight or ventilation.

It's been a year of this.

'Thoughts?' she asks, passing her phone to me.

This house is on the outskirts, nestled within a gated village. Semi-detached, beige and white. Oak columns at the front door, a small garden bed. Three bedrooms, small yard, all the basics ticked.

But it's a little too well-kept and I fear it'll sell for higher than predicted. 'Looks nice.' I hand her phone back.

'He's going to organise a viewing.' There's still a flicker of hope left in her voice when she talks about listings, and I wonder how long until that starts to sour.

It's remarkable, how much our lives are diverging. I'm negotiating a settlement with lawyers and she's attending house viewings and ultrasound appointments. I'm sleeping in her second bedroom and she's ready for maternity clothes and books on childbirth. She's hunting down three-bedroom homes and researching school catchment zones, and I'm learning what it's like to be alone after spending a decade with the same man. I'm also learning how much I *loathe* being alone.

For so long, we'd been on the same path together. But somehow, along the way, I turned around and Genevieve kept going.

'You know I'll move out, if you decide to stay in the apartment—'

'I know, I know, you've said.' She sips. 'But, baby or no baby, we can't stay in that place. It's just too small.'

But if you can't find somewhere to live, what happens then? It's something she won't acknowledge, no matter how many times I ask. No matter how many times I press.

Genevieve darts off to vomit behind a tall tree with white bark, the trunk so wide she can tuck herself behind it. I realise we're done here.

When she returns, I hand her some anti-nausea tablets.

'I'm totally fine.'

'You're totally not.' I wait for her to relent and ingest the tablets, then pack everything away.

'I felt really good on the way up,' she says, defensive, then wipes sweat from the back of her neck.

I hold her stare. 'Really?'

'No.'

And then we laugh.

'I should've cancelled this,' I say. 'I'm sorry.'

She shakes her head. 'I wouldn't have let you.' She pops a few mints into her mouth and sips more water.

Descending, I glance around. No other people in sight, and droplets landing on our heads as the rain rolls through. Out of habit, I check my phone again. No new messages. They really aren't going to say anything to me, after what I heard? *Put on your big girl pants, Josie, and apologise to me!*

Genevieve catches my mood and is quiet for a moment. Pondering. And then she turns towards me. Forces me to stop. 'Can I ask you something?'

'Anything.'

'You haven't contacted them in six weeks. But you've also not been in touch with anyone in the group,' she says, eyebrows rising. 'So does that mean *they* haven't contacted *you*, either? Haven't even checked in to see if you're okay?'

For a few moments, I say nothing. Digest her question. And then I step back and think about what she's asking. I'd been so focused on my marriage, and on Dave, that I'd only been thinking about *my* actions these past six weeks. Not theirs. And suddenly,

I feel small again. My chest constricts. My throat feels dry.

Slowly, I respond. 'Yes, I suppose you're right. Not one of them contacted me.'

Had I really not noticed? Six weeks of going through *hell*, and they didn't bother to reach out. Didn't ask if I was okay, didn't think to call. Didn't offer me their couch to sleep on. Didn't do *anything*.

Something about these friendships is different, now. Has morphed into a shape I do not recognise. And there might not be a way back.

'What *arseholes*.'

Genevieve is sympathetic. 'I'm sorry.' And then she covers her mouth with her hand, her eyes closing.

'How are you *really* feeling?'

After a moment, she speaks. 'Like trash,' she says. 'And I'm worried all this vomit is ruining my teeth.'

'Smile for me.'

She grins, cheesy and wide.

'All still there.' I tug on her arm. 'Come on, let's go.'

It's a quiet day on the mountain, but we eventually pass someone. A struggling young man, red in the face, sweat darkening his singlet.

Genevieve calls out. 'Not long to go!'

CHAPTER FIVE

The next morning, I am early to work. A ghastly kind of early. Three o'clock in the morning; what a disgusting time to be at the station. I am functioning on very little sleep.

Today, we find out how our breakfast show fared in the previous quarter and I fear the nerves might just be devouring my insides.

The radio station is torridly quiet. No music yet. After-hours lights, dull and flickering. And it's dark outside, nothing but streetlights illuminating the road. Every other desk on my floor is empty.

Usually, this place is bustling. Loud, lively. Laughter from all corners of the building, and rumbling chatter at every desk. Graham, our breakfast host, will sit inside his soundproof studio, tucked behind the microphone, and his commentary will project out here across the floor. Ad breaks, traffic reports, news updates, top forty music – it's a cycle, and I live for it. This place is a zoo, at the best of times. The walls are painted a deep purple, and the people are just as bizarre. Where I work is anything but ordinary, and I love it.

But, right now, I am alone.

Grabbing my headphones, I blast rock pop to disrupt the deafening silence. On my desk sits a half-eaten slice of toast – with butter and jam – now cold, and coffee. I'm wearing a new pair of boots not yet broken in. Brown with a small heel, deceptively painful. I rather hate myself for buying them.

I clear out some of my inbox from the weekend, then ready the segments for the day. Catch up on recent news to slide into the program. Read over my reminders from Friday, print out briefing notes for Graham. Research talking points for a segment we're running next week, and then take a sip of coffee.

It's gone lukewarm, and my lip curls. 'Ugh.' But I drink it, because I'm desperate. Because I'm exhausted, and tired, and I'll take anything to keep me awake – even tepid coffee.

Anxious, I flit between tasks: scour gossip websites for information to compile for our entertainment wrap, read through more emails, reply to publicists, go over my notes for the morning, then plot out notes for the rest of the week. Rinse and repeat.

Since my separation from Dave, there are two things I'm grateful for – Genevieve and my job. Genevieve, for obvious reasons. And my job, because of how busy it is. How easily it can distract me. Radio is never-ending, and if you really wanted to, you could work every hour of the day. It's what I've learnt in the six years I've worked here. If I arrive early and I stay back late, I can push everything from my consciousness, and let the station take over. The more I work, the easier it is to forget how different my life is. How much Dave hurt me.

Suddenly, as I'm deleting spam from the inbox, a ham and cheese toasted sandwich, wrapped and resting on a plate, appears before me. Placed delicately in front of my keyboard, along with a raspy directive.

'Eat.' It's Graham, pulling up a chair. His bald head is especially shiny today – what a gleam! 'I made it for you.'

'You're here early.'

'So are you,' he counters. 'Eat.'

'I've already eaten. But thank you.'

He spies the toast on my desk and raises one thick, bushy eyebrow. Gives me a *come on* kind of look, and I relent.

I take a bite, then another. 'Did you actually make this or did your housekeeper?'

He smirks, shoving a hand in his jean pocket. 'You know she doesn't start this early.'

At sixty-eight, Graham is best described as past his prime. And that's not me being cruel; he actually is referred to that way. Journalists, reporters, presenters – they argue he should've retired years ago, when he was still on top of the radio charts and people flocked to his program. Now, we're struggling to keep up with the competitors and he's struggling to stay relevant.

'Which kitchen did you use?' I ask, then smile. He's got four in his mansion, all fully equipped. Genevieve's entire apartment could probably fit inside one of them. 'Can't sleep?' I add.

He shakes his head, then wheels over a chair and sits down beside me. Crosses a leg, then crosses his arms over his chest.

This station was once number one in breakfast radio. For decades. Every quarter, we'd beat our competitors – all seven of them – and we'd toast to the win and congratulate each other, and then do it all over again three months later.

But it's been a while since that happened.

For two years, almost, we've been number two. And no matter what I've tried, we just haven't been able to reclaim the lead. And god, I've really tried. We've extended the show by an hour, increased listener calls, added in giveaways and competitions, doubled the entertainment segments and the interviews, slotted in more music, taken Graham on the road to news events and red carpets and sporting tournaments. Anything the team has suggested, we've tried it.

And it hasn't worked.

Each quarter, we're hopeful. *This time* we'll be number one again. *This time* we'll be back on top. But then it's—

Second, *again*.

Second, *again*.

Second, *again*.

If only I could figure out what's gone wrong. *Why* we're not number one. Because then I could fix it – get us out of this slump and back in the lead and I'd stop stressing for my job. For Graham's.

'You worried?' I ask, even though I already know the answer. Can see it in his frown and the bags under his eyes, in the way he's thrown on an old, creased shirt today instead of something ironed.

He holds my stare, then looks down. Readjusts his stance.

'We're going to be number one,' I say.

He smiles. 'You say that every time.'

'And I mean it, every time.'

'Maybe I'm too old for this.' He straightens, groaning, and runs his left hand over his head. 'Can you figure out a way to make me young again?'

'You'd still be bald.'

He lets out a laugh. 'Been bald since I was twenty-nine.'

'So you've told me, about twenty-nine times.'

That makes him chuckle. Then his face turns stony and he points at me. 'Eat.'

Three more bites of my sandwich and he's satisfied. Doesn't say another word about ratings, but I can sense his anxiety. The man dedicates his entire career to this breakfast program, holds the top position for decades, and then he hits his mid-sixties and his audience scatters. Diverts to other programs, with their younger hosts and their hot takes and their pranks. Their salacious, revolting humour. Maybe reclaiming the top spot means Graham would have to lower himself to their level, but that just doesn't seem fair.

'Jesus, absolute ghost town in here.' He rotates, looking around at the empty station. There's an eerie silence with so many desks unoccupied. 'Been years since I've arrived before the team.'

'Briefing notes are on your desk,' I say, nodding at the glass-encased studio to my left. 'I've updated one of the segments to discuss celebrity divorce, after the news on the weekend.'

He frowns, tilts his head. He has no idea what I'm talking about. Arguably the most famous couple in the world announces their split and he's oblivious? It annoys me, just sometimes, that he doesn't even *try* to keep up with all facets of the news. *I'm trying to make you relevant, come on.*

'Never mind. It's all there in the notes. Just read it before the segment and you'll be fine.'

'Is anyone going to care what I think about celebrity divorce?' he mutters, slipping into the studio to pick up the document and returning to sit down next to me. He flicks through the pages, skimming my notes, nodding as he follows our plan for the morning. And then he stops, narrows his eyes, scoffs and gives me an accusatory look.

'Seriously?' he says, gesturing. Then reads aloud. '"You can draw a connection to your own experiences here. Talk about one of your two hundred divorces."' His mouth twitches in a grin. 'I've only been divorced five times.'

'Only?' I match his grin, then ask, 'How was your weekend?'

He shrugs. 'Uneventful. Drank port.'

'Alone?'

'Of course alone.'

Good lord, he says things like this and it makes me berserk with stress that I'm looking at my future. Will this be me one day? Drinking alone, spending my weekends in an uneventful manner. Something about it makes me coil with shame. At least Graham owns a mansion! I'm sleeping in someone else's spare bedroom, for god's sake.

'You ever think about going out? Socialising?'

'Why would I do that?'

'Because it's fun.'

He counters, 'You telling me that fortieth you went to on Saturday night was *fun*?'

My smile falters, and he grins, smug. 'Well?'

'I enjoyed it.'

'Really?'

'I did, I really did,' I lie. 'Genevieve's pregnant, actually.'

His expression remains unchanged. 'Exciting. But I didn't ask about Genevieve. I asked about you.'

There's something about the way he's looking at me; I feel cornered. I can no longer harbour the energy to lie. 'I didn't realise things were going to change.'

He leans forward, elbows on knees. 'You went and hung out with *his* friends. After leaving him.'

Immediately, I am defensive. Borderline whiny. 'They're my friends too.'

'Not anymore, they aren't.'

I feel like he's sliced me. Two people now telling me my friendships are gone – irreparably changed. All these people I've come to love over the past ten years and now I have to let them go?

He stands. 'You've got us though. We're a team.'

'Speaking of.' I pluck a card from my handbag. 'Dora got engaged over the weekend.' Dora, our producer. Been at the station one year. Been with her boyfriend for five. 'Saw it on Instagram and picked this up yesterday. Already signed it from the team. Also have a bouquet arriving later this morning. You might like to suggest a lunch today, to celebrate? Your shout, given you're rich.'

'*Dora?*' Graham says, aghast. 'Got engaged?'

'She did.'

He's floored, mouth agape. 'She's twelve.'

'Twenty-three,' I correct.

'Is she religious?'

'I thought that too, but no. Turns out she and Cleaver are just really efficient people.'

'God.' Then he pulls himself together and nods. 'Yeah, a lunch, sure. *Christ*. Engaged at twenty-three. Imagine getting married that young?'

'Imagine getting married five times.'

He rolls his eyes before walking off.

Later, after the show has wrapped, the rest of the team depart for the pub to celebrate Dora.

Graham and I hang back. We tell them we'll meet them there later – after the ratings have been released. Good lord, I couldn't possibly read them with a beer in hand. My nerves wouldn't be able to handle it. No, I need to hide in a meeting room, head in my hands, gut on the floor. Armpits sweaty from worry.

At some point, Graham swings open the meeting room door with a stack of papers tucked into the crook of his arm. 'Mind if I join?' he asks, but then he slips inside anyway. 'Thought you might need some company when we come in second again.'

'We're going to be first,' I say, but now I'm not so sure. I've been awake too long, and my resolve has faded. People have been jittering about the office all day – men with gelled hair and pressed suits swanning about the hallways, in between board meetings and reading drab documents – and it has me nervous.

What if we *are* second, again?

How am I meant to bring this show back to the top if I've already used up all my tactics? I fear I've run out of ideas. I fear I am terrible at my job and I'll be fired and they'll bring in someone far younger than me whose greatest flex is being good at content creation. I'm going to be dumped for an influencer, and everything I've worked so hard for will have been for nothing.

'Are you crying?' Graham asks, now seated across from me. He's been skimming my briefing notes for tomorrow's show, his reading glasses perched on the end of his nose. He's looking up at me, frowning.

'No.'

'You look like you're crying.'

I check the time, just like I've done all morning. A mere ten minutes until the ratings results will land in our inboxes. My throat constricts.

'We'll be fine, Charlie. We always are.'

Here is something I've noticed about Graham since we started working together – he does not seem to fluster as easily as I do. No fanning about, no red cheeks or sweaty forehead. Everything seems to flitter over his head like dust.

'Seriously though,' Graham says, looking at my jiggling leg. 'Can you stop? Please? We did our best.'

'Three months isn't enough time between results. It's ridiculous. I could've done more,' I say.

'You've done plenty.'

'More entertainment, maybe. We know that works. Some big scandal, perhaps. When was the last time you took drugs? Recently? Maybe you grew reliant. Jesus Christ, I can't believe I didn't think of a drug problem! The tabloids would froth.' I push my laptop away from me in a frenzied mess.

He goes back to reading, and I check the time once again.

Two minutes until ratings results. I consider reading the email in the bathroom just in case I need to sob.

We're going to be number one.
We're going to be number one.
We're going to be number one.

'This means a lot to you,' he says, narrowing his eyes.

'Of course it means a lot to me, it's my job.'

'Well, yes. But you're ...' He searches for the right words. 'No other producer I've had has been this ruffled about the ratings.'

'This is very important to me.'

'Why?'

I struggle to articulate it, to confine it to just one thing. Why *does* this matter so much to me? Because I'm proud of what I do? Because I love what I do? Because I don't like failing?

He continues. 'It's collaborative,' he says, then points behind him. 'We work in a team of thirty people. Ratings aren't just on *you*.'

When I don't respond, he gives me one of his steely-eyed gazes until I can somehow form a response.

'My dad loved your program, tuned in every morning,' I say. 'I grew up listening to you on the radio. And the thought of you losing this because of me. Honestly, I can't stomach it.'

And then the email lands.

Ping.

Like a bomb.

Graham stands. Hovers over my shoulder, resting a hand beside my laptop. 'Go on,' he says, eyes on my screen. 'Open it.'

When I do, my hand shakes. Just like every other time. We take a moment to scroll through. To see the ratings breakdown – the market share, the percentages. To compare our numbers with our competitors'.

'Jesus,' he says, letting his head fall forward. His breath is loud and wheezy.

We're not number one.

We're not even number two.

We're number *four*.

'Oh god.' In all my nightmares, not one of them had us fourth. At no point did I think this was even a possibility. How is the religious channel ahead of us? How did we skip number three and just go straight to *four*?

There's a flaw in the system, and this is an error. I'm sure of it. This whole thing is a typo and if I keep staring at my computer, things will magically realign. I am filled with stress, all through my body and right down to the tips of my toes.

I swivel to face Graham. Go to speak but nothing comes out.

He cannot look me in the eye, continues looking down at the ground. His glasses slide a little further down his nose.

Then, he nods. Nods again. One more time. As if convincing himself that what he's just seen is real.

'What's going to happen to us?' I ask.

'Nothing is going to happen to us.'

'Graham, we're *fourth*.'

He snaps, 'I know that. I can read.' Then he corrects himself. 'Sorry.'

'They fire presenters for this. They fire *producers* for this.'

Hearing this, he is quick to rebut, pointing a finger at me. 'One dip isn't going to get us fired.'

'It's not just one dip. There have been many dips. *Lots* of dips.'

'Will you calm down, please?' He's clutching his head.

I shan't! I will not! We weren't good enough. *I* wasn't good enough. Is this not my job? Preparing a show that people want to listen to? I've failed here. For years, I've failed.

Graham grasps my shoulder. Pulls my attention towards him. 'Don't even *think* about blaming yourself.'

'Of course I blame myself.'

He throws his hands out – stretched, fingers pointed upwards. 'We've got a whole team of people: it's not your fault.'

'Aren't you worried for your job?'

'Charlie, I've been worried for my job since I turned fifty,' he says. 'I'm old and I'm *tired*. But I'm still here, every day. We're going to be fine.'

Assessing Graham's body language and facial expression, I decide he is not nearly rattled enough for this.

I press the inner corners of my eyes, because I'm imagining the worst. I'm picturing being called into a meeting and told I'm no longer needed. I'm picturing the team walking back into the station in an hour, having seen the results, and looking at me like a wounded bird.

Mostly, I'm thinking of Graham. Of what this means for him. And how I managed to ruin his standing in only a few years. He was the *best* and now we're in the middle.

On the table, my phone vibrates. *Genevieve calling.*

I cannot bring myself to answer – she'll know the ratings have come through. She'll be watching the clock and wanting to know how we fared. God, she's so supportive.

But telling her, telling anyone, might just kill me. I would rather wait for the news to break later tonight and let it swallow us all whole, like some gigantic whale in the deep sea.

'I don't understand how this happened,' I say.

One look at him and I deduce that he, too, has no idea what's gone wrong. But he's doing a far better job of processing it than me.

'You're amazing at what you do,' he says, and it makes me cry again. 'No, listen to me. You are *great* at what you do. And you've done an amazing job. And if they do fire you—'

I choke.

'*If* they fire you, I'll walk.'

'You will not.'

'I will. I absolutely will.' He sighs, then rolls his shoulders back. 'You're going to be fine. And I'm going to be fine. And when the dust has settled today, you're going to go home. You are going to close your emails and you're going to take the rest of the day off.'

I shake my head. 'My emails are a mess, and I'm still working through talking points for tomorrow's final segment—'

'I don't care.' He holds my gaze. 'You work harder than anyone else in this team. You'll leave on time today.' It's a statement, not a question.

'Graham.'

'Promise me,' he says. 'Promise me you'll leave on time today.'

Eventually, I whisper, 'I'll leave on time. Promise.'

CHAPTER SIX

I do not leave on time. I don't even *try* to leave on time.

The day stretches into late afternoon and I'm still in the office, well after the rest of the team have departed – after they tiptoed out, deflated by the ratings. Before they left, they gave me one final, sympathetic look, and told me to *hang in there*. It's the closest I've come to committing grievous bodily harm.

Fourth.

I need to prove myself. Better myself, and this program. Only three months until we do this all over again, and I can fix this. I can definitely fix this. I am not going to be responsible for tanking this show. It is not an option. We *will* climb back to the top.

When a young model out of Canada admits to a three-way tryst with a celebrity chef, I line up an interview for the next day and then spend fifteen minutes shifting the rest of the program. A subpar musician contacts us directly asking for an interview, and feeling generous, I slot her in for later that week. A pop group from twenty years earlier announce they're returning to the stage, and so I arrange an interview with their tour manager for Wednesday and negotiate a radio exclusive.

All the while, I think about the ratings. Wonder if there was anything I could've done differently – could've done better. I'm trying *so* hard not to check the news, not to read the articles. What they must be saying about Graham, I can only imagine.

To distract myself, I sporadically scan the group chat.

Two days since the party and not one of them has reached out. Not even to apologise. Not even to ask why I left Josie's fortieth so suddenly, or if I'm okay. All I've received is deafening silence, and I'm terribly hurt. Before I left Dave, this group chat would ping every couple of hours. And now, nothing. I imagine they've created a new one without me.

Not anymore, they aren't.

Graham's words haunt me and I feel it's official. By leaving Dave I have become Adolf Hitler and all association with me is considered frowned upon. I hadn't thought there'd be sides, but it appears they have all sided with Dave.

How many evenings have I babysat for Emmanuel and Diego? Listened to Emmanuel's work woes, given him relationship advice (hilarious to ponder, now that I'm en route to a divorce) – even went with him to trial new gyms because he needed a second opinion. Shaun and Josie assigned me godmother to two of their children, and I'm now worried they're going to revoke the offer. And *Cinar*. I've been to every art show, met every girlfriend, even arranged an interview with Graham to promote each collection.

And now I'm dead to them all.

These people shaped my twenties. Built me. When I moved here, ten years ago, Dave introduced us all and they made me feel welcome, in a city completely different to my hometown. Told me how much they loved me, how glad they were that Dave had found me. They brought me into their world and wrapped me up tightly in their arms. What a world it's been.

And in turn, I've been there for them through every major stage in their lives. Every wedding, every engagement party, every baby shower, every gender reveal. I've met every newborn, babysat them whenever they needed. Listened to Cinar whenever he decided to leave another girlfriend, helped Emmanuel when he and Diego were adopting – *literally* became his shoulder to cry on. I tested how many bottles of Josie's lotion? Most of it was gluggy and smelt like infection, but I still helped her. Dave certainly didn't. I purchased every birthday gift and Secret Santa present – did they know that? Dave organised *nothing*.

I've been nothing *but* supportive, and here they are treating me like I've got a transmissible disease. If I told them what Dave did, I'm certain their loyalty would realign. It'd be *me* they chose.

But why should I have to reveal Dave's betrayal to steal back their attention? That shouldn't be how life works.

I scan the group chat again. And again. And one more time. Still nothing.

This quiet office is doing nothing to settle my nerves. I look at those purple walls and I feel like I'm being shouted at, and then I look around at the empty desks, and ahead of me inside Graham's empty studio, and I think I'd actually quite like it if someone shouted at me right now.

Lord, give me *someone* to talk to.

I call Genevieve but she doesn't answer, so I try a second time. Then a third. Still no answer. Almost instantly, I switch to my contacts list and do something rare – I call my sister Naya.

She answers on the eighth ring, just as I'm about to hang up. 'I've been fantasising about going to prison,' she says, out of breath. 'Something white collar. Six months at the most. Long enough to have a rest.'

Naya's got four children under six. 'Is it the kids?' I run my hand along the fabric of my chair.

'Leonard,' she says. 'He tried to fix a cracked pipe and ended up hurting his hand. He said it's been sliced but I've looked at it and it's just a small cut. You'd think he's returned from war, the way he's going on about it. Keeps referring to it as a *wound*.'

Naya's husband is best described by his relentless injuries. If he hasn't pulled his groin, he's twinged his back. Perhaps his knee is clicking, or his ankle feels strained. He insists he bruises easily, and that he has off-centre hips. His core isn't engaged enough and it throws off his balance, et cetera, et cetera.

'I've told him if it's still bleeding tomorrow morning, I'll take him to the hospital,' she admits.

I check the time, do the conversion in my head. 'It's only lunchtime over there—'

One of her kids starts crying and Naya apologises. 'Hold on a second, just going to escape into the yard. Let Leonard manage them.' I hear her make her way through the house and out the back door. 'They're always crying, Charlie. And I love them, I do. But they'll cry about anything and I *know* that didn't come from me.'

Four years older than me, Naya is a stay-at-home mum. While I fled at twenty-one, she remained, living ten minutes from our childhood home and seeing our mother at least three times a week.

I can't imagine it, being with my family that often. When I met Dave, I was a university graduate and didn't need much convincing to travel across the country with someone I had only known ten months. Naya and Mum had been suffocating me since Dad died, all throughout my teenage years, so I welcomed any excuse to flee. I'd be lying if I said I hadn't been looking for some form of a getaway vehicle, and along came Dave. Perfect timing.

The crying stops, so Naya continues. 'Is everything okay? You never ring me.'

'I ring you sometimes.'

'You ring me *back* sometimes. And you never reply to my texts,' Naya clarifies. 'You're damn near impossible to track down. Something must be wrong.'

'Nothing is wrong.'

There's silence on the other end.

'So how are the kids?' I ask.

'They're fine, except for the crying. Lots of energy and we're constantly exhausted, but they're fine,' she says. 'Raphael's birthday party is this weekend, actually. Down at the park near the bike track. He'll be four, in case you'd forgotten.'

'I hadn't.'

'It makes me happy that all his friends from daycare are coming. Especially because he's bitten a few of them recently.'

'He's bitten them?'

She sighs. 'Nothing serious. Daycare is forcing us to see an occupational therapist. And the twins are testing us, which is actually a bit of an understatement. I had a twenty-minute argument with Camille about brushing her teeth this morning. Made me late to a doctor's appointment. And I can only put sunscreen on them if I use a make-up brush. I've realised at least sixty per cent of toddler management is marketing.'

A child starts crying again, this time a particularly heightened shrill sound. And then another starts weeping and Naya huffs. 'Hold on, better see if something serious has actually happened. Darla doesn't like to share anything and the twins have a tendency to steal things and it's honestly just a melting pot in this house most of the time.'

'Where's Leonard?'

'Assessing his hand, most likely. I keep telling him to stop looking at the cut, but he keeps stressing that he'll develop gangrene.'

Leonard works at a local hardware store and has done so since he was sixteen. He met Naya at the cash register not long after he'd started. She'd come in looking lost, because our father had just died and Mum was still glued to her bed in grief, and Naya needed something that was going to plug a leak in the shower. He helped her, they fell in love, and they were married before Naya turned twenty-one.

'Hold up, Charlie, just muting you for a moment.'

The line goes dead.

I use my shoulder to keep my phone rested against my ear and take the time to answer a few more emails. Then I trudge towards the kitchen, just for something to do, and pace around the place. Make myself a piece of toast – butter, peanut butter – and wipe down the kitchen bench while I'm there, since nobody else in the office seems to know how to do it. Have I always worked with such grubby people?

Naya then returns to the call. 'Just as I suspected,' she says, sounding rather defeated. 'Juliette and Camille stole some toys from Darla's room, so now I've put everyone on a time out—'

Naya is cut off rather suddenly.

'Do you think it's getting worse?' A muffled voice, gruff and husky. Leonard.

'You're fine, it just needs a band-aid,' Naya responds. 'Check my handbag if there's none in the drawer. I'm on the phone to Charlie.'

There's a pause. 'Your sister called you? That never happens.'

I cry out, 'I'm not *that* bad.'

But Naya isn't listening, because Leonard is asking her, 'How much antiseptic cream is too much antiseptic cream?'

When Naya suggests he go to a doctor if he's so worried about it, he says he couldn't possibly drive himself there and could she please do it for him?

'Who will watch the kids? I'm not dumping them on Mum again. Jesus. Sorry, Charlie, it's mayhem around here. I forgot you were on the line.'

'Do you want me to call back later—'

'*No*, it's fine. Really. Leonard, *stop* looking at your hand. Stop peeling back the band-aid, the cut is not that bad. Honestly, you and these injuries. Charlie left her husband for less than this – maybe I'm due.'

It's meant to be a joke, but the implication that I left Dave for insignificant reasons does pinch.

Leonard grabs the phone. 'Don't give her any ideas, Charlie! You know I'd never survive on my own.' He means it as a joke and I feel compelled to laugh out of obligation.

Naya snatches back the phone. 'Sorry, sorry. I'm escaping outside again. This house is too small for six people, I'm telling you. I daydream about being alone *all the time.*'

'You daydream about being alone? Really?' My face scrunches.

'Wait until you have kids, and you'll get it, Charlie, you really will. I wasn't kidding when I said I'd been fantasising about going to prison. It's a genuine concern that the next time you hear from me, it'll be from a holding cell.'

She pauses. 'Actually, hold on, I'm going to look it up. Offences that carry short prison terms,' she says, and for a couple of minutes, her end of the line is silent. 'Top result is . . . not stopping a boat when ordered by law enforcement. Damn, now I need to buy a boat.'

I steer the conversation somewhere else. 'Why are you seeing a doctor?'

'Prescription renewal, nothing exciting.' She plonks down on something. One of her outdoor lounges, probably. I'm imagining her left leg is now crossed over her right, and she's resting an arm up above her head, fingers deep inside her frizzy, chestnut hair.

'So why are you calling me?' she asks. 'Real answer only.'

'Do I need a reason?'

'Yes.' She clears her throat. 'I've got four kids and a Leonard and you always seem busier than me. Thought I was hallucinating when your name popped up on my phone.'

'Am I really that bad?'

Naya says nothing.

'Sorry.'

'Everything okay?'

In my chair, I swivel around and around. Let the purple walls dizzy me. 'The ratings came out today, and we're fourth.'

'Is that bad?'

Oh, bless. 'Yeah, it's bad.'

'I'm sorry.'

'It's okay.'

'You'll get it back, don't worry.' It's such a flippant comment, and coming from someone who has no grasp of what we do or why this fall in results is so devastating, it doesn't reassure me. I should try Genevieve again, after this. She'd understand.

'We will. I know.'

'And what about you,' she says. 'Are *you* okay?'

I can't say it feels natural to open up to my sister. 'I'm fine, I promise. Just wanted to hear a familiar voice.'

A moment passes before she speaks. 'You should come home and visit. The kids haven't seen you in over a year.'

The kids haven't seen me in eighteen months. I last visited just after the twins were born, and every time I remember that I feel like a horrid person. But I think of that house – of what it was like living there, after our dad died – and I just can't compel myself to go back.

'How's Mum?' I ask.

'Why don't you ask her? When was the last time you called?'

'Yeah, all right. A while.'

'Has she messaged you about the anniversary yet?' Naya asks.

'Oh god, no. Why?' *The* anniversary, a mere few months away. Twenty years since Dad's death. Just like the fifth, tenth and fifteenth anniversaries, I was hoping to ignore the milestone completely. Melt into the floor and pretend everything is fine.

'I'll let her chat to you about it. Just, call her, okay? Promise me.'

'I promise.'

Someone starts screaming from their naughty chair and Naya

apologises and puts me on mute again. My mind starts to reel. What could my mother want to chat about? What is it about the forthcoming anniversary that—

'Okay, okay, I'm here,' Naya says, returning. 'Sorry.'

'Do you need to go? I can call you back later.'

'You won't though,' she says. 'Once it's after nine, you're in bed.'

'My alarm goes off at three.'

'And? Try having four kids, Charlie.'

Time to bite my tongue. Time to stop myself from blurting out that she *chose* to have those four kids.

There's a scuffle on her end of the line, a muffling sound, and then she's back. 'Hold on one second, it's Leonard again.'

It's intended as a whisper, but Leonard's voice carries through the phone with surprising clarity. 'I just think I'd feel more comfortable if we take a quick trip to the doctor. Get this hand checked out. I don't want the kids to worry—'

'They're way too young to worry about your hand, Leonard. The twins aren't yet *two* and you've got a cut. Antiseptic cream and band-aids are all that's needed. It won't get infected, I promise. Just because Dad died suddenly doesn't mean *every* man dies suddenly.'

That makes me jerk upright. Loss, sadness, heartbreak – it hits me in waves, even after all these years. All it can take is a comment like that and I'm floored. Forced to self-soothe. It stings to hear Naya speak so flippantly about our father's death. As if it wasn't the most traumatic thing to happen in our childhood.

She returns to the phone call. 'So how much do we think boats cost?'

'Too much.'

We might be laughing off Leonard's eccentric behaviour, but I envy Naya a little. A house full of people, always chaotic, always busy. I think of how small my world feels right now and my throat constricts.

'I should go,' she says. 'If I don't take Leonard to the doctor, he's going to talk about that cut all night and I won't get any sleep.'

'Just chop it off.'

'Don't tempt me.'

CHAPTER SEVEN

Where is the engagement ring, Charlotte?

Dave's back. Only managed to hold him off for one week, unfortunately.

'Honestly,' Genevieve says. 'Of all the things he should be worried about right now, and he chooses the engagement ring.'

Sunday morning, we're standing in the far aisle at a baby superstore, discussing which pram is most suitable. I'm trying to explain to Genevieve why a flatback pram might be better than a foldable. Ignoring Dave, we continue.

'It's convertible,' I say. 'You can see the baby the entire time and they lie flat, so they sleep more easily. The front-facing ones are better for—'

But she's just not invested. Eyes in a daze, attention easily broken. Furrowed brows, hand clawing through her burgundy hair. She can be an indecisive person, but this is tipping over into extreme. So, I stop.

'There are just *so* many of them,' she says, overwhelmed. She flips over the price tag of a nearby double pram, and her eyes bulge. 'And some of these are outrageously expensive. Look at this! Two thousand two hundred.'

She's a helpless child herself, lost among all the pastels. Walking around aimlessly, distracted by all the products and the prices.

She's found another pram now, significantly cheaper.

'That's a jogger,' I point out.

She tilts her head, places a finger to her temple – I notice she's had her nails done recently. They're painted a deep teal. 'Maybe I could start jogging when the baby is born.'

I wait for her to realise her error. Only takes a moment.

'No, never mind, I'd hate that.' She leads me further down the aisle. 'How do you know so much about prams?'

'How do you *not*?'

It takes her a second to answer. 'I was so focused on the getting pregnant part, I hadn't really thought beyond that.'

Guilt gnaws at my stomach. 'Oh, right. Sorry.'

'Seriously though, you know a *lot* about prams.' She eyes me suspiciously. 'Were you and Dave thinking—'

'No.' I clear my throat. 'Josie and Emmanuel have two kids each, and Naya has four. And lord knows there's nothing a new parent loves doing more than talking about raising their child.' I catch her wary stare. 'No offence.'

'None taken.'

Actually, now that I think about it, in the week since I found out she's pregnant, Genevieve has barely spoken about her pregnancy at all. After years of trying, and a dozen rounds of IVF, Genevieve is *finally* pregnant. She's finally got what she wanted, but she seems determined not to draw attention to it.

My phone buzzes again, and I fish it out of my pocket.

> My lawyer will be in touch.

When I show Genevieve the message, she is instantly sympathetic. 'I'm sorry it's getting nasty.'

I run my hand over a nearby bassinet. 'You should've seen his reaction when I told him it was over. His body just . . . collapsed in on itself.'

Genevieve is silent.

'I like to remind myself of his annoying habits, whenever I have that image in my head. Helps it go away.'

'Like his obsession with golf?'

'No, more like, when he would constantly talk about what time of year it was. "Can you believe it's the end of October already? Christmas is next week. Oh god, it's mid-May! How did that happen? Sometimes I just cannot fathom how fast the year goes."'

Genevieve chuckles. 'I forgot he used *fathom* in sentences.'

'That's not the reason I left him, but I feel it should be taken into consideration.' I run my eye over a bright mural to our right – orange, green and soft hues of pink.

'What about when he ate?' Genevieve suggests. 'Chewed with an open mouth and food would drop out, like a child.'

'Oh *god*,' I say, mortified. And amused. 'One time he put too much mayonnaise on our burgers, and it just squelched out the corners of his mouth and dripped onto the plate. I can still *hear it*.' I shiver.

She's laughing. 'You never told me that story.'

'I think I'd repressed it.'

'Well, yeah. Naturally.'

We're in the next aisle now, and she's pulled out her phone. Replying to Bruce, then browsing her social accounts. As we pass through the toy section, I play with the interactive displays – the games, the stuffed animals, the motorised cars. This trip is starting to feel like a waste.

'Have you thought about bassinets yet?' I ask. 'Cots? Toys or a change table?'

Once quick glance at Genevieve and I can tell she's not into this. It's a little heartbreaking, to be reminded of how hopeless she'd become. How she thought it'd never happen for her.

'I feel like I'm playing catch-up.' She looks around. 'There's so much to *do*. So much to buy. I don't know how two people are expected to manage it all.'

'*Three*,' I say, nudging her. 'And your parents. That makes five.'

She's appreciative, I can tell, but it's short-lived. 'My parents don't live here, though. Do they count?'

'Of course they count.'

'I keep having nightmares the baby is going to fall out of me while I'm walking.'

'As in a miscarriage?'

She stiffens. 'No, like a fully formed baby just falls out one day and starts crawling. It just waddles around the grocery store and I'm standing there with no idea what to do.'

She grabs my shoulders then, her eyes desperate. 'Charlie, the baby was *huge*. Ready to graduate from daycare, I swear.' Holding her hands to her flat stomach, she glances down. Then back up. Leans in close for a whisper. 'You don't think my baby is going to be like, gigantic, right?'

I look at her, not sure how to respond. Although I can see why she's worried. Her husband Bruce is taller than a fridge and wider than anyone I've ever met, but his whole body is sponge, his belly like pudding. He's a human marshmallow, inside and out. He's got that bum chin American face, though he's not American. The square haircut, too. I once asked him if he has a favourite smell, and he said brand-new action figures. I have no doubt he'd be the first of us to die in an apocalypse.

As we make our way through the store, from the car seats to the nursery, and over to the other side where they sell the feeding supplies, Genevieve avoids making any sort of decision.

'I'm finding it hard,' she says. 'Doesn't feel quite real.'

'The pregnancy?'

She laughs. 'No, the pregnancy is real. The nausea is fucked.' We catch eyes. 'I meant the end of the pregnancy. The bit where you actually have the baby and it's alive and it's well and I get to take it home.'

She reaches out to a nearby rack and runs her fingertips over a cotton bib, dinosaurs stitched to the front. 'Like, what happens if I buy all this stuff and then I lose it?' She looks over at me, tears in her eyes.

'Oh.'

She tries to brush it off with a smile but fails. 'This was it. The final round, you know? And I have to wait another seven months before I know whether it's worked.'

Worked. What an odd yet devastating way to describe a full-term pregnancy.

'Why don't we start with something small?' I say, walking back over to the rack of bibs. 'We can buy a couple of these and then *if* something happens, I can mail them to Dave. And he can use them when he eats.'

She barks out a laugh, so hard her face goes red. Her knees turn inwards and I can tell, without her telling me, that she's at risk of a small pee. It makes me happy that when she's upset or stressed, I can still manage to make her laugh.

Once she's collected herself, she says, 'Deal. Thank you.'

CHAPTER EIGHT

Here is something interesting about my mother.

Her two greatest skills in life are attending to teeth, and cooking. A retired dentist who believes food cures everything – illness, grief, loneliness, anger, anxiety. And, most importantly, heartbreak.

When I left Dave, she called me every day. Texted by the hour. Left voicemails and voice notes, sent packages to the apartment door. And when I didn't answer, because I couldn't quite stomach it, she called Genevieve to ask how I was, make sure I was coping, pass on messages for me.

One day at a time.

Thinking of you.

Call me when you're ready.

There I was, catatonic at the kitchen table, and my mother was making sure I knew how loved I was. That I'd done the right thing. That she supported me. Most of all, she made sure I was eating, because if there's anything that terrifies my mother more than death, it's one of her children adorning an emaciated frame. She emailed recipes to me and Genevieve every single morning. Always at eleven o'clock, with a tail-ended message noting what wine it'd pair best with.

They were meals with simple ingredients, easy to find at the grocery store. Some nights it was a pasta, maybe with bruschetta.

A stew, or a curry. Something comfortable that she knew I'd love, and often meals she'd made for me and Naya when we were growing up. Some of them, actually, were recipes our father used to cook before he died – French onion soup, bourguignons and roasted lamb shank. It had been years since he left France, but he loved cooking meals from his home. And every time Mum sent me one of his recipes, it made me feel like it wasn't just one parent looking out for me, but both.

It became a routine for us – Genevieve, Bruce and me. It was like a lucky dip, waiting to see what my mother emailed each morning. What we'd need to buy from the store. How it might taste. We couldn't quite believe that, at seventy-two years old, my mother was taking the time to handwrite and email me recipes every single morning.

At first, Genevieve felt guilty. My mother was putting in all this work, and she and Bruce were reaping the benefits.

'These recipes are not for us,' she'd say.

And I'd correct her. 'They are, though. They *are* for you, as well as me. This is Mum's way of supporting me, but also thanking you for looking after me. For letting me sleep at your place. For keeping me sane. For keeping me company, when she can't.'

It was never about eating, I remember that much. In those first few weeks, Genevieve dragged me out of bed, forced a vegetable peeler into my hand and told me what to do. Bruce followed the recipe, Genevieve managed the meat, and I prepared the vegetables. Or the sides. Or the drinks. Whatever I had the energy to do that evening.

It kept me busy and my mind occupied. Helped pass the time.

And sometimes, on a bad day, when I felt the full weight of what I'd done, when I couldn't get Dave out of my mind and all I could think about was how drastically I had overturned my life, I simply sat on one of the kitchen stools and watched as Genevieve and Bruce managed it all. Let them fill the silence and talk to me about their day, their jobs, their families.

'What about this place,' I say now, leaning over the kitchen island, holding out my phone. Genevieve, wrapped up in a linen dress and slippers, is slicing chicken breast into strips and coating in cumin powder. Roasted chipotle and garlic chicken, one of my mother's favourite recipes. 'Three bedrooms and a small backyard.'

Looking up, she takes the phone from me, scrolling through the house listing. Then the photos. Her eyebrows rise, impressed. Her smile, widening.

Then she checks the address, and she deflates. 'Charlie, it's three hours south.' She says my name like one might chastise a child.

'Really?' I snatch the phone back, convinced she's wrong. Then clock my mistake. 'Oh, shit, you're right. Sorry. Been looking at too many, I think.'

She sighs. 'I've stopped looking, it's impossible. They're all too expensive. Or far away. Or small. Or ugly.'

I switch to a different real estate website. 'We'll find somewhere. And in the meantime, I'm going to pay more rent.'

'Stop saying that. No, you won't.'

'I will.'

'We love having you here.' She throws me a smile, her hands deep in raw chicken breast, turning it over in the oil and the spices. There's a *squelch* sound as her fingers grasp the meat.

She may love having me here, but it's certainly not *easy* having me here. The apartment is not meant to house this many adults – doesn't have the space or the storage or the layout for it. It's remarkable what she's done to maximise the place, with floating shelving and trailing pot plants hung from the ceiling, furniture with in-built hidden storage. We're cramped but we're cosy. Wooden baskets atop cabinets, vintage prints on the walls, mauve blankets over an olive-green sofa, floor lamps and trailing lights over the windows and scented candles on every surface. It's warm, here.

But we're constantly on top of each other, always waiting for someone to finish in the bathroom or squeezing onto a sofa that's already squeezed into the living room, and I'm starting to wonder if they're seeing too much of me.

Her phone pings, and it's Bruce letting us know he's running late. To eat without him. That he'll heat up leftovers when he arrives.

We return to what we were doing. 'There's got to be something,' I say, scrolling through pages and pages of real estate listings. It's remarkable how much is on offer and yet *none* of it is suitable. Houses so old and broken, they'd need to be torn down. Houses brand new but double the cost of what they're worth. Houses built in the backyard of another house. Houses the size of this apartment. It's all so defeating and yet I'm convinced there'll be something. *Let me do this for them*, I'm thinking. *After weeks of them looking out for me, let me do this for them.*

'Charlie, I'm really tired. Maybe we can look tomorrow?'

'If I move out, you'd have more space for the baby.'

'I've already said no.' She rolls her shoulders back, collects her thoughts. 'Even if you moved out, it's still not what we want long-term. I'd be surprised if the pram fit through the door.'

'You bought a pram?'

She corrects my mistake. 'Oh, no. I just mean when I *do*, where will it go?'

'Oh. Right.' It's been one week and she still hasn't revisited the baby superstore, hasn't bought anything online. In fact, if you look around this apartment, you'd have no clue a baby was on its way. The only sign would be the slew of parenting brochures I gifted them, which sit on the coffee table collecting dust.

'G,' I say. 'That baby is going to be happy and healthy and you and Bruce will find somewhere to live and one day we'll look back on this and realise we were worrying for nothing—'

'We might have to go for an apartment,' she says, voice sharpening. 'I've been doing the maths again and I just don't think we're going to be able to afford a house.'

Pause. 'But you've always wanted a house.'

'Yeah, well, things change.' Her mouth twists.

Genevieve tells me it's time for the next stage of the recipe, and I discard my phone. Peel the sweet potatoes, slice the green beans and listen as she reads out the instructions for the rest of the salad – toast the walnuts, drain the cranberries, rinse the baby lettuce. We rotate around the kitchen, doing our best not to bump into the other or knock something off the bench. Only once does a pair of tongs slide off the counter and onto the floor.

'Have you thought about asking your parents?' I suggest. She's pan-frying the chicken now, and my salad is complete. Tossed and coated and sitting in the middle of the kitchen table, ready for serving.

She looks defeated. 'We both know they wouldn't have enough.'

I'd suspected it but was hoping I was wrong. Most of their savings were spent on the IVF.

'And I wouldn't ask them, even if they did,' she finishes. 'I couldn't let them do that. Again.'

I offer up another suggestion, something I'd already been thinking about. 'Dave plans to stay in our apartment. He wants it, and I don't. And he has the money to buy me out—'

'*No.*' Her voice is sharp.

'You don't even know what I was going to say.'

She holds up a finger, silencing me. 'We're not taking your money.'

Okay, she knew what I was going to say.

'I can't be in debt to *another* person.' Her forehead creases with her frown. 'That's absurd.'

'Think of it as a loan.'

She says, 'That's what Mum said too.' And then she looks over at me and I realise she's on the verge of crying. Her eyes misty. 'Don't offer me your money again.'

'Okay.'

'I feel sick when I think of how much I borrowed from my parents. Physically ill.' Hand to her chest, breathing heavy. 'And I've tried to give it back, but they won't take anything, and now they tell me they don't expect it back, and somehow that makes it worse.'

I rise. 'I'm going to get you some tissues—'

'No, no, I'm fine.' She uses her pinky finger to wipe the corners of her eyes, then fans her face and lets out a few deep breaths, as if resetting.

'I'm just trying to help.'

'I know,' she says, reassuring me. 'And I love you for it.'

'I *will* find you somewhere. I promise. And if you won't take my money, I'll offer up my time. Help you pack boxes, wipe down the walls, clean skirting boards, whatever you need.'

She's plating up, quiet again. Her eyes are downcast, her lips slightly pursed.

'God, I'm sorry. I'm an arsehole, I shouldn't have said anything.'

'We just can't stay here,' she says, taking a moment to glance around the apartment. 'I thought we had time, but we need to get out. This place doesn't work for a baby. There's no airflow, everything has a sharp corner, the gaps between the railings on the balcony are so big that, once the baby starts walking, I'm terrified it'll slip through and fall over the edge. And that teenager down the hall blasts his techno music until two in the morning.'

'I think he's late twenties.'

'I *hate* him, Charlie, and I do not want my baby around him.' She clutches her forehead. 'I wanted a house so our neighbours wouldn't hear the screaming—'

'Who cares about the neighbours?'

'*I* care, Charlie. I *care*. This is exhausting. And I don't know if I have it in me to keep showing up at viewings every Saturday.'

She collects herself, placing her hands on her hips.

'Oh G, I'm sorry.'

She nods.

'Would it help if I murdered the teenager down the hall?'

She chokes out a laugh.

After dinner, I phone my mother. To thank her for the meal, to ask how she is, to give Genevieve some space. And because Naya said I should.

'How are you?' she says, voice soft and melodic. 'And how is Genevieve?'

I watch her slip into her and Bruce's bedroom – tea in hand – and close the door behind her. 'She says hi. We just finished dinner. Delicious, as always.'

Mum drinks in the praise. 'Oh *good*. That's great.'

I'm grateful for the food, I am. But I feel that I don't require it anymore, and that she's spending all this time on me that she doesn't need to. I'm better now. *I'm good, Mum, there is no need to do this for me anymore.*

But whenever a small part of me feels compelled to let her go, she cries retirement.

'Gives me something to do,' she says. 'And I *do* enjoy it. You should see what I've got planned for next week. Something new.'

That bright voice, that excitement. I can't stifle it. Can't bring myself to dampen her enthusiasm to assist. 'Can't wait.' There's something about it that makes me feel a little sick, like I'm exploiting my mother.

She moves the conversation in an entirely new direction. 'Been meaning to talk to you actually. Have you got a second?'

Here we go.

'The anniversary.' She pauses. 'Is coming up.'

'I know.' Got the date of Dad's death burnt into my memory. If I could remove it, forget about it, take some sort of pill that scrapes out that part of my brain, I'd take it immediately.

Twenty years. Has it really been that long? Part of me can barely remember him, and another part cannot stop thinking about him. How he'd dress in flannel, and how curly his hair would get if he went too long without a trim. Those faded loafers he'd wear, and the way he'd butter his bread.

'And I want to celebrate it.'

'Celebrate it? What does that mean?'

'A dinner, I think. The whole family.'

Whole family. What a ridiculous phrase. When did we start referring to our unit as whole? We will never be whole, again.

'And I'm telling you to fly home for it.'

'You're . . .' I trail off, processing, '*telling* me.'

'Yes, I'm telling you.' She holds steady. 'I've never done anything for the anniversaries before, and I think that's wrong. I regret it. And it's been twenty years and you've not been home in so long. We can't even get you here for Christmas! And I was going to *ask* you to come home, but I've done that before and it didn't make a difference. So, I'm telling you this time.'

This is the most assertive she's ever been with me. I fear I'm being disciplined, like I'm a child again. And *Christmas*. I knew she was going to mention that. I've told her I need to work through the holidays, but it's not really a *need*. Not a requirement from the station. I simply decided to do it. To busy myself. Genevieve invited me to spend it with her family, but that's not fair on Mum. It's home, or it's the station. And I chose the station.

I stare at Genevieve's closed bedroom door and desperately wish she'd resurface.

'But I don't want to come home for it,' I say. 'I think that'd make me far happier, if I stayed home and ignored the anniversary altogether.'

Mum is silent.

'You've never visited,' I say.

'Sorry?'

'You and Naya. I've been here ten years.'

'We visited after you moved.'

'*Once*. You visited *once*.'

She ignores me, clears her throat. 'I'm going to cook something he loved.'

Something French, then. Lots of butter, probably a red meat. Two baguettes. Even after twenty years, I remember how much he loved food from home.

Home.

That house holds so many memories and I've tried so hard to avoid them over the years. Moved across the country to avoid them. Never wanted to spend much time in that place, where he died. Where he lived. Where he loved us.

It's not that I don't want to see my family – I do. I miss Naya and the kids. I miss my mother and her mismatched outfits, the absurd ways she styles her hair.

But there's something about being in that house, and in that town, that is too painful. Even after all these years. I can still see Naya's face when she told me he was dead, frozen in horror after trying to revive him. Although I was not there when he died – did not see his body – Naya was. She painted a picture for me that I've never forgotten, her tiny hands pounding on his chest again and again while our mother cried out.

'You probably won't even recognise me,' Mum says. 'It's been that long.'

'Mum.'

'I'm serious. I'm seventy-two now. I fear the asteroid is on its way.'

'*Mum.*'

'It really could happen at any moment. Look at poor Leonard. His body is falling apart. Bruises one day, sliced fingers the next. Sometimes I lie awake at night and think about Naya being a widow.'

'Naya isn't going to be a widow.'

She is instantly defiant. 'I went to bed one night, sleeping husband next to me. I wake up the next morning and he's not breathing! Dead, just like that. It could happen to *anyone.*'

I have to hold the phone away from me for a split second. How incredibly blasé to speak about Dad's death like this. How easily it triggers something in me, even after all these years. A catastrophic, unforeseen heart attack and our lives changed forever.

'What if I say no?'

Mum is silent, for so long I fear she's hung up on me. But then she speaks. 'Charlie, *please.*' There's a wobble in her voice, and I know I've hurt her. Two people tonight, I've made cry.

'You can't pretend he doesn't—' She stops herself. 'I miss you. And I want to celebrate him. So I'm *telling* you.'

CHAPTER NINE

The following Saturday, at an apartment inspection, Genevieve tries to rationalise the situation. She's always held great determination to help me solve my problems. 'I think it's nice that they want to celebrate him,' she says. Then sees my expression. 'But I am, of course, wrong.'

We've carved out time this morning – Genevieve, Bruce, myself – to walk through an apartment I found after days of digging. Twenty-five minutes from where we're currently living. Further away from the city and deep in suburbia, but nestled firmly in their price range.

Beside me, Bruce cradles a piccolo – his second for the day. It's always comical seeing him with one, his gigantic hands wrapped around a minute cup like that. As if a giant were holding a kitten.

We greet the real estate agent – an affable man with wavy black hair wearing a pressed navy suit and clutching an iPad – and step across the threshold, inside.

'I'd prefer to forget,' I say.

'I know.'

'She's obsessing over it.'

Genevieve smiles. 'She's planned a dinner, Charlie. I'd hardly say obsessing.'

'And of course I couldn't say no, because then I'd look like an arsehole. She's cornered me, hasn't she? What are my rights here?'

She tries to hide her laugh. 'It's a trip home, not a murder accusation.' When I say nothing, she changes her tune. 'I can help think of an excuse for you? If we tell them that you've contracted some sort of vaginal rash, maybe they'd understand if you cancelled.'

'You're a good friend.'

'I know—'

A second real estate agent – tall, lean, with a cropped brown hairdo – cuts me off. 'Good morning.'

'Morning,' we recite, then make our way through the apartment.

It's bigger than our rental. An extra bedroom, bigger living area, larger laundry. But it's still a squeeze. I suspect the ceiling is lower, because of how close Bruce's head is to colliding with it. With a body that big, legs that long, he's at risk of clipping the door frame when he enters the first bedroom.

We go through the motions, avoiding the other groups of people as we progress. Kitchen, check. A bit clinical and sterile, with its white laminate cupboards and monochromatic appliances. Carpet, clean enough, but taupe and faded in the centre of the living room where the sun hits. Balcony, concrete and habitable, with a small bistro table and two folding chairs – wooden and splintering. Wardrobes, in-built and with a few scuff marks, but overall, thrilled to see they exist.

It's the first time we've viewed an apartment and so the list of things we're checking has instantly grown shorter. No backyard, no garage. No need to check retaining walls or ground drainage. Instead, it's strata and communal gardens. It's the safety of the entrance and the size of the post boxes.

It's not perfect, but it's certainly nicer than everything else on the market. And more affordable.

I feel a great sense of pride, having found this place. Bruce tosses his coffee cup in the bin and then throws me an appreciative look, because he knows how hard I've been searching. How many listings I've scoured, trying to find somewhere they might love. Trying to repay them for all they've done to help me. Genevieve might've given up on finding a place, but I'm convinced we can find them somewhere before the baby arrives. Somewhere great.

As the crowd grows, we duck out onto the balcony to debrief. Nearby, an older couple discuss buying the apartment as an investment.

'That'd be right,' Bruce grumbles. 'A rich person swooping in and adding another property to their collection.'

Over the railing, on the pavement, I see a couple walk to their car with a child at their feet, and I feel it's a sign. Those two people seem sensible, and they chose to live here. That could be Genevieve and Bruce! Perfect location for families, tick.

Turning back to Genevieve, I assess her. 'Thoughts?'

She nods, looking back inside. Shifting her weight into the balls of her feet and then back over the toes. 'It's nice.'

'I know it's not what you wanted. An apartment.'

Bruce adds, 'It isn't, but I could see us living here.' Then he looks down at her stomach. 'The three of us.'

Her eyes widen, and she nods. I cannot read the expression across her face, but she appears plagued with worry.

'You okay?' I ask.

'Just thinking.'

'What about—'

Someone inside suddenly shrieks to their partner. 'This place is *way* nicer than I was imagining. It'd be perfect for us.'

Bruce, Genevieve and I all turn to the source – a pregnant woman who appears near full-term. Genevieve stiffens.

Part of me is pleased that another pregnant couple can see potential in this place: it means I've done something right. The other part of me is focused on Genevieve, and how she's retreating into the corner of the balcony. She's taking a moment to collect herself, breathing in deeply.

'Everything okay?' Bruce asks.

After a moment, Genevieve nods. 'I think this was a mistake.'

'You don't like the place?' I say. 'It's the first decent one we've found since you got pregnant.'

I don't know why, but saying this somehow makes it worse. Genevieve chokes a little, tearing up. Turns away and rests a hand on the brick wall, hiding her face.

'Did I say something?' I ask. 'I'm sorry.'

Bruce throws me a desperate look over his shoulder. Mouths, *I don't know what's happening.*

'Are you feeling sick?' he asks Genevieve, placing a hand on the small of her back.

She shakes her head.

'We can go home,' I say. 'If this isn't what you want.'

'It's actually lovely,' she whispers. Rolling her shoulders back, she brushes the tears away from under her eyes. 'And it *is* the best place we've seen.'

'So . . .' Bruce treads carefully. 'Maybe we put in an offer?'

Turning back, Genevieve bites her bottom lip and pauses. Stares at her feet, then up and through the glass doors. Then she glances at me. 'I think you're right.'

I exhale, relieved. 'Good—'

'We should stay in the apartment. We should forget about this whole thing. We'll make our current place work.'

And then she walks off, back inside the apartment and towards the front door, leaving Bruce and me reeling.

'What just happened?' he says, eyebrows risen and hands outstretched.

'I have no idea.' I watch as she disappears out the front door. 'She hates the rental.'

Bruce is shocked silent, jaw open. 'I don't . . .' He clutches his forehead. 'I'm confused. She *doesn't* want to put an offer on this place?'

'That can't be right.' I feel like every ounce of energy has been sucked clean from my body.

Then, just inside the apartment, the older couple pop their heads out the sliding door. The man, inches from me, points at the tiled balcony ground beneath our feet. 'Oh dear, bit old. It'll need a renovation.'

Turning to his wife, he says, 'Those guys that fixed the tiling in our last place, can you remember the company name? They do good work – let's get them back again.'

Outside, further down the street, Genevieve hovers by my car while she waits for us.

Bruce stays by the apartment entrance, leaving us to discuss. He does that a lot, I've realised, letting us have time to ourselves. Perhaps he does it when he feels I can help the situation more than he can. Sometimes Genevieve doesn't need him, she needs me.

'We didn't finish our conversation about your mum,' she says. 'And the anniversary.'

'You're deflecting. Don't do that.' I step forward. 'Is everything okay?'

She is jittery. 'Yes, fine. Can we go?'

I make no move to unlock the car. And when I place my keys back inside my pocket, she lets out a frustrated groan. 'I'm *fine*, Charlie.'

'Don't insult me. You're not.'

'You've been saying this whole time we can stay in our current place. You'll move out and we'll turn that room into the baby's room, and we'll be just fine.'

'It's too small.'

'Well, it was time for a cleanout anyway.'

'And the lack of airflow?'

'I'll buy another fan.' She slaps her hands down against her thighs. 'And I'll get those padded strips for all the corners. And I'll get Bruce to build some kind of fencing for the balcony railing.'

'And the teenager down the hall?' I ask.

She opens her mouth, but nothing comes out. And then she collects herself. 'I really don't want to talk about this.'

'You're scared.'

'Of course I'm scared,' she shouts, head tipped back. Nearby, people on the sidewalk glance our way. 'I'm so fucking scared, *all the time*. Every minute of every day, I'm terrified. We've been looking for a house because we wanted to raise a family, and I've somehow only just realised that if this baby doesn't live, we won't need a bigger place anymore.'

Oh.

Oh.

'It'll be a waste of money. And I don't know how I didn't clock it before, but now I have and I'm even more terrified. This is my last chance, Charlie. And if I buy that place and lose the baby? That's all I'll ever think about when I'm living there.'

Stepping forward, I grab her hands and squeeze. Wait until her breathing steadies. 'G, I know it's scary, and I know you're preparing for the worst, and I know you don't want to get your hopes up and then have them completely obliterated, but this is something you can't control. You could buy a pram and lose the baby.' Then I gesture behind me. 'And you could buy that apartment and lose the baby.'

She looks away, closing her eyes. Her expression is haunted. 'I know.'

'It wouldn't be your fault. You know that, right? If something happened, if things didn't go to plan. It's never your fault.'

She says nothing.

'I'm trying to think of ways I can help. Things I can say.'

'I'm not sure there's anything you *can* say. I don't really know how to explain it, and I'm trying not to make it about me. But this isn't something you can understand unless you go through it.'

She's not trying to be cold, I know that. But it twists me inside. And she seems shocked to have even said it.

This isn't something you can understand.

CHAPTER TEN

'You ever think about having kids?'

Monday lunchtime, and Graham does not take well to my question. Across the kitchen, he looks up from his sandwich. Raises an eyebrow, slightly stricken. 'I think you might be too young for me.'

'Funny.' I pour my coffee and lean against the bench. 'I am absolutely too young for you.'

He discards the sandwich for a moment.

'I'm worried about Genevieve,' I say, stepping closer to him. 'She's terrified the pregnancy won't carry.'

'I think that's a fairly valid terror.' He reclaims his sandwich, bites into it. Then continues. 'And no, I never thought about having children.'

'Never?'

'No.' Something darkens in that expression of his – like he's plagued. Haunted. His frown, the creases in his forehead, the slight pull of his lips as they shift. Then, he points at me. 'Did you?'

I came here to discuss Genevieve, not myself. 'We'd talked about it.' I take a sip of my coffee. 'But we weren't there yet.'

'Right.' He eyes me over his lunch.

'Thank god,' I say. 'Leaving him would've been significantly harder if the two of us had a child.' But now I'm approaching my mid-thirties and I've no prospects for children and I may never have children and maybe I'll be the one doing twelve rounds of

IVF and feeling crippled with worry about miscarrying. It's something I think about, from time to time, but then I remember my only other option was staying in a decaying marriage, and I remind myself I did the right thing.

Swallowing the lump in my throat, I segue the conversation back to Genevieve. 'I've never gone through it, so I don't know what's normal. She won't even buy a pram.'

He thinks on it for a moment, as he chews.

'I thought you might have some advice. Like, if this were me, what advice would you give?'

He shrugs. 'I wouldn't give advice, I'd just tell you that I'm sorry you're hurting.'

'That's it? I'm sorry?'

'Sometimes that's all people want to hear,' he says, rising. Discarding his napkin and putting his plate in the dishwasher.

'You leaving?' I ask, checking the time.

'Not yet. I've got a meeting.'

'A meeting?' I follow him out of the kitchen and back towards the studio. 'You never have meetings.' Suspicion activated.

'Yeah, well, today I do.'

'With who? Doing what?' I've heard nothing since our rapid fall to fourth, and I've been paranoid ever since. My body reeks of it, I'm certain.

No word from the executive team, no whispers around the office. I'm terrified my time is up, worried they're going to replace me. The media coverage has dwindled, sure, but I'm convinced there's an agenda here at the station. Surely, *surely*, something is coming. A staff shake-up, or a new format. Maybe they'll move Graham to a different time slot, or get rid of him altogether. And me! What's going to happen to me? My colleagues look at me each morning like it might be the last time they see me, and with each passing day, I'm growing more and more agitated.

'You need to stop stressing.' He slaps his hands down against his sides.

'I'm physically unable to do that. Is the meeting about me?'

'You're not that important,' he says, then smiles. 'No offence.'

This does not placate me. I'm like a dog with a bone, I simply cannot stop. 'Who is it with? I'm stressing over here, Graham.'

'I'm sorry you're hurting,' he says, then smiles.

'You seriously aren't going to tell me?'

'No. I'm seriously not going to tell you.' He walks across the floor towards the elevator. Turns briefly, holds out his hand. 'But you're fine, okay? You're not going anywhere. I can promise you that.'

But it does little to ease my nerves.

Over a late lunch, Bruce and I meet to discuss Genevieve.

At a poky little café near my work, he arrives wearing chinos and a brand-new business shirt. It's a deep lilac, and it throws me. Not sure I've ever seen an IT consultant wear the colour eggplant before.

'Nice shirt,' I say, as he slips into the chair opposite.

Looking down, he casts an eye over it. 'I can't tell if you're being sarcastic—'

A staff member cuts him off, and we take a moment to order – coffee, cheeseburgers, juice – and then Bruce runs a hand through his hair, slouches back in the chair, crosses his arms and sighs.

'I'm worried about Genevieve,' I say. 'She's so terrified this pregnancy won't carry that she's too anxious to make a decision – won't buy anything. She's convinced you shouldn't buy a place. Hasn't chewed my ear off about stretch marks or rose-hip oil. Hasn't contemplated names yet. I had to make a joke about Dave just so she'd buy a *bib*, for Christ's sake.'

Bruce chuckles. 'I know, she told me. Always bothered me that man couldn't close his mouth when eating. Was like watching someone who'd been living underground their whole life enter society.'

I give him a look, unimpressed.

'Sorry, sorry.' He gestures to me. 'Keep going.'

'That's it!' I exclaim. 'You haven't noticed? Haven't thought something is odd?'

Bruce sits forward, ready. 'Have I *noticed*? That's a bit insulting. Of course I've noticed. I'm not Dave, Charlie. I *am* useful for some things and I do possess the ability of noticing when my wife is upset.'

Well, *ouch*.

'And we've talked about it.' Then he clarifies. 'Actually, *I've* tried to talk about it.'

'But she shuts you out?'

'Yes.'

'Me too.'

He runs a finger across his forehead, evidently stressed. 'I was hoping, as we progressed, she wouldn't be so worried. But then we passed six weeks. Then eight. And she's still—'

'Terrified.'

He nods. 'I don't think she thought this was ever going to happen. Twelve rounds, you know?'

'I know.' I think back on the IVF – the disappointments and the letdowns, the countless medical appointments, the negative pregnancy tests, how Genevieve changed with each round. She grew quiet, more reserved. Resigned to the fact that it might not happen for them.

'It scares me,' I say. 'How withdrawn she is. Like she's waiting for this whole thing to fail and each day, she's retreating more and more. Protecting herself, in case something happens again, and she can be like, "Well, I was right. I'm not meant to be a mother." But if everything *is* okay and she does have the baby? Well, she might regret it, one day,' I say, mid-chew. 'That she wasn't there for the big things.'

'Fuck, you're right,' he mutters. He expels a loud breath, rolls his shoulders back. 'I have no idea what to do. I thought she might just need more time.'

'Maybe.'

'You don't look convinced.'

Because I'm not. Because I *know* Genevieve and I suspect she will hold on to this fear the entire nine months. She will wind herself up and stress will slowly eat her alive.

Our coffees arrive and he grabs at his like a lifeline.

'I'll talk to her parents, when we're home for Christmas,' he says, between sips. 'I think it might be good for her to spend some time with her mum.'

'Yes.' Her *parents*. I feel myself relax at the suggestion, like Bruce just threw us a lifeline. 'That's a good idea. Talk to Cheryl when you arrive and ask her to speak with Genevieve. It'll help, it has to.'

Frowning at me, Bruce says, 'You're very bossy, you know.'

'One of us has to be.' I don't mean for it to sound cruel, but I hear it as it comes out of my mouth.

He winces, as if attacked. Silence befalls us.

And then, he says, 'I've really tried.'

'I know.'

'Every day, I've tried speaking to her. She's been so snippy with me, and we never used to fight, but we're fighting. She thinks I'm nagging her and all I'm trying to do is help her. It's been keeping me up at night. It's *my* baby too.'

He's haunted – sunken expression, body folded over his burger, devouring that meal like he hasn't eaten in days. I can't believe I didn't see it until now.

I reach out, grab his hand. Squeeze. In this moment I realise something – Bruce and I have been worrying about Genevieve, but who has been worrying about Bruce? I was so focused on my best friend, I didn't really think about how these years, and their miscarriages, affected Bruce.

'Are *you* okay?' I ask.

His eyes widen, and his chin tips up as he collects his thoughts. I can tell, and I'm ashamed in this moment, that this might be the first time someone has asked Bruce that.

'I really don't know.' Rather suddenly, he wipes his mouth with a serviette. Clasps his hands together, shakes away the tears forming in the corners of his eyes.

'Oh, Bruce. I'm sorry.'

CHAPTER ELEVEN

We're losing interviews.

The ratings results, which I try every day to forget, are impossible to escape. And for the first time since I've worked here, I'm struggling to pull interviews. Am getting ghosted by publicists, am getting told they have no space for me in the media schedule. When I ask for feedback they tell me there's limited availability but I'm certain it's because of the ratings. Because we're sliding. Talent managers only have so much time in the schedule and they're not going to waste a slot on a breakfast program that's no longer pulling in the listeners.

Today is no different. Sitting here, at the desk, after everyone else has gone home, and I find myself on the phone arguing with a music publicist. 'I'm sorry, Charlie, I can't justify keeping this interview,' he says. Voice strained. 'Not anymore.'

'Hamish, it was an *exclusive*.'

Pause. 'We can't do it, I'm sorry.' There's genuine sympathy there, but it doesn't do anything to settle this deep pit in my gut.

'Are you giving it to someone else?'

He doesn't answer, and I feel like crumbling. Collapsing onto the carpeted ground beneath me, crawling into my sweater and disappearing.

Our biggest interview of the year – something scheduled six months ago, something we've been promoting on air for the past week – has been pulled. One quick phone call and we're done. One of the biggest pop singers in the world and we had the national exclusive. We'd promised them a double slot, we'd promised to send through questions beforehand, and we'd promised to send the pre-recorded interview ahead of time to check it was fine. All these contingencies that we'd never normally offer, and we're still being cast aside.

'Charlie,' he starts. 'We get one slot in this market. *One* radio interview. I have to be able to justify where I place it.'

'But you *gave it to us*.'

'Yeah, before,' he says. *Before*.

'Hamish.'

Finally, he says it. 'You're fourth, Charlie. *Fourth*.'

I expected it, naturally, and I still find myself grimacing. Pinching the bridge of my nose. 'Who are you giving it to?'

He doesn't answer.

'*Fuck*.'

'I'm sorry, Charlie. I'm really sorry.' And then he hangs up, and I am alone again. In this quiet station, with an hours-old, half-eaten sandwich to my right, and a cold mug of coffee to my left.

'He cancelled?'

I jump. Turn around.

Graham is perched on the edge of my colleague Ivan's desk, hands crossed. Glasses resting on the edge of his nose. Bushy eyebrows drawn together, gaze distant.

'Yeah.'

He closes his eyes, crushed. 'Christ.'

'Why are you here?'

'I left my wallet in the studio.'

'Oh.'

'You told me you weren't going to stay back again.'

'I lied.'

He nods, and doesn't appear to have the energy to fight me on this. 'He's really cancelled?' he asks, and I nod.

For the first time since the ratings results, I see genuine fear flash across Graham's face. *What's going to happen to us?*

'Have you heard anything?' I ask.

He doesn't need me to elaborate. Apparently there's been no word from the executive team since the ratings were released, but that doesn't mean we're in the clear. Doesn't mean our jobs are safe.

What's
Going
To
Happen
To
Us?

'I meant what I said,' Graham replies. 'If they fire you, I'll walk.'

CHAPTER TWELVE

When my car needs servicing, I face a minor crisis.

Such an absurd, unforeseen crisis that I actually feel like a complete fool. Idiotic and reckless, really.

I'm parked across the road from my mechanic's garage and have been for the last fifteen minutes, psyching myself up. Motivating myself like one might before a public speech.

I'm not sure what the protocol is here, because Emmanuel's husband Diego has been my mechanic for eight years and does the service every six months for a discounted rate. Has even helped me find a new car twice.

What now?

I haven't seen the man since I left Dave. But he'll know if I switch mechanics. Not right away, but eventually. He might be at the breakfast table with Emmanuel at some stage and realise I've missed my six-month service, then deduce I've visited another mechanic out of sheer embarrassment at having to run into him.

Selfishly, part of me is wondering if he'd still give me a discount.

'Don't worry about any of that,' Mum says, on the phone. 'Just focus on yourself, okay? And maybe stop hovering outside in your car. They'll think you odd.'

She's called to ask if I've booked my flights home yet (I haven't) and gets absorbed in the tale of Diego. When I tell her I kept my servicing appointment but am parked kerbside across the road, working up the nerve, she chastises me.

'It'll be awkward for a *moment*. And you shake it off and you say hello and then you get on with it.'

One of Mum's favourite sayings for an awkward or tense situation. *And then you get on with it.*

I peer across the road, running an eye over all the workers. No Diego. Which is odd, for a Saturday. He's *always* working on a Saturday. Could he have seen my car on the schedule for today and called in sick? Could he and Emmanuel be on a holiday, travelling somewhere? Could he be hiding somewhere out the back, waiting for me to drop off my car and leave?

It's been five weeks since Josie's fortieth and I feel apprehensive about running into the group. Any of them. I'd been *so* confident knocking on Josie's door, and now that confidence is shot. And it's witless, I know, to be cowering here instead of pulling myself together. But when Dave and I separated, everyone else's lives just continued and yet, I'm still here, struggling.

I'd ring Genevieve to relay how daft I'm being, but she and Bruce have left to visit her parents for Christmas, and except for a few sporadic texts, we haven't spoken. I've been trying to give them space – let Bruce help Genevieve and let Genevieve be with her parents. And as such, I've been alone in their apartment, drowning in deafening silence and extreme loneliness. When I first moved in, after I left Dave, I felt unable to breathe. Wishing it wasn't so crowded. But now, I fear I'm experiencing too much of the place – I am simply not fit to live alone, I feel.

Genevieve invited me to join them, of course. She knows I don't enjoy spending Christmas with Mum and Naya, because it reminds me too much of Dad. Of his empty seat at the table and how I miss his loud, festive aprons, and the shortbread he'd bake every Christmas Eve. How I've spent almost every Christmas over the past ten years with Dave's family, purely to avoid my own.

But I declined, preferring to work through the holidays and better the show, come up with plans to reclaim our top spot. Keep busy and wait for the festive period to pass.

In the car, phone pressed to my ear, Mum speaks. 'Have you heard from him, recently?'

Dave. She doesn't need to say his name, with that cautious, careful, quiet tone.

'He's still asking about the engagement ring.' I glance down at my left hand.

She inhales sharply through closed teeth – a piercing noise. 'You still haven't told him you lost it?'

'Still haven't replied to his messages. Still haven't called him back.'

There's a silence on the other end of the line. Just for a moment.

'I think he's asking for it so that I'll see him,' I say. 'When I left, he wanted to work it out. Wanted to talk it through.'

'Oh.'

'But I was done.'

I haven't told her what happened with Dave – not yet. I can't trust her to keep it to herself. Genevieve stays loyal, like a vault. Knows all my secrets. But my mother would tell my sister the first chance she got. And then who knows where the information would end up?

'I'm sorry it didn't work out,' she says. 'I know I've said it before, but I feel like—'

'Tell me something that will make me laugh,' I interrupt, as I continue searching for any sign of Diego. For any sign of my old life. 'Something funny.'

I'm wondering why I didn't just switch mechanics. Find someone else. Ignore the fact that Diego would've realised at some point. But I've already changed so many things in my life – can't

I keep this one small thing the same? Maybe it's because I want him to tell the group that he saw me. Remind them I exist, so that they'll reach out, apologise and invite me back into the fold. Or it could be that I need to prove I can do this. Prove I can face these run-ins and come out the other side, stronger. That I'm not going to let what happened at Josie's birthday change who I am.

It might just be all of the above.

Mum picks up on the topic change. The need for a lighter conversation. Says 'Oh' in a perky tone and then thinks on it for a second. 'Well, Leonard's hurt himself again.'

It makes me smile. 'Of course he has.'

'Nothing serious.' It never is. 'He was regrouting outdoor tiles yesterday and tripped over. Got a bruised chin.'

'Naya's furious?'

'Fuming. He's been at the doctors twice already. I took him an ice pack this morning and let him unload his woes for a while, to give Naya a break.'

Mum might be the only person who can stomach Leonard when he's injured. She lets him ramble about his cuts or bruises or scrapes. Has always had a soft spot for him, because he helped take care of us after Dad died. When Mum was deep in grief and couldn't leave her bed. When we needed help with cooking and cleaning. When I needed someone to drive me to school. It was Leonard.

He may seem ridiculous, but she wouldn't have it any other way.

'You're very good to him,' I say.

And then I spot Diego, reversing a car out of the shop and parking it down the back of the lot.

He's here.

My chest constricts, my throat closing up. Wearing that dark blue jumpsuit, patterned with grease and oil. A rag draped over his left shoulder. Thick, black hair tousled and standing to attention.

Four-day stubble. Emmanuel once told him if he ever fully shaved his face, it'd be grounds for divorce.

I wouldn't say Diego and I were super close, but he's certainly the most interesting of the group. The most layered. When he shares stories of his family – scattered around Brazil – it's clear he had a lively upbringing. Rich, flavourful music. His mother the heartbeat of the family. He talks to his extended family – aunts, uncles, grandparents – almost as often as his own siblings. They eat together, venture together, consume culture together. When he drinks, he and Emmanuel start to samba. Dancing is something he could never live without, he once told me, and one Sunday a month he volunteers at the local community centre teaching locals all that he knows. Community is everything to him.

Not long after I met him, I told him my father died when I was twelve and he pulled me into a hug and shed a tear. Told me he couldn't imagine what that would've been like. Called it an unimaginable horror. It was the most empathy I'd received from anyone.

Maybe *that's* why I'm actually here. Because he's a good person, and I like talking to him. Because I've enjoyed coming here every six months, spending time with just the two of us, away from everyone else.

'Are you still parked across the road?' Mum asks.

'Yes.'

'I'm hanging up now. You're worrying too much. I'll talk to you later. About to send you tonight's recipe.'

She cuts in with an afterthought. 'And book your flights, please.'

'Tonight. I promise.'

Then she's gone.

*

Diego isn't there when I park the car. Isn't there when one of his colleagues greets me, checks me off the schedule, and takes my car keys.

I scan every corner of that shop trying to spot him, but no luck.

'You need something?' his colleague asks. A short, lanky boy. Early in his career, I suspect. Not an ounce of dirt or grease on his jumpsuit.

'Diego? I thought I saw him, earlier.'

'Oh, yeah, he's here somewhere.' He turns around, lowering his clipboard. 'Bathroom, maybe. Or the back room on brea— Oh, there he is.'

The boy points, says 'Diego!' in an unnecessarily heightened volume. So, of course, Diego hears. Of course he looks our way, caught unawares.

And then he freezes.

Body rigid, feet no longer moving. He gives a trying smile, a half-wave, and then darts off. Scurrying away like a beetle.

And he doesn't return.

CHAPTER THIRTEEN

Two days later, still reeling, I relay the story to Graham in the hallway of a posh hotel as we await our turn at a press junket with a touring celebrity actor.

'He ran away?' Graham says, dumbfounded. We're seated by the elevators on the fourth floor. A row of chairs lining the wall, we move forward every time a journalist at the front steps into the junket room. 'Like, actually ran off? You sure he wasn't just in dire need of the loo?'

'No, the little fucker *ran off*,' I say. 'Should've seen his face. Had no idea I was coming – looked like he'd been slapped across the nose.'

Graham's eyebrows rise, shocked. 'And you never saw him again? He didn't send you a message afterwards?' he asks, left leg crossed over the right. Arms folded. His frown tells me he's rather invested in this story.

'No. He just slithered off somewhere.'

The time reads three o'clock and a flustered publicist wearing black tells us it shouldn't be too much longer.

'Right, well. There you go. And the price? What did they charge you?'

'No discount.'

He is empathetic, offering me a gentle smile. 'Shame.'

After Diego disappeared, I was gutted. I'd expected there to be an awkward conversation, of course, but was completely thrown when there was no conversation at all. What kind of adult runs away from another person? Am I riddled with an infectious disease? A witch dancing with the devil?

I haven't stopped thinking about where he even went, when he slipped away. I picture him cowering in some office, under a desk, and it just doesn't seem like the Diego I know. The jovial, social, helpful Diego. The man who sends money home to his parents every month, who dances while he eats, who wears orange tracksuit pants to dinner and spends the entire evening trying to convince us all that it's *far-shun*.

I just never thought I'd be a person someone ran away from.

'You want to talk about it?' Graham asks, shuffling through the interview questions and briefing notes that sit nestled in his lap. Beneath our feet is plush navy carpeting with gold trims at the base of the skirting boards. Scattered along the walls are bone-white sconces.

'Not really.'

'Understood.'

But then, instantly, I change my mind. Realise it's dangerous to be left alone with my thoughts at a time like this. Left alone at all, really.

'You've done this five times,' I say. 'You ever had anyone run away from you?'

'Thanks for the reminder,' he says, giving me a look. 'And no, never.'

'Must be me, then.'

'Must be Daniel.'

'Diego.'

'Right, Diego.' Then he chuckles. 'Still can't believe he ran away from you.'

We're moved up the line into the next seats. In front of us

sits a television entertainment reporter, and in front of *her* a print journalist I don't recognise.

'You lose people,' he says, quietly. 'It's kind of inevitable.'

'I've lost *all* my people.' Dave, my friends. Haven't seen my family in over a year and a half. It's like somebody clicked their fingers – *snap!* – and everyone I love evaporated. Disappeared into thin air, leaving me behind. Then, I remember Genevieve. 'Well, almost all of my people.'

'Not me,' Graham says. Then he is sombre, his face still. I've known him long enough that I can pinpoint the exact moment he moves into deep thought – he grows quiet.

'You've lost people?' I ask.

And he nods. 'Every time,' he says, leaning back into the chair. 'You never see their friends again. Their family. I've made friends with their colleagues before, but they didn't survive the divorce.' He shrugs. 'Life, I guess.'

Josie, Shaun, Emmanuel, Cinar, Diego. Are they really all gone?

Perhaps Graham realises how nonchalant he's being about it all, because he starts to backtrack. 'But I get it. I remember how shocked I was the first time around. After Leona . . .'

Leona, his first wife. The one I suspect he misses the most, and the one he loved the greatest. He talks about her the least, but when he does, it's always good things. The way she laughed, how often she laughed. How beautifully she dressed, and how superb her taste was. How kind she was. Caring. Thoughtful.

I didn't know him then, of course. This was a lifetime ago – thirty years, maybe more – when Graham was co-host of a community radio music station. He was somewhat known but not famous. Not rich. Just another bald white man working in radio, who'd been married for ten years and loved his wife so fiercely he complimented her on air on a regular basis. Spoke about how he was punching, how he couldn't wait to have children with her.

And then it ended, and Graham was blindsided. He went underground for a while, took a leave of absence. And the tabloids went berserk for it – how in love he was, quoting old audio of him raving about their perfect marriage.

And the whole time, she was cheating on him.

The widely sordid tale of Leona leaving Graham for a café worker sped around the country, and when Graham emerged from his isolation four months later, thinner and haunted, everyone knew who he was. Everyone was tuning in to hear what he had to say.

Leona leaving Graham was the worst thing that happened to him. But it was the best thing to happen to his career.

Back in the hotel hallway, we're shuffled forward to the front of the queue and are one step closer to our interview slot. If Graham knew how hard I had to beg for this, he'd be sickened. I sent so many emails, called the actor's management and pleaded for time – any time – in the press junket.

But if this helps keep our breakfast program alive, I'd do it all again.

The flustered publicist returns. She has a slick ponytail, darkened eyebrows, and her phone appears stitched to her hand. 'You're next,' she says, then disappears into the hotel junket room.

'How long did you say our slot was?' Graham asks.

I swallow. 'Five minutes.'

He frowns, checks his watch.

The journalists before us have each had longer allocations – ten minutes – and I am hoping Graham won't notice. Hoping he won't say anything. I'm just so sickeningly grateful we've even got a slot at all.

'Any plans this weekend?' I ask.

After a moment, Graham disregards the time and shakes his head. 'Nothing.'

'You say that every week.'

'Well, I mean it every week.'

'I've tried calling you on weekends, and you never answer.'

'I'm not glued to my phone the way you lot are.'

'Careful, you're showing your age.'

He smiles, then looks back at me. 'I drive a lot. Get out of the city.'

'By yourself? Why?'

His chin snaps back with the question. *Why are you alone most of the time?* And it takes him a second to answer, but rather poorly.

'I don't know, I think I just prefer it that way—' He checks his watch again. 'You know, everyone else has been in there longer than five minutes.'

'Oh, really?'

At my feet sits my handbag, and I grab out my water bottle and take a sip.

'You told me the publicist emailed *us* about this junket.'

'She did.'

He holds my gaze.

'She didn't,' I say. The way he's looking at me – narrowed eyes, upper body tilted forward – and I know that lying to him is not an option. 'Someone dropped out, that's how we got in.'

He looks down, running his hands over his knees. Nods a few times, deflating each time. His body is like a balloon and I just popped it.

My phone alerts me to a text message – loud and shrill – and I realise it's not on silent. I fish it out of my bag. Switch it to silent, intent on ignoring the message until the press junket is complete.

But it's Josie.

And I cannot possibly ignore it, when it's been *weeks* since I've heard from her. When I'm desperate to know what she's thinking, even though I know I shouldn't.

'Charlie? Graham? We're ready for you now.' The publicist is back.

Graham is already standing, three steps ahead of me. He's managed to mask his disappointment.

The publicist is waiting for us, impatient. She's giving me a narrowed look, then glances down at the phone in my hand.

'Charlie.' Graham grows huffy.

'Sorry!' I stand, collect my things. 'Coming.' Scrambling after him, nodding an apology at the publicist.

I step inside the room, and as I hear Graham introduce himself to the agent, and then the actor, I sneak a glance at the message.

> Charlie, let's get coffee. Tomorrow? Usual spot?
> I'd like to apologise in person.

CHAPTER FOURTEEN

True to form, Josie arrives late. Her shirt untucked, handbag swinging from her forearm, her fringe scattered at all different angles.

'Oh my gosh, hello. Hi.' She plonks down on the chair opposite me. 'I can't believe how late I am.' Checking her phone, she baulks. 'Twenty minutes, horrendous, I'm *so* sorry. There was a bit of drama at home and I lost track of time.'

We've met at our favourite coffee shop four blocks down from her house – a suburban corner café, rattan seating, wooden white tables, overgrown fronds and potted palms in corners, windows stretched floor to ceiling, staff wearing crisp white aprons, cream-coloured cushions on seats.

Josie's sporting a new haircut – chopped below the ears, darkened strawberry colour, shorter fringe – and I'm so floored by it, I do nothing but stare.

It's the first time I've seen her stray from the long, flowing waves and I'm caught off guard. That ethereal look is gone and now she looks, well, ordinary. Conventional, I guess. The crown has toppled off her head and she is now like every other person on the street. Reminds me of my own hair change, six weeks before I left Dave. Dyed it all white then realised the relationship couldn't be salvaged, so changed it back to ash blonde.

'Your hair,' I say, dumbfounded.

'Oh *right*, you haven't seen it.' She reaches up and fingers the ends. 'I needed a change.'

'One hell of a change.'

'You like it, right?' she asks, nervous.

It takes a moment to get used to it. After so many years looking like Galadriel, she now resembles D.W. from *Arthur*. 'Of course.'

Her hair delays discussion about the text, but not for long. Josie, plagued with guilt, sits forward in her chair, places her handbag on the ground at her feet, then grabs my hand and squeezes it.

'Charlie, I'm sorry. *So* sorry. I'm a horrible person. An awful friend. It's unforgiveable. I think I was shocked when you and Dave split and just assumed you wouldn't be coming to that party. And I don't know why I said what I said, but I've spent weeks kicking myself for it.'

Her apology seems genuine, which is a shame because I'd planned on yelling at her and making her feel all sorts of uncomfortable. And I didn't realise how much frustration I harboured until she just said all those things. I can feel my body unwind.

'You could've called,' I say. 'To apologise.'

'I know, I know. And I should've. But I was furious with myself. I felt sick. And I couldn't face you. I was embarrassed.'

'But you're here now?'

'Yes, I am.' She pats my hand. I wait, but she has nothing to add.

'I've missed everyone.' My voice is quiet and it wavers, because I'm trying not to tear up. I didn't even plan to say it.

'Oh god, Charlie.' She pulls me into a hug. 'I'm going to message them all after this. Tell them off. We've been horrible, haven't we? Real arses.'

'It's okay.'

'It's not.'

'Okay, it's not.'

She is satisfied and sits back in her chair.

Over the past few years, Josie and I have spent hours here. It's like our second home, somewhere just for us. She runs a hand through her new hair, and I can tell she's still getting used to it. 'Gosh, there's so much change happening at the moment.'

And I remember, now, what she said. About drama. About losing track of time. 'Is everything okay? At home?'

'Oh, yes, all fine.' She exhales with an intensity I'm not sure I've heard before. 'The twins are being tiny brats, but what else is new?' Her reddened cheeks are returning to their natural colour but the skin under her eyes looks sunken. She rubs her eyes. 'Emile's teacher told us he's struggling with his spelling, so I've been getting up with him every morning to help him with the workbook. And *obviously* he hates it, so it's this whole palaver. When I was seven, I swear it was "hat" or "cat" but the boy's got words like "dance" and "rinse". And he can't work out if something has an S or a C and so he just guesses. And when he gets it wrong, he starts crying and it's this whole thing.' She waves her hands about, then leans in close, whispering. 'And of course Shaun's no use. Doesn't help unless I ask him to—'

A staff member appears to our left. '*Oh*,' Josie says, perking up. 'Marvellous. I'll have an oat latte.' She turns towards me, hand extended.

'Flat white, please. Regular.' The staff member scoots off.

'What were we talking about?' Josie asks. 'Oh, the kids. Boring. Let's not. How are *you*?' She pokes my leg. 'These pants are cute. They new?'

'They are, actually.' I run my hands around the pinched waist.

I've had coffee with Josie enough times to know how easily she flitters between topics. How often she'll moan about her husband, tell me her kids are exhausting her, and that her mother-in-law is once again meddling in their family life. And then where I bought my outfit, how my mother is enjoying retirement, how my sister manages to keep up with four kids when she's struggling so much with two, and how I'm finding my job at the radio station. All in the space of ninety minutes, often less.

'How's work?'

Josie is a mediator. Has been doing it for as long as I've known her. She waves off the question with a flick of her hand. 'Oh, same old.' Then she toys with the question a little further, lets it sit. Her body tilts to the side while she muses. 'Actually, the company's been struggling a little. There have been a few layoffs, but I've been reassured I'm safe. Been there the longest, after all.'

'Oh, shit.'

'Sounds worse than it is.' She brushes her hair behind her ear, runs a hand down her linen pants. They're thin and seem like they might tear with the slightest pull. 'Mediation is just taking a bit of a dive at the moment, it seems.'

'People trying to solve their own problems?'

Josie shrugs. 'Or just not solving them at all. It'll pass though; it always does. There are *so* many psychos out there. And they all work office jobs, for some reason.'

Then, she segues to her new assistant. Early twenties. Gen Z and insufferable. 'Just no awareness. No understanding of hard work. Been out of uni for, like, one minute and wants an outrageous salary she hasn't earned. I'm really harsh with her, if I'm being honest. But it's necessary! Sorry. If I could flush her head down the toilet, it'd be so satisfying. She'll say something sassy and I just think, *If it meant I wouldn't get fired, I'd totally haze you.*'

After a moment, she continues. 'The entire time she's been alive is how long I've been in the workforce. Respect your elders, you know? The older I get, the more I turn into a Karen. And it's completely inevitable. I. Am. A. Karen.'

Our coffees arrive and she drinks almost half the cup at once. Closes her eyes and sighs, like she'd been craving it all morning.

'So, tell me everything,' she says, perking up. 'How *are* you? I've been thinking about you a lot. Must be so hard, what you've been going through.'

'It's getting easier.'

She nods profusely. 'Of course, of course. It'll take time, I'm sure of it. Separating after that long? I couldn't imagine.'

'For the best though.'

'So, no regrets then?' she asks, watching me with a keen eye.

'No.'

'That's great. Really great.' Her face falls, and I think she was expecting more – a bigger download, perhaps. 'Must be difficult. I feel for you, going through this.' She places a hand to her chest.

I'm wondering if this coffee date is just an opportunity for Josie to relay how sorry she feels for me. It's not nice, to be constantly reminded. I want to be distracted. I want to talk about something else.

When she realises I've divulged as much I'm going to, she changes the subject. 'Diego mentioned he saw you.'

Ha, knew it. They've definitely got a new group chat without me.

'Did he tell you he ran away from me?'

Josie is prepared for this, placing a hand to her chest again. 'Poor thing was *so* unwell.'

Of course he was. A likely story. 'Convenient.'

She sips her coffee, shifting uncomfortably. And then her phone *pings* and she glances quickly at the incoming text message. Lets out an almighty groan. 'Shaun, honestly. I leave the house for ten minutes and he's asking me something about the twins. He can't function without me, I swear.'

There's silence while she taps out a text to him. And then she speaks. 'The kids are at that horrendous age where they're being crude with us. Sometimes when they catch me on a bad day, I wonder if I'm capable of murder.' Then she laughs, waving it off. 'Kidding, obviously.'

'Obviously.'

'And I know I've said this before, but Shaun is a complete sucker. They walk all over him.'

I fidget with the edges of my blouse, run my hands over my thighs, clear my throat. There's something about our conversation I can't quite place. Something *off* about all of this. Josie's always been one to moan about Shaun and the kids, but I don't remember feeling this agitated by it. And I can't place what the issue is. Is it that after three months of my own personal hell, I'm not interested in hearing about hers?

But I push it down. Ignore the sick feeling. Because I've got Genevieve and Bruce in the back of my mind making me fear that this is too good to be true. *You never see their friends again.* I want to prove them wrong.

'And how is Shaun?' I ask.

'Oh, he's fine. The usual,' she says, finishing her coffee. 'He's started cycling with the kids on weekends, to lose a bit of weight. Did you notice at the party? He's a bit heavier at the moment. Built like an unemployed alcoholic uncle, is how Mum put it.' She laughs.

Thinking back, I'm not sure I noticed any weight gain at all, no.

After a moment, Josie continues. 'Certainly not something you would've faced with Dave. Why can't *my* husband run marathons?' She offers up another laugh, then quietens, face turning serious. 'Although, I did always wonder if that bothered you? Dave out every Sunday, training.'

'To be honest, I preferred not having him around.' Now it's my turn to laugh. 'Probably a sign that something wasn't working.'

'Interesting.' She is quiet but seems satisfied with the information.

And it triggers something. A light bulb moment. *There it is.*

'Oh.'

She tips her head. 'What?'

'You're waiting for me to complain about Dave. That's how we used to do it. Tit for tat – you complain about Shaun, I complain about Dave. We go back and forth.'

It's ridiculous how simple it is, now that I've figured it out. In the past, I'd listen to Josie's woes, she'd listen to mine, and then we'd laugh it all off and go back home to our husbands. Except I went and did something about it, and here she is, still complaining about Shaun.

'Oh,' Josie says. 'Probably.' She looks like she's been struck. Like she genuinely had no idea how much she complained about Shaun until I wasn't there to offer up Dave. We are no longer equal in our unhappiness, and she no longer has my own woes to make her feel better.

'So you don't really have any updates, I guess.'

Her face changes after that. Blank expression, eyes unfocused, jaw slackened. Like she possesses a huge level of regret.

Silence ensues for far too long. It's remarkable how long I can pretend to be sipping from a coffee mug that's already empty. How have things changed so much in such a short amount of time? This stillness, it's killing me.

'Actually, I *do* have something about Dave.' I straighten in my chair. 'He's been hassling me for the engagement ring.'

'*Really?*' She perks up, like balance has been restored, now that I've got something to offer.

'He hasn't mentioned anything to you?'

She shakes her head. 'Nothing.'

Surprised, I pull out my phone and show her the text.

> I still don't have the engagement ring, Charlotte.

Her brow furrows, the corners of her mouth turning down. 'Is that how he speaks to you now? Like a business transaction.'

I nod, and her face darkens. 'That's awful.' I wonder if it bothers her, to see one of her closest friends speak to me like this. I wonder if she's seeing a side to Dave she never knew.

'Might be time to tell him you lost it.'

'I've been ignoring him. Hoping he'll forget about the ring entirely.'

'That's not Dave at all.'

I stare down at the message.

'Could you buy a new one? Something that looks similar?'

Bless Josie for offering a solution. Ever the mediator, trying to find a compromise.

'It'd cost thousands. And it probably won't work. Not unless I find an exact replica.' I tuck my phone away. 'I'll figure something out.'

The conversation lulls now that I've taken my turn discussing Dave, and she's got what she came for. Perhaps not as much as she was hoping for, and certainly not as much as she used to receive, but enough to placate her.

She's agitated though. Won't stop picking at her nails. 'Shaun's not that bad. I'm far too harsh on him,' she says. 'He took me out for our anniversary the other month, which was lovely. Italian, by the beach. Beautiful.'

'That sounds nice.'

'And he's great at getting the kids out of the house – down to the park, that sort of thing.' She leans forward, enthusiastic to divulge more. 'He cooks most nights, too, and even organised a trip for next year. Just us two. A *wine* tour, which will be fantastic. His sister is going to babysit.'

'That's really nice, Josie.'

'Right?' She sighs. 'I'm very lucky to have him.' And then she's flustered again, eyes darting around the café. Fidgeting endlessly with her outfit. Cannot stop touching the ends of her hair.

She grabs at her bag and rises. 'I actually need to head. I'm sorry.'

'Oh. Okay.'

'Yes, sorry. We've got a few things on today.' She offers a small smile. When she reaches out and grasps my wrist, she squeezes it firmly. 'I'll call you. I promise.'

Shortly after, I'm sliding back into my car on the street, watching Josie's figure retreat as she walks briskly back home. She's glancing down, phone in hand, punching out a text message.

I feel hopeful after seeing her. Reassured. It was different, sure, and perhaps I'm annoyed at myself for forgiving her quite so easily, but she's still one of my oldest friends in the city. I want Genevieve and Graham to be wrong about them – we *can* still be friends – and I feel moved that she reached out and organised this. I love that she apologised, and I feel heartened that she's holding the rest of the group accountable. She's probably messaging them right now, telling them to get over whatever issues they're having and to reach out to me. Things are looking up.

On my way back to Genevieve's apartment, my phone pings in my bag. One, two, three messages, then more. Too many to count. An absolute flurry of texts that have me worried there's an emergency. I pull over kerbside a few minutes from the apartment, dig around in my bag and find my phone.

There's an onslaught of messages in an old group chat, one that hasn't been active for months.

> **Emmanuel**: well??? how was it?

> **Josie**: Awkward. The whole thing is just so awful. What are we meant to do? Divide our time between the two of them?

Cinar: Did she say anything about Dave?? Tell you why she ended it?

Josie: Didn't get that far. I tried but she barely spoke about him

Diego: Did you tell her I was sick last weekend

Josie: Yeah. Don't think she bought it though, sorry

Diego: Damn

Josie: She's upset we've been avoiding her. She started crying . . .

Cinar: Oh god

Shaun: We should all feel terrible

They've got the wrong group chat, I realise, and the irony isn't lost on me. They finally start messaging, but it's the wrong forum and they've not yet realised.

It's gutting, seeing all this, realising what they truly think. That this was all an act, that they pity me. Acting like I'm contagious, like they've forgotten I was once a close friend.

Is that why Josie wanted to go to coffee? So she could find out, on behalf of the group, what happened between me and Dave? Was she elected, or did she take one for the team? My mind is reeling, my thoughts completely overtaken.

Emmanuel: i'd love to know what happened. you don't think she's found someone else, do you?

Josie: Starting over at thirty-two? Who could be bothered?

ISN'T IT NICE WE BOTH HATE THE SAME THINGS

Cinar: Um, scusie me? I'm starting over at thirty-eight

Emmanuel: and you'll be starting over at thirty-nine. and forty. and forty-one . . .

Cinar: Bitch

Josie: Maybe Dave found someone else

Emmanuel: doubt it, the guy is barely functioning

Josie: She's really trying though, I feel for her. What do we do about couples night? Do we invite her? Dave's coming

Shaun: Of course we invite

Emmanuel: definitely do not invite

Josie: What if she asks?

Cinar: Lie to her. It's the only way.

Diego: Do not invite. I ran away from her!!! It's awkward

Diego's comment earns a splattering of laughing emojis, and with each one I feel like someone is piercing my skin.

And the couples' night! I'd completely forgotten that was coming up – was so preoccupied with everything else it slipped through. I should've known I wouldn't receive an invite. I should've known this is what they actually think. Completely unlike Dave to cheat, but not me? If they found out what Dave did, they'd be inviting *me*. They'd be apologising to *me*. It'd be *Dave* left in the lurch. It'd be *Dave* who ceased to exist.

Cinar: What are we going to do?

Josie: No idea

Emmanuel: so nothing about dave at all?

Josie: Just that he's chasing the engagement ring

Diego: Have they finalised the settlement yet?

Josie: Not sure

Emmanuel: do they speak at all?

Josie: Don't know

Cinar: Any update on what's happening with their apartment?

Josie: She didn't mention

Emmanuel: josie! ridiculous. i'm taking over

Not thirty seconds later, my phone alights with a text message from Emmanuel.

> hiya, been thinking about you. miss you! sorry i've been MIA, i'm a terrible friend. let's get dinner next week? love you!

And I'm done. Feeling utterly defeated. Like someone has scooped out my insides and left my shell behind.

It's remarkable how much this has floored me – I fear I'm *more* surprised by how my friends have reacted than by the actual end of my marriage.

I'm cursing them all. Thinking of ways I can destroy Emmanuel's collection of Egyptian artefacts without him finding out it was me.

Let me tell you, if any of *them* go through something lifechanging, I suspect I'll think twice before offering my support.

Like if Emmanuel's marriage ever breaks down, or Cinar's artwork stops selling, or Josie discovers material other than French flax linen.

Charlie: Wrong group chat guys!!

I watch as they all view the message. One by one, until the tally marks five. And then I wait ten minutes, to see if anyone is going to say anything.

Josie starts typing, then stops. Shaun starts, then stops. Diego, even, attempts to say something but ceases his attempt.

And then, nothing.

I imagine the real group chat is going *off*. Makes me smile, thinking of them panicking. Re-reading their conversation to see just how bad it was. To see whether it's fixable.

After twenty minutes, there's still nothing and I've realised that my message has well and truly murdered our friendship. They must've decided, together, that this is not salvageable. That we're done for. That it's best to make a clean break and say nothing.

Genevieve and Graham were *right*. My friendships are over.

CHAPTER FIFTEEN

When he finds out I'm not headed home for the holidays, and that Genevieve and Bruce are away, Graham invites me over for Christmas Day lunch.

It's awfully nice of him. Without Genevieve and Bruce in the apartment, I fear I'm slowly dying from the quiet. I feel like an inmate who has been granted a day pass.

Graham's mansion is stunning, like something out of the Hamptons, with its beige shingle aesthetic. Fifteen bedrooms, gated like Fort Knox. Three-storey stone, and natural wood bordering all windows. Triangular roof with two chimneys. Manicured garden out the front stretching fifty metres, leggy monsteras, flowering philodendrons, clipped evergreen shrubs and tall, elongated Cypress trees lining the motor court driveway.

The front door swings open and I cheer, 'Happy Christmas!'

Graham waves me through, reading glasses perched atop his nose. He wears dark-wash denim jeans and a white linen shirt.

Inside, I marvel. 'Jesus *Christ*.'

Grandiose artwork with golden frames, plush sofas and armchairs with velvet cushions, and sheer, white curtains that stretch to the ceiling. Sparkling glassware, overgilded appliances, glittering chandeliers, four-poster beds – honestly, I could go on.

'Graham, you don't need to make your wealth quite so obvious.'

I'm dazed, tottering through the place. And I wouldn't have pegged Graham for someone who loved Christmas, but the decorations are madness. It's a sea of tinsel (on cabinets and benches and tables, and just about any surface that exists), and I count four trees in the first ten minutes of the tour. Fairy lights over railings, baubles in bowls, and glass gingerbread homes lined up on windowsills.

I've brought a bottle of champagne with me, but when I reach one of the many bars in his mansion, I scoff. He's got boxes of the stuff, and better brands, too. I feel I'm no longer worthy of an invite; I'm showing my wage. 'Well, my contribution is a waste.'

'Steady on,' Graham says, reaching forward and grabbing it from me. 'I'll put it in the fridge.' Then he points me in the direction of the main kitchen. That's how big his place is – he has to *point* so I don't lose my bearings in the maze of corridors and nooks.

'You live here by yourself?'

'I do.'

'What if you get lost? You take a wrong turn and get disorientated, who knows where you'd end up?'

He wears an amused expression. 'It's a house, not a fairytale forest.'

Graham insists on doing the majority of the cooking. Glazing the ham, prepping the meat, slicing and oiling the vegetables. All I have to do is sit on the kitchen stool and drink champagne, and it's making me feel all sorts of rich.

'You like cooking?' I ask.

'It's calming,' he says as he seasons the vegetables with rosemary then takes a sip from the champagne flute to his right.

'And Christmas?'

'I like what it does to the world. People stopping and celebrating on the same day. There's something about that, I can't quite explain it.' After a brief pause, he adds, 'And my mother loved this time of year.'

This might just be the first time he's ever mentioned his mother to me. 'Thank you for inviting me.'

'What would you have been doing, if I hadn't?'

'Cooking ham for one,' I say, chuckling. 'My mum sent through a recipe.'

'Sounds depressing.'

'You'd be alone too. If I'd said no.'

He smirks. 'I meant *ham for one* sounds depressing. Not being alone.'

'Oh. Right.'

He straightens, rolls his shoulders back. Even his apron is festive – an enlarged green Christmas tree with flashing lights attached – and it reminds me of my dad. He loved wearing those loud, silly aprons at Christmas. 'You should've gone home for the holidays.'

I stop mid-sip, and place down the glass.

He continues. 'We would've survived without you. And I could count on one hand the number of times you've visited home since we met.'

Now I feel guilty, which I'm sure was his intention.

'Please tell me you've spoken to them today.'

'Yes, I've spoken with them,' I say. 'Called them both this morning.'

Mum was prepping cocktails, and Naya was dressing the kids and listing out all the gifts she and Leonard had given them this morning. Leonard, somewhere, was fastening a new, Christmas bowtie around his neck.

It's been so long since I've spent Christmas with my family,

I'm afraid I can't picture what they'd be doing right now. It'd be too early for lunch, I'm sure, so perhaps Mum is giving the kids her presents. Or maybe they've already unwrapped them and are playing in the yard. Or maybe—

'Charlie? Did you hear me?'

'Oh.' I readjust myself on the bar stool. 'No, sorry.'

'I was thanking you. For the year,' he says. 'I know how hard you've tried.'

He's thinking about the ratings again. *I'm* thinking about the ratings again. Even on Christmas Day, of all days, and we're morose about it.

'You've had more meetings,' I say. 'Don't think I haven't noticed.'

It's all I've been stressing about these past couple of weeks, really. Graham staying later at the station, walking into meetings with suited men and their gel-parted hair.

He holds my gaze for a beat, then glances away. 'I've been negotiating my contract for next year.'

'Oh. *Oh*.' Relief floods through me. 'So you're staying then? We're okay?'

'We're okay.'

'They're keeping you? Oh, Graham, that's such good news.' Hand to my chest, I feel ten pounds lighter.

We're safe. We're okay. All that hard work wasn't enough to keep us in second place, but it was enough to keep our jobs, and suddenly I'm not as distraught that we fell so far in the ratings. Because we're *safe*, and Graham still has a job.

And then I'm heavy again. Because if Graham is okay, what does that mean for me?

He senses my discomfort. 'I already told you, you're fine. I've made sure of it.'

Why do I not believe him? I still feel uneasy – wound up.

'We don't need to talk about this today,' I say. 'It's Christmas.'

'I know.' Looking me in the eye, he adds, 'I just want to make sure that you know you're the best producer I've ever had. And I'm glad I get to spend Christmas with you.'

'Oh. Graham, me too.'

CHAPTER SIXTEEN

Two weeks later, a freakishly hot day in January, and the air is already thick and sticky when I wake.

Of all the days to hold a gender reveal in a *park*, and it had to be today. Today! I'm already feeling so clammy, so deflated by the heavy heat in the apartment that I experience pockets of rage as I flitter around collecting everything for Genevieve's party.

I fear the heat might kill me. My pasty freckled skin is not prepared for this – I'm going to crisp and crumble near a rusty outdoor barbecue and there'll be nothing left of me except my spaghetti-strap summer dress and chunky silver sandals.

I'm late to arrive because it took me three attempts to leave the apartment this morning. The first time, I realised I forgot the present – a lush size 00 bodysuit from a boutique near our building – and had to dart inside again. And then Mum called just as I was stepping back out the door. We'd been playing phone tag all week, so I chatted with her long enough until I could excuse myself from the conversation. Turns out, she just wanted to discuss how one of her neighbours, who I cannot remember, sold their home after forty-five years. And, also, that she was contemplating buying a clothing steamer.

'Charlie! You made it! We were about to send out a search party.'

Bruce's wave is entirely unnecessary. His head peeks above the rest of the crowd like a lighthouse. He emerges from the group of people and approaches me in the carpark. 'Need a hand? Christ, what *is* all this stuff?'

Flowers. The present. A hat. Genevieve's hat, because I noticed it on the kitchen table and realised she forgot to bring one. Sunscreen, in case others need it. My handbag. A two-litre water bottle that Bruce calls monstrous.

'Oh, good thing you brought that.' He points at the water bottle, then behind him. 'The lake's looking low, might need a top-up.'

'Funny.'

He grabs a few of my belongings and I take the opportunity to glance around the park. Hectares of open space, with manicured gardens and at least two different playgrounds, children crawling all over them like ants, which reminds me of Naya's house. There's an oval, a sports field, bushland and a small artificial lake in the distance. I hear the distinct sizzle of meat on a hot barbecue. All over the park, people use paper to fan their faces and women are tying their hair into top buns. One man clutches the front of his shirt and jolts the material *out and in, out and in,* to try and cool his body down.

'We moved everyone to a shady spot,' Bruce says, then grabs my forearm. 'Don't say anything about the heat to Genevieve. I'm trying to keep her positive.'

'I feel like my make-up is melting off my face.'

He runs his eyes over my forehead, nose, then down to my chin. 'No, you look fine.'

'*Charlie.*' Genevieve appears from behind Bruce (an easy hiding spot), wearing a fitted beige cotton dress with thin straps. Her face is red, and her skin dewy. Her bump is small but prominent. Fifteen weeks. She cradles it instinctively. 'I've been trying to call you. Was worried you'd melted or something. Fuck me, it's hot.'

'Is it?' I say, tossing my hair over my shoulder. 'I hadn't noticed.'

'I think the weather is quite nice, actually,' Bruce adds.

Genevieve narrows her eyes, glancing between the two of us.

I assess her for any kind of indication of how she's feeling. Is she excited at all? Embracing the pregnancy? Or still annoyed her parents organised a gender reveal without consulting her?

In this moment, I'm also thinking of how Genevieve might feel if things do go awry. I don't want to think, even for a second, that her pregnancy will have complications. But, what if it *does*? Her parents meant well planning this, and I know they're not malicious people, but what if they put on this party and then something unexpected happens? How will she cope then?

Genevieve runs an eye over my olive-green dress, right down to the flared skirting and brown stitching at the hem, and back up. '*Love* this.'

'Sorry I'm late.' I extend the present towards her. 'Where do the gifts go?'

'The invite said no gifts.'

'And I ignored.'

Genevieve chuckles, then takes it from me. Places a hand on Bruce's shoulder. 'I need to check on my parents. They keep touching the cannons and I'm worried they'll set them off early.'

The *cannons*. A concept so absurd I twist my body because I *must* get a good look at them over by the barbecue. Bio-degradable powder cannons from Etsy, intended to erupt in blue or pink when it comes time for the big reveal. Something I'd have never guessed until I saw them. And there they are, looking like male genitalia.

After Genevieve darts off, I step closer to Bruce. 'How was it? Seeing her parents.'

For a split second, his face stills. Then he masks it with a smile. 'It was good,' he says. 'She really needed that time with her family, I think.'

'Good, good.'

And then he winces, sympathetic. 'She told me about the group chat.'

'Oh. Yes. Awful.'

'Have you heard from them?'

'No.' It's been almost three weeks and with each passing day, the hurt dulls. Graham was right – I'll never see them again. 'Thank god Genevieve's back or I'd be struggling.'

A quick flash and I see it again, on his face. Guilt, I think. Lines appear on his forehead as he frowns. The inner ends of his eyebrows flick up like tails.

'Everything okay?'

'Of course, of course.' He looks across the park at Genevieve. 'Big day.'

'How is she?'

'You should talk to her,' he says, face grim. He's not even trying to hide his expression now. Something is wrong.

'She's okay, right?'

He raises his hands to calm me. 'She's okay. Her mum really helped. They went out and bought some things, and she has an ultrasound picture to show you. I mean she's still terrified, and it's an uphill battle, but she's okay.'

My body instantly relaxes, my stomach knot gone. 'Okay, good. That's good.' Across the park, I watch Genevieve as she chats with other guests. Directs them to the food – iced cupcakes, sandwiches, cheese platters, cob loaf, three charcuterie boards and an ice bucket filled with beer – chastises them for bringing gifts, and laughs when they notice the cannons.

Bruce rubs his forehead, and I notice his fingernails – painted a sharp shade of blue. Surprised, I point.

'Oh, it was Cheryl's idea,' he says, extending out his hands. 'Bit of a last-minute thing. They've got pink and blue nail polish over there on the table. Guess what you think the gender will be and paint your nails.'

I glance across at Genevieve, but her hands are now in her pockets. 'What colour has she painted?'

There's a pause, and then Bruce speaks. 'Neither. She won't do it.'

As I wait for the right moment to speak with Genevieve, I mingle.

Bruce's sister is so beautiful that I hate her and walk away after a couple of minutes because it's just too saddening staring at her face – high cheekbones, smooth skin, arched black eyebrows and a set of veneers. Her forehead is always fresh with botox. She once told me that when you get to her age (forty-six), you must choose between your body and your face.

It's a bit of a blur after that – a couple of the teachers from Genevieve's school (one of them runs phys. ed. and is mighty jacked, has pink nails), her parents (excited to be here, both guessing a boy), her dentist (not sure how he scored an invite, Genevieve has not once mentioned him, nails painted pink) and some of Bruce's colleagues (all IT consultants, names include Gary, Jon, Xavier and Ny, all nails painted pink). Lastly, a former roommate of Genevieve's named Julia, nails unpainted. 'Bit presumptuous to have *boy* and *girl*,' she says, biting into a cupcake. 'What if the baby identifies as something entirely different?'

I'm quiet for a moment. 'Oh, yes, I suppose you're right.'

Just before the announcement, while Bruce is working out the final touches on those powder cannons, I swipe the nail polish from the tables and pull Genevieve aside.

'Having fun?'

'People are fascinated by the cannons, for some reason.'

'Because they look like circumcised penises.'

She frowns, her mouth making an O. Looks back at them. 'Oh damn, you're right.'

'And they're *cannons*, G.'

She winces, and a flash of embarrassment crosses her face. 'Dad organised them.'

'I don't think anyone at this party believes *you* bought those things.'

She smiles, laughs, then reaches out to me. 'I missed you.' Then she points at the nail polish in my hands.

'I thought we could do ours together?' I suggest. 'Although, I'm sorry, there's only blue and pink—'

'Ignore Julia,' Genevieve says. 'I mean, she's right, and my parents wouldn't really understand, but it's fine.'

I hold them out to her again, but she dismisses me with a shake of the head.

'Come on.'

'I don't want to,' she says, placing a hand to her stomach. 'I'll be happy about whichever sex it is—'

'It's just a guess.'

'Okay, alive and healthy. That's my guess.'

I lower the nail polish, embarrassed.

'Sorry,' Genevieve says. 'That was harsh.'

'No, you're right.'

I lead her to a nearby table, far enough away from the group that we're not overheard.

'I bought a pram,' she says. 'Thought you'd be proud. And a bassinet. And some other things.'

'That's great, G.' I slide in opposite her. 'Do you want to start looking at listings again? Not now, obviously, but maybe tomorrow?'

She looks down, her face resembling the same expression as Bruce. Guilt.

'Unless you definitely want to stay in the apartment? Because if you need me to move out, I can be gone tomorrow. Can help you put together furniture, paint walls, whatever you need.'

She shakes her head. 'It's not that.'

I wait for her to continue. Run my hands over the backs of my knees – they won't stop sweating.

'I actually need to talk to you about something but didn't really want to do it here.'

'Then you should've married someone with a better poker face,' I say, jerking my thumb at Bruce, over by the cannons. 'He told me to come talk to you.'

She groans. 'Jesus, Bruce.' Then she straightens, placing her hands flat on the table. Closes her eyes, exhales. 'We're—'

My phone erupts. An onslaught of text messages come through at once, the alerts so loud it startles both of us.

I pull my phone from my back pocket to see who's trying to contact me. Two of my colleagues – Dora and Ivan. How odd. I never hear from them on a weekend. Then it's my mother. My sister. And finally, Graham.

I open his message first.

> It's not your fault.

And then another, not ten seconds later.

> You're safe. I made sure of it.

'Everything okay?' Genevieve asks.
'Not sure.'
I open Naya's text.

> Just saw the news. Are you okay?

'Oh god,' I say. 'Something's happened.'

Genevieve is alert, and, I suspect, grateful for the distraction. She tucks her hair behind her ears and darts around to my side of the table so she can read over my shoulder. 'What news?'

'Don't know.'

I switch to the internet, search the first news outlet I can think of, and wait for the homepage to load.

And it's right there: breaking news.

Gone! Veteran radio host Graham Jackson axed after atrocious ratings quarter.

Genevieve clasps my shoulder, squeezes so tight I fear I might bruise.

Fired.

He's been fired.

'He'll finish before the end of the financial year.'

I was wrong; he wasn't safe. *We* weren't safe. Graham is getting fired.

This man I've known for six years. Someone I look up to, someone I genuinely love seeing every morning at the station. Someone who has become my sounding board when I've been struggling. Has been one of my biggest supporters.

And now he's leaving. 'He lied to me.'

Fired.

He'll be gutted. Distraught. I'm picturing him alone, at home, with no one to talk to. If I weren't at this gender reveal, I'd be driving to his house.

I don't say anything for a second, then close the article and lay my phone on the table. Feel my heart beating so fast I need a second to calm myself.

'Should you call him?' Genevieve asks.

Nearby, I sense Bruce getting agitated. He's impatient for the reveal to start.

'After,' I say.

Genevieve nods.

And then I remember. 'Oh god, what were you going to tell me? Sorry.' It's hard to pivot when my mind is reeling, when I feel this blindsided, but it's not lost on me that I'm here, at this park, for Genevieve. That she was gearing up to tell me something when the news came through.

She tries to wave it off, dismissive. 'Another time. Tomorrow?'

'No, now.' I tap the seat next to me. 'Come on.'

Genevieve resembles a wounded animal.

'Are you okay?'

She readjusts her position on the bench. Sneaks a look at Bruce, who clocks it and grows sheepish, turning away.

'Is someone dying?' I ask.

She grabs my hand. 'We're moving, Charlie. To be near my parents.'

It's remarkable how quiet everything suddenly seems – I can no longer hear chatter from the group, or the squeals from the children playing in the distance. No birds, no laughter, nothing.

It's hard for me to form words.

'I'm sorry.'

'But that's interstate,' I splutter. 'Hours away. And I can find you listings. I *will* find you listings. Let me help you.'

Let me help you like you helped me. Let me be there for you after all these years of you being the best thing in my life.

'We already found somewhere, actually.' She fidgets. 'When we went home, my parents showed us a house nearby. It's really beautiful. We bought it.'

I have to say it aloud to believe it. 'You bought somewhere already.'

What I really want to say is, *You bought somewhere already and I had no idea.* Something monumental in your life and I wasn't there for it. It's selfish, I know, to feel cut out of such a big moment. I didn't know she was considering such a drastic move, didn't even think that was a possibility. She's never once mentioned it – wouldn't that be something she'd want to talk about with me?

But that's not something I'd ever say aloud. I've got nothing to do with this. Genevieve is checking off all the things she's been dreaming about since childhood – marriage, children, house. Who am I to make her feel anything but ecstatic?

'Congratulations.'

She offers a warm smile. 'I realised I was missing my family,' she says. 'And we couldn't afford to buy here. And I know that things might not go according to plan, and then we'll be in a house we don't need, but—'

'You don't have to explain. I'm happy for you, I'm just—'

'Sad?'

'Yeah. Really fucking sad.'

Sad because my best friend is moving away. Sad because my marriage didn't work out. Sad because of those group chat messages. Sad because my family live on the other side of the country. Sad because Graham got fired, and I don't know what this means for my job.

I'm going to have no one left.

Nearby, a child starts crying. Genevieve winces. 'This is terrible timing, telling you here. I'm sorry.'

'When do you leave?'

Her silence, and that crushed expression, tells me it's soon. She pulls me in for a hug. 'I'm going to miss you.'

All I can muster is a nod.

'I've been wanting to tell you for days, but I couldn't do it.'

'Can I see it? The house?'

'Of course.'

But we're interrupted by Bruce, who comes over to reiterate

Genevieve's apology. 'Charlie, *so* sorry. But we're going to come down and visit, obviously. Fly down as often as we can.'

Everyone always says that, when they move away. It's what I told Mum and Naya when I left home, and even then I knew I was lying.

Bruce taps Genevieve's shoulder. 'We should probably start.'

'Right, yeah, okay.' Genevieve turns to me again, her eyebrows lifting in an empathetic expression.

'Don't apologise,' I say. 'I'll be fine.'

Will I be fine? Will I? I honestly have no idea what life is going to look like for me now. I feel like I've been left behind while everyone else is moving forward.

'I'm always going to worry about you,' she says. 'You're my family.'

I grab the ends of her wispy hair. 'Well, as your family, I feel I need to be honest with you. Let's buy you some product before you leave. Because this will *not* survive the humidity.'

'You think I should just shave it all off?'

'Yes.' We laugh, then I ask, 'Can you do something for me?'

'Anything.'

I pluck the nail polish from the table and drop it into her hand. 'Paint your nails both colours.'

She smiles. 'Alive and healthy?'

'Alive and healthy,' I repeat. She does what I tell her, before being whisked away to fire off the cannons.

Turns out, the baby is a girl.

PART TWO

Two months later

CHAPTER SEVENTEEN

Naya cannot quite grasp that I've elected to attend a book club. 'But you barely read,' she says over the phone while one of her kids calls for her in the background. 'Not now, Mummy's on the phone to Aunty Charlie.'

My phone pressed against my ear, I stare at the terrace house before me. Old, paint-stripped, charming. Door painted a deep red, with black detailing around its rim and a thick, bristled door mat. I hear the sound of buzzed discussion on the other side.

'I read plenty.'

'Really?' she says, sharply. 'What books?'

I laugh, but only a little. That raised pitch in her voice, and the pointed nature of her questions. She's the reader in the family, always has been – self-confessed bookworm with shelves stretched to the ceiling. I can tell I've encroached on her territory. Now that she has kids, I know she wishes she had more time to read. Dad always said that one of his favourite things about her was how much she loved books – falling into other worlds, other perspectives, other lands – and I know it's something she still thinks about.

A child calls for her again, and she groans. 'Charlie, sorry, I have to go. Tell me how it goes. Where is it?'

I shrug. 'Just some house. I'll send you a picture.'

'I assumed it'd be, like, a pub or a café or something. Not

someone's *house*.' She groans. 'Lord, one day you're going to turn up to one of these things and get murdered.'

One of these things.

It's been one month since Genevieve and Bruce left, and four weeks of exploring as many different methods as possible to fill my time. Distract myself. Meet new people. Wine tours, pub crawls, music festivals, anonymous meet-ups I found on the internet, soap-making classes (a low point), ocean swim races, tennis clubs, dinner parties, bar-hopping with colleagues. The list goes on. And while I've met some *great* people, something about each interaction has left me feeling unsatisfied.

'You're going to be turned into a podcast, I can feel it.' One of Naya's children screeches and she lets out another frustrated groan. 'Sorry, I'll call you later. Be careful, okay?'

And then she's gone, the line dead. I'm left alone with my thoughts and the paperback copy of a book that I did indeed read but couldn't understand. One of those literary books that definitely had a hidden meaning – if only I could figure out what it was!

Once inside, I'm greeted by a tall, pencil-thin woman about ten years younger than me with six books under one arm and a glass of prosecco in the other. An icon.

Closing the door behind me, she flashes me a smile. 'Welcome.'

She introduces herself, and then about six other women standing nearby. I instantly forget all their names, but I am grateful when they pass me a glass of wine and point out the various cheeseboards laid out around the room.

'Head through to the back,' she says. 'The girls are there somewhere. They're wearing white trainers.' *The girls*. Alannah and Francine, book club founders. Sisters. I remember their names from social media – their beaming profile photos, hands curled into a wave.

'Thank you.'

The house is open and bright. White walls, high ceilings, cool air coming in through open windows down the back of the house. Oak bookshelves line the back of the house by the kitchen, rugs along the floorboards don rich colours – plum, teal, a pumpkin tone.

Rising onto the tips of my toes, I scan the room. If I had to guess, I'd say there are about thirty women in here. Youngest around twenty, oldest in their late forties. It's eight o'clock and I'm going to regret this in the morning – the late weeknight, the alcohol. But when I contemplate heading home, I promptly change my mind. Genevieve isn't here anymore. I am, begrudgingly, alone. We no longer live together, and I am missing her something stupid. It's like a limb has been removed and I'm learning to live without it. Floundering, stumbling, doing anything I can to acclimatise.

Before she left, Graham offered me one of the many empty rooms in his mansion. Just temporarily, he said, while I figure things out. It was very altruistic of him, but I also suspect he wanted company after news broke of his firing.

And so, somehow, I've survived four weeks without her, and with each day that passes I feel like I am still in mourning. Like I am a wealthy, teary woman at my husband's funeral staring at the ground as his body is lowered beneath it – except for the fact that I do not have much money at all and my clothes scream common folk. And I really do look like a swollen panda bear when I cry.

Nearby, someone lets out a high-pitched laugh and it makes me wince. Spurs me forward, through the property. Draining half my wine, I shoulder my way through the people. Past the living room, the bathroom, the kitchen and the bookshelves. Beeline past a group of girls each discussing their mother-in-law ('I'm very lucky to have her. She's very nice. Very welcoming. But she's also a nosy mole.').

Doesn't take long to find them, in merino sleeveless tops. Alannah and Francine are on the balcony, standing in the open doorway. The close resemblance is remarkable. Their mouths dip in the same manner, their body shapes identical – average height, barrel-chested and busty but lean in the legs. Borderline translucent skin. Both are wearing wide-leg jeans, although different (dark blue denim, khaki corduroy).

'Charlie, right?'

After we've introduced ourselves, they describe themselves as *girlies in their thirties*. Then they ask me how I feel about the book.

'I have *many* thoughts,' Francine says, dimples flashing, her hair the colour of soot.

'All of them good,' Alannah adds, then clutches her chest. 'I cried at the end.'

Francine tips her head back. 'The *twist*. Ugh, gutting.'

Oh god. Help! I can't remember a twist. Can't remember the last one hundred pages. I completely zoned out. Barely knew what was happening. Only finished it because of this meet-up.

'I really struggled, actually.'

'You *did*?' Francine says, horrified. Then she holds out a hand to stop me from speaking any further. 'Let's save this until we're with the others.'

Together, they lead me back into the house to introduce me to some of the other members. They start with Lily, who they've known since the first meet-up a couple of years earlier. She's recently cut her hair into a bob and she's not so sure about it. She strokes the ends while Alannah compliments the style.

Cordelia and Sally joined the club at the same time, and work together at a nearby media agency. Cordelia says she doesn't read as much as she used to, and makes some sort of distraught face when she says she's only been able to read five books this month. Five! In the same month! And she's not trying to be funny.

I lose track of the names after that. One girl recently graduated with a degree in nutrition and another asks for my star sign. 'Cancer,' I respond, and the girl nods. 'Thought so.'

Another member runs marathons on her weekends, evidently by choice, and the girl next to her – round face, glasses, arms and neck coated in fake tan – works as an event manager at a library not too far from here. She shakes my hand, the only one who does, and tells me she lives and breathes books. Another woman is a self-confessed yogi who calls her friends her *tribe*.

It's a blur, and incredibly hard to keep tabs on everyone. Their names slip out of my memory almost as soon as I'm told them. This is the most ambitious event I've attended since Genevieve left (and that's including the podunk carols singalong in a dimly lit park just a couple of weeks back!). More people than any other night. More faces and more conversations, more glasses of wine.

It's selfish, I know, but I search each of them for some hint of familiarity. Just something that reminds me of Genevieve – her dry humour, her optimism, her class. Sporadic insults she throws out when I'm in need of a laugh.

Here, just like every other event I've attended, I want to meet someone and think, *Yes, it's you. I don't have Genevieve but I'll have you.*

Because the easiest way to move on from her is to try and find a *new* her. A new Genevieve. And it's not going to be easy, I know that. Genevieve and I have known each other for a decade. We've been friends since I had bad eyebrows.

Back at the house, Cordelia is updating the group on a dating disaster. 'I lied and told him I could ski, and then found out he went to the *Olympics* for it.' She sighs. 'So, yeah, didn't really work out.'

At some point, and I promise it arises naturally, the conversation shifts towards chest size and Francine moans about her own. 'If I had the money I'd reduce them,' she says, looking down. 'People look at me and just think, *boobs*.'

She's right. I did think *boobs* when I first saw her.

'But I didn't *choose* the DD life.'

'If I had money, I'd do a lot of things,' Alannah says. 'I should've bought a house in 1990 instead of learning how to walk.'

Sally adds, 'I wasn't even born then and I'm mad at myself.'

I chime in. 'Only thing stopping me from a drug problem is a money problem.'

The group erupts into laughter. It was a risk; they might have genuinely thought I could have a drug problem. But I've been doing this for weeks – embedding myself into friendship groups, meeting new people – and I'm getting better at it each time. Have learnt the best moment for a joke, and what questions to ask. How to ease seamlessly into a group that's long been close.

We've moved on to careers now. Sally's pushing for a promotion, Cordelia is considering full-time influencing, Francine dislikes her new boss – calls him a slob, and a battler – whilst Lily dislikes her job altogether. Or maybe it's *Francine* who dislikes her job, I think I might be getting the names mixed up. Alannah feels like she's been cheated in her career, because she was an overachieving child and now she's just an average employee working five days a week.

Someone asks me where I work, and then show pity when I tell them about the station and the breakfast show. They join the dots and remember Graham has been let go.

'He's not gone *yet*.' I am quick to clarify.

'Still horrible,' Cordelia says.

'Agreed,' Francine (potentially Lily) adds.

'Do you know who's going to replace him?' Lily (could be Francine, who the fuck knows) questions.

'Not yet.' And I won't find out until the rest of the country does – the station is secretive like that.

'What a job though,' Sally says. 'Graham Jackson is a media legend.'

I've learnt from my attempt at joining a craft club that I shouldn't tell these women I live with Graham. Not yet, anyway. Because the conversation will be dominated by questions and fascination. What does his house look like? How many rooms? Tell us about the furniture and the pools and the tennis courts. Tell us how big your bedroom is. Tell us how many cars he owns. Are you two dating? Is he holding you against your will? Blink twice if he keeps you locked in his wine cellar.

It feels like a betrayal to gossip about him like that. And, also, it really isn't as marvellous as people might think. It's remarkable how we can live in that place, together, without actually seeing each other. Bedrooms and car ports on opposite sides of the property, a wine cellar he won't reveal the entrance to, and three separate living rooms I never seem to find him in. Some days, I wonder if he's in the house at all. Some weeks, my only glimpse of him is his car triggering the front gate.

And, despite living in what will probably be the grandest house I'll ever encounter, I am reticent to spend long stretches of time there. I thought living with Graham would be a dream. I thought I'd love it, and that it'd be easier than living alone, but I fear it's made no difference. It's too quiet – too empty. Too easy for me to feel completely and utterly alone. Too easy for me to miss Genevieve – to ring her, text her, bother her when she's busy forging a new life.

The marathon runner places a hand on my shoulder. 'I'm sure he'll be fine.'

I'm wondering when we'll start discussing the book, because I'm on my third glass of wine and am starting to feel woozy. Tired, with achy shoulders. Aware I'll have a headache tomorrow, because I haven't drunk enough water.

Then, Cordelia says *terrible person* mid-sentence when discussing a colleague, and it reminds me of Genevieve. Like a punch to the gut, I'm alert.

You're not a terrible person, you just left a terrible marriage.

I'm thinking about her again. What's she doing right now? Have they settled on a baby name or are they still on the shortlist of four? Above all else, I wonder if she, too, is trying to find a replacement.

My phone pings with a message from Naya.

> Checking you're still breathing?

And then a follow-up text.

> Also, meant to ask. Have you booked your flights home yet?

'Shit.' I'd completely forgotten.

> Sorry, soon.

At some point, conversations break off and I'm alone with Lily. She's someone I could slip inside my pocket – tiny and timid. Voice like a bird, she cannot stop rubbing the ends of her hair.

'I like it,' I say, pointing. 'The bob.'

'Oh. Thank you.' She folds in like she's wounded. 'My boyfriend broke up with me.'

I stifle a laugh. Drastic hair change – I should've known there was context.

'It was blue on the ends,' she adds, hands level with her collarbones to signal where the colour would've altered.

'*Blue?*'

'When I arrived tonight, no one recognised me,' she says.

'Me neither.'

She frowns, then clocks the joke. Chuckles. 'Oh, right. Because you're new. I get it.'

'You've been here since the start, right?'

'The book club?' she clarifies. Then nods. 'Since day one.' Then she looks down and away, and won't stop touching her goddamn hair. I suspect the blue looked ridiculous anyway, but I can't tell her because I sense she might just topple over and die.

I'm wondering if we have anything in common, or if this conversation is going to be a struggle. 'Did you like the book?' I ask.

After a moment, her mouth twists. 'Not really.'

And I realise we have a chance. 'Me neither.'

She is instantly relieved. 'I don't really understand what it meant. I felt stupid reading it, like everything was going over my head.'

'*Yes*.' Instinctively, in a moment of finally being able to relate to her, I reach forward and grab her wrist. Then retract. 'Oh. Sorry.'

She waves it off, then touches her hair again. 'I feel naked.' She runs her fingertips over the back of her neck.

'How recent was the breakup?'

'Couple of weeks. This is my first time out, since it happened.'

'Were you together long?'

She nods. 'Quite a while.'

She doesn't elaborate, so I'm left pondering what *quite a while* could mean. A few years? Or less? If I think *quite a while*, I'd guess minimum four.

'Do—'

My phone vibrates, and our conversation is temporarily halted. It's Naya, again.

> Mum's so excited to see you. Please don't bail.

'Something wrong?' Lily asks, and I realise she's clocked my expression. The way my shoulders have sagged, and I'm biting my lip. Maybe she's sensing my guilt, because it's been almost two years since I've seen my mother, even longer since I was home for the holidays, and I've always known how much that pains her.

'My sister,' I say. 'Asking if I've booked my flights home.'

Lily nods, pensive. 'Do you head home often?'

'No, not really.' When I look up, I see how inquisitive she is now. For the first time since we've started speaking, she's dropped her hand. 'My father, he . . .'

'Oh.' She glances down. 'I'm sorry.'

'I find it hard to go home. Reminds me of him.'

I say nothing more – I'm not one to divulge much about my father. The only people I really spoke to about him were Genevieve and Dave.

I think I was lucky, perhaps, that Dave had not yet gone through a great loss. For most of the time that Dave and I were together, he didn't know what that felt like and couldn't possibly relate. And I think I preferred it that way. He knew enough about my father to help me when I needed, but also did his best to distract me. On Dad's birthday, or the anniversary of his death, Dave would plan a drive somewhere, or tickets to a musical. Something long that had at least two acts, and a longer interval. He'd get spirits from the bar, rather than something milder, because the more I drank the easier it was to forget what day it was and how long it'd been since I'd seen my father.

'My brother talks about it all the time. Death,' Lily says, pushing her wine glass aside. 'He's a nurse, sees it often.'

'What does he say about it?'

'How it can look, and smell. How slowly it can happen, when life is being particularly cruel.'

'Does he ever talk about how fast it can happen?'

By the soft, understanding expression on Lily's face, she has realised that my father did not die slowly. 'It has the biggest impact. The ones you don't see coming. The operations that should go smoothly and don't, the car crashes that wouldn't have happened if someone left their home one minute earlier or even thirty seconds later. Because people aren't expecting the worst, and so there's this distinct before and after. Before, someone was alive, and now, they're not.'

I think of my own before and after. Before, we were a family. Loud, chaotic, bustling. After, it was silent. All the time. And I did everything I could to escape.

I don't realise I'm cracking my knuckles until Lily winces. 'I'm sorry about your father,' she says.

'We were never really the same after that.'

'No, I imagine you weren't.' And then she straightens, goes back to touching her hair.

If Genevieve were here, she'd know I need a laugh. She'd say something witty, poke fun at someone. 'Maybe we should go back to complaining about the book,' I suggest. 'Alannah and Francine really liked it.'

Lily groans. 'They *all* liked it. I asked as soon as I walked in. Couldn't believe it. I'm glad there's someone else here who struggled.' Collecting her wine, she takes a generous sip.

'I didn't buy the relationship,' I say. 'The boyfriend was thick. I don't really know why she was with him.'

Lily is brushing away a tear, and I've been too slow to notice that I've upset her.

'Oh god, I'm sorry.'

She waves it off. 'Totally fine, totally fine. Every now and then I just remember, you know?' She points behind her. 'Francine got engaged over the weekend and I cried when she told me. And she thought I was crying because I was happy for her, but I was actually just really sad for me.'

'Don't think too much about her engagement.' I hold up the book. 'She likes *this*. Her taste is questionable.'

Lily laughs, covering her mouth with her hand.

'It helps if you remember things he never liked doing, and then go do them. Don't know why, but it works.'

'He didn't like threesomes.' Then she looks me up and down.

Not at all where I thought the conversation was headed. The room feels like it's quietened, somehow. 'Oh. I—'

'I'm fucking with you,' she says, smiling. 'He was sugar-free and it was depressing. I've been eating candy nonstop. You're right, it does help.'

I laugh. *Really* laugh – a loud cackle. It's so unexpected that a couple of the other girls glance our way. Lily delivered that quip so quickly, so effortlessly, and it was exactly what I needed. It's the kind of joke Genevieve would make, and I feel like this could be something. Could be *someone*. I could ask for her number, suggest a coffee. Maybe go see a film. Propose seeing a play or a musical.

And then she ruins it.

Well, Alannah ruins it. Walks over to us, wraps an arm around Lily's shoulders and dons a sad expression. 'Did Lily tell you she's leaving us? Travelling overseas for two years – we're all devastated.'

Lily smiles, raises her hands in a *sorry* kind of way. Casual though. Like she doesn't really care that she's leaving book club – leaving the country.

And there goes my chance.

'Oh. How exciting,' I say. 'When?'

'Monday,' she replies. 'Bags all packed. Came here to say goodbye.'

The other girls join us now, each hugging Lily. They tell her they're going to miss her, that she better keep in touch. That she can read the book club selections from afar.

She promises the group that she won't be a stranger – that they'll talk every week – and I think of Genevieve. How she reassured me as well, in the beginning. And I look at these other girls and I see that they believe Lily. They think things aren't going to change.

But everything is going to change.

Plucking out my phone, I send Genevieve a text.

Miss you.

CHAPTER EIGHTEEN

After they announced Graham's impending departure, I began socialising with colleagues after work – Dora and Ivan, mostly, for happy hour on Fridays. We drink spritz and beer and wine at our local until I stumble home alone.

The three of us realised, almost instantly, that we needed each other if we were going to get through this. Graham's departure, and all the media attention. A new host, the ratings results. Suddenly, as if overnight, we bonded.

Tonight, we're perched on bar stools around a high table. Above us, on the television screen spanning the entire width of our table, is a basketball game that none of us are watching.

Dora, ever the optimist, tries to reassure us that Graham needs a break, that he must be exhausted, and that his departure is a blessing in disguise. Tucking her hair behind her ears – a sleek, auburn bob with a blonde balayage – she incants the phrase 'everything happens for a reason'.

Ivan takes a different route. 'He's a crusty old geezer about to crumble into dust,' he says, then senses our reaction. 'But yeah, it's sad. I'll be bummed to see him go.'

He's sturdy, Ivan. Tall, muscle-less and pudgy with perfectly crafted hair – shaved on the sides, polished blonde quiff on top, and he's obsessed with ensuring every strand of hair stays in its rightful position.

'Is anyone going to drink this?' he adds, pointing to a spare cider on the table – an error from the bartender who accidentally made an extra one without charging us for it. Dora and I shake our heads, still nursing our third drinks.

'Wonderful.' He grabs it, taking a sip. 'All I'm saying is the other stations are lapping us. No one wants him anymore.'

'I want him,' I say. Dora nods in agreement.

Ivan looks me in the eye, then jokes, 'Yeah, but you've been around almost as long as he has. You're *paid* to like him.'

His logic is flawed, and incorrect, but I'm not going to argue. Too exhausting. The man once told me we shouldn't need farmers because we have grocery stores. Sometimes I remember he's got a fully formed frontal lobe and it's all I can think about for the rest of the day. How beautiful it'd be if, just once, he stopped describing male sports players as men with no necks. He's our social media manager and I'm worried he's accidentally going to post from the work account one day and we'll make the tabloids.

'He'll be fine,' Ivan says. 'The man's house has, what, fifty bedrooms? Plenty of space to wallow. And decompose.'

Dora slaps his arm but laughs at the same time. 'You're so bad.'

Neither of them asked where I moved to after Genevieve left, and I didn't want to tell them. Didn't want the questions, or the envy. Didn't want them asking if they could come over to see the place.

'Okay, make sure I stop after this one,' Dora says, placing her hand on top of her glass. 'Need to be up early tomorrow.'

She hasn't told us what for, but I'd bet money it's related to the wedding. It's remarkable how quickly she and Cleaver have managed to pull everything together – how easily they were able to lock in a venue, a planner, the dress, the guest list, the menu. Dora's always been efficient like that.

'Oh,' she says, perking up. Swivels towards me, placing a hand on the table in front of my drink. 'You're coming to the hens', right? You haven't RSVPed.'

'Oh god, sorry. Yes, yes, I'm definitely coming.'

'Great.' She raises a finger in the air, taps the side of her forehead. 'Making a mental note to add you to the seating plan.'

Ivan makes a face. 'Devastated I'm missing out.' His mother's sixtieth is on the same evening. Flapper-themed. He rises. 'Bathroom,' he explains, darting off.

The bar is not quite as busy as usual, but we're still lucky to have nabbed a table. The place is a smorgasbord of finance men – six-five, pressed suits, brass rings, polished brown shoes – and I watch as Ivan slips through the crowd, running his eyes over some of the men as he does.

Suddenly, Dora is switching to the stool next to me. Placing her drink next to mine. 'How is Graham feeling about the whole, firing thing?' She says *firing thing* so flippantly, and it reminds me of her age. That this is probably the first colleague she's ever known to get fired. 'Been meaning to ask you.'

'Why?'

Her head tilts, suggesting I'm silly. 'If there's anyone he would've talked to, it's you.'

Well, yes, this is true. But that doesn't mean we've talked about it. Doesn't mean he's divulged. 'I don't know that he's ready to talk about it.'

'Oh.' She's disappointed, deflating. Eyes downcast. 'Okay.'

Should I be pressing him about it? The man isn't a very open person, and even after six years there's a lot I don't know – he's revealed very little about his family and his childhood. Outside of the station, and his career, he's quite guarded.

'I imagine he's very disappointed,' I say. 'That job is his world.'

'Do you think he'll go somewhere else?'

I shrug.

'Or maybe he'll retire.'

I say nothing.

'Maybe he'll switch careers, do something else. That'd be me, I reckon. I'm delulu like that.'

Delulu. Another moment that reminds me of her age.

'I wonder if he'll be relieved.'

I counter it immediately. 'He won't.' Because I'm picturing his face when he found out, like that morning he saw the ratings. I'm imagining how he'd feel knowing this could be his last job in the industry – that he may not receive any offers after this. That he's tainted, with those ratings. That people think him a has-been.

Ivan returns from the bathroom in a furious mood. Running his hands over his belly, his face a permanent frown. 'Some little fucker in the bathroom called me chunky. I know I'm not *skinny skinny* but I still go all right.'

We're horrified, even though it's a little bit true.

'Chunky? Seriously?' Dora asks.

'I know,' he says, looking down. He doesn't ask us if we agree, or seek validation. He's reeling from the encounter, drink forgotten.

'I'm sorry,' I say. 'That's awful.'

'The man was probably feeling insecure and took it out on you,' Dora offers.

'Was the other guy big too?' I ask.

'*Too?*' Ivan asks, upset. 'What do you mean *too?*'

Oh god. 'Sorry, that's not what I meant—'

He holds up a hand, and I stop. Dora catches my eye and I can see she's trying not to laugh.

Ivan downs the rest of his drink. 'What an utter *fuck*,' he says. 'Can't believe it. Just wanted to piss in peace.'

Dora announces she now needs the bathroom. 'All this toilet talk and I'm suddenly busting.'

'Careful,' Ivan warns. 'The toilets here come with body shaming.'

After she's gone, Ivan takes her spot on the stool next to mine. Comes in real close – so close I can smell the cider on his breath. He's intense. Eyes alert, body rigid. He's going to talk about something very important.

'Tell me the truth. Do you think I'm chunky?'

'I don't like where this is headed.'

'Tell me.'

'I feel like there's no right answer.'

'There is,' he says, desperate. 'There *is*.'

'Okay, well. No, you're not chunky,' I say, fibbing. 'You look great.'

'*Liar*,' he says, pointing at me.

'Okay, well. Yes, you've gained a little weight recently.'

'Bitch.' Then, suddenly, we're laughing. Ivan running his thumb across his chin, and me chuckling into my glass of wine.

Ivan glances down at his belly. 'It's getting harder as I get older. I have this constant desire to be skinny but the complete lack of motivation to do anything about it.'

Later, long after Dora has left, I head for the bar. 'Two gin and tonics, please. Double shot.' The bartender nods, turning to assemble the drinks.

'Two doubles? I respect it.'

I turn, looking for the source, and come face to face with an older man. His forehead is at eye level, his body puffed in a buttoned-up business shirt. A golden necklace clasped tight around his neck, and a rugged beard stretching down from his face.

He's got a pointed face like a bird that's been extinct for millions of years. 'I'm Vance.'

'Charlie.'

'Nice.' He looks – no, *peers* – at me, like he's attempting to crack a code. 'You work nearby?'

He's well-dressed, but it's a certain vibe. His shirt is rich green and tailored, but oddly patterned. Botanical designs – oversized flowers, shrubbery, seeds. All overlapping and repetitive and far too chaotic. Like Gucci in the '70s. Like the kind of man who'd wear cowboy boots with a tasselled jacket.

'The radio station,' I say, then point behind me. It's entirely unnecessary to do that, because it's eleven o'clock, we're too many drinks in, and he doesn't need to know the direction of my workplace.

'Oh?' he says, voice rising. 'Interesting. I work across the road actually. I'm in sales.'

'What do you sell?'

'Insurance.' Then he leans forward, chuckles. 'It's actually *very* boring. Please don't judge me for it.'

Laughing, I step closer. 'You didn't say what *kind* of insurance it is. Could be body part insurance. Could be cyber insurance.'

He pouts. 'It's dental insurance.'

I turn away. 'Oh no.' I smirk. 'You're a lost cause.' Tapping with my credit card, I pick up my two drinks and pretend to slip past him. 'Couldn't possibly be interested now.'

He laughs, and it doesn't match his exterior. It's rather angelic – delicate. Quiet and reserved, but sharp and detailed, with a slight rise at the end.

The crowd is even louder now, and for someone with a voice that soft, he has to lean forward to be heard. His hand grazes my elbow in the process. 'So, what do you do at the radio station?'

'I'm a producer.'

His lips part, and there's a glimmer to his expression. 'Whoa, okay. Love that. Very interesting. Love music then?'

'Love Graham Jackson,' I clarify. Then I add, 'And music, I guess.'

'Can you play anything?'

'Musical instrument? I played the recorder in school,' I offer. 'You?'

He pats his chest. 'Drums.'

'Any good?'

'For a nine-year-old playing in my bedroom, yeah.'

'Got any siblings?'

'Three.'

'Bet they *loved* you.'

His mouth twitches, amused. 'We had our moments,' he says. 'My brother dabbled in the saxophone for a couple of years.'

'And your other two siblings?'

'Bought ear plugs.'

I hold in a laugh, but the smile escapes. And he uses it as an opportunity to step closer. The way he looks at me – and only me – triggers something. Reminds me of Dave, and the first time we met. In a pub, not too dissimilar to this one. We'd bonded over a quip, too. Made each other laugh. He'd looked at me with the same eager, wide smile that Vance currently has across his face. And it frightens me, how easily I could be that to someone else. How easily I could start something with a new person, after a chance encounter in a bar.

It's all too easy. And far too quick.

'I don't want to leave my colleague waiting, but I'll come find you later.' I have no intention of finding him later, but I cannot bring myself to reject him. Cannot bring myself to disappoint him, and that wide smile, like I've just recently done with Dave.

This is too much too soon. Flirting with him, flirting with *anyone*, has me feeling trapped. Claustrophobic. So uncomfortable that when I slip away from him, I don't even hear his objections – don't hear what he says to try and stop me.

When I return, Ivan pokes a finger at me. He's fuming, his frown back. 'What do you think you're doing speaking with him? That short greasy geezer is the one who called me *chunky*.'

CHAPTER NINETEEN

Once at home, I search for Graham.

All I know is that I do not want to be alone here. I'm always alone in this place, and it fills my body with remarkable dread. I do not want to think about the bar, and that man, and how it felt when I realised I could start over, if I chose to. Instead, I want to mindlessly drink. Spirits, preferably. And with someone who *gets* it. Not Dora or Ivan. I want someone who has been through what I'm going through, and who can tell me what this means.

It's absurd how long it takes me to find Graham. I spend fifteen minutes walking through bedrooms, corridors and living rooms calling out his name. His house is ridiculous in size. To think I grew up in a settler's cottage and somehow ended up here, even if only for a short amount of time, forces me to contemplate: I've either done something very right, or very wrong, and I'm not sure which.

I give up and call him. 'You're home, right? Your car is outside.'

'I'm by the pool.'

'Which pool?'

'North-facing.'

I hang up, swivel on a heel and go back the other way, swiping a bottle of Japanese whisky and two glasses from one of the bars. The bottle has already been opened, so I unscrew the lid and take a swig. Then another.

A couple of minutes later I exit the downstairs living area onto the patio, walking over flecked paving and then pebbles. They *crunch* under my feet.

Doesn't take me long to spot Graham lying on the outdoor sun lounge, fully clothed in trackpants and a faded grey T-shirt, slides still on his feet.

Of course, he's already got a drink with him and a bottle down on the floor. He's cloaked largely in darkness, except for the faint, warm glow coming from fairy lights behind him – wrapped around a shrub, half of them not working.

'Never noticed those before.'

He looks over his shoulder. 'Been there a couple of years. Shayna put them up for Christmas.'

Shayna. The fifth ex-wife.

'So this is where you hide,' I say, sinking down onto the sun lounge next to him. I adjust the recliner and look up at the starred sky.

He sips from his glass.

'Want some more?' I ask, jiggling the bottle in my hand.

His eyebrow arches. 'Bad night?'

'Went drinking with Dora and Ivan.'

'Went babysitting, you mean.' He swallows a smile, and I notice the sunken skin beneath his eyes. The man doesn't sleep much since he was fired. And these last few months on air seem like such torture, I'm wondering if it would've been better if he'd been dismissed immediately, instead of given notice.

I pour myself a generous serve. 'A man hit on me at the bar.' The way I say it, pitch slightly piqued, is like I'm surprised it even happened.

His smile turns sly. 'And how do we feel about that?'

'At first it was exciting. And then it was terrifying.'

His expression suggests he's been there before, the way his body softens and his mouth pinches in the corners.

'Does that go away? Feeling terrified?'

'Eventually.' He kicks off his shoes. 'Sickening at the beginning, though. My first date after Leona, my body ran so hot I was melting at the table. The woman was ten minutes late and I spent the entire time googling that surgery to make your hands stop sweating.'

'Is that a thing?'

'The surgery? It is. An enormous amount of money though. Even for me.' He sips.

Our conversation takes a pause, Graham switching up his drink. Reaches for the second glass from the ground, fills it one-third with whisky.

I look down, fiddle with the whisky glass and then take another sip.

'Young people are terrified of being single.' He glances across at me, reaches out to *cheers* my drink. 'What you did was a good thing.'

Are young people afraid of being single, or is *everyone* afraid of being single? Graham's been married five times. Josie won't stop complaining about her husband but has no plans to leave him. Cinar is always in a new relationship, and then ends them three months later so he can find someone else. Dora is getting married at twenty-three.

'It doesn't always feel like a good thing.'

He is silent.

'I feel like I wasted all that time with him.'

'You didn't know.'

'I think I did.' I sink further into the chair. 'On some level, I knew something was wrong.'

He looks across at me, sympathy crossing his face. He reaches out and squeezes my shoulder. 'You ever going to tell me what he did? Did he murder someone?'

'No.'

'Human trafficking?'

I shake my head.

'Mass poisoning with that awful wine of his?'

I whirl on him. 'I liked his wine.'

Graham corrects himself. 'That's mean, actually. His wine is okay.'

'Just okay?'

One of his eyebrows rises. 'That's me being generous.' He pauses then drains his glass. 'Charlie, did he cheat?'

'No.'

He is shocked quiet. Then his upper lip curls towards his nose and he makes a *hoomph* sound. 'Well, shit. Okay. I was certain I had that one.'

I swivel around, planting my feet back on the ground. Take my glass and rest it on my knee. Think about all that happened between me and Dave – all I went through – and realise that with Genevieve gone, maybe I *should* tell someone else.

'He—'

'Don't.' Graham holds up a hand.

'What?'

'I actually think it might be best if you don't tell me.'

'Oh.'

'It was bad, what he did.' He eyes me, his expression softening. 'Sensed it when you first told me you'd left him. Could see how much you were hurting. And I always thought he'd had an affair, but if he *didn't*—'

He looks to me to triple check, and I shake my head to confirm.

'—then he did something even worse. And I don't want you telling me unless you really want me to know.' He points to my drink. 'And not when you've done nothing but drink.'

He continues. 'I have so many regrets about how I handled my separations,' he says. Not divorces. *Separations*. 'I told anyone who'd listen what happened. Blabbed to the heavens. And now I look back and realise I wasn't being very smart. So many people out there know my business, are free to pass it on to whoever they choose.' He looks over at me. 'If you tell me, you need to be sure.'

I go to speak, but come up short. My mouth hanging open, no sound coming out.

I love Graham, always have. And I trust him, but not like I trust Genevieve. And maybe I'm not ready yet to let him in. To give him this one final piece of the puzzle, and have him realise just who I was married to. Dave did something unforgivable, and I judge myself every day for missing it. For marrying him, for being so blind. Do I want to give other people the opportunity to judge me too?

Refilling his glass, Graham pivots the conversation. 'So, Ivan and Dora. How were drinks?'

'Dora's getting ready for her hens' party.'

'Just what you need,' he says. 'Sipping cheap prosecco from a dick straw. Do people who have hens' parties realise they don't have to?'

'She asked me how you were feeling about it all, and I didn't know what to say.'

He's quiet, running his fingertips over the rim of his glass.

'How *are* you feeling?'

Shrugging, he sinks back into the lounge. 'It is what it is. All fine. I'll survive.'

Guarded, as suspected. 'Because—'

My phone buzzes in my pocket and our conversation takes a pause. I fish it out. Genevieve.

How are you? What are you doing? I MISS YOU.

CHAPTER TWENTY

I am living in the eastern wing of Graham's mansion.

Eastern wing.

How posh of me. How foul. Sometimes I will stand perfectly still in one of the corridors, and tell myself not to move until I hear a noise. Any noise! But then I'm standing for so long I worry I'll turn geriatric before I hear anything, because it's a fortress and could even be soundproof. I could emerge from the house one day and discover every other person on this planet has perished, and have zero idea what happened to any of them. Or what year it is.

Most nights, I pace through the halls. Back and forth, like some crazed lunatic in an asylum, I trudge down the centre hallway, with its stark white walls and its plush grey carpet, and then when I reach the end where the cinema room meets a living room, I turn on a heel and make the journey back to my room. Just for something to do.

For the first fifteen minutes of my pilgrimage, I am usually on the phone to my sister. She always starts the call with a rolling update on her kids like they're models down a catwalk – one by one. 'Darla is a poltergeist, I swear,' Naya says. 'I came out of the shower this morning and she was just standing there in the corridor, completely in the dark. She yelled at me for getting out of bed before her.'

From there, the conversation diverts.

'You only call me because you have no one else to talk to,' she says.

'That's not true.'

It's totally true.

'I get so worried about you. I've started memorising the names and numbers of a few crime reporters,' she says. 'In case I need media coverage to solve your disappearance.'

'Please,' I say. 'I'm not that bad.'

I am that bad. I simply cannot stop signing up for ridiculous activities. With Genevieve gone, I must find ways to fill my evenings. Search for people who could slot into her space.

For a very brief moment, I considered Dora and Ivan. Wondered if it could be them I needed. But then Ivan, drunk on gin and tonic, described me to a friend as middle management, and I realised I needed to cast the net a little wider. Needed to socialise with people my own age.

Earlier in the week, I attended an urban wine crawl and met two women obsessed with talking about their busy jobs. In the middle of the conversation, I realised that being an adult is just saying 'after this week things will slow down a bit' until we all die.

One of the women, an alarmingly pale person whose veins showed at the wrists and neck, told us that she'd recently got back together with her troubling ex-boyfriend. 'I love a good relapse,' the other woman replied.

My sister clears her throat. 'Did you hear me? I asked if you'd booked your flights.'

'Oh, god. Sorry. No, not yet.'

'You're terrible.'

'I know.' I pass one of the many bathrooms as I walk, and run my hand over the sleek, gold-coloured door handle.

'You're coming, right?'

'Of course I'm coming.'

'Good, good.' She sighs. 'Mum's garage has flooded.'

'Again? She needs to get that fixed.'

Naya is quiet, then says, 'I hadn't thought of that. Thanks, Charlie.'

'Sorry.'

'Leonard thinks he can fix it.'

Of course he does. 'What's causing the flooding?'

'I don't know,' Naya says. 'I just know it's causing me grief.'

In the background, I hear squealing. Laughing, playing, the occasional snort of a child. One of them is running, I can tell from the *thump thump thump* of their little feet on Naya's floorboards.

I look down at my own feet, bare, on the carpet. And around me, nothing but silence and pristine walls. Reminds me of home, after Dad died. When whatever fun we'd had together, whatever laughter, was sucked clean out of the house and we all simply co-existed.

I keep pacing. 'How is Leonard?'

'Leonard is the same. He's headed around to Mum's tomorrow to help her with a few things. She's driving us a bit nuts, Charlie. I don't think she suits retirement.'

'She's seventy-two.'

'And bored.' She huffs. 'You're coming home, right? Like, actually coming home?'

'Naya, I just said—'

'I know what you said,' she replies. 'I need to hear it again.'

'I'm definitely coming home.' Begrudgingly. Forcefully.

'Great. It's just been a really long time.'

'I know.'

'Do you miss us?'

'Of course I miss you.'

'But you're never here. And I don't understand.' There are more squeals, more *thump* noises as the kids are off on their game. It's so loud and I crave more of it. Crave it as I look around Graham's eastern wing. As I reach the entrance to the cinema room and run my hand over the closed double door – polished rich wood, painted a deep red.

'Charlie—' Naya's voice wavers. She sniffles, clears her throat.

'Are you okay?'

'Yes, yes. Just, excited.' She clears her throat again, and I'm picturing her pressing her fingers into the corners of her eyes. 'I need you to—' She stops herself.

'What?' I ask.

'Never mind.' Her children are loud again, and she excuses herself. 'Charlie, I have to go.'

'Oh. You can't stay?' I say, as I step through into one of Graham's living rooms. Cast an eye over the stone interior and the fireplace. The hanging, rustic chandelier and the plush cream sofas. Over at the window, I place a hand on the glass and stare out at the grounds – pitch black.

'Yeah, I do,' she says. 'Need to put the kids to bed.'

'Talk tomorrow? Same time.'

'Yeah, sure.'

And then she's gone.

CHAPTER TWENTY-ONE

Wednesday evening and I attend a speed dating meet-up event – fast friending, they call it.

The event is held inside a derelict warehouse south of the city. Prime real estate for murder. The sun has long set and the wind whistles in my ears. I fear the CCTV footage from the area will be shown on the news tomorrow. *Final footage of missing radio producer*, it'll say. There will be interviews with my mum and my sister, maybe my colleagues, and then maybe they'll track Dave down and he'll be like, *Yeah, it's sad, but while you're looking for her, could you also look for my engagement ring?*

While the outside of the building looks rundown and rusted, the space inside is anything but. I'm pleasantly surprised. Comforted, even, to realise that it is unlikely I will be killed here. I had expected trestle tables with wooden, stiff chairs on either side – parent-teacher night vibes. A pop-up bar, with a limited selection, perhaps one person manning it. Maybe a few women milling about, forced small talk while everyone waits for the night to begin.

I was wrong.

Seating is lined up in a semi-circle and each place to sit is different. Leather armchairs or suede lounges. Some of those garden egg chairs, padded with pillows. I spot a couple of stools, a few beanbags, and some rattan chairs overstuffed with thick cushions. My favourite is the navy daybed down the end.

There is quite a large cohort of women here, and I find it ironic how many of them are already connecting, chatting over a wine while they wait until the event starts. Wouldn't it be a twist if there was no speed-dating, just the bar, and that's how these friendships were orchestrated?

At the bar, I somehow become trapped in a heated discussion with a group of women about the etiquette of weekend holidays.

'I just don't want a *bar* of it,' one of them says, when the conversation ventures towards the grocery bill. 'None of this "Oh well I don't like soy milk and I only had one square of the chocolate and I didn't drink as much wine as the rest of you, so I'm not contributing to that." We're all functioning adults with jobs and far too much anxiety. Let's just split everything evenly and try not to insult each other, shall we?'

When the event starts, I'm paired with a woman whose black hair has blonde tips; she introduces herself as being attracted to red flags. 'That's my downfall,' she says, and laughs. 'Need to start hanging with friends instead of men.'

The woman seems perfectly polite. Cordial. She shakes my hand when we meet, and when she relays that her name is Katie, there's a rise in tone at the end. *Kay-TEE*. Her voice goes squeaky.

'After Katie Holmes,' she clarifies. And then we find ourselves talking about *Dawson's Creek* until we're halfway through and I realise Katie hasn't asked me a single question about myself.

If Genevieve were here, she'd want to discuss Katie's sandals, which are faded brown and far too small for her feet. Her little toes are jabbing out the sides of the shoes.

'My sister is Demi, after Demi Moore, and I grew up in this hippie, loving home. Real free-spirited kind of community, you know? No rules, all home-schooled. There was a river near home that we learnt to swim in – it's all dried up now – and sometimes when I go home, I sit in the riverbed and think about my childhood. Do you ever do that?'

She doesn't wait for me to answer.

'It's cathartic, isn't it? There's something about this city that isn't quite the same as home – wouldn't you agree? Where did you say you were from?'

I didn't.

'There are just *so* many places I haven't been yet,' Katie cries, slapping a hand down on her jeans. 'Can you believe? It's criminal. So many people I haven't met, so many cities I haven't seen. Beautiful, rural land I've never set foot on. Isn't that funny? And I firmly believe that we were put on this earth to explore. Move around, discover new things. Feel sand in our toes and wind in our hair.' She exhales, closes her eyes. 'Life is pretty fantastic.' She clasps her hands together, intertwining her fingers.

God, I miss Genevieve. I want to call her up so we can laugh about Katie.

How is it possible that four minutes can feel so long? So mentally and physically draining? I feel a twinge in my back. Swivelling my torso, I hear a *crack*. Instant relief.

Katie's now speaking about her nephew. 'He's *adorable*, of course. He's seven, and always making me laugh. Kids are funny, don't you think?'

I have no time to answer.

'Last time I flew home, he waved me over and told me he had a serious question to ask. A big question! Something important that absolutely could not wait. And then he hands me this note and it says, and I kid you not, *Have you ever seen a bomb?*'

The buzzer sounds, and Katie laughs. 'My god, I've done nothing but *talk*. Sorry about that. When I'm having fun, I just can't seem to stop.' She rises, and then sticks out her hand for me to shake. 'It's been so nice to meet you . . .' She trails off at the end, having forgotten my name.

'Well, bye.' She darts off in search of her next victim, and I pull out my phone. Instantly search for a message from Genevieve. But there's nothing.

I've already messaged her many times this week. Even tonight, before coming here, I'd texted:

> Genevieve, what the fuck am I going to do about this engagement ring?!? Ronald The Lawyer won't stop hassling me! Dave texts me every week about it (the man forgets his retainer every night but THIS he remembers).
> How deep is the harbour do we think? Should I just swim down there and get it? Maybe hire someone to do it for me! What the FUCK am I going to do.

Five minutes later, after I'd processed my meltdown, I'd sent a follow-up text.

> But how are things with you?

No response yet, but it's still early. And her life is different now. She's got her family there, and a house, and she's just joined a mothers' group. I bet she's got a suite of new friends – I bet she's replaced me already. I'd cry, if I weren't in public right now.

Wine is required.

At the bar I buy two glasses, and down half of the first one almost immediately. Look back over at the group of women finding their next seats and realise this event has me feeling uneasy. It feels forced, and uncomfortable. Are things really this dire?

When I fish my phone back out of my handbag, there's a new alert. *Missed call from Genevieve.*

CHAPTER TWENTY-TWO

Back at happy hour, Dora updates us on the wedding planning. The menu and the cake and the bridesmaids' dresses. She's stressing about the budget, and the weather forecast. She thinks vendors are taking advantage because she's young.

'I just can't believe how much it costs to get married,' she cries.

'Imagine doing it more than once,' Ivan says, smiling. 'Graham's been married five times.'

'Graham has money though,' I point out. 'Too much money.'

Ivan suddenly remembers something – I can see it flash in his eyes. He points at me. 'You've been married before, right? How much did it cost you?'

He stinks of wine, like Henry VIII.

'A lot.'

'Right.' He wants to ask me again how much. I can tell by the way his beady little eyes dart between looking at the table, and looking at my face. The way his mouth twists, as he tries to think about how best he can repeat the question without seeming like an arse.

Dora continues. 'Anyway, it's absurd, that's all I'm saying.' She sips at her wine, and the table falls silent. My shoulders feel heavy, like they might just sink down into my body if I let them.

We're glum this evening because rumours are circulating at the station that they're close to securing a new host – that it's down to three options. Who exactly, we don't know. But with each piece of information we overhear, we realise we're one step closer to losing Graham. And it wrecks me each time, knowing that.

I check my phone to see if Genevieve has replied to my latest message.

Nothing.

'How do we think he's coping?' Dora asks. 'Graham.'

'Not well, I'd guess.' Ivan readjusts his position on the stool. 'Imagine if they replace him and in twelve months we're still fourth. Or worse.'

'Charlie?' Dora asks, and they both look my way.

'He hasn't said anything to me.' Which isn't a lie: he really is keeping everything to himself. Pretending he's fine, acting as if he's processed the news.

I don't buy it. Not for one second.

He keeps disappearing on Saturdays. Every week, he slips away.

When I ask him where he goes, he tells me he just drives. Gets in the car, picks a direction, and keeps driving. 'Helps clear my head,' he says.

There is something there, under the surface, that I cannot place. Something he's not telling me. And I wonder how hard I'll have to peck to find out.

Ivan buys the next round and I realise how glad I am to have these two. The routine of it all – seeing them at work every day, drinking with them on Friday evenings. They're not Genevieve, but they're *something*. Something to make me feel less alone.

Once again, I check my phone to see if Genevieve has replied.

Nothing.

There's a natural lull in the conversation, at some point. At ten, or maybe eleven o'clock, Ivan ducks to the bathroom and Dora is on a call with her fiancé. So I grab my phone and open Instagram. Mindlessly scroll while I sip.

It's my crutch, I realise, to automatically look for Genevieve's name. To seek out her profile picture in a line-up. Maybe it brings me comfort to know what she's up to. To know how she's spending her time.

And when I see that she has posted something new to her story, I open it immediately. Practically stab my phone with my finger clicking on that icon.

'Oh.'

She is with three other women, seated at a restaurant. Crisp white linen, gleaming gold cutlery. Half-eaten pasta in front of them, and a meaty pizza nestled in the middle of the table. Genevieve is wearing a flowing dress and cradling her growing bump, and she looks so happy – wide grin, hair brushed behind her ears.

Who are these women? How does she know them?

I click on all of their profiles in a desperate attempt to solve this great mystery, but their profiles are on private and it makes me murderous.

'Fuck.'

CHAPTER TWENTY-THREE

Two days later, another attempt at meeting new people. This time, a martial arts class. One man tells the group he's adopted a former racing greyhound called Dougie.

'His favourite stuffed toy is a carrot,' he explains. 'And he won't let me wash it. I'll be on Zoom calls for work, and he'll come into frame and show everyone his nasty carrot. My colleagues think it's adorable.'

'Interesting,' another man says. His eyes are close together, and I can't look away. 'If I showed *my* nasty carrot on a Zoom, I'd get fired.'

CHAPTER TWENTY-FOUR

Over the course of one week, I text Genevieve eleven times. She replies to six of them.

I can feel her drifting away from me. I'm constantly wondering if she still loves me as much as she used to.

I hope she does.

I hope that will never change.

CHAPTER TWENTY-FIVE

Late on Saturday evening, Graham finds me repainting his kitchen walls.

'What are you doing?'

He's come from the cellar, a bottle of Irish whiskey in hand, expression amused. Trackpants, T-shirt, bare feet. He leans against the doorframe and watches me.

'What does it look like I'm doing?'

I'm crouched on the ground, perched atop a bedsheet I found in a cupboard along the western wing, holding a paint roller. Hair pulled back into a low bun, wearing a stretched bed shirt I was considering tossing. I've started with the wall by the dining table and have almost completed the first coat.

'Did you mark the walls?'

'No.'

'Then why are you painting?' he asks. 'And where did you get all this stuff?'

'Found it in the basement.' I continue painting.

'You know I pay people to repaint my interiors? Every couple of years.'

But we both know it's not about the painting. Not about the kitchen or the eggshell colour of the walls. It's not even about this house.

It's simply a way to occupy my time.

Graham pops off the bottle cap and sips the whiskey. Then, heads further into the kitchen, opens a cupboard and takes out a glass. Pours himself a generous serving.

'Want some?' he asks.

I shake my head.

He's drinking more, I've noticed. Didn't think it was possible, but there's definitely been an increase. He's still pretending everything is fine. Still assuring me he's okay with being fired, even though I suspect he's not.

'Are you okay?' I ask.

'Perfect.'

See? Pretending. 'Have you thought about what you're going to do after you finish for the year?'

'No. Have you thought about what *you're* going to do?'

'After you leave?'

'No.' He looks over at me, takes a sip of his drink. 'About your engagement ring. And Genevieve being gone. What are you going to do the next time you have to see Dave?'

I don't quite know how to answer that.

'You're going to have to figure it out eventually.'

That's hardly news. Of course I'm going to have to figure something out. As much as I wish it, Dave is not going to disappear – although sometimes I imagine him evaporating, nothing left but a puff of smoke, and it makes me giddy.

'Do you regret getting married?' I ask.

'No.'

'Not even the fourth one?' I say, knowing that wife took photos of him drunk and sold them to the tabloids not long after they separated. She told him she did it for the money and he said he would've given her the cash, if she'd just let him know.

'I find it hard to trust people,' he says. 'But the ones I do trust, I like being around.'

He looks at me then, with this expression I cannot place. Pensive, small smile. 'I thought every single one of them was going to last.'

'Do you keep in touch with any of them?'

He looks down, shakes his head, then glances around at the kitchen bench, where I've left mess from dinner. I hadn't yet harnessed enough energy to clean up. 'Another Penelope special?' Graham notes.

'It is.' I run the roller down to the base of the wall, and back up. 'You going to join me one evening?'

He shrugs, takes a sip. 'Maybe,' he says. 'Have you booked your flights home yet?'

'No.'

'Charlie.' He sighs. 'You've got a family that loves you and you barely even see them. It's really sad.'

'Excuse me?'

Sensing my tone, he holds up his hands in defence. 'They care about you. And you never see them. That's all I'm saying.'

'They never visit either,' I counter. 'Been here ten years and I think they've visited once.'

He shrugs, as if to say, *I don't know anything about that.*

'I've never seen you with *your* family.'

When I was preparing for my job interview, I read as much about Graham as I possibly could. Every interview, every segment, every snippet I could find. And nowhere, in any of the information I found, was there a mention of his parents. He's mentioned his mother to me once or twice, but never talks about them on air, in the station, to the press. And even though we've all wondered at some point whether they were still alive, none of us has dared ask.

'It's like you just appeared one day. Rose out of the ground, all on your own.'

He doesn't reply.

'I'll book the flights, I promise.' Can't quite bring myself to stomach the task, but just another thing I'm going to have to face eventually.

Fastening my grip on the roller, I rise and look at my handiwork. The smell of paint always does make me feel like I'm starting something afresh. I feel cleansed.

'Genevieve finished her nursery,' I say. 'She sent me a photo. Want to see? They've put stencilled stars next to the window and they've painted the walls lilac.'

I can feel him behind me, can feel his comforting presence as he steps closer.

He does not answer me. Instead, he grabs holds of my upper arm and gives it a gentle squeeze. 'I think I'd like to pretend for just a little longer.'

'Pretend?'

'You asked me what I'm going to do after I finish,' he says. 'And I actually think I'd like to believe I'm not leaving. At least for the time being.'

CHAPTER TWENTY-SIX

I'm reminded of Genevieve when I least expect it. I'll be packing my bag for work and remember that time she hit her head on the elevator when leaving her apartment building. I'll be grocery shopping and see her preferred brand of almond butter. I'll see that book on my shelf that she recommended to me twelve months earlier, that I still haven't read. I'll be at the gym and see that rotund man who once gave unsolicited advice on how she was using the row machine.

My stomach lurches when it happens, and I feel like it's my body reminding my brain that I miss her. That I want us to make dinner together and laugh about something absurd her students did that day. Buy coffee and pretend we're going to the gym when, really, we're just wearing activewear. Joke about the absurdity of Bruce's silk pyjamas. Sing belter music in the kitchen. Talk about baby names and work schedules and our families – the good *and* the bad. I want to tell her about Graham and what it's like living with him.

Mostly, I want to talk about my marriage, and my friendship with Josie, and dissect what went wrong. And when I get yet *another* text message from Dave and *another* call from my lawyer asking about the engagement ring, I want her to brainstorm ideas with me and reassure me I've done nothing wrong. I want her to look me in the eye and say it. *You're not a terrible person, you just left a terrible marriage.*

And I think about this all the time. Every day. When I wake up, when I go to bed, when I have a moment to myself at the radio station, when I'm waiting for her to return my call.

Even at Dora's bachelorette party, I'm thinking about it. While blindfolded, playing a game of 'pin the dick' on an A3, blown-up printout of a naked man. Photoshopped to have Cleaver's head.

'*So* close,' someone says, as I pull off my blindfold and realise I've pinned the penis to Cleaver's left nipple. '*Next.*'

We've taken a bus down south for the day and there must be twenty of us stationed inside this rustic mahogany winery barn with an endless supply of bubbles and wine. There are canapés on plates, and waiters in aprons. It's raining ferociously, so the outdoor element has been cancelled (group photos on the hill, overlooking the lake, panoramic views of the vineyard, wind in the hair, et cetera).

Inside, the girls are getting rowdy. Drunker by the minute. 'Did anyone else spot that guy working the bar? *Ca-ute.*'

'Slay, girl. Go *get* it.'

With the exception of Dora's mother, Rue, and Cleaver's mother, Florence, I am the oldest here. By at least ten years. And it might not seem like much of an age gap, but it's exhausting trying to keep up with the cultural references. Someone uses Gucci as an adjective and then later, when I'm at the bar, a girl in knee-high white cowboy boots and a necklace with '2004' across the front hands me a new glass of sparkling.

'Thank you.' I point at her necklace. 'What's so special about 2004?'

She grabs at it, fiddles with it. 'I was born.'

'Oh, right. Of course.'

Normally, I'd message Genevieve to laugh about this. Born in 2004! Wasn't alive for the turn of the century but old enough to have her own baby, if she wants.

I fear it's time for a nerve tonic and a constitutional.

When the first game starts, we're directed by Dora to take our seats at the tables. 'Look for your name,' she says.

It's a little hard, with all the streamers and flowers, the heart-shaped confetti, plastic costume glasses and penis straws. But I find mine, eventually, to the side of the barn. I'm at the same table as Dora's and Cleaver's mothers, and an empty seat next to me is assigned for *Quinn*.

I stretch in my seat and crane my neck, watching as everyone else finds their seat and there's still no one next to me. When I gesture to the empty stool, Dora's mother leans across. 'Cleaver's half-sister,' she explains. 'She got caught up at work, but she'll be here soon.'

Across the room, the girls cheer. Toast to the celebration, take photos with their commemorative glasses (pink, shaped like love hearts, with sparkly cocktails on the sides), and ask Dora all about the wedding planning.

It stings a little to hear her discuss the flowers and the seating and the dress. I didn't think it'd bother me this much to be here. How easily it'd bring back memories. But it's only been two years since my own wedding. And I, too, had one of these hens' parties. Genevieve, my maid of honour, booked out an entire floor at a tapas restaurant and instructed everyone to wear coloured sequins. We wore the sparkly hats and the plastic penis glasses and sang pop hits at an obscene volume.

And of course, we played all the games. The guessing games, the truth or dares, the Pictionary, true or false, the pin the penis on the fiancé. The game to see how well you know the bride, the one where you ban a word and have to drink if you accidentally say it, that collage game where there's photos of the bride and everyone has to guess how old you were at the time. And my personal favourite, where everyone guesses if the name being read out is the title of an adult film or a nail polish.

And *because* I know them all, when the maid of honour Issy sets up a television towards the front of the barn, I'm aware of what's coming.

The Mr and Mrs Quiz.

This would be the perfect time to hear from Genevieve. *You're not a terrible person, you just left a terrible marriage.* Because watching two people talk about how much they love the other is enough to make you feel horrible about your own relationship ending.

When Cleaver's face appears on screen, the group cheers. Shouts his name. He's wearing a long-sleeve shirt, and his reading glasses are perched atop his nose. Two-day stubble, if I had to guess, and dishevelled hair like he's just woken up. He's smiling at the camera, and when Dora sees that, she breaks out in one too. It's immediate, how happy she is to see him on the screen – hands clasped together, chest puffed with pride, the ends of her auburn bob flicking back and forth as she shimmies in her seat.

I'm not sure I would've smiled like that at Dave. In the beginning, of course, but not towards the end. At my hens' party, when *we* played this game, I don't remember feeling as happy as Dora. Deep down I think I knew, even at my own hens', that Dave and I weren't going to work out.

And yet I married him anyway.

Issy commences the game, explaining that they've already asked Cleaver a set of questions about their relationship, and she's going to ask Dora the same.

'Let's see how they measure up,' she says, which prompts a *woo* from one of the girls on the table to my left.

It's pretty seamless after that. Issy asks a question, Dora answers it, then she plays the video to check if she and Cleaver have said the same thing.

Who cooks more? Dora says Dora, Cleaver says Dora.

Who initiates sex more? Dora says Cleaver, Cleaver says Cleaver. One of Dora's girlfriends yells out *bullshit* and the friendship group laughs.

Who said 'I love you' first? Cleaver, unanimously.

Who is the better kisser? They each say themselves.

What Disney character is Dora most like? This is on brand for Dora, whose favourite movies are all Disney. She says Snow White, but he says Sleeping Beauty (then makes a joke about what she's like when she hasn't had enough sleep, and it cues laughter from the crowd).

And so it continues.

When listening to the game, it's impossible not to think of your own relationship. I'm almost certain the other girls – the ones in a relationship, anyway – are thinking about their own partners right now. What *is* their weirdest quirk? Who *is* the better kisser? Who *is* the tidiest? The most efficient? The one most likely to become famous? Mainly, they're thinking, how well do I actually know my partner? How compatible are we?

I cannot help but think of Dave as each question is asked.

He cooked more.

He initiated sex more.

He said he loved me first.

I was the better kisser.

The Disney character? It stumps me, for a moment. Who would he be? He's considerate. And caring. Quite wise, when he wants to be. So at first I think of Rafiki. But Dave's emotional understanding, his ability to read other people, is not as sharp as it could be. Maybe Genie from *Aladdin*? Wise-guy. Fast-talker. Keeps everyone entertained and keeps the conversation flowing.

But unhappy. Trapped. Confined. In desperate need to be set free.

You're not a terrible person, you just left a terrible marriage.

'Q! You made it!'

The game pauses, Cleaver's latest answer halted. My fingers move away from the phone.

Dora's hugging her sister-in-law, who has finally arrived, small and the only one dressed in dark colours. Her hair is saturated from the pelting rain outside, and Cleaver's mother runs off to find something that might help dry her.

The sister-in-law exits the hug and turns to the group to wave, and I recognise her immediately. Her chopped locks and her pointed nose. That warm smile and keen, observant eyes.

Quinn. Cinar's Quinn. Visual artist divorcée who used to dress like Frodo Baggins. *That* Quinn.

'You're over there,' Dora says, pointing my way.

And we lock eyes. Quinn's face warms as she recognises me, offers a half-wave, and then makes her way over.

'I'm saturated,' she says, stopping just short of the table. She wrings out her hair, lets it drip onto the concrete floor below. 'Couldn't find my umbrella.' Her nose crinkles with her smile. 'How *are* you?'

I'm about one inconvenience away from a mid-tier meltdown. 'I'm really good.'

'Yeah? That's good.' She doesn't believe me. A frozen smile and a forced nod, I bet she knows I'm in a wretched place.

She shifts the conversation, looking down at my tasselled dress – gold and sparkling. 'You look great.' She wears a long-sleeved dress, sparkled but black, with beads stitched around the neckline and red pointed shoes.

When she takes her seat next to me, her stepmother arrives with a roll of paper towel. 'Sorry, this is all they had.' And immediately, Quinn tears off sheets to dry her hair, her face, her neck and then pat dry her clothing.

'Have I missed much?' she asks, looking up at me.

'Just some games. And the first round of drinks.'

She pauses, looking around at the rowdy girls. 'This is them after *one* drink?'

'Oh, them? No, they drank the entire drive down. *We* are on our first round.'

She tips her head back, as if to say, *Yes, that makes more sense.* Discarding the paper towel, she tucks her hair behind her ears, clears her throat and grabs the champagne on the table in front of her. 'I was worried I wasn't going to make it.'

'Working?'

She nods. 'I work part-time at a local gallery. One of the girls went home sick, so I stayed back.'

'What gallery?'

She names it, then asks if I've heard of it. Of course I haven't. 'Sounds familiar.'

'Liar,' she says, then laughs. 'How's *your* work going? I heard about Graham. I'm sorry. That must be hard.'

I appreciate her empathy, and the way her face softens when she speaks. 'We've still got over a month left.'

She nods. 'And then?'

I shrug. 'No idea.'

She lets out a low whistle. 'Ruthless,' she says. 'But he's a legend, he'll bounce back.'

'Thank you.'

'And he's always seemed like a decent person. I like that. You switch over to the other stations and the hosts are so—'

'Inappropriate?'

'Was going to say inexperienced. Graham seems genuine. Cares when people call in.' She sips her drink, then continues. 'Is he like that in real life, too?'

'He's letting me crash at his house.'

'So, yes.' She pauses, staring at a girl nearby. Swivelling back to face me, she leans in close and lowers her voice. 'Has that girl got 2004 on her necklace?'

Grinning, I nod. 'It's the year she was born.'

Quinn makes a horrified face. 'I feel old.'

I wonder if Cinar makes her feel old, now that he's dating someone age-appropriate. Does he think that, when they're together? Does he ever look at her body and feel surprised, because it's been so long since he's been with a woman his own age?

It's almost like she can read my mind. Knows I'm thinking about him. Because she places a hand on my forearm, looks me deep in the eye as her face turns sympathetic. 'I'm *so* sorry about the group chat. Cinar told me.'

Oh, great. The group chat. That horrendous exchange I've been desperately trying to forget.

'I told him how awful it was. Did he reach out and apologise?'

When I shake my head, she's shocked. Mouth agape. 'Serious? He told me he would. He *promised* me.' She turns away, then back again. 'Have they invited you to couples' night next week?'

Oh god, she's really skewering my feelings today.

Couples' night. I guess it's happening. The first one I won't be invited to, after *years*. All those nights at Josie and Sean's making cob loaf and cocktails and screaming Pictionary guesses at Dave while he displayed such horrendous drawing skills, I knew we had no chance. Balderdash was the only game we excelled at. All those nights laughing with the group about Cinar's dating history, or Emmanuel's fashion decisions. Trying new batches of Josie's lotion, and listening to her latest work woes.

All of it, gone.

'No,' I say. 'Haven't heard anything.'

She makes a disapproving noise, raising her hands. 'I'm so embarrassed,' she says. 'I'm going to say something to him, I'm *so* sorry.'

'It's fine, it's fine.'

'It's not, Charlie. It's not fine.' She's clasping my wrist now, her eyes boring into mine. Her focus is rather intense. 'I've been there. It's not fine.'

She's right.

It's not fine that my friends never spoke to me after I ended things with Dave. That Josie said those things about me in the group chat. That Cinar promised his girlfriend he'd reach out and he didn't. That Cinar can break up with every girlfriend he's had and we don't bat an eyelid, but I end my relationship and suddenly, I'm an outcast. It's not fine that Genevieve moves interstate and I'm out here looking for all these different ways to keep myself busy, just to distract myself from how incredibly lonely it is ending a marriage.

'It's not your fault things didn't work out. And it's certainly not your fault for leaving.'

You're not a terrible person, you just left a terrible marriage.

'Tell me something funny, please,' I say, desperate. 'Anything.'

She doesn't even need to think on it.

'I had a boob job when I turned thirty, and the first time I went through airport security, the whole machine reacted. Beeped, signalled. Hooted its head off. But my shoes were off and I had no jewellery on, and we couldn't work out why it was reacting like that. And then security said, "Do you have any implants in your body?" And I thought oh shit, and I just grabbed my boobs, you know? Just grabbed them and said, "Yeah, I do, actually." And the poor man looks at me. Like, right in the eye, and says, "No, ma'am. I meant metal implants."'

I spit out my wine, cackling. Hand to my mouth, eyes wide. 'And then?' I splutter.

'I don't know. I was too mortified. Did you not hear the part where I clutched my own tits?'

I decide I'd like to spend more time with Quinn. That she's

a hoot, and she's insightful. That she's quick-witted and genuine. That she could fill the hole left by Genevieve.

Reaching out, I clasp her arm. 'We should get dinner sometime,' I suggest. 'Just you and me. You can tell me about this gallery which, I admit, I've never heard of. Or set foot in.'

She smiles, then nods. 'I'd like that.' Then she rises from her chair. 'I'm going outside for a vape – want to join?'

Only now do I realise Mr and Mrs Quiz is over. That I was so invested in Quinn's arrival, and her airport story, I didn't notice they restarted it. That the other guests have all been distracted while Quinn and I talked.

I look outside, cast an eye over the rolling fields, and notice we're still in the middle of a downpour. 'In the rain?'

She shrugs, unbothered.

Nearby, Issy is preparing us for the next game. 'Little break, everyone. Little break. Top up your drink, go to the bathroom if you need. When we come back, we'll be playing "Drink if". I say something, and if you've done it, you drink. Easy, right?' Everyone cheers, and then she continues. 'I'll give you the first one now, get everyone excited. You ready? Drink if . . . you've ever been married.'

I grab my glass and stand. 'Okay, let's go.'

CHAPTER TWENTY-SEVEN

The next afternoon, my sister is flustered when she answers my call.

'Charlie, hi. Sorry. It's noisy. Got the kids with me. Everyone, say hi to Aunty Charlie.' She's in the car, on speaker phone. I hear Raphael talking about trucks and Darla calling for her mother's attention. The other two are quiet. 'Not now, Darla, I'm on the phone. Charlie, sorry, just headed to Mum's for lunch.'

I'm getting ready for dinner with Quinn. Applying foundation while sitting cross-legged on the bedroom floor, make-up bag in my lap, tall mirror leaning against the wall in front of me.

Naya waits, then asks, 'Everything okay?'

'Yes, just calling to see how you are.'

'Oh.' She makes a slight squawk sound. 'Thought you were calling about something.'

I pause. 'No.'

I hear her flick on the indicator in the car, and Raphael yells out about a dog he can see. 'Yes, Raphi, a puppy dog,' Naya says.

'Is Leonard with you?'

'No, he's injured his back.' Exasperated, she sighs. Turns off the indicator. 'My sympathy is growing thin, Charlie. I don't understand why he's always injured. This man isn't yet forty, why is he spending so much money on the physio?'

'How did he injure it?'

'Playing with the kids.'

'I'm sorry.'

'Me too.' She clears her throat. 'Before we left, I told him to hang out the washing. If he's going to stay home today, he can do some chores. Am I a bad person?'

'No.'

'I told him I don't have time for his injuries.'

'Oh.'

'I know, it's bad.' And then she's quiet.

'Are you okay?'

'Yes, fine. Just a mum with four kids. How are you?'

I feel if I imply in any way that I'm busy, I'll regret it. 'Why don't you visit? All of you. Graham wouldn't mind, he probably wouldn't even notice you're here.'

She laughs. 'Tempting.'

'Or come alone. You and me.'

She is quiet for a moment. 'Have you booked your flights home yet?'

I stop applying blush and say nothing.

'Charlie, I can't keep chasing.'

'I'll book them, I promise.'

She ignores me. 'I can't look after *another* person.'

'Excuse me?' She hasn't looked after me since I was a teenager. Since Dad died. Since Mum was grieving and she needed to teach me how to use the stove to make dinner. 'I'm not asking you to look after me.'

'You are. You really are.' She lets out a groan. 'By calling me every second night. By not booking your flights. By never calling Mum but expecting me to update you. You might not realise it, Charlie, but you *are* asking me to look after you—'

One of the twins starts screaming, a real snotty, tantrum kind of belt.

'Christ, okay. Charlie, two seconds.' And she mutes herself, and

I'm suddenly listening to white noise while I thicken my eyebrows with setting gel.

I do not expect her to look after me; what an absurd thing to say. I'm the one who calls her! Listens to her woes about Leonard and Mum, bites my tongue when she uses her children to justify her chaotic schedule.

I'm brushing my hair now – still wispy, still a nightmare – into a sleek ponytail, and with each stroke of the brush I grow more and more irate. I'm trying with all my might to see it from her perspective and I just can't. Don't speak to me about not booking flights when you and Mum have only visited me once—

'I'm sorry, Charlie.' She's back, the car now much quieter. 'It's just been a day. We're almost at Mum's now. Can we speak tomorrow?'

'Do you really think you're looking after me?'

'It's fine, Charlie. Ignore me, honestly, I'm just not having a good day. We really do have to go. Is that— Is there anything else?'

Is there anything else? Like I'm her colleague, not her sister.

'No, I think that's it.' I zip closed my make-up bag and rise. 'I'm heading out, anyway, so yeah, all good. Busy day for both of us.'

'Great! Okay, talk soon.'

CHAPTER TWENTY-EIGHT

Quinn takes me to an Italian bar she's fond of – shabby, rundown, dimly lit. Finds us a booth, orders two gin cocktails and a bowl of crisps. Then some pasta.

When she takes off her coat, it reveals two arms coated in tattoos. They'd been covered up at the hens' party, but here they are, shoulder to wrist, both sides. Almost complete coverage, dark blue and red. It's hard to see all of the tattoos without better lighting, but I spot flowers and mosaics, sculptures and spirals. There is something rather mesmerising about the shapes and the angles on her arm.

She catches me staring. 'I've got space for another,' she says, pointing to the only blank area left on that arm that isn't tattooed. It's the size of my hand. 'Not sure what to get.'

'It's impressive. When did you—'

'Since I was eighteen.'

'What about the rest?' I glance under the table, but she's wearing jeans.

'Nothing yet,' she answers. 'Just the arms. Might go for the back next. Or maybe one of my calves.' When she flips over her left hand to reveal the initials *PV* on the back of her wrist, she smirks. 'My ex-husband. Peregrine Vance.'

'His name was Peregrine?'

'Ridiculous, right?'

'Do you keep in contact?'

She shakes her head. 'You?'

'Not really,' I say. 'He used to call me *Charlie* and now he calls me *Charlotte*.'

I haven't acknowledged that aloud until now – haven't allowed myself a moment to speak about how awful that is, for someone to call you something different after so many years. No matter what happened, he says *Charlotte* and it feels like the last ten years have been erased.

'Well, last I heard,' Quinn starts, 'Perry was living on a tree farm and learning to grow eggplants.'

Later, when we're four wines deep and I've divulged far too much about my predicament with the engagement ring, she considers it her responsibility to offer a solution.

'So here's what you should do,' she says, straightening. Fork in her hand, spaghetti wrapped around three-fold. She's wobbly on the chair. Body like a noodle. 'Turn up to his apartment, shove a finger in his face and tell him to fuck off.'

'And option number two?'

'Turn up to his *workplace*, shove a finger in his face and tell him to fuck off.'

It doesn't sit right with me, either suggestion. Telling Dave to fuck off, when *I'm* the one who lost the engagement ring?

She clocks my uncertainty and softens. 'Or you could just tell him the truth.'

I gesture to her empty left hand. 'What did you do with your rings?'

'Sold them,' she says, chuckling.

When her phone rings, the screen lights up between us. Vibrates next to the bowl of crisps.

Cinar.

She pulls her phone to the other side of the table, throwing me an uneasy glance.

So I guess they're still together then.

If Genevieve were here, we'd laugh about it all. She'd tell me, again, how horrible the group was. How they don't deserve me. She'd turn petty and call them *ghouls* and tell me Josie's hand lotion isn't that good, that Cinar's artwork looks like a child's, and that Emmanuel's clothing needs tailoring. She'd pin anything she could on them to ease my anxious mind.

'You can answer that, if you need to.'

Quinn considers it, but ultimately declines the call and slips her phone into her bag.

We fall into an easy silence, and I think about how I haven't heard from Cinar in weeks. How, in the group chat, he acknowledged that lying to me was *the only way*.

I wonder if he lies to Quinn.

'How is he—'

'He's good, really good.' She gives a tight nod. 'He's got a show coming up, in case you want to . . .'

'Probably not.'

'Right.'

'But thank you for the invite.'

She nods.

'Things seem to be going well, between you.' I don't actually know that, not for certain.

She hides a smile, looks over at me. 'Because he hasn't broken up with me yet?'

'Yes.' I sip from my glass.

We laugh, and the tension between us eases. I like that we can laugh about these things, that we seem to be on the same page. I like that she seems like a sensible, well-rounded person. That she, too, made a mistake and married the wrong person.

And seems to be doing better because of it. Most of all, I like that she sympathises. That she understands. Josie, Cinar Emmanuel and Diego, they just couldn't seem to understand why I left. Couldn't seem to hide their judgement – their distaste, at what I've done to Dave.

I take a moment to look at Quinn's tattoos again. Those shapes and colours – the flowers and the architecture. I don't need to know much about tattoos to admire them; I cannot help but lean towards her to take a better look.

An arched eyebrow tells me Quinn is surprised by my curiosity.

'Just interested in this one.' I point at her forearm. Cursive writing – *Ohanna*. There's something shadowed across Quinn's face when she looks down at that word.

'It's Armenian,' she responds, quieter than before.

'A name?'

'My mother,' she answers in a whisper. 'That was actually the first one.'

'Your first tattoo?'

She nods. 'After she died, then I started decorating around it. The orchids, the tree roots.' She twists her arm to show me the other side. 'I've got a clock around her at the back—'

'Does it mean anything?'

'My tattoos? Or my mum's name?'

'The clock.'

She shrugs. 'Just saw one I liked. It was cut-out, with berries and mountains. Kind of charming and rather unique, so I photographed it. Got it inked on my arm a few years back.'

My attention diverts back to *Ohanna*, and the way it kickstarted all of Quinn's tattoos.

'You want to ask about her, don't you?' She gives me a pointed look.

I didn't realise I was being so obvious. 'A little,' I respond. 'But

I know what it's like, people asking questions about someone you've lost.'

I hate it. Always have. A few people have asked, over the years. *What happened? How did he die?* Like those weren't intrusive questions. And when Father's Day rolls around, I just want to disappear. Close my eyes and wake up when it's over.

'It doesn't bother me. I like talking about her.'

'You like talking about her?' I echo, unable to process it. 'Really?'

'I don't like forgetting about her,' she says. 'Each year, I can feel her memory shrinking. And I don't like it. It scares me. And so, if you want to ask about her, you can. I don't mind.'

I do ponder it, for a split second. For Quinn to have her mother's name tattooed on her body means she must've been somebody special.

'It's okay.' I retreat, leaning back in my chair.

I'm still thinking about what she said, that her memory is shrinking. That she feels her mother fading.

I cannot remember what my father sounded like. What his signature cologne was. How often he'd get his hair cut or what his favourite films were. All I remember is how he made us feel – *loved, safe.*

'So, your engagement ring,' Quinn says. 'The more I think about it, the more I think you need to buy a replica.'

CHAPTER TWENTY-NINE

'I miss you.' It's the first thing Genevieve says to me when she calls.

Friday afternoon and I'm seated, alone, out by Graham's north-facing pool. A crisp white wine in my right hand, my phone pressed against my left ear.

'Sorry, who is this?'

She chuckles. 'Tell me you miss me too.'

'Of course I miss you.'

I recline in the chair as the sun sets behind the house. Graham is out this evening, and I've escaped out here for a moment to recollect myself. I never thought I'd say this, but living in a mansion is not what you'd think it to be. It's a bit dull. Still and silent, much room for self-loathing.

It's been such a strange week. I've seen Quinn twice since that dinner, and each time I've come to appreciate her even more. She's no-nonsense and brazen. Assertive, but also the first to laugh. Sometimes I stare at her face and feel this great sense of astonishment that we crossed paths, then I remember she's dating Cinar and find it all a little confusing. What does she see in him? He's flippant and vague, loves to fool women. Quinn is far too smart to be fooled.

Truthfully, Quinn has taken my mind off Genevieve.

'How are you?' Genevieve asks.

In front of me, ripples line the pool.

'We've almost chosen a name,' she continues. 'And we had a scan today. Twenty-five weeks. I'm getting big.'

'Big and beautiful?'

'No, big and sweaty,' she counters. 'But the nausea has stopped.'

'Finally,' I cry.

'I know, I know.' I hear her shuffling about before collapsing down onto something comfortable. 'I no longer vomit when I see raw meat.'

When she laughs, I drink it in.

I'm aghast at how long it's been since I've seen her in person. Since I've hugged her, smelt her citrus perfume, cuddled her little body and felt her arms crush me from behind.

'You've met new people,' I say, remembering the restaurant photo.

Genevieve knows who I'm speaking about. 'I joined a mothers' group. It's early, but a lot of us are new to the area—'

'You don't have to explain. I think it's nice.' I feel my insides coiling from jealousy as I say it. 'I've been doing all sorts of silly things since you left. A book club.'

'Since when do you read?'

'I tried a martial arts class.'

'Bitch, *I told you*. Martial arts is not for you. How many times have I said that?'

'You were totally right. The experience was harrowing.'

'Thank you,' she says, smug. And then there's a moment of silence – a slight inhale, then a choking exhale.

She's quietly crying. 'I just need a minute.'

'Oh, Genevieve.'

This makes her cry even more, like my empathy has given her body permission to blubber. 'I'm okay,' she says.

'No, you're not.'

'I just really miss you,' she says. 'My parents are great. And these women, they're nice, but they're not you. One of them dresses like she sells Bibles.'

All this time, I thought she was learning to live without me. Moving on. I thought it was just *me* struggling. I clutch my chest. 'You can come home.'

'No, I can't,' she says, sniffling. 'If I could've stayed, I absolutely would have.'

'I know.'

'And I want to see you. Why haven't you visited?'

I gasp. 'Because you haven't invited me.'

'Oh, Charlie.' I can feel her physically deflating. 'You don't ever need an invitation.'

My heart feels hard – squeezed tight – and I feel awful. Like a bad friend, like I don't deserve her. 'I'll visit. Of course I'll visit.'

'I've been waiting.'

'I'm sorry.'

'I didn't realise it'd be this difficult. Moving,' she says. 'I've been trying so hard and I think it's only just hit me that this is going to take longer than I thought. To settle in.'

She calms herself, then asks, 'Was it like this for you? When you moved?'

Ten years ago – what feels like a lifetime. 'No,' I say. 'But that's because I had you.'

CHAPTER THIRTY

A week later, I fly interstate to visit Genevieve and we hug in the airport terminal for ten minutes, maybe more. She rotates her body to the side because she really is *big* now and we no longer fit together quite so easily.

'Hi there.' I glance down at her stomach. Genevieve is wearing a loose fitted linen dress – high neck, sleeveless, oat-coloured – and sandy-toned sandals fit for a Messiah.

'I told you I was going to have a giant baby.'

She's right. Her baby is going to be monstrous. 'How many times has someone asked if you're having twins?'

'Every fucking day.' She runs a hand over her hair, which is brushed back into a low bun. As expected, it's battling the humidity, little strays poking out at all angles.

'She's going to walk out of there,' I say.

'Bruce keeps joking she'll have a boxy head.'

'She's going to be gorgeous.'

That silences her, quells her fears. She nods, smiles, and then pulls me in for a hug again.

She seems much happier than when we spoke on the phone last weekend. I certainly felt that it was my duty this week to check in on her every day – to tell her I love her, to plan my visit. Perhaps, selfishly, a small part of me is hoping she'll miss her old life so much she might eventually come back. Maybe part of me is using this weekend to see if I need to intervene – redirect her back home. Resume my endeavours of finding her and Bruce a place in the city they love.

It is early evening by the time we arrive at their new house – a two-storey white brick home, with a black garage door and charcoal plantation shutters across the front. The first thing I notice when Genevieve pulls up in the driveway is the cherry tree in the centre of the front yard, striking in its size. The branches, bare, indicate it's been some time since they last flowered.

'We're here,' she says.

As she walks around to the front of the car, I take another look at her bump, because she's grown so much since I last saw her and this is everything she wanted – family, children, a home. It's bittersweet to witness it now. I feel incredible pride.

Once inside, she is excited to tell me about her new cashmere runner rug, and the low-lying linen beanbag that rests at the end of the hallway. And the terrazzo side table nestled to its right.

'How *good* does it look?' she says, admiringly. 'Bought everything at the local markets from a woman who makes ceramics in her basement. And then she invited me to join her pottery class.'

'You've started pottery?' I ask, hiding how that makes me feel. Slowly, over time, we are learning to live apart. I realise I am not learning new information about her as it happens but, instead, weeks after the fact.

She holds up two fingers. 'Only gone twice, but I like it. Tried to bring Bruce but it's not really his thing.'

Speaking of Bruce, he materialises at the top of the stairs with a wave. 'Charlie!'

'Bruce.'

He has not changed at all – same towering, stocky body, encased in linen shorts and a cotton shirt. Once he's descended, we come together in a hug and he squeezes me tight, rocks me side to side like he always does. 'It's good to see you,' he says.

'You too.'

He disappears to grab my bags from the car, and only now do I notice the grey floorboards beneath me. I'm not sure why, but when she described the house, I imagined white tiles.

Perhaps I stare too long, because Genevieve points downward. 'Burnt gum. Like a brown and a grey, mixed together. Different, don't you think?' Then she points to the plantation shutters, which are white on the inside of the house. 'These are my favourite.'

Of all the properties we viewed back home, nothing was as nice as this. Not even close. It's open, with stretched ceilings and draping sheer curtains. It's homely, with a spotted gum staircase and floor lamps in corners. She's decorated it how she always imagined, too – shades of beige, olive green and brown. Jute rugs in the living room and dining area. Photos framed and rested atop cabinets.

In the kitchen, she's got a marble benchtop island – she's always wanted one of those. Always commented on them, when someone else owned them. Once told me they look chic and expensive.

I grab her hand. 'You did good. This place is beautiful.' And you are beautiful in it, I want to say.

'I can't believe you're here.'

Beside us, back in the hallway, there are at least six cupboards for storage. I run my hand over the varnished door, then search for the sofa again and clock how big it is. Triple the size of the last one. 'Makes you realise how small the old place was. Bet you don't miss it.'

She holds my gaze. 'I miss it all the time.'

Outside, with a cheeseboard, we sink into her new outdoor furniture – navy, six-seater, wooden benches attached to the sides for drinks. I glance out over the yard, with its plush green grass stretched far, and palm trees lining the edges.

'Tell me everything I've missed,' she says, tipping her head back and letting the breeze fan her face. Beside her, Bruce cradles a tea.

'You've missed nothing.'

'I was trying not to message too much,' she says, averting my gaze. 'Thought it might annoy you.'

'Why would you think that?'

Bruce places a delicate hand on her thigh. They glance at each other, and something is mutually understood, and then he rises. 'I'm going to lie down for a while. I'm not feeling too well.'

And then he's gone, and it's just me and Genevieve.

I take another look at the bump. After watching her struggle for so many years to fall pregnant, it's near impossible to look away.

'I'm still terrified,' she says, catching me looking. 'Not sure that will go away until the baby arrives.'

'Not sure that will go away even when the baby is here.' Then, looking up, I say, 'You scared me last weekend.'

She nods. 'I know.'

'It's okay to love it here.'

'I'm worried I shouldn't have done this. I don't want to feel like this was a mistake.' As Genevieve tears up, she presses her fingers to the corners of her eyes to try and stop them falling. I slap her hand away. She's always been someone who has tried to hide their vulnerability.

'You tried so hard to find us somewhere,' she says.

'So?'

'And I left you.'

'So? Genevieve, look where we're sitting—' I gesture around me, swivel in the chair. Then reach over and place my hands on her stomach. '—look what you've got. I am not upset with you. I am not mad at you. I *miss* you, and I wish I could still see you but do not feel bad for living here if that's what you want.'

She tries to brush off her tears and I slap her hand away again. 'Stop.'

'It's been hard,' she says.

'I know.'

'I don't know many people. But I love Bruce, and my parents. And I love this house. And I love *you*—'

'And I'm one flight away.' I grab at her hand, clutch it tight in my fist. 'You need me, you call me.'

'Okay.'

'Okay?'

She nods furiously, letting tears fall down her cheeks. And this time, I reach over and swipe them off her cheeks for her. Cradle her face in my hands, and say, 'Now tell me what you love about being here.'

She smiles. 'It's warmer,' she starts. 'And there are markets at the end of our street. And the neighbours are all friendly. They invite us over for dinner every month. And—' She stops herself, works to collect her thoughts.

Then, finishing, she says, 'And I can see this being a really great place for a child.'

A really great place for a child.

It's quietly devastating to hear. In the back of my mind, I'd hoped there might be a possibility that she and Bruce would move back at some point. Perhaps in a few years. But she can see a future here, for her family, and that changes things.

'And I really want a dog,' she says.

'A puppy and a baby?'

'Yeah.' She spits out a laugh. 'A great, big fluffy German Shepherd that I want to call Sheriff. I looked on Google and apparently dogs reduce stress and increase life expectancy.'

ISN'T IT NICE WE BOTH HATE THE SAME THINGS

'Did dogs tell Google that?'

She slaps my arm, laughing. A little cackle of a laugh that has me smiling. And it feels so *good* to hear her laugh like this – to see her happy. As much as it pains me, because I'd love her back in my life, things are going to be different now and there's nothing I can do about it. As I sit here, I know.

She's never coming back.

'I'm happy for you. You know that, right?' Now it's my turn to choke up, and she reaches for me.

She knows I'm struggling. Can sense it. Pulls me into a hug, resting her head on my shoulder like she would always do at home.

I say, 'You don't need this, not at all. But you have my permission to be happy here.'

CHAPTER THIRTY-ONE

Tuesday morning, and I'm in the midst of a schedule rejuggle.

We're still struggling to book interviews. I'm trying, really trying, but the publicists are telling me there's no time left in anyone's schedule. Then I hear the talent on every other breakfast program.

They just don't want us anymore.

We're on the countdown until Graham leaves. A few more weeks and he's going to depart and we're not worth anyone's time until that happens. Until a new host comes in, and we're given a fresh start.

Graham doesn't seem as crushed about it as he should. 'It is what it is,' he says, after we wrap an ad break and I tell him about the latest cancellation. 'It's fine.'

Ivan, nearby, makes a confused face. 'He's so delusional.'

'Surely it's a mask,' Dora offers.

'Of course it's a mask,' I say.

Ivan smiles. 'He'll crack soon. It's inevitable.' He's been saying that for weeks.

Later, my sister rings. Normally, I wouldn't answer calls while the show is on air. But, well, my sister never calls me at this hour. My sister never calls me, full stop.

'Naya, hi. Is it Mum?' I rest the phone between my ear and my raised shoulder while I rewrite briefing notes for Graham.

'No, Mum is fine.' Naya is short of breath. 'It's me, Charlie. It's *me*.'

'What's wrong? Are you okay?'

'Leonard's back is still hurting him, and I love the kids but they're hard work, Charlie.' Her voice wobbles, and then there's a pause and I know it's because she's crying but doesn't want me to hear it. 'And I got upset and told Mum she relies on us too much and now things are strained and it's really hard. Really hard.'

'Oh shit, Naya.' I hold the phone in my hand, wheel back from my desk. I signal to Dora and she takes over the notes for me.

'I know, I know. I feel terrible. But it's all a lot right now . . . I don't know the last time I was calm. Are you calm?'

It's such an odd question – I'm not entirely sure how best to answer.

'Are other people *calm*?' she asks.

'I'm not sure anyone is calm, Naya.' Graham's getting fired, Dora's organising a wedding, Genevieve's got one chance to have a child and she's terrified it won't go to plan. 'Are you okay?'

'No, I am not *okay*. You have no idea what it's like. You're never—' She stops. 'Have you booked your flights home?'

Shit. 'God, I'm sorry. I haven't, but I promise—'

'Jesus *Christ*, Charlie. You're impossible.' She lets out an exhausted, passionate cry. I know better than to try and defend myself. 'Everything we do here, everything we do for Mum and all you have to do is book some flights. How hard is it, Charlie? Your life is so *easy* and you have no idea.'

She hangs up on me.

Not ten minutes later, she sends me an apologetic, embarrassed message.

> Let's forget that happened, okay? I'm having a bad day.

I respond,

> Yeah, sure, okay.

But I can't forget it happened. It's the first time she's said anything like that to me in years. Since we were teenagers, and she'd rouse on me for just about anything.

What does she mean by impossible? The anniversary dinner is ridiculous, anyway. Let's all sit around a table and talk about Dad like he's not been gone from our lives for two decades.

Still, being forgetful isn't a good enough excuse and I know it.

The first thing I do when we wrap the show is book my flights home.

CHAPTER THIRTY-TWO

Graham's final red-carpet event for the year is a television and film awards night. *The* awards night. Biggest, most-watched and streamed live across the country.

'Do I really need to do this if I've been fired?' he asks, beside me in the back seat of the car. He's attaching his cufflinks while I read through briefing notes. It's two o'clock in the afternoon and we're still a few minutes away from the venue.

'Yes.'

'Says who?'

Gosh, I don't know. I'm just a lowly producer, I don't make the rules.

Grumbling from beside me, he runs a hand over his bald head. He wears a navy suit – his finest – and I've squeezed into a strapless burgundy gown. Low heels, black. A silver necklace resting on my collarbones. Matching silver earrings.

I've got the briefing notes in my lap but also a spotter sheet – photos of all the talent expected to attend tonight. Actors, filmmakers, influencers, composers. It's an extensive list this year, and I feel it's going to be a massive night.

'Last one,' I say, looking up at him.

'Thank god,' he says, squirming a little to get comfortable. 'Hate these kinds of things. They're stuffy and crowded and loud.'

I don't believe him for one second. He once told me this was his favourite event of the year, and right now the man cannot stop leaning forward to check the GPS tracker in the front of the car. Keeps looking out the window as we approach the venue.

I reach out and rest a hand on the top of his back, bringing his attention to me. But also because I know it calms him. 'Are you worried people are going to say something?'

He frowns. 'No.'

'Graham.'

He relents. 'It's embarrassing.'

'It's your job.'

He looks at me, challenged, and I can tell from his tight expression what he's thinking. *For three more weeks.* But he says nothing. Then, he runs an eye over me. Head to toe.

'I like what you're wearing. You look nice.' Then he runs a hand down his own suit. 'Mine's a little tight.'

'You look very handsome.'

'Not too bad for an old guy.'

The red carpet is stationed at the front entrance of an exhibition centre, stretching from one end of the carpark to the other. Studio lights line – and illuminate – the entire stretch of carpet, with bollards and rope to section off the media from the talent. On the other side of the carpet sits a four-level tiered grandstand for fans, who have already started taking their seats.

When the event publicist shows us to our allocated position in the media line, we realise that something has shifted. It's immediate, like someone has thrown a bucket of iced water down our backs.

We'd usually be stationed towards the start of the carpet, near the television crews and the sponsors. It increased our chances of access to the biggest names – because we were the second most sought-after radio outlet in the country and we could catch the talent before the media line exhausted them.

But tonight, they've placed us down the back with the tabloids. With the shady journalists and the trashy magazines, known for asking inappropriate personal questions. With the bloggers and sub-par freelance journalists.

I know we're not as valuable anymore, with the ratings slipping. With Graham being fired. But being placed *here*? We're going to get skipped by the talent. The publicists will take one look at who is standing next to us and veer their actor away.

Before she slips away, the event publicist throws me a sympathetic glance, then shrugs, as if to say, *What did you expect? What was I supposed to do?*

This is a disaster, and there's nothing we can do about it. It's enough to make my chest constrict.

'Well, fuck.' Graham is blinking at a rapid rate; that's how he composes himself when he's upset.

'I didn't know. I'm sorry.' I assumed we'd have the same spot as last year. And the year before that, and the year before that. And every single year before that, for the six years I've been working with Graham.

He rolls his shoulders back. 'How long until it starts?'

Looking at my watch, I wince. 'We've got an hour for set-up.'

'And then the two-hour carpet.'

I nod.

'Jesus, okay.' His mouth twists as he steps behind the bollard and rope, as he glances down at the floor and reads all the media outlet labels written on paper. Slowly, he steadies his breathing.

It's only a matter of time before Graham's facade falters, and I fear it is imminent.

*

Over the next hour, as other press arrive, the media line squishes. Journalists in their floor-length gowns, some with trains and far too much equipment. Lights, camera stands, everybody's bags on the ground behind us – it's all far too busy. We're squeezed together in such a small space – how are we all going to fit? In our old spot, up the front, it was spacious, and we felt royal. But down here, towards the end of the line, we're pressed up against everyone else. Edging our path with elbows.

Normally, I'd love this. The people, the conversations, the company. After a few quiet nights at Graham's, I was looking forward to this. Now, all I want to do is turn around and go home.

With each body that's added to the media line, the temperature climbs. We're undercover but we're outdoors, and it's already too humid. Warm and sticky. The backs of my knees are sweating, and I can see that the top of Graham's forehead is starting to glisten. I smell body odour, but can't tell who it's coming from.

There's another grandstand on the other side of the carpet, directly facing us. Five tiered rows of fans, all waiting to sight their favourite celebrity. Phones out, cheers ready.

And so, we know instantly when the carpet has started. Not because we can see the arrivals ourselves, but because the fans have a better view than we do and their squeals alert us.

Graham reads his briefing notes and spotter sheet one more time. Then straightens and turns to me. 'I've decided I'm fine with this. I'm being positive.'

That's great, because I'm not. I was trying to be positive, but that was an hour ago and now I feel awful. After everything Graham's done for radio and *this* is how he ends his career. My upper lip curls.

To really twist the knife, I realise how long it takes for anyone to reach us down here at the back. It's at least twenty minutes, maybe more, before an obtrusive dress is in view.

And then, it's a sea of people, floor-length gowns and fitted bodices, silk column dresses and sequined mermaid cuts. Sleek ponytails and hair extensions, drop earrings and obscurely shaped metallic clutches. Publicists with lanyards hustle the media line, adorning all black and pulling their talent over for interviews.

The noise reaches an unbelievable height. How have I never noticed that?

We bank a couple of interviews, but as suspected, we're largely avoided. We watch as publicists read media outlet names on the ground, see who surrounds us, then give their talent a quick head shake and move right along towards the photo wall.

'It's because they can't properly see me,' Graham says, elbowing a couple of the people beside him. 'If they could just see me.'

That's definitely not it.

'Hold on. I'm just going to nudge forward.' He tries to readjust his stance, leans out over the bollard a little further, and in the process, he somehow loses his footing.

He tumbles forward onto the carpet.

Hand over head, belly smacking down on the carpet. He takes down a bollard as he does it, causing an almighty racket. The air shifts. Before, it was hot and stuffy – far too much noise, far too many journalists and media crews. But when he falls, suddenly it's just the two of us. And it feels like the carpet freezes. Everyone around us turns to see what's happened. Jaws dropped open, hands covering mouths. Phones extended, filming.

'Shit.' I rush forward, stepping over the rope to help him. So do scores of other people, which I know is making it worse. Making it become more of a scene.

Talent have stopped walking the carpet, instead pausing to stare. Publicists hold grimaced expressions. Around us, media are shouting out, asking if he's okay. And then, to my left, two security guards jog over.

All eyes are on us.

Graham makes a strangled groan as I hook my arm underneath his shoulder and help him up. 'Are you okay?'

My god, this is awful. With each person who comes over to us, and joins this crowd, my body tenses up even further. I should've stopped him from stepping forward. The pitying looks cause me to sweat even more than I already am. We're on live television now: I can sense it without even looking over at the camera crews.

'I'm fine, I'm *fine*,' Graham snaps, pulling himself up. Swatting our hands away as we try to assist. Keeping his head down. Blinking like crazy.

Everyone is looking at us – at Graham. And anyone who's been in the media for a long time is giving us softened expressions, because they've noticed where we've been placed. Seen what media we're surrounded by. Clocked what this means.

Graham straightens his jacket, which has torn along the armpit.

'You can't notice it,' I say, after he runs his fingers along the tear.

He closes his eyes. 'I'll just keep my arm down to my side.' Then he tips his head to the side to crack his neck and rotates his torso to crack his back.

'You sure that you're okay—'

'I'm fine. Let's just, forget it happened, okay?'

'Okay.'

He won't look anyone in the eye, just keeps hold of the microphone in his hand and works to control his breathing. I want to tell him it's not his fault the ratings slipped, and that I'm sorry he's been fired. I want to tell him that something will come up for him, because this simply cannot be the end of his career.

But he keeps fighting back tears and he keeps touching the rip in his jacket – running his fingertips along it and poking his finger through the new hole – and I know this isn't the right time.

'Maybe take the jacket off?' I suggest. 'If you're worried about it.'
His mouth twists. 'This is my best suit.'
'A tailor will fix it.'
'That's not what I meant.'
I know what he meant.

For the rest of the night, most of the talent bypasses us. Don't even see us, just get whisked away by their publicists and steered inside to get seated.

We're calling out their names, but so are the other media outlets. And with each familiar face that walks by, I see Graham grow more and more depleted. Is this what it's come to?

I am determined not to check my phone, because I *know* it's blowing up about the fall. God knows what people are saying about him. God knows how many have viewed the footage.

'Are you sure that you're okay?' I ask.

'Stop asking me that.'

'I'm worried about you.'

His mouth forms a thin line, but he shrugs off my comment. And it's really tiring, I'll admit, trying to coax the truth out of him. I'm so, so exhausted.

'Graham, what are you going to do after you leave the station?'

He flinches, then stumbles over the words. 'It'll be fine. I'll figure it out.'

'Really? Look where we are.' I extend my arms to prove a point. 'You might be the first radio host I've heard of to get fired but given notice. You know that's worse, right? You have to stick around while they find your replacement. Are they going to make you do the onboarding, too?'

His eyes widen. Looks up at me with this challenged expression. *I didn't know you had that in you.*

People are staring. Listening. We're packed too tight for conversations like this to go unnoticed. Graham's eyes dart around.

'Graham, you got *fired*. Doesn't that bother you—'

He simply holds up a hand to silence me.

And I'd argue, I would, but a commotion is starting to build over the evening's biggest arrival. The crowd on the other side of the carpet recognises a famous face, and judging by their reactions, we know instantly who it is.

Graham presses his fingers into the corners of his eyes, and shakes his shoulders as if resetting.

Pauline Sandringham, a seasoned actor who's been in the industry for almost as long as Graham. Rich, black hair trailing down her back. Pale skin peppered with freckles. She's wearing a purple number – lilac, low-neck, sequined and draped over her shoulders and down her arms, paired with silver, beaded heels.

We've had her on the show a dozen times – she and Graham have known each other most of their lives.

She's barely doing any interviews, breezing down the carpet. But as she nears the end, she spots Graham from afar and comes charging towards us, beaming. 'Oh, *Graham*,' she says, breathless. Pulling him into a hug. 'I was hoping to see you.'

Graham is so relieved to have nabbed an A-lister, I fear he's about to cry. 'Pauline, thank you.'

'How *are* you?' she asks. And he lies, of course, tells her he's doing very well. That it's a blessing. That he's going to be just fine. And she buys it. Visibly relaxes. Says, 'Good.' Tells us that our show is her favourite in the country, and she doesn't know what she's going to do without him.

Realising we're running out of time, Graham thrusts his microphone under Pauline's chin and the interview gets underway.

'How are you feeling tonight about your nomination?'

'Talk us through your outfit.'

'Who are you excited to see here?'

'Will you be going to the afterparty?'

'And finally, any projects coming up that you're excited about?'

And then the interview is over, and she's being directed to the photo wall. But before she leaves, she reaches out and touches Graham's side. Angles her body and lowers her eyeline so she can get a better look at him. Then clicks her tongue.

'Oh, Graham, I think your suit is ripped.' She dons a saddened expression. 'What a shame.'

And then she's gone, waving and blowing us both air kisses – two, three, four times – as she slips away. After she's out of sight, Graham hands me the microphone and yanks off his jacket, discarding it on the floor.

CHAPTER THIRTY-THREE

As suspected, the footage of Graham goes viral. Within twelve hours it's across every social platform, seen in every corner of the world.

In the background of the video, frozen in shock, is me, watching on as he tumbles, his legs flipping over his body.

The comments are a mix – some caring, some ruthless. The headlines are worse. If people didn't already think he was past his prime, that he was too old to be doing his job, they definitely do now.

Ivan is the first person to message.

> Old geezer is popular again.

Then Dora.

> Painful to watch. Your dress is slaying though!

Finally, Genevieve.

> Oh god, poor Graham. Is he okay?

Nothing from Naya.

Graham comes to find me just after nine o'clock as I'm pulling together some breakfast in the kitchen. No doubt he's seen the video – his expression is withered and deflated, bags under his eyes, hands sunken inside jean pockets.

We glance at each other, and he mumbles, 'My suit is too small.'

'Sorry?'

'My suit,' he explains, stepping forward. 'I didn't realise it until I saw the video. It doesn't fit me anymore. Why didn't you tell me?'

'I didn't notice.'

'Liar. What are you eating?'

'Are you okay?'

'Yeah, why?'

Why? Because we got demoted last night on the carpet. Because everyone bypassed us. Because your suit jacket tore and you fell over on the carpet and now everyone is laughing at you – more than before. Because you've been fired, and you've only got a few weeks left in your job.

'Just checking.'

He pulls out a bowl of grapes from the fridge, pops one of them in his mouth. 'You free today?'

'I don't like to drink during the day.'

He rolls his eyes, then laughs. 'Not to drink. I'm going for a drive. Would be nice to have some company.'

His mysterious Saturday drives. I feel honoured to be invited, like I've been accepted into some sort of secret club. 'Where?'

He doesn't answer, just eyes my oversized T-shirt and khaki leggings. 'You wearing that?'

'No, I sleep in this.'

He checks his watch. 'Can you be ready in ten minutes? Meet me downstairs.'

He doesn't tell me where we're going. Not when we get in the car, not when we enter the highway, not even two hours later when we exit and drive through a small town that has certainly seen better days – dilapidated housing on the verge of falling apart, broken windows, cracked driveways, overgrown lawns with grass to the knees, tarps over roofs to stop water seeping through cracks.

I'm yet to see a single person. It's deathly deserted around here. Like the start of an apocalypse movie, after people have fled.

'Is this where you go?' I ask, filling the silence. He doesn't need me to finish the sentence. *Is this where you go, all those Saturdays you disappear?*

'Yes.'

He seems more relaxed than normal, I'm now realising. Softer expression, head resting against the driver's seat. And when he looks over at me, he stills.

'I've loved having you in the house,' he says. 'I want you to know that.'

'Okay.'

I wait for him to continue, but he doesn't. A moment later and we're pulling into the driveway of a sports centre.

Graham parks, and I see the lot is half-full, busier than anywhere else in town.

The sports centre itself is dated – 1980s, if I had to guess. Retro neon lights bordering the building. Colourful graphics on a wonky entrance sign. Gardens full of weeds. Faded flyers on the brick wall by the door. Basketball and squash courts, aerobics, tennis and a gym. Behind the centre are stretched barren fields – brown and desolate – and industrial buildings, with crispy shrubbery lining the sidewalks.

'The people here,' Graham says. 'They do good work. Try not to say anything insensitive.'

'What would I say?'

He glances behind us, at the rest of the town. Gives me a pointed look, as if to say, *You know what.* Then exits the car.

Inside, reception is unmanned, so Graham rings the bell three times, then shoves his hands back inside his pockets.

Glancing around, I feel I've been propelled back in time. Bold carpets with zigzags and geometric shapes, patterned tables, floor-to-ceiling mirrors along the outer walls, old motivational posters from the end of the twentieth century, and a set of teal lockers in the lefthand corner. I take a moment to scan photos lined on walls behind the reception desk – sporting teams all the way back to when the centre first opened. Sepia tones, everyone seated in rows with hands on their laps.

'You ever wonder where these kids are now?'

Graham is sombre. 'Long gone, I hope.' He runs a hand over the chipped concrete wall to his left.

Then, a great *wheeze* erupts and the double doors next to reception are pushed open.

In walks quite possibly the tallest man I've ever seen. Well over seven-foot. Dark-skinned, thick black hair plaited and pulled into a ponytail at the base of his neck.

'Graham,' he says, reaching out for a handshake. 'Good to see you again.' He's got a gruff voice, gravelly. 'And you must be Charlie. Graham talks about you a lot.'

'He does?'

We shake hands. Firm but brief. He's wearing one of those boxy singlets with basketball shorts, red shoes with blue socks. 'I'm Zane. Come on through.'

Graham slows a little as we follow him.

'You could've warned me about the height,' I say.

He hides a smile. 'More fun this way.'

Through the doors, it's a hot, sweaty, loud place. Like entering the belly of the sun. Courts line the right-hand side – we're surrounded by the distinct sound of basketballs slapping against vinyl flooring – and a glass-encased gymnasium adorns the left. The building stretches ahead, beyond. Signage points to tennis courts and a swimming pool. For how old this place is, and considering the rest of this town, I'd assumed it would be run down in here too. But the flooring looks new, the walls recently repainted. There's gloss to it all. A sneak peek at the gym reveals it's modern – recently renovated, I suspect.

And kids are everywhere. This place is *alive*. Chatter and laughter. Children playing in every corner, on every court. Barefoot, wearing old, tattered clothing, maybe socks with holes at the toes, and they're having the best time. Making friends, inventing games. One boy has a broken arm, the whole thing sheathed in plaster, but he's playing basketball with the rest of them. Injury be damned!

Zane steers us towards the back corner, to the dodgeball team, eyes following us the entire way. No – eyes following *Graham* the entire way.

Awe. Excitement. Whispers behind hands, palms curled in ferocious waves, toothy grins that follow us all the way to the back basketball court. Graham is incredibly loved here.

'How are they?' Graham asks.

Zane nods. 'Good. Great, actually.'

Turning towards me, Graham explains, 'Zane's a volunteer. Coaches here on weekends.'

'Dodgeball?' I ask.

'And tennis,' Zane says.

'And basketball, and squash, and swimming,' Graham adds, then points to the gym. 'Runs some of the classes too.'

I'm impressed. 'Every weekend?'

Zane's clearly modest, doesn't like drawing attention to himself. Can't quite look me in the eye when I compliment him, or when Graham calls him the soul of the centre.

'This place would be closed if it weren't for Zane.'

He scoffs at that, then gestures around to the other volunteers, voice hardening. 'You *know* that's not true.'

Looking back at Zane, only now do I notice the scar on his chin – short but deep, wiggly like a worm. It trails his jawline like a cord.

'You didn't get that from dodgeball, did you?'

Rubbing his palm along his chin, he chuckles slightly. 'No.'

He rallies the dodgeball team. Introduces us to the kids, speaking about each of them like they're his own. 'Randall is six – he's got a wicked sidestep and incredible speed; Mitsy is nine and has a strong left arm; Trinity is ten and a gun on the tennis court – you should see her backhand.'

This continues long after we've met the team, because other kids come up to greet us and Zane introduces us all. And it just keeps going.

The kids are buzzing – impatient. Desperate to see Graham. And Graham is smiling. Good lord, it's actually a little alarming. I'm not sure I've seen him grin like that.

When Graham's busy with the kids, Zane pulls me to the side of the court. Asks me how Graham's doing. 'You know, with everything that happened. And last night. The video.'

'Oh. You saw that?'

Zane smiles. 'We do get internet here, yes.'

I glance over at Graham. 'I tried to ask him.'

'Me too,' Zane says. 'Was calling him all morning. Didn't know if he'd still turn up. I worry about him. We're friends.'

'He's never mentioned you before,' I say, then clock his expression. 'Sorry, that came out rude.'

'I've known him since I started here four years ago.'

Looking over at Graham, I see he's high-fiving the kids. Testing out his dodgeball skills. Pretending to duck but deliberately getting hit by a ball, feigning pain as Mitsy celebrates. 'I didn't know this place existed, before today.'

Zane runs a hand over his stubble and seems to understand

what I'm trying to ask. *Why this place? What's so special here?*

'You'd have to talk to him about that.' Then, straightening, he adds, 'He owns this place. Bought it like ten years ago. I don't even want to know how much money he sinks into it.'

'He owns this place?' I ask.

Seconds pass. It takes a moment for my brain to comprehend. 'Why?'

A stray basketball hits Zane's ankle. He picks it up and lobs it over to court three.

'He pays for all of this?'

Zane nods. 'The renovations. The food. The classes. Pays the wages, too. We'd do it without the money, but he insists.'

Soon, Graham and I catch eyes across the court, and there's an unspoken understanding between us. The way his shoulders relax when he sees me, the small smile.

On the way home, later that day, Graham fidgets with the steering wheel, the volume knob, then adjusts his posture in his seat. Shifts the height of the open window at least four times – up, down, further down, up all the way. His breath is shallow.

'Are you going to tell me why you own a sports centre in the middle of . . .' I look out the window. 'I don't even know where we are.'

He smiles. Rubs a hand over his jawline, glancing out the window at the desolate land around us. 'I didn't have that as a kid. And I wish I did.'

I wait for more, but apparently he's done. *Nothing further, your honour.*

'That's all I get?'

His lip twitches, amused. Then he elaborates. 'It's hard to find places like that.'

'A sports centre? For kids?' I ask, sceptical.

'Most of those kids have nothing. Some of them have slept there, in that building. Look at this town, you know?'

He's trying to tell me something, now, in the way he can't look me in the eye.

'I know this isn't just about me. I don't want to make it about me. That's why I've never . . .' He trails off, looking out the window. 'I know your dad died, and I know there are other people out there who've lost a parent. But both my parents were dead by the time I was eight, and I had *no one*. Nowhere to go. Your dad died in his sleep, didn't he? I *wish* that's how mine went. My dad died with a needle in his arm on the sofa, and my mum had a psychotic episode and walked in front of a truck one month later. Right out the front of our unit, so I had to watch paramedics walk up and down the street collecting body parts like some kind of easter egg hunt.'

An uncomfortable silence ensues, and Graham cannot seem to look anywhere but straight ahead. Doesn't appear to be blinking. Clenches his jaw so hard I'm worried his teeth are going to crack.

'I didn't know.'

'Don't exactly broadcast it, do I?'

'I'm sorry.'

'Don't be.' He straightens. 'I got very good at relying on myself. And handling things myself.'

'You didn't have any other family?'

'All gone. Or dead. Never really knew. Went through foster care for a long time, and I spent two years living in that town. That place saved me.' He points behind us, signalling the sports centre. 'If I didn't have it? Growing up? I don't think I'd still be alive.'

He clears his throat. 'I made it, you know? Despite everything. Been alive a long time now, and I've survived a lot. Gives me perspective. Reminds me that I'm fine. That I can battle just about anything.'

Then he holds my gaze. 'So the next time you're wondering if I'm okay, know that I mean it when I tell you I'm fine. Getting fired or falling over on a red carpet, in the grand scheme of things, is nothing.'

'Okay.'

'I mean, it's embarrassing, but I'm an adult. I can handle myself.'

'I'm sorry.'

'Don't be.' He smiles.

CHAPTER THIRTY-FOUR

Friday night and I'm headed for a kerbside pick-up after drinks with Dora and Ivan. They spent the entire evening discussing Graham's on-air stumble, and I spent an equal amount of time remembering how excited those children were to see him.

It was a completely different side to Graham than I've ever seen before. How severely I've been underestimating him! Here we all were, thinking him some sorry, sad geezer wheeled off to die (forcibly retire) and he's motivating disadvantaged kids.

It's all tumbling around in my head as I depart the pub – Graham and his sports centre, and how little time we have left with him at the station. I'm also thinking about Dave, and how my lawyer has once again chased me for the ring, and Naya, who has been avoiding my calls since we last spoke. She's still embarrassed, I suspect, that she snapped and said all those things. She's usually such a composed person. But I've forgiven her, I've decided. In fact, I hardly think about the conversation at all.

I'm so lost in my own thoughts, I walk straight into someone as I exit the bar.

'*Fuck*.' I grab at my head, throbbing where the other woman's chin collided.

We're both clutching at our bodies, wincing.

'My *god*, this hurts,' she whispers, then lets out a nervous laugh.

Her voice is familiar, but I'm so distracted by my own aching forehead, I don't quite catch it.

Not until we both look up.

'Josie.'

'Charlie.'

And then I let out a laugh, because honestly, what are the chances? What are the actual *chances* that it'd be Josie I walk into, at night, in an area far from where she lives or even frequents.

'Oh god,' she says again.

This might be the first time I've ever seen her so flustered, wringing her hands, unable to look me in the eye. She's usually so composed, so melodic. Her fresh haircut has grown out a little, and it falls in front of her eyes.

Nearby, a man calls out, 'Jose? You coming?'

He's got a brisk kind of voice and wears a tailored suit, vape in hand. He resembles a gopher. Round face, stubble, thick bushy eyebrows. Pudgy and short.

Looking over her shoulder, Josie waves him off. Dismisses him. 'I'll meet you all in there.'

All.

And I realise it's not just the one man with her, but four. A collection of suits. And two women. Colleagues, I'd guess. They shuffle off in the direction of the bar next door.

Josie loses her balance and staggers, and I realise she's been drinking. Heavily. Her eyelids flutter, and her body sways. She clocks my expression and explains, 'Shaun's with the kids tonight. And it's Roger's last day, so . . .'

I don't know which one Roger is. 'You hate being called Jose.'

She winces, then rubs her head again. It must still be aching and part of me feels happy I walked into her – caused her some pain.

'And you hate after work drinks with your colleagues,' I add. 'You've told me that, like, ten times.'

'It's been a long week, Charlie.' She fumbles my name. Slurs it a little, and shame crosses her face. She hates people noticing that she's drunk. Doesn't want people to see her when she's not poised and perfect.

'I'm fine,' she says, even though I didn't say anything.

She tucks some of her hair behind her ear gently, then does the other side. Clears her throat, attempting to look a bit more sober.

'So, how are you?' she asks with a thin smile. It's a mask. It seems that she's expecting us to pretend we're doing very, very well, when in reality we're all doing very, very poorly.

'Since that group chat conversation? Or just, in general?'

There is a brief moment of silence, and then her face crunches in on itself. The smile is gone, and her composed expression is replaced by complete shame. 'God, this is so awkward. I'm really sorry about all of that. Shaun told me I should be ashamed of myself.'

'Cinar told Quinn he would reach out and apologise. But he didn't.'

She's confused, for a moment. Her brow furrowing, as if to say, *Why are we suddenly talking about Quinn and Cinar?*

Her phone rings in her hand. *Shaun*. She declines it immediately, as if by habit, then realises I saw.

'I'll call him back,' she says, although I'm not convinced.

'How is he?' I ask, because he was the only one who defended me in the chat. Because he's always been kind to me. Because I feel sorry for him.

'He's driving me insane today,' she says, then clocks my expression. 'But he's good, really good.'

'Still looking like an unemployed alcoholic uncle?'

It's a cheap shot, I'm aware. And she's silent after I say it, because she's remembering our conversation at the café. That she laughed when she told me about Shaun's weight gain. And even for her, she knows that was too far. That Shaun doesn't deserve it. That Shaun might not be the problem here.

I wasn't as bad as her, right? When I spoke about Dave – when I complained about him. It wasn't quite to the same level, was it? Now that I've realised what our conversations used to be like, I feel deep shame.

'Charlie, I'm sorry.' She runs her hand down her dress – white, pleated, midi-length. 'I should've called or reached out, but we were embarrassed and we felt awful.' She reaches towards me, then retracts her hand, letting it fall by her side.

'Jose?' Her gopher-colleague is back, poking his head out of the neighbouring bar.

She signals at him to go back inside. 'Won't be long.'

'Got you a pint,' he calls, then disappears inside.

Josie's eyes find mine.

'You hate beer,' I point out.

'I've told him so many times,' she says, with a sigh. 'How hard is it to order a gin and tonic?'

'That Roger?'

She nods, then smiles. 'I just got a promotion, actually. With Roger leaving, I'm stepping up into his role. And he recommended me. So, I kind of owe him.'

What about your husband? What do you owe him?

Instead, I say, 'Congratulations.'

And she thanks me. Then she sighs. 'I really hate Roger, though. I think I've got two more drinks in me before I head home. Need to be up early tomorrow morning.'

Tomorrow. Saturday. 'You driving up to see Dave?'

Her head tips to one side, and she frowns, confused. 'No, the twins have swimming lessons. Did Dave not tell you he's back?'

'Sorry?'

'He's back in town. Drove down last weekend. He said he was going to reach out.'

'Why on earth would he reach out?'

'He said he wants to see you.'

I feel tired hearing this. Tired of Dave and Josie, and the group. Of course he wants to see me. Probably wants to ask about the engagement ring in person, probably wants to try and explain – again – why he's not a terrible person. Why I should forgive him.

'He thinks we're still friends,' Josie says. 'We didn't tell him about the group chat.' She's looking at me with an expectant expression, as if trying to assess my loyalty. *You won't tell him, will you?*

'And we are still friends, right? It'd be such a shame to lose this, we miss you,' she says. 'Things won't change, will they? Just because of what we wrote?'

My Uber arrives, and I pull my handbag further up my shoulder. 'We can't afford to lose friends, Josie, not at our age.'

She visibly relaxes. 'Exactly.'

'Starting over at thirty-two?' I fling the question over my shoulder as I walk away. 'Who could be bothered?'

CHAPTER THIRTY-FIVE

'Sorry I'm late.' Quinn finds me perched on the front steps of the state museum. 'You been waiting long?'

It's been ten minutes. 'Just got here.'

I always think two things whenever I see Quinn.

What on earth are you wearing?

How do you look so good in it?

This time, it's wide-leg silk black pants. And I mean *really* wide. You could fit another person in there. Polished black loafers on her feet. Cropped white knit top. Khaki leather jacket. She's a work of art.

The museum was her suggestion. I said I wanted to go somewhere that might distract me. I'd proposed a walk around the lake and she'd countered with this. 'I'll introduce you to my world,' she'd said, and I thought, *Yes, good*. Introduce me to your world. Let me escape mine for the afternoon.

'So funny you've never been here before,' she says. 'I must be here at least once a month.'

From what Quinn's told me about her art, she's had mild success. Small-scale shows. Enough interest to help her pay bills, but nothing of great note yet.

I've googled her, of course. Trawled her social media. Her art is graphite pencil portraits, mainly. Emotional, moving drawings of faces. And bodies. Sometimes hands. I can't pretend I understand anything about art, but when she told me she's not had much luck with her career so far, I remember feeling great surprise.

She waits for me to purchase a day ticket at the box office, then steers me to the right side of the museum, past the Egyptian collection and the zoological specimens, and through to the historic objects. Extending a hand towards the collection in the far corner of the museum, she leads me to walls of oil paintings. Of river gullies and stretched, open land. Of horses and farmland, men in wide-brimmed hats looking out over clifftops.

'Aren't they striking,' she says, framed as a statement, not a question.

She steps closer to one of the artworks and her head tips to the side as she examines it. A faint smile crosses her face. 'I've tried it before.'

'Oil painting?'

She nods. 'When I was younger. Starting out. I knew I wanted to create, I just didn't know what kind of art it would be.'

'Were you good?'

She turns back towards me, an amused expression across her face. 'At oil painting? God, no. I was terrible. Couldn't get the blend right.'

'I've seen your drawings online. They're beautiful. You're very talented.'

She appears uncomfortable at the compliment, fingers fidgeting with the zipper on her jacket. 'Thank you. Cinar tells me I should post more. On socials. Said it might help me find my audience.' She looks at me. 'It felt very patronising.'

'Cinar doesn't even have socials.'

Quinn raises her eyebrows. *Exactly*, she's saying.

'And you've got more of an audience than his previous girlfriends.'

'Got more years on me, too.'

We laugh, moving through the collection.

'I wouldn't worry what about what Cinar says. He's so focused on himself, he doesn't notice much about those around him.'

She seems mildly annoyed, her brows slightly furrowed. 'I'm not worried. Just would love to see my art on walls like these one day.'

I don't know what that's like, pursuing something creative. Making art for years, hoping it'll resonate. To come in here, look at what's possible, and wonder if it'll ever happen for you.

'I bartend on weekends,' she says. 'Not sure if I've mentioned?'

'You haven't.'

'To make extra money.' She looks away. 'Need to pay the rent, and all that.' Waves her hand around as if to say, *You get it.*

My phone vibrates with a message from Genevieve. A photo of her recent pottery creation – a miniature jug with a spout. Squished, lopsided, wonky. Looks like shit.

LOVE it.

After sending the message, I turn back to Quinn. 'Did I tell you I ran into Josie the other day?'

'No, but I heard.' She catches my eye and sniggers.

'She was drunk.'

'Really?' Quinn says. 'She left that part out.'

'Her colleagues call her *Jose*. And she was drinking beer.'

'And you're sure it was her?'

'In the flesh.'

Around us, the exhibition grows busy. We're in the photographic collection now – negatives and rolls of film from the 1800s.

'I never heard from Cinar. Or Emmanuel.'

And then suddenly, as if sliced, she straightens, body swivelling to face mine like she wants my full attention.

'Something that surprised me when I split with Perry, something that I never realised until later, was that it's never about you. How people react, what they think. It's not about you at all. And I wish I'd known that earlier. I think it might've helped.' She folds her arms across her chest, then continues. 'Cinar's parents are divorced, did he ever tell you that?'

'They're divorced? No, he didn't. He told us his dad left. That he hasn't seen him since he was—'

'Ten,' she finishes. 'But they were divorced before it happened. A few years earlier. His dad was a drinker. And a cheater. And his mum got sick of it and left. Took Cinar and served divorce papers.'

'Oh.' We've stopped in the corridor.

'Cinar was shuffled between the houses, but his dad stopped minding him as often and then eventually disappeared altogether. Cinar blames the divorce for his father leaving the country. Blames the divorce for a lot of things, actually.'

'You couldn't expect his mother to stay, though.'

'I agree.'

The fact that he's told this to Quinn, and not the group, means he must be serious about her. And the relationship. More serious than any of the other girlfriends we've met (and lord, have there been *a lot*). And selfishly, I'm wondering how this is going to work, if those two are going to last. Me and Quinn, being friends, when she's with Cinar. What are the rules here?

'He told me it ruined his childhood. He told me he'd never get a divorce,' Quinn says. 'No matter what.'

I glance at Quinn and detect no lie. No exaggeration. She offers me a sympathetic smile.

'What?' I hate hearing this. It pinches my body and makes my chest contract – like it's been sucked of nutrients. Cinar would rather stay miserable in marriage than explore the chance of being happy alone. Is that what he thinks I should've done? Stayed unhappy with Dave? Spent the rest of my life with him while each part of me slowly died?

'He said that?' My voice is strained.

'He did. So don't take it personally. It's not about you. It's about him.' She places a hand on my shoulder and it feels genuine. When her thumb runs over my skin in a reassuring movement, I feel comforted. So comforted I might just cry in front of her.

'But *you're* divorced,' I point out. 'It's fine for you to be divorced, but not me?'

'I don't get it either.'

Reflecting, I say, 'It explains all the women.' And his limited experience with long-term relationships. The man's trying so hard to avoid a divorce he just flitters between partners instead.

Quinn continues. 'And Emmanuel's a practical man. Very matter-of-fact. Can't sympathise for things he doesn't understand. You leaving a marriage without telling him why? I suspect that's why he's distant.'

How has Quinn figured out my friends quicker than me? How has she read them this well, this soon? *Is* that why Emmanuel doesn't message anymore? Because he doesn't understand the decision? Does he even have a *right* to understand the decision?

'And Josie? What about her?'

She muses. 'I need a little more time to figure that one out.'

Driving home that night, I call everyone to see who might be available for a chat – Genevieve, Dora, Naya, Ivan, Mum. But no one answers.

Ten minutes later, once inside Graham's house, they all start calling me back. But my window for being social is over.

CHAPTER THIRTY-SIX

At work, my phone vibrates as we close the final segment. It's Dave.

Charlie, I'm back in town, and I'd like to see you. Please.

Well, fuck.

CHAPTER THIRTY-SEVEN

Later that night, by the pool, peated whisky in hand, Graham is little help with the situation.

'You think I should see him?'

'Sure.'

'So that's a yes?'

'Okay.' He's distracted by the fireworks display let off by a neighbour down the road. It's loud and constant – a crackle of pink, blue and red in the sky.

I wave my hand in front of his face, and he startles. 'Sorry, what were we talking about?'

'Dave's text.'

'Still going on about that engagement ring, is he?'

I glance down at my phone, re-reading it. He hasn't said anything about the ring, but I know that's what he's implying. Know him well enough that he wants to settle this in person. That he's sick of messaging. Sick of dragging this out. I've tried calling my sister, because I'd like her opinion, but she's still not answering.

'Is he even going to care that you lost the ring?' Graham asks. 'The man never noticed it was gone.'

Pondering his question for a moment, I sip my drink. *Will* he care? I don't know. Hadn't really considered it, just felt such guilt for losing it in the first place I didn't want to tell him. And then, after the separation, I didn't want to see him.

Fireworks erupt again, higher in the sky, and louder. Small green bursts then wider orange explosions. With each beat, Graham's face is illuminated. He looks pensive. Complacent.

'Charlie.' He turns to me, holds my gaze, smiles. 'I've decided to leave, after I finish the show. Travel overseas, for months. Maybe years. Sell the house. Sell all my things and just go.'

There is silence for a moment. And then an explosion of fireworks – the short, sharp *pop pop pop* as it continues on and on.

'Fuck.'

'Language.'

'You're leaving? But . . .'

He's leaving. Another person, gone.

Pop.

Pop.

Pop.

I slump, feeling a great heaviness travel through my body. Right down to my toes. Do I laugh at this point? Is there someone, somewhere, playing some cruel joke on me, as they rip everyone from my life?

'I'm sorry, Charlie.'

'How soon after the show? How much time do we have?'

His head tips to the side, and his smile is sympathetic now. 'House goes on the market tomorrow.'

I choke a little. He must've been deliberating on this for some time. He's not going to change his mind. And with that, my disappointment grows.

'Oh.'

'I know.'

'That's . . .'

'I know.'

I'm excited for him, of course. What kind of person would I be if I wasn't? 'I can't believe you're leaving.'

He bends over to grab the whisky bottle and tops up the glass in my hand. I hadn't even realised I'd finished it.

'Sorry to kick you out,' he continues. 'I've liked having you here.'

'We live on opposite sides of the house. Sometimes I don't even know if you're home.'

Small smile. 'I know.' Then he clinks his glass against mine. 'Regardless, I've loved living with you. More than I did with four of my ex-wives.'

'Ex-wives two, three, four and five?'

He makes a face. *Of course those four – don't be daft.*

'Selling your house, though,' I say, looking back over my shoulder at the grand exterior. I fear I might've taken the place for granted. 'I can't believe it.'

'The news will hit tomorrow. Finally, something else for people to say about me, instead of that video.'

'And being fired.'

'So thoughtful of you to remind me.' The corner of his mouth lifts.

'I'm going to miss you.'

'You're going to be just fine,' he says, warmly, sinking further into his lounge, looks up at the sky. Closes his eyes, as if letting the evening fall over him. 'We're all going to be just fine.'

I'm not sure I believe that, but in this moment I choose to accept it. I imagine Graham hopping around the world. A part of me questions whether he'll return, but then the rest of me fears I'm only thinking this because of Genevieve. Because she's not coming back. Because I'm worried history is repeating itself.

'You and Genevieve,' I say. 'I think I'm sadder about both of you moving away than I was about ending my marriage.'

'That's because you grieved the end of the relationship while you were in it,' he says. 'By the time you left, you were fine.'

Remarkable how much this impacts me. Hits me like someone striking my face. How right he is, and he says it so plainly like it's the simplest thing in the world. I was thinking of leaving Dave for months. Was tossing it over in my mind, mulling it over night after night, until I found out what he'd done.

'So you think I should see him?' I ask.

Graham releases an exhausted groan. Rubs his brow. 'Charlie, if I'm being honest, I'm a little tired of talking about Dave. Go see him, or don't. Tell him about the engagement ring, or don't. But please, *please*, make a decision.'

CHAPTER THIRTY-EIGHT

Quinn doesn't quite share the same position as Graham.

'People can be so impatient,' she says, as we stand in Graham's kitchen. 'You've still got time. You don't need to see Dave if you don't want to.'

She drags out the word *impatient*, hisses it. Makes me think there's a wound there – raw and recent – and I consider pressing it. But then she moves on.

'Okay, done, what's next?' She places her hands on her hips. Looks around the kitchen while I re-read the recipe – Mum's latest.

'Teaspoon of butter in the pan, then fry the sliced onion until brown,' I say, stepping towards the fridge. 'I'm going to season the meat.'

Tonight's meal is beef and vegetable stew, one of my favourites, and it's the first time I've cooked it with someone other than Genevieve and Bruce. It feels comforting, to have Quinn here sharing the kitchen.

When she first arrived, parking her car in the driveway, she leant over the steering wheel and stared at the house, mouth agape. It might've been the first time I've seen her genuinely shocked. Unable to compose herself. When she stepped out of her car, she breathed out, 'Holy hell. You live here?'

On the kitchen bench sits an opened bottle of merlot; we've

recently topped up our glasses. 'I'm going to tell her not to send the recipes anymore,' I say. 'Mum.'

'Why on earth would you do that?' Quinn snaps, frowning. She's cutting the onion with such ferocity, I feel intimidated.

Her reaction throws me for a moment – her disagreement, her distaste. 'Because I'm okay now,' I say. 'Because I don't need her to do that for me.'

'Might not be for you anymore. If she enjoys it, let her do it.'

'But I feel bad.'

'Don't,' Quinn insists. 'I'd give anything to have this.'

She says nothing further, but I am reminded that her mother passed many years ago.

Meat seasoned and vegetables frying, Quinn tells me she loves cooking but has never had anyone to share it with. 'Cinar just doesn't understand it,' she says. 'I find cooking therapeutic. And he just wants it to be ready.'

Impatient. The connection is not lost on me. 'How is he? How are you both?'

She pauses, and for a moment the only noise in this kitchen is the sizzle of the vegetables on the pan. 'He's asked me to move in with him.'

'Holy shit.' I choke a little on my wine. 'He's never done that before.'

She doesn't look nearly as happy as she should, instead resembling a frightened animal.

'So people keep telling me.' She makes a face. *I get it, all right?*

'You don't want to live with him?' I ask. For months I've limited how often we talk about Cinar. I was salty about how the group treated me, but I also didn't think this relationship was going to last. I thought I'd give it a few weeks, it'd end, and then I'd never really need to know about their relationship. Could forget all about Cinar.

'I don't know what I want,' Quinn says. 'Is it weird that moving in with him makes me feel trapped?'

Yes.

'No.'

'Because I didn't feel like that with Perry, so it scares me. But Perry and I didn't work out anyway, so maybe that doesn't mean anything.'

'You never talk about Perry.'

'Because we were little idiots. So young. Stupidly young. I'm not surprised he had all those affairs, actually. Poor guy must've realised pretty early on that he'd made a huge mistake.'

'And what about you? Did you think you'd made a mistake?'

'Not at first,' she says, watching as I transfer the vegetables into a pot then place the beef in the searing pan. It sizzles, smoke rising up. She turns on the exhaust fan and it whirs loudly. 'Not for a long time. I was obsessed with him. His long curly hair, his dance moves. He always wore these service-station sunglasses and I thought his confidence was inspiring.'

She sighs, then continues. 'And then, you know, life happened. We were different people by the time we were approaching thirty. The man didn't want responsibilities and spent every dollar he had. And he was *so* fun, but he also couldn't hold a serious conversation. And that was fine when we were twenty, but not so cute eight years later ... And he gave his opinion too freely on what I wore. How I dressed. Told me I looked dowdy.'

'It's always the service-station sunglasses who have an opinion on aesthetics.'

She laughs, guttural, head tipped back. 'Oh, I needed that, thank you.' Then after a brief pause, she adds, 'You know, I really like spending time with you.'

It's the nicest thing she could say to me. The biggest mood booster, and she doesn't even realise. She twirls around to look for the salt and pepper and I'm here holding my hand to my chest.

I really like spending time with you. The first genuine friend I've made since Genevieve left. My heart swells.

On the bench, her phone lights up, and as if on autopilot, I look down at it. A group chat is erupting – messages incoming one after the other. Josie, Emmanuel, Diego, Josie, Josie, Cinar, Emmanuel. And finally, Dave.

So there *is* a new group chat. Of course there is. And now Quinn's in it, instead of me. It feels a little like she's taken my spot in the group. Is it growth, that I don't feel anything?

'Sorry,' she says, turning her phone over. 'Josie's trying to organise a dinner now that Dave's back in town.'

'It's okay.' I straighten.

Quinn eyes me, and I know the topic is about to shift. 'Dave's text ... Any chance it's not about the engagement ring? What if he wants to try and convince you it was a mistake leaving? Try and fix things.'

Assessing her, I stammer. 'W-why? Has he said something?'

She holds up her hands, innocent, and dismisses it. 'No, not at all, I'm just thinking. It's what Perry did. Tried to piece us back together.' She grabs the wooden spoon, stirs the pot.

I look down at my hand, where my ring once lived. Then, I shake my head. 'If anything, I think he'll try and convince me that what he did wasn't that bad.'

She looks up, fast, and I know it's because I've never revealed what he did. What I found out. And I can see it in her widened expression that she would love to know.

'I've only told one person,' I say. 'Genevieve.'

Her head tips. 'Who's Genevieve?'

'Oh.' The small sliver of silence between us is the only indicator of my surprise. 'A friend.'

Genevieve is such a big part of my life, and I hadn't realised that I'd never mentioned her to Quinn. Was I trying to hide her? Or simply build a new life without her?

'You've got more self-control that I do,' Quinn continues. 'I told everyone about Perry's mistakes. Made sure they knew that the divorce wasn't my fault.'

'Even though you got married too young,' I say, and she returns my smile.

'Well, yeah, but I'm not the one who had the affairs.'

Later, after we've eaten, Quinn talks about the house. 'A shame he's selling it,' she says. Then she turns towards me with a pointed smile. 'A shame you have to move out.'

'I've been looking at rentals.'

'Apartments?'

'Studios.'

She swallows a laugh. 'Going from *this* to a studio, I can't imagine.'

'Sometimes I'll drop something and say "Oops" and realise that's the first time I've heard my own voice since getting home from work.'

Her smile fades.

'I miss Genevieve's apartment,' I say. 'It was small, and we were on top of each other. But then I moved in here and I realised I prefer it like that.'

She pours me another glass of wine and her phone, now beside her, lights up again. I'm expecting it to be the group chat, but it's someone else. A name I don't recognise.

'Would you have done anything differently?' Quinn asks me, and I realise she's talking about Dave. About our marriage.

I think it over, for a moment, because I've never been asked this before. Never even contemplated it myself. *Would* I have done anything differently? She gives me a second to think about it – to process a decade-long relationship in a matter of seconds to determine if I'd do it all over again.

'The relationship, no.' I run a finger over the edge of my wine glass. 'But I would've changed other things.'

'What other things?'

'I moved here for him. Was so desperate to leave home I think I would've followed him anywhere. And my friends were . . .' I point to her phone, and she knows who I'm referring to. 'His friends.'

'It was his life.'

'All of it,' I say. Then I hold up my glass. 'Even the wine we drank, was always from his family's vineyard. I'd suggest buying something else and he just couldn't understand why I'd bother . . . Might not make much sense, but—'

'No, I get it,' Quinn says.

'It was just always, kind of, about him.'

She points at my phone now, before sipping her wine. 'Kind of still is. Can't get rid of him until you figure out what to do about that engagement ring.'

Tell him about the engagement ring, or don't. But please, please, make a decision.

'Do you miss him?' she asks.

I take more time to answer this one, because it's complex. 'I don't miss *him*. But I do miss having someone. Having the company, and the support of another person.'

'But that could be anyone.'

Like Genevieve. Like Graham. Like you. 'It could. But it's different, I guess. I don't know how to explain it.'

It's being alone at night, for the first time. And dividing your belongings. It's telling your family that you've split, and your friends. It's seeing people get married and have children. Watching as everyone moves on around you, and you're still processing.

It's losing your best friend.

'I think he's a good person,' I say. 'I just don't think we were right for each other anymore.'

Quinn understands, nodding.

'If I told you I've enjoyed stringing him along, would that make me a terrible person?'

She smiles. 'Because you're mad at him?'

'No.' I straighten. 'I'm annoyed I'm here, in this situation. Wasted all that time on a relationship that was probably doomed from the beginning. And then he goes and . . .' I trail off. 'Never mind.'

'I don't think you're a horrible person. But it's not his fault, though, right? Not his fault things didn't work out. That you stayed together for so long.' She pauses before continuing. 'I don't know what he did, of course, but before you found out about it, were you happy?'

I contemplate whether to lie here. Tell her I was head over heels. But this is the person I've most connected with since Genevieve left. And I know I need to trust her. I need to trust *someone* if I'm going to build my own life here, without Dave. Or Genevieve. Or Graham.

'No,' I say.

Her eyebrows rise, but the rest of her is still.

'But I kept convincing myself that maybe we could be saved. That it was a hassle to leave.' I take a sip of my drink. Then another. 'And then I found out something about him, and suddenly, he was the worst person I knew. And I couldn't look past it. So I left.'

She nods, running a hand through her hair.

'I think about him, and I feel sorry for him,' I say. 'Because I think he's weak, and I think he's going to regret so many things when he's older. And when he texts me, and I see his name, I feel exhausted. Does that make any kind of sense?'

She doesn't say anything at first, just reaches across and picks up her phone. Opens something, then slides the mobile across the bench towards me.

A picture of an engagement ring – sapphire, marquise, teardrop diamonds either side. 'What am I looking at?'

'I've been meaning to send this to you,' she says. 'Looks similar, right?'

The tapered band is a little thicker than my own engagement ring, but apart from that, it looks almost identical to the one I lost.

'Oh. You're right, it does.'

She gives me a pointed look, and suddenly I understand.

What if I did what everyone has been suggesting, and I bought something similar? Maybe I don't need to tell him I lost the original one. Dave's lawyer could finalise the settlement and then he'd stop pestering me with text messages. It's been so long since he's seen the ring, maybe, just *maybe*, he wouldn't notice it was different. He didn't realise that I'd lost it, didn't even clock when it disappeared from my finger, and maybe he'll be so relieved to get back *a* ring he won't realise it's not *the* ring.

I grab my phone from my back pocket. Let it rest in my hands for a moment. And then, I message Dave. After all these months, I reply.

Let's meet at the apartment.

CHAPTER THIRTY-NINE

Responding to Dave's message seems to unlock something between us. Something I didn't intend. He takes it as evidence – as confirmation – that I want regular communication. Maybe he thinks I miss him (I don't), maybe he thinks I want *us* back (also don't), but as we progress through the week, his messages grow frequent.

> How have you been?
>
> I'm looking forward to seeing you on Friday.
>
> I'm sorry about Graham.
>
> I'm sorry about Genevieve.
>
> The anniversary is this weekend, that must be hard.

God, I'd forgotten how chatty he gets over messenger. Only once do I respond.

> Have you visited her?

It silences him, as I suspected. Because if there is one thing guaranteed to mute him – render him incapable of responding – it's *her*. I don't need to name her for him to know who I'm talking about.

I check my phone a few times throughout the morning, watch as the three dots appear. Then disappear. Then reappear. It's a dance, one that repeats itself many times. I think of him trying to work through a response and then imagine him changing his mind over and over again.

'Charlie? Hello?' Dora waves a hand in front of my face, blocking my view of my phone.

I look up, realise how much time has passed, and apologise. 'Shit, sorry.' I toss my phone to the side of my desk and return to work.

At the end of the week, on the day I'm scheduled to see Dave, it is also Graham's final shift at the station.

We all agree that his exit has come far too quickly. Even Ivan, who thinks him past his expiration date, looks glum. Graham progresses through the final segment of the morning – his goodbye – and we're all utterly bereft.

'Well, this is it,' Graham says. Hunched in his studio chair, running a hand over his head. He takes a breath, to calm himself. 'My last show here at the station, after thirty years. Can't believe it.'

Behind us, a crowd has formed. People from all areas of the building – every department. Marketing, Creative, Reception, HR, Finance, Tech – even the executive board make their way down to watch Graham's sign-off.

'These have been the best years of my career,' he says, choking a little. Then he corrects himself. 'Of my life.'

Another deep breath. He doesn't like people seeing him upset, and so I imagine it's killing him right now that he can't hold it in.

And it's killing *me*, to see him in there, saying goodbye. Makes me angry all over again, that he's been fired. That someone will step into his role. Sit in his chair.

In my back pocket, my phone starts ringing. *Dave.* Likely checking that I'm still coming.

Graham continues. 'I've loved every minute of this job. And I'm grateful to all of *you* out there, in your cars, in your homes. Listening to this crusty old geezer.' He throws Ivan a look and we all laugh.

'How does he know I call him that?' Ivan whispers.

'My team,' Graham adds, looking across at us. Giving us a nod. 'Charlie, Dora, Ivan, the whole crew there. They do so much of the work for me and I'm so thankful. And I know that the new host, whoever they may be, is going to step in and love this place just as much as I do.'

Once the final song of the morning is underway, Graham takes off his headphones, placing them on the desk in front of him for the final time.

Forty-five minutes later and Graham still hasn't left the studio.

At first it was sweet, him sitting there, subdued, as if saying goodbye to the place. We all gave him a moment, said nothing. Just waited. And then, after the rest of the crowd grew bored and walked back to their desks, we assumed he just wasn't ready yet. Wasn't ready to leave. Wasn't ready to say goodbye.

But it's been almost an hour, and I'm running *so* late to see Dave. I can see my phone on my desk, buzzing like mad.

'Now it's just sad,' Ivan says. 'Do you think he's going to stay there until his replacement starts?'

'Poor guy,' Dora says. 'He's been broadcasting from that chair longer than I've been alive.'

Christ.

'Charlie just rolled her eyes,' Ivan says, laughing. 'You made her feel old.'

'Oh. Sorry.' Dora lets out a squeaked laugh and then lowers her voice. 'Seriously though, he's been in there for ages.' She's got a scone on her desk, recently heated in the microwave, that she's spreading jam and cream atop.

I'm trying not to look at Graham, but I also can't stop looking at him. He's just not doing anything. Just sitting there, looking at the controls in the room. At his microphone. At the notes in front of him, now irrelevant. It's incredibly sad. I couldn't possibly leave when he's looking like that. Dave will have to wait.

'Someone should definitely go in there,' I say.

Ivan and Dora look at me, expectantly.

'Yeah, okay.' As I rise, Ivan goes back to his computer screen.

Dora, who I suspect was born forty years old, takes a bite out of her scone and moans a little. 'How good is a scone? I cannot *wait* to retire. I would eat them all day.'

Inside Graham's studio, I notice he's tidied up. Papers and briefing notes, usually strewn around the table, are all stacked neatly in one pile. The desk looks cleaner, like he's wiped it down. And the spare pair of trainers that had been sitting in the corner of the studio for months are now gone. Tossed away, perhaps.

On the wall beside him sits a poster of the show – Graham in the forefront – and I wonder how long it's going to be until the station takes that down. Tomorrow? Or when his replacement starts?

'Sorry,' he says. 'I know I've been here a while.'

'Came to see if you're okay.'

I realise he's not okay. Far from it. On the verge of tears.

'This place has been my life for thirty years.'

'I'm sorry.'

He looks around, does his best to pull himself together. 'Will you tell me something that's guaranteed to cheer me up? Please.'

'You've worked here longer than Dora's been alive.'

He splutters out a laugh for a moment, and then swallows it. A few seconds and he's reserved again – hunched, overcome with sadness.

'You told me you'd be fine.'

'I am fine.' A brief moment and then he reiterates. 'I am fine, really. This just isn't how I thought things would end. And I'm allowed to be sad.'

'You're running away.'

His eyes narrow.

I double down. 'You're running away instead of giving yourself a chance,' I say, firm. 'And I refuse to believe this is the end of your career.'

'No one is going to hire me after this. I'll be left to desiccate.'

His self-pity sparks something in me. Infuriates me, right down to my bones. 'I'll give you one more minute of whingeing, and then you can shut the fuck up, honestly.'

This alarms him, jolts him upright.

'You have lost all ability to see how loved you are,' I say. 'The self-pity is embarrassing – pull it together. Something will come up. Something you'll love.'

He goes to speak, a mischievous grin forming.

'And I don't mean a sixth wife.'

He laughs, then rises and pulls me into a hug, letting out an exhausted sigh. 'I'm going to miss you.'

'You'll be having far too much fun.'

'I'm thinking of getting a hair transplant in Turkey.'

His flight leaves this weekend. He's letting me stay at his place for another fortnight while they try to find a buyer, and I'm still deciding where to live. Still can't bring myself to rent a place alone, but am dreading being in that mansion by myself until I figure things out.

'You're far too old for that.'

'But not too bald, right?' he says, and then he laughs into my shoulder. When we pull away, he smiles. 'I hope my replacement tanks the ratings.'

'No, you don't.'

He looks away, through the glass and out to the team. All of us, who have been with him for years. Who have worked our hardest, to bring this show back from the brink.

'I'm going to miss you most of all.'

Back at my desk, I realise just how late I am to see Dave. Unacceptable levels of late.

'Your phone has been going *off*,' Ivan says, his eyes not leaving his computer.

And he's right. Over fifteen missed calls, and just as many text messages. Fuck.

> Checking you're on time? I've got to leave for work soon.
>
> Charlie?
>
> Are you still coming?
>
> Seriously?
>
> You said you'd be here by now, where are you?

> I need to leave for work in 5.
>
> Honestly ridiculous.
>
> You owe me this.
>
> You were already planning to leave, did you know I knew that?
>
> I've known this whole time.
>
> Before you found out about me, before you snooped through my things, before you deserted me in that hospital bed, you were already planning to leave me.
>
> Don't act like this is all my fault. Don't act like I'M the bad guy for hiding ONE tiny secret from you.

Oh god. The office chatter around me seems to still while I read the last two. While I process. While I attempt to piece together how he knew – how he found out.

Before I ended things with Dave, I only ever told one person that I was thinking of leaving him.

One person.

I swallow hard, feeling my throat close up. Suddenly, my body is hot and my mouth is parched.

I only told *one person*.

Right now, I should be explaining to him why I'm not going to make it today. Why I got held up. I should be telling him to shove his attitude, and to stop being an arsehole.

Instead—

ISN'T IT NICE WE BOTH HATE THE SAME THINGS

How did you know I was planning to leave?

His response is immediate.

Genevieve.

CHAPTER FORTY

When I disembark the plane, it's my mother I see first, her head poking around the terminal doors. She needn't have waited by the gate, but of course she is here. As close as possible to the plane – to me.

It is only natural I spot her first, with that hair. It's like an ice-cream – short, rounded mounds, sprayed stiff. The colour of honey and just as thick, Mum's signature style. People have described her hair in all sorts of ways. Peculiar, interesting, distinct. Someone once asked me how Naya and I had hair so different from our parents – me, wispy and ash blonde, and Naya, a frizzy wave of chestnut brown. With Mum resembling confectionary and Dad plagued with thinning black hair, we could never figure it out. For a fleeting moment when I was ten, I wondered if I was adopted. Perhaps my real parents were out there somewhere, searching for me. I imagined being switched at birth or accidentally lost in a shopping centre. But Dad would not let me think that for a minute.

'You may not have our hair, but look at what you *do* have,' he'd said, tapping my nose. 'That's mine.' He ran a hand along my pointed chin. 'That's your mother's.' He pointed at my knobbly knees. 'And I dare say these came from both of us. If you look closely, you'll see that your sister has them too.'

And so I never entertained the thought again.

*

Mum mirrors a buzzing animal as we make our way through the airport – jittery, unable to keep still.

'Look at you.' She gives me a once over, offers to help with my belongings, but it's just a handbag and one carry-on with wheels.

'I got it,' I say.

'How was the flight? How are *you*?'

'The flight was fine. Thank you for picking me up.'

'Nothing to thank me for. Nothing at all.' Mum turns to me. 'It's a shame you can't stay longer.'

My lips twinge.

Naya's kids – they must be so big now. Will they even recognise me?

'Big weekend,' Mum says, then reaches across to drape an arm over my shoulder. Squeezes me like I might disappear.

Big weekend indeed.

Family dinner tonight. Naya, me, Leonard, the kids, all of us seated around Mum's mahogany table. It'll be nice to see Naya, and to reassure her. Tell her I don't blame her for what she said to me. That I forgive her.

Tomorrow, Mum wants to drive to the cemetery. The three of us, together, visiting Dad's grave. There'll be flowers, I'm sure of it. It'll be the first time I've visited his grave in years. The last time I went, Darla was one. I loathe going – I dread the very thought of it. The silence, the still air. The graves long forgotten, cracked and fallen over, next to ones covered in flowers and memorabilia – I'm not sure which saddens me more. And finally, tomorrow afternoon, an afternoon tea at the house before Naya drives me back to the airport. Three events over two days, and then I'm back on a plane and can forget about Dad for another year.

A couple of minutes and we're through the airport and out the other side, in the carpark. 'Naya mentioned the two of you speak a fair bit now, which is nice.'

Mum must not have the full debrief on what's occurred. 'We do.'

We're now mere metres from her scratched sedan – not a single panel on that thing that isn't damaged. 'She mentioned you saw Genevieve.'

Somehow, we both know to stop.

'How is she?' Mum asks.

She told Dave I was planning to leave him. I don't know when, or why. But she did, and now I don't know how to talk to her, because I don't understand why she would've done that. I feel hurt, and resentful. What could possibly have allowed her to think that was an acceptable thing to do? I'm completely broken-hearted. Like she's stomped on me and broken all my bones.

'She's good,' I say. 'She'd be thirty weeks now.'

Mum's eyes bulge.

'You must miss her.'

I turn. 'I miss *you*.'

She melts a little and says it back. Gives me a warm smile, then takes my bag and loads it into the car.

In my pocket, my phone lights up. Vibrates like crazy. And only once I'm inside Mum's car do I take a second to look at it.

Two missed calls from Genevieve. And one new text message.

> Is everything okay? I feel like you're ignoring me.

I've always loved our family home – a charming settler's cottage, weatherboard and painted white inside. Built in the 1960s. Sandstone steps leading to the front entrance, and then continuing behind the house through to the backyard. Mum has a knack for killing any plant – indoor or outdoor – she attempts to pot, and so everything decorative is plastic.

The inside of our home has not changed since I last visited. In fact, I cannot remember the layout of the furniture, the artwork on the walls, nor the colour scheme of the rugs and the pillows ever being any different. Even the diffuser is filled with the same essential oils – lavender, rose, cedar.

It always feels so bizarre arriving home. Everything is exactly the same – right down to the dark sandy shade of the welcome mat – and it deeply unsettles me. Part of me wants things to change. I want to come home and say, *Wow, look what you've done*. But instead, it's like no time has passed, like I left mere moments ago. And I hate that.

The house pivots around a honeycomb colour palette – yellows, browns, a mustard-tinged vanilla, the occasional steel grey. The lounge is plush eggshell white, with an earthy red woollen blanket draped over the armchair. To others, the colouring may seem a little niche – perhaps a bit off-putting, as Dave once described it. But for me, I've always found Mum's decorating to be quite welcoming. Warm, light.

'Spare bedroom is all set up,' she says, dropping my bag by the corridor cabinet.

The cabinet catches my eye, in that moment. Something about it seems odd, but I cannot place it right away. The colour is the same – cream with brass handles – but there's something askew. Something bare, like things have been moved around and they don't quite fill the space.

Framed photos sit atop the cabinet, always have. But they're different this time. Leaner. I think back to the last time I was here. Most of the photos atop this cabinet were of me and Naya. And the kids. I remember pictures of Naya and Leonard at their wedding and on holidays. And there were about half a dozen photos of my dad, Marco. Didn't matter what age he was, he was always recognisable by his thick, black moustache. He said it tickled once, when Naya asked, but that he couldn't imagine removing it. When he met Mum, she told him it suited him, and so he never considered shaving it off.

I run a hand along the cabinet, paying particular attention to the photos of my father. Work to remember his face so it doesn't ever feel like it's slipping out of my memory.

And then I realise. Suddenly clock why this cabinet looks so different – so sparse.

Beside Naya and Leonard, there used to be photos of me with Dave. At our wedding, at Darla's christening, when we bought our apartment.

But now all traces of Dave have been removed.

I glance around the living room, and down the hallway, to the other spots where Mum likes to display photos. Naya and Leonard are still there. Their kids too. There are still photos of Dad around the house, even after two decades.

But all of my photos with Dave are gone. Not replaced, just *gone*.

There was a photo of us at the end of the hallway, from when we attended Genevieve and Bruce's wedding. And by the television, there used to be a small polaroid that Dave gave Mum a couple of years ago, from when he accompanied me to a Christmas party.

But they're all missing.

'I wasn't sure what I should do,' Mum says, hovering by the front door. Wringing her hands. 'Naya told me you might not want to see them. So, I pulled everything down.'

Somehow, it feels sadder than it should, seeing all traces of him removed from the house. As if he never existed in the first place. I feel like Mum loved him as much as I did. I'm imagining her expression when she did it – her sadness as she collected all the frames, stored them all, somewhere hidden.

'I considered cutting him out,' she says. 'Of the photos.'

'That would be weird.'

'I know,' she agrees. 'I thought about what might happen if you got back together. Could hardly sticky-tape him back in, could I?'

I soften. 'We won't be getting back together.'

Her posture sags. 'I had assumed so.' Her head tips to the side. 'A shame it didn't work out. I'm sorry, Charlie.'

Then, Mum reaches out, grabs my shoulder. 'I know I've already said this, but it makes me happy that you've been ringing Naya. I've often wondered what would need to happen to bring you two closer.'

'You've wondered that?'

'Of course.' Her face stills, as if she cannot believe I even questioned it. 'You left for a good reason. You met Dave. But you hardly visited. You never called. And so yes, sometimes I did have moments where I wondered what it might take. For you to call us. Reach out.'

'I'm sorry.'

'I never guessed that it'd take a divorce,' she says. 'I feel for you, going through it. But at the same time, it's brought you back, in a way. And now, with this anniversary, you're here. Home. Gosh, not sure I'm making any sense. Do you know what I mean?'

I ponder this, for a moment. 'I left rather suddenly, didn't I?'

'You did. She's missed you.' Mum straightens. 'Since you left.'

Collectively, we step back. 'I can't believe it's been twenty years,' I say.

Mum nods. 'Sometimes it feels like it's been twenty minutes, and other days I realise just how long it's actually been. Just how many people have forgotten about him.'

'Why now?'

'Sorry?'

'Why *this* anniversary? We've never done this before.'

Mum looks away, not meeting my eye. She goes to speak. Tries to work up the courage to talk about it—

Her cuckoo clock, hanging on the wall above us and somehow

still operational, erupts. 'Oh my *lord*,' she cries, hands to her cheeks. 'I need to start on dinner.'

All talk of the anniversary forgotten, Mum swivels on a heel and charges towards the kitchen.

Later that day, five minutes past four, we're making predictions on how late Naya and the family will arrive. I suggest twenty minutes, believing the twins will make a fuss upon departure and it'll take extra time loading everyone into their people mover.

'Controversial,' Mum says, tapping her chin, 'but I'm going to say forty minutes.'

'*Forty?*' I reply, aghast.

'Raphael insists on dressing himself at the moment and it's always something wildly impractical. Leonard tries to reason with him, but of course that never works, and so Naya tells him that he can't wear only *one* shoe outside the house, and he needs to wear a shirt. That's when the shrieking starts.'

Again, I'm reminded of how little I know about my own nieces and nephews. My chest feels like it's caving in.

And, of course, Mum is right, as it turns out.

Naya's silver people mover is kerbside at exactly four-forty, Mum hurriedly slipping out the front door. I was planning to wait a moment and let the family exit in their own time – if my memory is correct, it's always a ten-minute disembark as they unbuckle children, pull out toys and bags, the electronics – but evidently, Mum doesn't hold that same reservation. She is full steam ahead to the car, barefoot and all.

'Right,' I whisper, following.

Mum goes straight for the children in the back seat, sliding open the kerbside door and popping her head into the car.

'Look who's *here*,' she cries. 'At *grandma's* hous— *Oh*, they're

ISN'T IT NICE WE BOTH HATE THE SAME THINGS

all asleep.' She covers her mouth with her left hand, lowering her voice to a whisper. 'Would you look at that. Charlie, they're asleep. Completely out of it. How funny. Come see!' She peers into the backseat again. 'Although, I only count *three* children in here.'

Raphael, the four-year-old, sits in the far seat with his legs and arms splayed out wide, his mouth open to a cavernous size. Drool bubbles at the corner of his mouth. He's still got that spiky black hair that I remember, and he's wearing an outfit that does indeed suggest he dressed himself that day – black swimmers pulled up over his pants.

And then there are the twins, Juliette and Camille, almost two years old and dressed in matching outfits – yellow and white frilled dresses and velcro white shoes. Ankle-high socks. They're triple the size since I last saw them. They look somewhat angelic, fastened in child seats, chins resting on their chests, Camille's head tipped to the left.

Searching again, my brow furrows. Mum and I catch eyes. 'No Darla?'

Leonard is stretching on the other side of the vehicle. He bends down to lengthen out his back. Then he sinks into his right hip and extends his left arm to the sky – after a moment, he repeats.

It appears that Leonard has finally accepted his fate and has shaved his head. Before, with his shoulder-length, shaggy grey hair, there was a bald patch forming on the crown of his head and Naya spent a solid amount of time biting her tongue about it.

Finally, my sister steps out from the passenger side. She's got Dad's long legs, wearing black leggings and an oversized, white buttoned-up shirt paired with ballet flats, her hair pulled back into a high bun. Her fringe seems frazzled, unsure of where it should sit.

She hesitates, then pulls me in for a tight hug. Awkwardness aside. 'I was convinced you wouldn't come.' Releasing the hug, she continues, 'Sorry we're late, Leonard forgot his phone and we had to turn back. And Raphi insisted on swimmers over pants, so we were late to begin with.'

Mum and I share a look, and then she points to the back seat of the car. 'Any chance you forgot a child, too?'

Naya smiles. 'Ah, sorry, forgot to mention. Darla has a sleepover tonight. And no offence, Charlie, but a dinner with you wasn't enough to lure her.'

'None taken.'

Leonard has stopped stretching now, making his way around the bonnet of the car. 'Charlie, you made it. Welcome back, great to see you.'

We hug, and then I point to his head. 'Love the new style.'

He runs a hand over it. 'Yeah, still getting used to it. A bit chillier now, with the mane gone.'

'Still got the beard though.'

Naya smirks. 'Couldn't get rid of that even if I paid him,' she says, winking at Leonard.

The conversation stills and Mum places a hand on Leonard's forearm. 'How are you? How's the hand? And the back?'

Leonard attempts to reply but Naya cuts him off. 'He carried a case of beer from the car to the fridge – he's fine.'

Naya turns to me. 'I birth four kids and it's only ever *Leonard* she asks about.' There's something stilted about how she is around me, and I wonder if she's replaying our last conversation in her mind. *You're impossible. Your life is so easy and you have no idea.*

Raphael is awake, now. Eyes open, wiggling in his car seat.

Naya points at me. 'Raphi, you remember Aunty Charlie?'

He does a double-take but says nothing. Head tilting, confused.

Then, frustrated, he continues to wriggle, and Mum dives in to release him.

'I'm sorry,' Naya says, sympathetic.

Once inside, it's like three tornadoes in the middle of suburbia. Children running through the house, out the back, around the yard, into the bedrooms. They must touch everything, question everything.

In the kitchen, Naya starts preparing meals for the twins. 'They won't eat Mum's cooking, unfortunately.'

'Because they're fussy?'

'No,' Naya responds. 'Because they're two.' She chops up an assortment of fruit. 'If it looks strange, they won't eat it. If it smells strange, they won't eat it.' She points to the slow cooker. 'If it comes out of some oversized machinery like that, they definitely won't eat it.'

'Tricking them doesn't work?'

Naya is amused. 'Want me to try and convince them Mum's chicken confit is actually chocolate? Tricking them can work, but it has to be realistic.'

'At least sixty per cent of toddler management is marketing,' I recite.

She points at me. 'Exactly.' Then she smiles.

I reach across and grab her hand. 'It is *really* good to see you.'

Her facade falters for a moment, and I worry that she's so overwhelmed, she might just crumble before me.

'I'm worried about you,' I say. 'I've been ringing.'

She looks away. 'Let's forget about it.'

'You asked me if I'm ever calm. You were trying not to cry.'

She gestures around her. 'I'm always trying not to cry.' She's pressing ahead with her task, but I know her well enough to sense it's a distraction. If she can focus on something else, she'll stop herself from getting upset.

'Are you okay?'

Raphael runs inside, asking how long until the food is ready. Naya tells him he needs to wait. To go back outside and play.

And then the kitchen is quiet again.

Still, she chooses not to answer my question, which I feel hanging over us in silence.

'They've got so big,' I say instead.

'Destructive, too.' Naya plates up their food and covers it in cling-wrap before putting it in the fridge.

'I'm sure you get that all the time. Shows how long it's been since I've seen them. Too long.'

Naya nods. 'I'm sorry Raphi didn't recognise you.'

'Can I help with anything? Give me a task.'

Naya frowns, clicking her tongue a couple of times while she thinks. 'Mum has a couple of highchairs. The girls are a bit old for them now, but it helps keep them still a bit longer. They're in the hallway, in that tall cupboard where she keeps the ironing board. And now that I think about it, I don't think Leonard got out all of the toys we brought. There's an iPad, too, in one of the bags. That'll help keep Raphi occupied during dinner—'

'Maybe I'll grab Leonard too? To help?'

Naya is quick to dismiss that – desperate, arms outstretched. 'No, please don't.' She peeks out the kitchen window at Leonard and Mum, deep in discussion in the backyard. 'They keep each other occupied.'

'Oh.'

'Don't get me wrong, I love Mum. And of course I love Leonard. But Mum is a lot. And Leonard just loves talking. Mostly about himself. And she feels sorry for him and putting them together seems to just work, so I let them be.'

In this moment, I see how exhausted she is. Four kids and all. The tired way she holds her body, her hair thrown back into a bun, unbrushed. The darkness under her eyes.

'He knows that's his job,' Naya says. 'Keeping Mum busy.'

I didn't think that was a task she'd need. Looking out the window, I see Leonard is watching the children, but he's also pointing to something on his calf.

'What do you think they're discussing?'

Naya takes a generous sip of her wine. 'Whatever it is, I'm just glad we don't have to listen to it.'

Later that evening, Leonard settles the twins in their highchairs first, slipping their wiggly bodies down beside Mum's mahogany dining table.

The twins barely fit, and they look somewhat ridiculous sitting in those highchairs, their bodies grown quite tall.

'Next time you're here, Charlie, the girls won't need these anymore,' Mum says from the kitchen. She's slicing up some chicken into smaller, bite-sized pieces for Raphael. 'They might be sitting at the table here with the rest of us.'

Leonard chuckles. 'Or they might be off to uni.'

Naya's lips twitch as she suppresses a smile. I guess I deserve that.

Mum serves a plate to Raphael first, who is rather short for his age and needs a booster seat to be able to see his food. His attention span, like most four-year-olds', is atrocious, and so Leonard passes him the iPad – sound off – to occupy him.

'What games does he play?' I ask.

Naya shrugs, running a hand through her hair. 'We'll give him anything, as long as it keeps him quiet.'

When Mum returns again, placing the chicken confit down

onto the table served in a golden, oval bowl, we all know to marvel. Make the appreciative noises.

Chicken confit was Dad's favourite. Salted, cooked in fat. Something his own father made for the family when he was growing up.

And yet, it's one of my least favourite meals.

The smell makes my nose curl, and it feels blasphemous, to have grown tired of something that my family loves so much. And my mother adores it because it reminds her of him. Of us, as a family. Before he died. So I dare not say anything, even though, inside, my body feels like it's shivering – recoiling. The memories this meal evokes, how easily it thrusts me back into my childhood, when Dad served this dish in that exact bowl. It's been twenty years but, in some ways, no time has passed at all.

I detect the blackened herbs, the garlic and the ginger. That tangy aroma tells me that Mum slipped in strips of citrus fruit.

'Looks great, Penelope,' Leonard says.

Naya murmurs in agreement. 'Thanks, Mum.'

'You didn't need to go to all this trouble for me,' I say. And then Naya's eyes meet mine, and her expression is unreadable. A little sad, perhaps? I cannot tell.

And then, it's gone. She's masked it.

'Yes, I did,' Mum says, sitting down on the other side of Raphael.

'We would've been happy with anything.' I start topping up wine glasses.

Mum smiles. 'I know. But it was his favourite.'

Slowly, we begin filling our plates. Leonard starts cutting up the breadstick. And then, collectively, we extend our wine glasses towards the middle of the table.

'To Marco,' Mum says.

And we follow suit. 'To Marco.'

Mum places her glass back down on the table and lets out a sigh. 'Twenty years, my god.'

I try and catch Naya's eye, but she's looking down at her plate. I feel for Mum in these moments, bringing up the past. Reflecting on someone I struggle to visualise. Elbows on the table, hands clasped together, Mum rests her chin in her palms.

'What are you thinking about?' Naya asks, reaching across to squeeze our mother's hand.

'Everything,' she says tenderly. 'His cooking, his singing. The way he would tap his foot under the table while he ate. How his favourite time of day was dawn.'

'His singing voice,' I add. 'Always off-key, and a bit sharp.'

Mum looks at me, perplexed. 'He was a baritone.'

One look at Naya, who nods, and I realise Mum is right. He did *not* have a sharp singing voice. And I'm overcome with shame, that I didn't know that. That I could've got that so wrong. I shift in my seat, pick at my food. Push the chicken around the plate so it looks like I've eaten more than I have.

'The last time we saw him,' Mum continues, 'he'd just bought a new scarf, even though he owned so many. I always thought it was absurd, how easily he felt the cold.'

I feel my body start to overheat. The chicken feels thick in my throat. Must his final moments be brought up at dinner? We can talk about anything – *anything* – but that day.

Naya adds, 'He was too skinny, not enough fat on his body. Could eat anything he wanted and it never made a difference.'

Mum looks down at her meal and suddenly, as if bulldozed in the face, I remember that he'd cooked chicken confit the night he died.

'You're thinking about the last time *you* saw him,' I clarify, looking at Naya and Mum. I cut into my meal. 'The last time *I* saw him was earlier that morning when he told me he was disappointed in me because I'd yanked on Naya's hair until she cried. Which I only did because she'd pushed me to the ground.'

'I pushed you to the ground because you were being a brat,' Naya says. 'You pulled so hard my hair ripped out of my head and I started bleeding.'

'Yeah, well, you must've deserved it.'

Naya is unimpressed. She looks quickly at Mum. 'And you wonder why we barely spoke to each other.'

Mum starts to eat, her eyes downcast. The room feels quieter than it did before, even with three children munching away on their food. The twins make popping noises with their mouths and Raphael drops his fork onto the table every thirty seconds.

'So, Charlie,' Leonard starts, pulling everyone's attention towards him. 'Graham has finished up now, I see. That's a shame, I always liked him.'

Bless Leonard for changing the subject. 'I'm going to miss him,' I say. 'Genevieve leaves, then Graham. Not sure how I'm going to manage without them, to be honest.'

Naya and I lock eyes, and again there's something in hers I cannot place. This time, it feels accusatory.

Mum throws me a smile. 'I'm glad you're here,' she says. 'Might not be the most upbeat of occasions, but we got you here.'

'You got me here?'

Mum's mouth parts, and her eyes dart to Naya. 'I just meant it's nice to have you here. And you can visit anytime.'

'Yes,' Naya says, jumping in, the most animated she's been since I arrived. 'You *could* visit anytime.' The look she's giving me is more pleading than anything else. *Please visit anytime*, she's saying. *Please*.

The way they're both looking at me, and sneaking glances at each other, I'm trying to decipher it. *We got you here*.

'Is that why you put this on?' I ask Mum. 'To get me to come home?'

Mum raises her hands in defence. *You caught me.*

No one says anything for a moment, but I feel all eyes on me. What a numpty I was, not realising the ruse. I cannot face anyone, cannot bear to look them in the eye.

My own family, *tricking* me.

I feel enraged. Around me, there's the *squeak* of cutlery on the plates, the dull *tap* of Raphi's finger on the iPad, and *munch munch* as the twins devour their food. *Somebody say something, for Christ's sake.*

Turning to Mum, I ask, 'You organised an entire weekend just to get me here?'

'Actually, no.' She points at Naya, who straightens.

'Guilty,' my sister says, pointing to herself. Looking smug. 'Worked though, didn't it?'

I can feel anger building in my chest. No, not anger. Embarrassment. Shame. It's like I've just walked into my own intervention. Three other adults at this table, all scheming to get me here. Talking about it. Strategising. Makes me think of Josie and her group, dissecting my marriage. Genevieve and Bruce, working out how to tell me they're leaving. Graham, disappearing from the country, never to return.

I look around the table. 'You could have just, I don't know, asked?'

Naya drops her cutlery onto her plate, immediate and loud. We all jolt. 'Oh. Really? We could've just asked? Why didn't I think of that?' Her voice is deeper than normal – guttural, gravelly. Coming from the gut.

Leonard taps her arm. 'Naya.'

'Sorry.' She picks up her knife and fork again. 'That was rude. But we did ask, Charlie. So many times.'

'It's hard, with work. I don't always have time off.'

'I've got four kids, and I have time.'

'We get it, you have children.'

She looks up at me, eyes narrow and sharp.

'It's like no one else is allowed to be busy or tired or poor or unwell, because you have four kids. We get it! You have four kids! Sorry I'm *calm*, Naya. Sorry I have a calm life and you don't. Sorry you can't arrive on time to a dinner because you chose children and I didn't. I'm still allowed to be busy.'

The room is painfully, awfully silent, except for the sound of Leonard chewing chicken confit inside his closed mouth. He's slowing down the chews to try and quieten it, but it's not working. I can sense that oiled piece of chicken stewing in his mouth and it makes me want to vomit.

'I'm going to pretend you didn't just say all that,' Naya says. Taking a deep breath, she attempts to calm herself. 'You are not going to ruin this night. After all we've done.'

Oh, she's fuming. Holding a lid on her emotions so tightly, her body must be quivering. I want to reach out and poke it, to watch her go off.

'You seem like you have more to say,' I reply.

'Don't, Charlie.' Mum looks at me. 'Don't provoke. Now is not the time; we're having a lovely meal.'

Are we?

Naya is back to eating. 'I knew I shouldn't have told you that. I was having *one* bad day.'

'You lured me here,' I continue. 'You used Dad's death to guilt-trip me.'

'I'm not saying anything further,' Naya snaps. Then, she turns to Leonard, who is still. 'Eat your chicken confit please.'

And now, with permission, he resumes chewing and swallows.

Naya glares at me. 'Can you stop staring at me, please? It's creepy.'
'Creepy?'
'Yes. I'm not used to having you here, looking at me so much. Look somewhere else.'

Lord, it's all getting a bit out of hand. I'm now staring at my chicken. 'You called me impossible, remember? And I didn't get angry at you. In fact, I forgave you.'

'*Forgave* me?' she cries. 'For what? Telling the truth?'

'I think you're being a little ridiculous here, Naya—'

And then she explodes. 'I shouldn't have to guilt-trip you into coming here. I shouldn't have to try so hard to see my own sister. You don't get to forgive me, because there's nothing I need to be forgiven for. You *left* us and you pretend Dad doesn't exist. You pretend his *death* doesn't exist. We all loved him too, but you disappeared and you never called, and you married a man who was exhausting and unobservant and nowhere near good enough for you, which was just *so* insulting. You didn't love that man, Charlie, you just met him when you needed someone – *anyone*. My kids don't even recognise you, and I miss you all the time but I also hate that you left us. And honestly, sometimes, when it's been months since we've talked, I think of you as dead, too. Dad's dead, and you're dead. That's how I see it.'

Leonard's eyes bulge. Mum has her hand over her mouth. Naya's looking down at her meal because she cannot seem to meet my eye. These past few weeks, I thought she was embarrassed about what she'd said to me. But no, she's furious with me.

She'd know how much this guts me. Drains me of anything I had left. My stomach feels like it's fallen through my legs, to the floor below.

And then one of the twins starts screeching, slamming their fists down on the tray below them. A high-volume tantrum ensues, and it triggers the other children.

Screaming.
Crying.
Screeching.
The dinner is now, most certainly, ruined.

CHAPTER FORTY-ONE

You're dead. That's how I see it.

The next morning, Naya cancels on the cemetery trip. Tells Mum that Darla is sick, and she's not up for the visit. Darla *could* be sick, but I'd rather accuse Naya of being ashamed. Of needing space. I'm picturing her practising her apology and working out how best to mend this. Between last night, and that horrid phone call, my sister has a *lot* of grovelling to do.

She thinks me deceased, and it's all I can think about. I leave home and she considers me as good as dead.

'She's still coming this afternoon, before your flight,' Mum says. 'So, that's something.'

They didn't stay long last night – not when the kids were playing up like that – so there was no time to confront her.

'You two, honestly.' Mum is near the door, buckling her tan sandals. She's very well dressed, for a cemetery visit, in a sleek black shift dress. 'She shouldn't have said those things last night, I've told her that. But I still think it's a nice thing she's done, getting you here.'

'She tricked me.' I'm still irate about it. A couple of times this morning, I thought I'd processed it, and then I circled right back to where I started. *Furious.*

'Well, maybe you needed to be tricked. I was starting to forget what you looked like.' She opens the front door. 'Come on, we'll be late.'

'Late?' I say. 'Mum, I don't think he's going anywhere.'

She throws me a look, unamused.

There is only one cemetery in town, nestled on the side of a towering hill. It's where everyone around here ends up.

Hectares of graves and family plots. Manicured grass and hedges, angled with precision. Some might think that Mum picked Dad's spot for its beauty, but I know it's because of the view. She spent half her savings for a grave near the top of the hill. She felt he deserved it, after the life he lived. After he was cheated out of so many years.

I've always detested this cemetery. All cemeteries, really. But this one in particular, because I have so many memories here – so many mornings when Mum dragged me and Naya to visit the grave. Speak to our dad. Reminisce about him. I understood it the first couple of years. His death was still so raw, and it made Mum feel better to come here. And there was a time when Naya enjoyed it too – once admitting to me that she felt comforted being near his grave. But that was years ago now, and I wonder if that is still the case.

'When was the last time you were here?' Mum asks. There's something routine about how she moves, placing fresh flowers on the grave. Collecting the dead ones. Placing a delicate hand on top of the headstone and whispering something I cannot catch.

I think back. Before the twins, I know that. When Darla was a toddler – not long after her first birthday. 'About five years.'

Mum makes a noise – a short, blunt whistle with her tongue.

It's quiet this morning. Quieter than I was imagining. In the past, there have been other cars moving through the grounds, but today I don't see any. We're alone, and this place makes me feel uncomfortable. How many people are here, forgotten by their families?

Looking at the dead flowers in Mum's grasp, I step closer. 'How often do you come here?'

'All the time,' she admits, without pause. 'Four times a week. Sometimes less, sometimes more.'

I catch my breath. 'Jesus, Mum. That is a lot.' Fidgeting, I lean forward and place a hand on top of the tombstone. As if to say, *Hello, I'm here. I know it's been a while.*

'You don't consider me dead, right?'

'Oh *god*, of course not. She shouldn't have said that. She was upset.' Pause. 'It's becoming a habit. She said some things to me recently that she's since apologised for.'

'I know.'

Her expression softens. 'She told you? That I rely on them too much? Maybe she's right, on some level. But I do it for them. They need me.'

I grab the dead flowers from her hands. 'I should come home more often. And call.'

'We can't expect you to visit. You have your own life, and we're proud of you.' Then she looks me in the eye and repeats, 'We're proud of you.'

The subtext is clear. *We're proud of you for doing something others wouldn't. For leaving him, and leaving that life.*

She sneezes, then coughs, then clutches her head.

'Are you okay?' I ask.

'Just a headache,' she says. I'm sceptical, watching as she clears her throat and straightens.

'What do you usually do when you come here?'

'I talk to him.'

'What do you say?'

'Oh, it could be anything. My day. My work. I find myself talking about Naya a lot these days.'

'Naya? Why?'

The corner of her mouth jerks down. 'Sometimes I wonder what her life might be, if things had been different.'

'Different how?'

'She took care of me, that's all. When she didn't need to.'

After Dad. Naya was sixteen and Mum didn't get out of bed for weeks. Someone had to feed me, get me to school. Wash everyone's clothes. Naya got so good at running the household that even *after* Mum resurfaced, she was still helping our family in ways that should've been reserved for Mum.

'You were probably too young to remember,' Mum says.

'I was twelve when he died. I remember it all,' I respond, irked. 'And I'd give anything to forget.'

She glances across at me, pity on her face. The sky is overcast now, the sun tucked behind a thick sheet of clouds. I'm still holding the dead flowers.

I lower my gaze, picking at my fingernails. 'I was at a sleepover. Kristy Le Voun's house. Dad told me he was going to cancel it, to punish me for what I did to Naya. But he didn't. I'm not sure why.'

'Because I told him not to,' Mum says. 'I thought it'd be cruel. And I saw Naya push you, so I kind of understood.'

'Kristy's mum made milkshakes that night and her sister kept following us around. I remember thinking she was annoying.' I smile. 'She's a scientist now, did I ever tell you?'

'Kristy? Or the sister?'

'The sister. She studies diseases. Or fungi. Can never remember.'

'Impressive.'

'She was a pest back then, that's all I kept thinking. And then Dad died and everything changed.'

Mum places a hand on my shoulder, and squeezes. 'It didn't make a difference, you not being there. You wouldn't have been able to say goodbye, even if you were home.'

My mouth twitches. 'It made a difference to *me*. Not being

there. I got home and Naya was stripping your bed. The house just felt empty. Like everything had been ripped out of it. I felt so . . .' I gather my thoughts. 'Alone.'

'You're never alone.'

'You should see where I'm living. I feel alone there.'

'You miss living with Genevieve and Bruce.'

'I think it's good for me to learn how to be on my own,' I say. Then, I think about how I've been acting in Graham's house – pacing back and forth, constantly trying to fill my time. 'But I don't think I've handled it very well. I don't like when things feel so . . .'

She waits, then prompts. 'Feel so?'

'Empty.'

Immediately, she understands.

'Naya told me what he'd looked like, and how you sounded when she was trying to pull you off him. The ambulance took six minutes and she said it felt like twenty.'

Mum's jaw clenches, but not out of anger. Like she's trying not to cry. 'Naya got so used to helping us, she never lived her life. *That's* why I feel for her. And it's why I help with the children when I can, and why I talk to Leonard as much as I do.'

'We survived,' I say. 'Sometimes that's all you can do.'

Mum nods.

'And Naya is fine. She'll be fine.' Will she? I'm ashamed to admit I don't really know my sister at all. *You're dead. That's how I see it.*

Mum looks at me. 'You don't remember what she was like before your dad died, do you?'

I hesitate.

'If you did, you'd understand why I worry.'

'Tell me.'

She wipes her brow. 'Later. I'm feeling tired. Shall we?' She makes her way back to the car. I take a minute before following, placing a hand on his headstone again.

It'll be years before I'm back here. Who knows what our lives will be like then, what kind of people we'll be?

In my back pocket, my phone rings. *Genevieve.*

I stare at it for a good moment, before declining. Even if I weren't at the graveyard with my mother, I'm not sure I'd answer her call. I feel betrayed and embarrassed. I'm at a complete loss as to what I would even say to her.

Mum falls ill not long after we return from the cemetery, clutching her forehead and complaining of headaches. Her nose is blocked and her voice is deeper than usual. She retires to her bedroom for a nap, apologetically. On the way, she rattles off a list of the food she has in the kitchen for afternoon tea later today – scones, tarts, chai tea bags and some shortbread. She asks me to wake her when Naya arrives.

I don't.

Hours later I meet my sister at the door, hushing her quiet. 'She's sick.'

Naya slips a hand inside her jacket pocket. 'Damn. Flu?'

'And migraines.' I step out of the house, locking up behind me. 'Let's go for a walk. The weather is nice.' *And I want to talk to you about last night,* I want to say. *Want to pepper you with questions about the things you said, the hurt you felt. Want to understand what Mum meant about the kind of person you were before Dad died.*

'No afternoon tea.' Naya's lower lip puckers. 'I was rather looking forward to it. My house is a germ zone at the moment.' And then she glances up, as if only just realising that it *is* a lovely day – no clouds or wind, just sunshine. She closes her eyes, lets it warm her face.

'Here.' I extend a hand, unwrapping paper towel to reveal an assortment of our mother's treats. Naya's excitement is immediate, eyes widening, the corners of her lips lifting. She takes a tart and a piece of shortbread and leaves the rest to me.

We turn right out the front of the driveway, and for a few minutes we say nothing, biting into Mum's baked goods. The shortbread is a winner, as it has always been.

'How is she today?' Naya asks, her voice muffled as she swallows the final bite of her tart.

'I didn't realise she visited him so much. Did you know?'

She gives me a look. *Of course I knew.*

'Four times a week is a lot.'

There's a chuckle. 'She's lying to you. She goes almost every day. And I go with her most Sundays. Largely so I can get out of the house, but also because I don't like the thought of her being alone so much.'

'Every day? Seriously?'

'She likes to visit him,' Naya says, defensive.

'It's been twenty years. At some point I thought she'd move on. *Every day?* She's one step away from sleeping by his grave.'

'I don't think it's possible for anyone to move on completely.' Naya runs her hand through her hair, brushing it over her shoulders. 'Leonard and I thought she might've met someone else by now, but I guess not.'

I frown. 'She told me something today. At the cemetery. About you. She said that you were different before Dad died.'

'Of course I was different. We were all different.'

'No, she didn't mean it like that. It was more like, if I knew what you were like before it happened, I'd understand how it'd affected your life. What it . . . changed about you.'

The wrinkles on Naya's forehead smoothen out, her face still and her posture alert. 'She shouldn't have talked to you about that.'

I'm desperate to push, but Naya picks up the pace, hands shoved deep inside pockets.

'I'm worried about her.' I struggle to keep up. 'About Mum. Aren't you?'

Naya stops. 'I've done nothing *but* worry about her. And as much as I love her, it can be tiring taking care of her all the time. I'd appreciate some help.'

'Taking care of her all the time? Why do you need to take care of her?'

Her eyes narrow. 'I can't tell if you're being serious or not.'

'Naya, she's an adult.'

She gestures back to the house. 'She's seventy-two and lives alone. Why do you think I take the kids around every weekend? She has, what, three friends? No parents, no siblings, just us. And the grandkids.'

'Oh.'

'I need a break, Charlie. I have—' She stops herself.

'Four kids?' I say, swallowing a smile.

'That's not what I was going to say.'

'That's absolutely what you were going to say.'

'You're never around. Have you honestly never thought about what it might be like for her since Dad died, living by herself?'

I glance back down the street at our mother's house, and picture it. Isolating. Quiet. For a moment, I think of Graham in his mansion. I think of *me* in his mansion. Alone and deeply uncomfortable, like I've been left behind. Like I'm missing something.

When I got home from that sleepover and Dad was dead, I'm ashamed to admit that I felt left out. Distraught at having missed it, when the others were present. It's odd, I know, and I can't explain it, but that's how I feel when I'm alone.

Like I'm missing something.

Like I've been left behind.

So I surround myself with whoever I can – whenever I can – and pretend that feeling never existed.

'Guess not.' Naya squares her shoulders, her upper body turning rigid. She is, evidently, not done yet. 'Who do you think helps her maintain that backyard? And the garden? Who is mowing the grass and trimming back her trees every year, and wiping the dust off all her artificial plants? Leonard.' She lets out a measured breath to calm herself. 'Half of his injuries are from helping Mum fix something or build something. I know we laugh about Leonard, but I love that man *so* much for everything he does for us. Mum needs something and he's there for her. He's too nice to say no.'

'But *you* could say no,' I retort. 'No one is forcing you to do any of this.'

'You've been gone a long time, Charlie,' she says, flustered. 'You disappeared and you left me here with her.'

'And I'm dead to you, right?

Guilty, she looks away.

'I'm waiting for your apology.'

She baulks. 'Apology? I'm not apologising. *You* apologise.'

'I should apologise for you calling me dead?'

'You know what I mean.'

'No one asked you to stay.' I turn, walking back towards the house. Naya is close on my heels. 'Aren't you tired of taking care of everyone around you?'

'I took care of everyone because I had to,' Naya snaps. 'When Dad died, Mum wasn't getting out of bed and you were too young to do anything about it. Who else was going to make sure you had food to eat? Who else was going to make sure you woke up early enough to catch the school bus?'

'And I'm grateful for it, I am. But you don't need to take care of us anymore. I'm not in school and Mum gets out of bed by herself now. And you're still taking care of her. And Leonard.

It's like they can't survive without you. Or you don't *let them* survive without you.'

This fires her up. 'You have no responsibilities, Charlie. *None*. You have no idea what it's been like for me here, without you. And I never said anything because we barely spoke anyway, but then you left Dave and you lost all of your friends and suddenly I can't get rid of you. Suddenly you're calling me all the time, wanting to chat, and I can't think of what to talk about with you, because we've never really *talked* to each other.'

She pauses, then continues. 'I shouldn't have called you dead. That's not how I feel. It came out wrong. What I meant is . . . What I meant is, I barely know you. I've done the best I can with Mum. But if she wants to go to the cemetery seven times a week, or even *seventy* times a week, I'm not going to stop her. And if she wants to make confit every week, fine. I'll eat it. I'll compliment that monstrous slow cooker and tell her that I love her rubbery chicken. I make sure she has someone to talk to, and things to do. She minds the kids, and I like that.'

She pauses to catch her breath. 'But I can't do *everything* for her. So, yes, she hasn't moved on and she probably should've, but if you want to change that? It's *your* turn. You're the one who has a lot more time on their hands. You've left your marriage and your friends are gone. You have all the time in the world to help Mum out. If you're truly worried about her, do something about it.'

We're back at the house now, and Naya is so flustered she's shaking her hands, as if trying to calm herself.

'I was so mad at you last night I could've flipped that table. Talking about Genevieve and Graham leaving. How much you miss them,' she says, laughing bitterly. 'Now you know how it felt for us. When *you* left.'

She pulls her car keys from her back pocket. 'I can't stay, not when I'm this angry. And I know I said I'd drive you to the airport, but I'm not going to do that anymore. That would be taking care of you, wouldn't it? You can find your own way there.'

It all happens so fast I don't have a moment to process what she's said. Naya slips into her car, starts the engine and drives off, and it isn't until she is gone from view that I realise we didn't say goodbye to each other.

Later that evening, I'm still thinking about the conversation with my sister. I was still thinking about it when Mum woke from her nap, and when she chastised me for letting her sleep too long. I was still thinking about it when I packed my bag, and when Mum drove me to the airport. And then I thought about it for the entire plane ride home, and then again when I landed, turned on my phone and found four missed calls from Genevieve but nothing from my family.

Suddenly you're calling me all the time, wanting to chat.

I barely know you.

I'd never realised what my sister really thought of me, and how trapped she might feel. And now my friendship with Genevieve is damaged – perhaps long-term – and Graham has left and Dave's back to being furious with me. And I can't call Quinn or Ivan or Dora because they couldn't possibly understand any of this.

Somehow, in all my efforts *not* to be alone, that's exactly how I've ended up.

I almost forget my bag as I exit the plane, and then I pass the flight attendants with a curt, albeit distracted, nod. My phone, nestled in my hand, is giving me grief. What do I do here? I'm attempting to craft a message to Naya, but I'm not sure what to say.

Sorry?

Call me?

I barely know you either, so how do we fix this?

Everything feels inappropriate, and like it won't make a difference. Maybe I call her when I'm home. Maybe I just call her now. That'd be better than a text, right?

Walking through the departure lounge, I'm so lost in my own thoughts that I'm not paying attention when I step onto the escalator. So distracted that I step too far forward, heel sliding off the edge and then my leg crumbles beneath me, propelling my body forward.

My phone flies out of my hand. My bag drops off my shoulder.

As I tumble down the escalator, my body flips faster than I thought possible. Two or three times. It's a blur. I think I hear a crack, maybe two. And then finally, I land on the tiles on the ground floor.

Immediately, I know something is broken, that my arm shouldn't be at that angle, and that my leg is twisted.

The airport is quiet when it happens and even quieter after it happens – there's a split second as everyone turns to assess my fall. The pain isn't immediate, but when it hits, I cry out. It is *excruciating*.

A crowd forms, fussing.

When the paramedics arrive, they ask if there's anyone they can call. Faces flash in my mind. Genevieve, Bruce, Graham, my mother, my sister, Ivan, Dora, Quinn. People I need but cannot call. People who are gone.

It destroys me, realising this. My mind and my body feel detached from each other, my heart like it's been sliced and squished and pressed into the smallest thing it can be. All these years on earth, and in my greatest moment of need, I cannot decide who to call.

When the paramedics ask again, I tell them the only name I can think of. The only person still here, in town, who I know will definitely answer the call.

DAVE

I met Dave by chance one night in the back corner of our local, hometown pub.

It was a fluke we crossed paths at all, given I wasn't meant to be there. Wasn't planning on it, until I received a last-minute dinner invitation from two girls I'd made friends with at university. Our cohort was only twelve people, including me, and these two girls wanted to celebrate the end of their first week at a journalism cadetship at the local newspaper – something I'd unsuccessfully applied for. I considered declining the invite so I could wallow in peace, but my mother was smothering me and I desperately wished to escape the house.

I was envious of the girls. That's the main thing I can remember about heading to the pub that night – that I liked them, and I wanted to see them, but I was devastated and upset, and thus prepared for a cry in the pub bathroom at some point in the evening.

As they ate, the girls did their best not to speak of it. They asked me how I was, apologised that I couldn't join them in the newsroom. But then, as the night progressed, conversation steered towards their work. And of course I needed to be happy for them. Needed to support them.

'How is it going?'

They told stories of editorial meetings, by-lines and journalist mentors, and the chance to earn enough money and move out of home. And here I was – working twelve hours a week at a corner store, volunteering at a community radio station, and living with Mum, Naya and Leonard in a cottage on the other side of our small town. No freedom in sight.

Even being there, in that pub, I felt like a failure. I was overwhelmed by the musky stench of old beer mats, and the wooden table between us looked about as weathered as I felt. The staff around us worked in cargo shorts and singlets, with slip-on sandals and tussled, unkept hair. There were only four meals on the menu – fish and chips, cheeseburger, chicken schnitzel and a meat pie – and I almost felt angry, in that moment, for being born where I was born. If I'd grown up in a larger town, maybe my options would've been better.

I tried to tell myself that their success wasn't that exciting – small-town newspaper and all. They were probably working on articles about lost animals and council regulations, maybe the occasional crime. But I was still filthy with envy. Small-town newspaper was better than no newspaper at all.

When we finished eating, I suggested a round of cocktails. My treat, to congratulate them. And, allowing me to slip away, to collect my thoughts, shove down my disappointment about the cadetship and carve out whatever encouragement and excitement I could muster for them.

And then I met Dave.

Seated by himself at the bar, one bite into a cheeseburger and a plate of fries to his left. Intermittently sipping a large glass of red wine. He had long, shaggy brown hair with the top half pulled back into a bun and the rest grazing his shoulders, flicking outwards at the edges. Such messy hair mixed with such a smart outfit – an ironed and pressed buttoned-up deep blue shirt. Tailored for his frame, and matched with cream pants and brown slip-on shoes. If I had to guess his age, I would've said twenty-nine. Thirty, at a stretch.

He must've sensed my stare. In a rather swift motion, he looked around to his right, his body perfectly still. He glanced at me out of the corner of his eye.

'Just waiting for my drinks,' I said, pointing to the bartender. Dave nodded and took another bite of his burger.

And it took some waiting. The bartenders were flurrying around with other orders.

So I turned back to Dave, because I just couldn't place him. This well-dressed worker in this small-town pub. He looked too important for here. Like he'd stumbled inside by accident.

'Do you live around here?' I asked, which was horridly unoriginal. But he just couldn't possibly. There was something about him – the way his hand wrapped around that burger felt territorial, but then he sipped his wine so slowly and delicately, two fingers pinching the stem.

Wiping his mouth with a serviette, he swivelled his body around to face me. 'No, just passing through.'

Called it. 'You here for work?'

He nodded. 'I'm in sales.' He extended a hand, and as we shook, I tried to remember the last time I ever shook a stranger's hand. 'David.'

'Charlie.'

'You live here, I gather.'

'I do,' I said, then asked, 'What do you sell?'

He smiled, lifting up his glass. 'Wine.'

'Seriously?'

'Seriously.' He took another sip, and I pulled up a stool. 'My parents own a vineyard.'

'Your parents are winemakers?'

'My father is,' he clarified. 'My mother used to help out a lot more, but it's got a bit more difficult lately.'

I waited for him to clarify, but he didn't.

'There was a wine fair this weekend. Up north,' he said. 'We have a stand every year.'

Why on *earth* would anyone choose to travel here? I wondered.

For a moment, I was distracted by the bartender, who'd finished making our drinks. I accepted them, but made no move to leave.

'How often are you here?'

He didn't immediately respond, instead glancing over my shoulder to my friends. 'You aren't going to go back?' he asked, nodding at the cocktails.

'Not yet.'

He grinned, straightening. Grabbing his fries, he extended them towards me and I plucked a couple from the pile.

'So you sell wine,' I said. 'That seems like a fun job for . . . I want to say, a twenty-nine-year-old?'

He was amused. Pinched cheeks and a deep, guttural chuckle. 'Are you fishing to find out how old I am?'

'Maybe.'

'Twenty-eight.'

The discussion moved seamlessly for the next little while, even after the girls came to collect their cocktails (I'd completely forgotten about them, at this point. And I never saw them again).

'So, journalism?' Dave said.

'You were eavesdropping?'

He shrugged. Done with his food, he pushed the bowl of fries to his side and rubbed a napkin across his lips. He cleared his throat. 'Fresh out of uni. That'd make you about . . . twenty-two.'

'Twenty-one.'

'Close.' He leant an elbow on the bar. 'Sorry you didn't get one.'

'Get what?'

'A spot at the paper.'

'Oh. Thank you.'

'Do those kinds of opportunities come often?'

I choked back a laugh, and he understood. *No.*

'You ever thought about moving?'

I frowned. Leaving home? I had only just graduated. 'No.'

'Might need to consider it.' His eyes didn't leave mine. 'What's keeping you here anyway?'

'Are you fishing to find out if I'm seeing someone?'

He looked away, shy.

'Not sure I could leave my mum,' I continued.

'Why? Is she sick?'

'Oh. No. She's just . . .' I struggled to finish my sentence. Why *couldn't* I move away? Because Mum still hadn't moved on from Dad's death? Because she was pretending everything was okay when it wasn't? Or maybe because I'd feel guilty leaving her. It wouldn't be long until Naya and Leonard saved a deposit for a house, and then they'd be moving out. And if I left too? Mum would be all alone.

'I just . . . hadn't thought about it, that's all. Where would I go?'

Dave checked the time on his phone. Froze in his seat. 'I'm sorry, but I'm on the red eye.'

'You're flying home *tonight*? It's like . . .' I pulled out my own phone and glanced down at the time. 'Oh god, is it only eight-thirty?'

'I'm afraid so.'

Dave rose from his stool, almost knocking it over in the process.

'What time is your flight?'

'Ten-thirty, and I still need to pick up my bag from the motel.' He thanked the staff. Pulled on his coat. 'And to answer your earlier question, I'm here every second month. Same weekend each time.' He took a quick sip of water and then handed the glass back to the waiter.

'That's a lot.'

'I always eat my dinner here on the Saturday night. Maybe I'll see you next time?'

Was this sleek, gentle man asking me out? I barely had any time to consider the possibilities. He was rushing to collect himself. As if he'd meant to leave earlier. As if I'd delayed him. This was the first time all evening I'd seen him frazzled.

'Have a great night.' And then he was gone, slipping out the door.

For eight weeks, Dave sneaked into my thoughts sporadically – his scent, his hair, his woollen jacket, the way his lips pursed when he smiled and he then looked away, as if embarrassed.

When things at the house felt strained, I thought of him. Like when Leonard complained of neck pain and ankle aches, and when he told me to be mindful of the back step because he was convinced it was no longer level. When Mum picked up a new hobby – scrapbooking – and suddenly, the dining room table was a sea of paper and stickers and tape, and we all had to eat dinner on the floor for three nights because she was determined that the table stay as it was. When Naya insisted that she and Leonard still didn't have enough money for a house deposit, even though she was on a psychologist's wage and told me one evening – after finishing a bottle of red – how much they'd managed to save and I spat out my pinot noir.

'My god, what are you still doing here?'

'Leonard is being cautious,' she responded, mildly defensive. 'He wants to wait a little longer. Just in case.'

In case of what? I knew it was impolite to laugh whenever Leonard was being ridiculous, but the frequency made it rather difficult.

In these moments, when the place felt cramped and my patience grew thin, I found myself pondering. *Would* I ever move? Leave my family behind?

The night Dave was due back at that pub, I was still tossing up whether to go. Perhaps I'd heard him incorrectly. Would it be strange to attend? I mulled it over all day. During work at the store and in the car home.

When I arrived and found Naya and Mum in the kitchen, my sister was trying to keep her from packing the dishwasher. 'Let me do that,' she said, manoeuvring the plates and the bowls and pushing Mum's hand away when she tried to help.

I caught my mother's eye and could tell that she wasn't going to argue. There was a slight smile, a couple of questions about my day, and then Mum slipped out of the kitchen.

'Leonard's out the back about to mow the lawn,' Naya said. 'And Mum mentioned that she heard a squeak in one of the bedroom door hinges. Yours, I think. Had you noticed it?'

'No.'

'I might get something for that squeak, might check the shed—'

'Let's go out for dinner tonight,' I said, cutting in. 'You, me, Leonard.'

'Dinner?' She said it with such a perplexed tone, like she couldn't quite comprehend the suggestion.

'Yes, dinner.'

Naya contemplated it, biting her upper lip. 'Where?' She waited for an answer. Hands on hips, expression held.

'Just a pub. A friend of mine might be going.'

'Which friend?'

'From the radio station.'

Her head tipped and she frowned. 'You said there was no one else your age there. That you barely see anyone all day.'

Christ, I'd forgotten how good her memory was.

Mum returned to the kitchen, having slipped into a pair of runners and changed into shorts. 'I'm going to help Leonard.'

Naya's facial expression – etched with concern – made me want to laugh. If there was anyone we should be worried about around a mower, it was Leonard. Not Mum.

'I'm taking Naya and Leonard to the pub tonight,' I said. 'You'll be okay on your own, right?'

Mum shrugged. 'Of course. Why wouldn't I be?'

When we arrived, I was hopeful. Searching the bar for a glimpse of a messy top bun and a burger with red wine. But he wasn't there.

'Has your friend arrived?' Naya's tone was light and insinuating.

'Not yet.'

Leonard jumped in. 'And how do we know this *friend*?' he asked, hands on hips. It was remarkable how boyish he looked.

'Let's get a table.' I gestured near the fireplace. 'And a drink.'

Leonard offered to pay for the first round, disappearing into a sea of patrons.

'Seriously though, who are you meeting?' Naya asked.

'I'll tell you who I'm meeting when you tell me why you're so reluctant to move out of the house.'

Naya was still.

'You have more than enough money to buy somewhere.'

'You sound like Leonard.' She sighed, resigned. 'I'd feel bad, leaving Mum.'

'Why?'

'Because I'd worry about her.'

'You're always worried about her,' I responded. 'And she's fine.'

Naya's mouth turned into a flat line. 'She'd miss us, don't you think?'

'Probably.' My stomach pinched. 'But Naya, you're a psychologist.'

'So?'

I chuckled. 'Come on, you *know* you need to move out at some point.'

There was a pause in the conversation as Leonard returned, bottle of white and three glasses in his arms. Naya was pensive, for a moment, and then caught my eye. 'I don't *need* to do anything.'

Exhausted, I looked away. And that's when I spotted Dave.

By the entrance, a little flustered and red in the face, glancing around the pub like he might, in fact, be searching for me. He was visibly out of breath, chest rising and falling at a rapid rate.

When we caught eyes, his body relaxed. He sighed, smiled, and ran a hand through his hair – that same shaggy length, messy bun and all.

Naya followed my eyeline. Craned her neck, desperate to get a better look.

'That him?' The rise of her eyebrows suggested she found him more attractive than she'd anticipated.

'Yes.' I rose from my chair, glass of wine in hand.

Naya seemed disappointed at the little information I'd given. Like she'd been short-changed. But then she wiggled closer to Leonard and the two of them started reading the menu together. Leonard made a joke about something – I couldn't hear – and Naya let out a laugh. Placed a hand on his shoulder. Smiled at him, carefree and light.

At the bar, Dave and I slid onto the same stools as last time.

'You came back,' he said.

'I came back. Another wine fair?'

A sly smile on his lips, he shook his head. 'A yearly meet-up with some of our suppliers.' He glanced at Naya and Leonard. 'Didn't bring the girls this time?'

'That's my sister and her husband. You look like you ran here.'

'I did.' He pointed his thumb over his shoulder. 'Cab dropped me up the street.'

I held out the menu, but he shook his head. 'I get the same thing every time.'

'Really?'

'The burger is the only good thing here.'

'Still.'

Dave sipped his wine. 'Is it strange?' I asked him. 'Drinking this' – I paused, looking at his glass, trying to find the words – 'this basic stuff when, I imagine, your family makes better?'

He chuckled, then he put down his glass and pointed to a bottle behind the bar – the label was eggplant in colour, with a black illustration of a pear tree. 'This is from our vineyard. This bar is one of our stockists.'

'Oh.' I cringed. 'God, sorry. I've never tried it, I just assumed it was—'

'Terrible.' His mouth twisted, amused. 'It's not terrible, actually. Nicest wine here.'

'I'd say you're biased.'

'Probably.' Then, smiling, he added, 'Should I put basic in my tasting notes?'

'Sorry.'

'Don't be. Pubs like this are where we make a lot of our revenue, if you can believe it.' He took another sip. 'So where do you work?'

'At a corner store.'

His eyebrows rose.

'But it's fine,' I said. 'I'll figure something out. I'm volunteering in community radio at the moment. It's small, but maybe it could lead to a job. You never know.'

He seemed unconvinced. 'Is the industry hard to break into?'

I gave him a look – chin tilted down and one inch to the left – that told him what he needed to know. *In this town? Yes, yes, it is.*

Glancing over my shoulder, I watched Naya and Leonard for a moment. They shared a bowl of peanuts, deep in conversation. The side of Leonard's mouth tipped up in a smile, and then Naya grasped his upper arm. Ran a thumb across it and looked at him like she adored him and only him. Like they'd only just met.

Turning back to Dave, I changed the subject. 'Tell me about the vineyard. It must be beautiful, living there.'

'I don't live there. I visit a lot, but I live in the city and just drive up when I need to.' He slipped out his phone and slid it towards me. 'Here.'

Photos. Hundreds of them. *Stunning.* The rolling green hills, the varnished back veranda, vines wrapped around telegraph poles, and a small pocket in the distance where I could spot a lake. Zooming in, I see how it glistened, even when still.

'Christ, why *don't* you live there?'

'It's beautiful but it's remote.'

'When did you move out?'

'I'd just turned eighteen.'

'That's young.'

He nodded. 'Moved between a few share houses, but yeah, I left as early as I could.'

I wondered how he felt, being away from his parents. 'Do you miss home?'

'Sometimes.' He continued to eat. 'They're the only family I have.'

'I get it.'

'You do?' he asked.

'It's my sister, and it's my mum.'

His gaze stayed on me, searching my face. He'd clocked the absence of a father. Realised I've never mentioned one. He nodded, then, as if understanding. 'My mum is very sick. MS.'

'Oh. Dave, I'm sorry.'

'Thank you.' His posture had changed – rigid now, tense.

Our meals arrived, and Dave seemed grateful for the interruption. I worried that I'd upset him, bringing up his mother like that. He grew quiet and pensive while he ate.

'Do you like working for them?'

'It's fine,' he said, but I wasn't convinced. 'I've done it to help out Dad. I always knew they weren't going to be able to keep up the work, and I'm the only one around to pitch in. One day they'll hand the place over to me, and I'll move back.'

'And you seem thrilled about it.'

He smiled, then shrugged. 'I didn't have time to consider any other career. Mum and Dad needed help, so I helped.'

I couldn't decide if I felt sorry for him, seemingly forced into a career he may not have wanted, or if I admired him for stepping into a role he hadn't necessarily chosen. There was something about his selfless nature that drew me in. Something about his loyalty that I found comforting and safe.

He grew quiet again after that, and I wondered if I'd steered the conversation into the wrong direction. I felt this innate desire to cheer him up. Make him laugh. Keep him happy. Keep him thinking about me.

'If you'd like to tell me more,' I started, grabbing his phone. He flinched as I did it, just for a millisecond. I input my number. He clocked what I was doing and made no move to stop me. 'There's my number.'

He extended a hand towards my coat pocket, waved his fingers in a jolty motion and then he waited as I handed over my phone. A few seconds and he'd reciprocated the action.

And then he noticed the time. Winced.

'You have to go?' I asked.

'Sorry.'

'I'll see you next time, right?'

He met my eye, paused. 'Of course.' There was a strange expression on his face that I couldn't quite place, but then it was gone. He wiped his mouth with a napkin. 'How about a nicer place to eat, though? A restaurant, maybe, with wine that hasn't been made by my father.' He let out a laugh. When he pulled on his coat, he noticed my glass was empty, signalled to the bartender for another, and then covered the charge. 'Say hello to your sister for me. And her husband.'

The bartender handed me the wine, and I thanked Dave.

'Until next time,' he said. He seemed to contemplate a hug, but ultimately decided against it. With a slight nod, he brushed past me and out the front door.

'Until next time.'

Two months later, we met at a grill restaurant. He'd said *nicer place* and that was really the only one in town. Somewhere with linen tablecloths and material napkins, waiters who took your order at the table, and a wine list longer than half a page. Rustic decor, high ceilings, and dark, polished timber. Black rattan lamps. Charcoal-coloured ladders along the bar. Moody, geometric tiles.

I'd been there once, before Dad died. For his fiftieth. And as I stood there at the door, wearing the nicest outfit I owned – ironed, too – a part of me felt like Dad was with me. In my ear. *You did good, kid.*

Dave was already seated, and when I joined him, he told me his suitcase was behind the bar. 'This place is different, isn't it?'

I didn't tell him I had to book it in advance – that I reserved it right after he left the bar, two months earlier. But as he looked around at all the tables – full – I sensed he knew. I'd been caught out. He knew, without me saying it, that I was eager for this, keen on him. That I was *in this*, with him.

'New hairstyle,' I said, because he'd brushed everything back into a low bun. I almost didn't recognise him when I arrived, but then I saw the pressed black trousers and the crisp, aqua button-up shirt and thought, *Ah, yes, there you are.*

He ran a hand through it, sheepish. 'Not sure how women do it. Hair this long? Drives me mad.'

'Why not cut it?'

'I'm considering it,' he said. 'I grew it out on a whim. Josie told me it'd suit me, but not sure I want the maintenance. It's always falling out – is that normal?'

'Josie?'

'My flatmate. One of them, anyway.'

'Ah.' All those messages we'd been sending to each other, for two months, and he hadn't once mentioned flatmates.

'Cinar told me I'd look homeless with long hair.' He touched the bun again, self-conscious.

'You don't look homeless.'

'Emmanuel said I look like Jesus.'

'Cinar, Emmanuel and Josie,' I recite.

He nodded. 'Flatmates.'

When I leant across the table, he held my gaze. 'I actually like the length, but if you were looking to cut it shorter, you could . . .' I brushed my fingertips over the top of his ear. 'Trim it back to this kind of length. Much easier to maintain, and could still do a top knot, if you wanted.'

Our faces so close, I noticed how much darker his eyebrows were than I'd initially realised, how thick his hair was, and that his shirt might have been dry-cleaned with too much starch. It was stiff, like cardboard, and could probably stand on its own if he stepped out of it.

'How have you been?' he said, voice soft.

I thought on it, for a moment. I was fine. Intrigued by Dave, curious to know more. Where he was living, what his flatmates were like.

But I was also losing my grip on home. On my career. On my life. 'I work at a corner store.'

He was quick with a retort. 'You volunteer in radio.'

'There are no jobs, and I can't find work.' I slumped in my seat. 'I'm going nowhere.'

'You know what I'm going to suggest, don't you?' he said, before taking a sip of wine.

'I can't afford to move out.'

'Not move *out*. Move *away*.'

'To where?'

He shrugged, then placed his glass on the table. The silence between us was suggestive, and I joined the dots. How preposterous! I barely knew this man. Didn't even know he had flatmates, until now. Had only seen him three times. We hadn't even kissed.

Was he actually thinking I could move across the country for him?

'You'd be able to find a job,' he said. 'One you like.'

'It would break my mum's heart if I left.' And yet, I was considering it. Thinking of what it'd be like, to pack a suitcase, step on a plane, and build a new life somewhere new. Somewhere with Dave. Really, I wasn't thinking about my mother at all.

'But she has your sister,' he said.

She did. We'd had countless conversations and Naya was still firmly rooted at home, with Mum. Treating her like porcelain, doing everything for her. And Mum was letting her. It was utterly suffocating.

'Is it like this with your mum?' I asked, then immediately regretted it.

'It's a bit different, I think,' Dave said, a little clipped in his tone.

Mortified, I apologised. 'Oh god, I'm sorry. I don't know why I said that.' His poor mother had MS for god's sake and here I was, trying to compare that situation with my own.

'It's okay, it's fine.' Was it? And then he changed the subject, grinning slightly. 'You haven't commented on the wine yet.'

'Oh. Is it yours?'

'No.' He lifted the bottle and ran his eye over the back of the label. 'But this grenache is a favourite of mine.' He tapped the glass with his fingernail. 'Not too far from here, lovely Dutch family. They always save a couple of bottles for me.' Then he winked. 'Don't tell my father.'

From there, the conversation flowed. We said more to each other that evening than we had during our previous two meals together. Dave told me about his flatmates and their terrace house, and what it was like growing up on a vineyard. When I mentioned that my father died nine years earlier, Dave's sympathy felt genuine. And when I mentioned *how* he died – sudden and unexpected, warm in his bed – he looked heartbroken. I wondered if he was thinking of his mother.

Later, when it came time for Dave to leave, he plucked his bag from behind the bar and led me out onto the street. Here was where we separated, once again.

'Until next time?' he said, and I smiled. Never could quite explain how much I loved hearing that phrase.

'Until next time.'

He reached across for a hug this time, and I wrapped my arms around his torso. God, I always forgot how tall he was until I was standing that close to him. I gave a gentle squeeze and he nuzzled in closer.

When he pulled away, we both glanced down. His cab was approaching, and he was retreating. Stepping closer to the kerb, getting ready to flag down the car. I felt a little disappointed. It'd be another two months before I'd see him again. I watched him wave to the driver and signal for the boot, lifting up his suitcase inside. He then slammed the boot shut.

I waved. A small wave – light, a few fingers jerking. But perhaps it was enough to spur him into action, because he abandoned the car – momentarily – and leapt back up onto the pavement. He grabbed my waist, pulled me towards him. One hand rested on my cheek as he gave me the gentlest of kisses, like he wasn't sure what he was doing but maybe a brief, nondescript kiss was better than no kiss at all.

And as quickly as it happened, it was over. 'That's it?' I asked, as he walked back to the car.

He threw me a smile. 'Until next time.'

Six months later, I moved across the country.

Told the family over dinner one evening, when Leonard was out. Waited for them to finish their meals, waited until they'd drained their glasses. Waited for the right moment.

'When?' Mum asked, her face frozen in surprise. A moment later, she hid her disappointment with a plastered smile.

'Next week.'

Naya leant across the table. 'But you don't even know this man. And you're just going to move in with him?'

It made me foul with frustration, when she said that. Who was she to comment on how much I knew this man? We'd been speaking every day. And for the first time since Dad had died, I didn't feel so alone.

'I *do* know this man. And I'm not going to move in with him.'

'But you're moving *for* him?' she asked. 'This is outrageous.'

'Naya,' Mum said, chastising.

'He's the love of my life.'

My sister was bewildered, arms flailing about, fingertips pressed to her eyebrows. 'Oh *please*, he is not the love of your life. He is just the man you've loved the most so far.'

I ignored her.

'This is ridiculous. We haven't even met him.'

Perhaps it was rash. But for the first time in a long time, I no longer felt trapped. I'd be living somewhere else, away from this house and its memories. Away from Naya and her mothering. I wouldn't need to walk down the corridor and see inside the room where my father died. I wouldn't need to be reminded, every day, that he was gone. I wouldn't have to walk through the supermarket, run into a neighbour or one of my schoolteachers, and have painful small talk with someone who pitied me.

'Well, this is *great*, isn't it?'

As it turns out, Naya wasn't angry. Wasn't worried for my safety. Was simply annoyed that I'd snuck in ahead of her. Because not five minutes later, she told us that she and Leonard had found a house. In need of fixing up, but with four bedrooms and two storeys and they were excited about the renovations.

And so, in one evening, Mum had gone from a house of four people to an empty nest. I watched her face fold in at the realisation, tears build in her eyes, and I worked hard to convince myself that I was doing the right thing.

'I'll visit all the time,' I said. 'Promise.'

When I first moved, I crashed at Dave's place while I looked for a room to rent. And it was overwhelming to be in the city, after a small-town existence. The thin walls and creaking floorboards, the sound of traffic all through the night, raucous youth stumbling home from a boozy night, buses and ambulances at wee hours of the morning as they descended his street. During quiet moments,

I wondered what my family were doing, but I convinced myself I had made the right decision. I might've been cold every night, but at least I would never again have to walk past that room.

One week after moving, I arrived at a two-storey terrace house for an inspection, and the tenants didn't answer the door. Didn't pick up my calls. I must've been knocking on that towering wooden door for over a minute before the neighbour came outside, wondering what all the noise was about.

And that neighbour was Genevieve. Hair long and pulled back into a low ponytail. Thin lines for eyebrows, an amused expression. 'Are you okay?'

I pointed at the door. 'I'm meant to be inspecting a room.'

'They're away at the moment,' she said, frowning. 'They must've got their days mixed up.'

'Great.'

I'd spent almost a week inspecting rental properties. And they were all either too expensive or too messy, or the people were strange, or the vibe was off. Each time I'd go back to Dave's place and tell him it didn't work out and he'd look at me and say, 'Well, you could just move in here?' And I'd say, 'It's too soon.' Rinse and repeat.

'I've got an empty room, if you'd consider it?' Genevieve said, then introduced herself. 'I hadn't had a chance to post it online yet. I've been overseas.'

She seemed normal. She was dressed, unlike one of the places I'd attended, and presentable. Red hair brushed, striped trainers on her feet, ceramic coffee mug in hand. The bar was low, but she'd cleared it.

'Well, all right.' I walked around to her front gate, and she let me through. 'I've been having the worst luck.'

She gestured to her neighbours' house. 'You dodged a bullet. It's like a revolving door there,' she said. 'They're big on crack and they party a lot.'

Then she took in my blazer and blouse and my slip-on shoes. 'You don't . . . strike me as the same kind of person.'
'The blazer too much?'
She looked at the shoulder pads. 'You look forty.'
'I'm twenty-one.'
'Damn, okay.'
As she waved me inside, my phone buzzed in my bag and I fished it out. My sister, checking in.

> Everything okay? How are the inspections going?

When I stepped inside, Genevieve's house smelt like chamomile. And it was vacuumed, which shouldn't have excited me so much, but I really had been walking through some filth that week, so it did. White tiles, with bohemian rugs. Plush beanbags in the living area. A mid-century reading chair. Coloured artwork and blankets draped over furniture. Stone coffee table. Floor cushions. Hanging planters and terrariums on the back veranda.
'My parents are hippies,' she said, as if explaining the decor.
'Cosy.'
Another message from my sister.

> ???

Then another text, concurrently, from the neighbour.

> Sorry, slept in. Are you still at the door? We're here.

I looked up at Genevieve, who was now in the kitchen making me a coffee while telling me about her job as a teacher and her overseas trip and how she expected a flatmate to clean up after themselves. Made me think of Naya, cleaning up after us all. Even now, texting me every day. Checking I'm alive. Looking after me, from thousands of miles away.

'How soon can I move in?'

If I had to pinpoint the moment I suspected Dave of hiding something, it was when I first asked him about wanting children.

'What?' he'd said, stiffening.

'Kids,' I repeated. 'Do you want children?'

'Yes of course,' he said, but his body language said otherwise. Twitchy, eyes darting, body straightening. 'But not yet. Not for a while. Why? You don't want them yet, right?'

Of course I didn't want them yet. At twenty-two, I was working in a low-paying admin role at a public broadcaster and could barely afford my rent. But I was proud of myself. I was out on my own. I was independent. I was happy. I'd talk to my sister on the phone and she'd relay her worries about our mother and I'd think, *Thank god I'm not you.*

'No.'

He relaxed. 'Good. That's good.' We were eating brunch at a corner café and he took the moment to bite into some toast. Then, wiping his mouth with the back of his hand, he clarified. 'I just don't want them young. Want to wait as long as I can.'

His response triggered a mixed reaction in me – happy I wasn't dating someone desperate for children, but worried he'd never want them at all. Worried I might waste my youth on a man who ended up changing his mind.

Right then, a bus passed by. The advertisement – bright and orange – wrapped the entire vehicle and caught my eye.

Graham Jackson.

The Graham Jackson.

It felt like something stomped on my chest and ripped me open.

My father had *loved* Graham Jackson.

And I'd completely forgotten, until I saw that bus. It was like I'd reached inside my brain and opened up a tiny compartment that had been locked shut for nine years.

Every morning, while he buttered his toast, my father would turn on the radio and listen to Graham Jackson. Nod along to his insights and laugh at his observations. One time he turned to me and said, 'I respect this man for how hard he's trying to find love,' after Graham announced his third divorce. Dad loved Graham's raspy voice and his music selection, loved how hard he'd worked to build his career. Loved the way he spoke about toast spreads.

I'd completely forgotten about Graham Jackson in the years since. Had not heard his voice, had not seen his face, had not thought about him at all, since my father died.

And there he was, face adorning the side of a bus.

Reaching across the table, Dave clasped my hand. 'Did I tell you what Josie said to me last night? That she likes you. That she thinks you're good for me.'

Somehow, the years passed. I barely flew home, because I couldn't afford it. And that promise I'd made seemed like a distant memory.

I turned twenty-three.

I turned twenty-four.

The public broadcaster promoted me to a producer role and Dave booked a top-tier French restaurant for lunch to celebrate. We toasted with cocktails.

It was the role I wanted but not the company.

Every day, on my drive to work, I listened to Graham Jackson's breakfast program. Imagined my father in the passenger seat, listening with me.

I told myself I'd work there one day.

Over time, calls with my mother grew infrequent and Naya's texts turned brief.

> How are you going? How have you been?

Sometimes I forgot to reply, and eventually she stopped bothering at all.

I knew it was my own doing, that it was my fault. But my life took over. My job got busy, and I grew close with Josie. And Cinar. And Emmanuel. I spent so much time with Genevieve, I lost track of it all. Lost my way, a bit.

And Dave was changing.

His mother deteriorated and he was struggling. Couldn't quite articulate how he was feeling. It was the first time we'd gone through something difficult together, and he wasn't the same person I'd met. When we had dinner with his parents, he'd watch his mother like one might watch someone with terminal cancer.

One morning, I heard him crying in the shower. Silent, small sobs that told me he didn't want me knowing. When he exited the bathroom, I hugged him. 'Are you okay?'

He pushed me away, and I felt like I'd been stabbed.

'I'm worried about you.'

'I'm fine.' His voice was gruff.

'Are you?'

He looked at me with a blank expression and a tense jaw, and I felt like an inconvenience. It was baffling, how these conversations always went. I'd start the discussion irritated with him – with his unwillingness to let me in – and I'd end the discussion worried he was irritated with me.

'Mum will get better,' he said.

But what if she doesn't? I wanted to ask.

Eventually, Dave retreated into a shell, and no matter what anyone did, we couldn't get him out.

Josie. Cinar. Emmanuel. We could all see it, but we couldn't do anything about it. He just wasn't the same person that I'd met in that bar. Not all the time, anyway. I'd wake up in the morning and wonder which Dave I'd be seeing that day. And I could feel myself changing, over time. I was so vibrant when we met, but along the way, I'd dulled.

One night, Josie and I were watching a film. Just the two of us. And she turned to me and said, 'You better not break his heart. You wouldn't leave him, would you?'

They were best friends, and she was always looking out for him. Reminded me of Naya and Mum.

'Charlie?'

I took too long to answer, judging by her face. Her eyebrows rose fast, and it was frightening. Her face hardened with genuine concern. On the precipice of anger.

'Of course not.'

She relaxed, and I remember worrying that I couldn't turn back if I ever wanted to. Couldn't change this path I'd walked down.

I got a glimpse then, of what it'd be like if Dave and I split. How fast Josie might choose a side – how quickly I'd be made to feel guilty for leaving. And then I thought about how the others might react – Emmanuel, Cinar, Genevieve. Would I lose them too?

I wondered if Dave would get better. Wondered how he'd react if his mother passed. *When* his mother passed, as that was bound to happen at some point in our lives. What *would* Dave be like when faced with any kind of tragedy?

And in that moment, I knew that Naya was right.

I do not know this man.

Dave's mum did get better, for a time. And the man I knew returned. I started forgetting about what it had been like before, instead focusing on what I'd loved about him.

How selfless he was, how compassionate.

His shaggy hair.

How often he helped care for his mother.

How he prioritised his family's business.

How he made me feel when he looked at me (on a good day).

How little he criticised others.

The list went on, because I was trying to rationalise. Someone can be hurting and *also* be other things. Great things. And it was easy to dismiss the parts of this relationship that weren't working. Because all relationships have issues, right? And I did not want to feel that I'd uprooted my life and left my family for something that crumbled within a couple of years. I did not want to ring my sister and tell her that we didn't work out.

Everyone moved on around us. Josie froze her eggs, then met Shaun. Emmanuel started dating Diego, then moved out. Cinar didn't change at all, but the girls he slept with did. When the IT system at Genevieve's school broke down, Bruce attended the call out to fix it. They started dating the following week.

When Genevieve told me she was moving out to live with him, Dave and I found an apartment to rent. Both houses disbanded, all of us scattering in our own directions.

*

When a producing role opened up with Graham Jackson, I spent days on the application. Read it over and over again – aloud and in my head.

Dave told me not to get my hopes up. Assured me the job would come up again, at some point, if I was not successful. At the time, I thought he was protecting my feelings. Now, with distance, I see the negativity.

I knew the role was hotly contested. The most popular breakfast radio program in the country – I had fierce competition.

But I was *good*. Really good.

And ahead of the interview, I spent every waking hour prepping. I studied the show and the segments, scrolled through months of social media posts. Read about their ratings share, their exclusive events and red-carpet coverage, even the publicity scandals. I poured over the news articles and tweets, every speech Graham had ever given, and compiled all my work from the public broadcaster to bolster the application.

And when the time came for the interview, my leg jiggling under the conference room table, sitting opposite HR and the chief of staff, I knew I nailed it. Could sense it immediately. They talked about 'next steps' before I'd even completed all of their questions.

I started working at the Graham Jackson Breakfast Show not long after my twenty-sixth birthday. Finally, I had secured a job that I loved – truly loved. Something that made me think, *You did good, kid. You made it.*

The first time I met Graham, he was standing in his studio reading something on his phone. And I walked in, introduced myself, and immediately he reached out to clasp my hand. His was bigger than mine, and warm, and I let the handshake last longer than usual because I just wanted to look at him a little while longer.

My dad loved you, I thought. *Really loved you.*

'I'm looking forward to working with you,' I said.

He returned my smile, and the sentiment, and then slipped out of the room. It was such a small moment in his life, but one of the biggest in mine.

And every morning, when my alarm screeched and I slipped out of bed in the early hours, I'd feel this incredible surge of pride. This boost I'm not sure I'd ever had before. Dave and I were doing well, and I'd convinced myself that all relationships needed work. That's what that rough patch was – work. His mum was well, the business was thriving, and Dave was happy. *We* were happy.

And then Naya fell pregnant. And my confidence splintered.

It wasn't that she was having a baby – of course I was thrilled. It was that she told me in a text message. A photo of the ultrasound, no accompanying message. Is that what we'd come to? A huge moment, shared like this.

I called and called and called, to no answer. Sitting in the studio that morning, the breakfast show wrapping up, Graham was on his final segment of the morning and I was swept up in my sister's news. She'd told me over *text*.

I couldn't stop thinking about it, for days. What I'd lost in pursuit of all this.

The second time I suspected Dave of hiding something was when I was freshly twenty-seven, and I proposed the idea of merging finances. Joint accounts.

'What?' he'd said, giving me a sharp look from across the kitchen table. 'Why would we do that?'

'Because we've been together six years?' I said, as if that should be enough. 'Because we're talking about buying an apartment together?'

I had an ulterior motive for suggesting it, of course. The man was struggling to save any money and I couldn't work out why. For years, he'd complained about money, but his earnings were good, his expenses were moderate, and he barely bought anything. His mother's medical bills were covered by insurance, so he didn't contribute. And yet, he had no money. *If only I could look through his accounts, I'm sure I could solve it.*

'I don't want to do that.'

His face was growing red and his neck splotchy; he was nervous about something. He was anxious and his body was making it known.

'I just think it's best if we keep all that separate.'

Later that evening, a few minutes shy of midnight, I received a text from my sister with a photo of a baby swaddled in a knit blanket.

> Your niece, Darla. Hope you're well.

One year later, Dave's mum died.

It was worse than I'd imagined. His grief was a flood that blew into our apartment one morning and, no matter what I did, it wouldn't drain. God, I tried. Our friends did too. Josie, Shaun, Cinar, Diego and Emmanuel all turned up. For days. For weeks. Cooking for us, cleaning, helping us plan the funeral.

Dave barely left the bed; he was growing sullen. Practically mute, barely speaking to me.

In a moment of desperation, I turned up at Genevieve and Bruce's apartment. Lay down on their couch, hands lost in my hair. 'How long do you think I should wait? If I were to leave him.'

'You're thinking of leaving?' Genevieve said, shocked.

'It's bad, G.' I was crying at this point. 'We barely speak to each other. We're not even friends. Just two people sleeping in the same bed.'

'He needs time—'

'I've given him time! Years of it,' I snapped. 'Sorry.'

'Don't be.' She reached out. 'I'm sorry.'

'I've been staying late at work and he keeps texting me asking when I'll be home,' I said. 'And then I get home and it's like he hasn't even noticed. We cook, we eat, we sleep, we go to work. How long does this last?'

She didn't have an answer for me, but I could tell she was concerned. 'Would you like me to speak to him?'

'No! Don't tell him I said anything.' Then, pausing, I continued. 'Sometimes, when I get home, I just sit in my car. On my phone, reading old text messages we sent. Like, I'd rather do that than go inside and see him. Is that sad?'

She didn't answer.

'I enjoy being at work more than at home.'

Her reaction – widened eyes, pressed lips – told me that there was something very wrong.

Early one morning, at the radio station, Graham caught me crying.

'Want to talk about it?' he asked.

'You're here early.'

I watched as he pulled up a chair next to me. Rested his elbows on his knees, his head in his hands. 'Are you okay?'

'How much time have you got?' I asked, and then I told him everything.

Afterwards, he told me he was sorry. 'I've been through this. More than once. Sometimes things just don't work out.'

'I love him, though.'
'Do you?'

I ignored every instinct in my body telling me something was wrong. And somehow, time progressed. We passed eight years together. Dave was better, had come to terms with his mother's death. And every time I sat down on Genevieve's couch, I'd remember what I'd told her – that I had considered leaving him. And every time Graham asked me how Dave was, how *I* was, I knew he was waiting for things to sour.

How absurd that was, I'd thought. What a good thing I'd be throwing away. What a good man. What kind of person would I be if I'd left him when he needed me most? Deep in grief, missing his mother, and I'd told Genevieve that I wanted to leave him. Did she and Bruce talk about me when I wasn't there? Were they convinced this relationship was doomed? They didn't know how *good* it was. How good Dave could be. What things were really like between us.

And so, when Dave proposed, and I said yes, she was the first person I called. Because she was my best friend, but also because I needed to convince her. *Look at us. Look how good we are.*

When I saw her in person, and showed her the ring, she'd looked me in the eye without one ounce of judgement. 'I'm happy if you're happy.'

At our wedding reception, on the grounds of Dave's family vineyard, Josie gave a speech.

'Something Charlie doesn't know about Dave is just how smitten he was after they first met,' she said. The guests made an *Oooh* noise. Nearby, my mother wore a draped olive-green dress

ISN'T IT NICE WE BOTH HATE THE SAME THINGS

with a shawl. Naya and Leonard, whose two children were with a babysitter, were enjoying a night to themselves – one of the first, since becoming parents.

Josie looked me in the eye. 'Dave flew across the country every two months just to see her.'

I rotated to face Dave, and he was sheepish. He hid his smile but clasped my hand under the table. Our eyes met. 'But the wine fairs.'

'Only one a year, actually.'

'Oh.'

'You didn't notice?' he said. 'After you moved here, I've barely been back.'

I hadn't noticed. Had I made such an impression on him, that he sought me out so many times? That he paid all that money, spent all that time, just for me? Across the table, Mum's mouth was parted. Naya was shocked. A little teary, both of them, and then Mum looked at me with an expression that said, *You've got a good one there.*

Josie resumed her speech. 'That's how we knew Charlie was the one for him. That they were perfect for each other.' She held my gaze. 'That they'd never part.'

It went downhill very quickly. Only a matter of weeks. We'd been married for two years by this point, together for ten. But it's remarkable just how quickly something can unravel beyond repair.

It started when Dave had that accident at work. He was working with the barrels on the vineyard, when one slipped and crushed his hand. His own fault, I later learnt. Rigged wrong. Distracted, not monitoring his work closely enough.

When I arrived at the hospital, flustered, he was wincing in pain as they realigned his fingers. He'd crushed most of the bones in his hand and he was heavily drugged. Couldn't tell whether I was real or a hallucination. Couldn't explain what had happened. Wanted someone to ring me, not realising it was me standing in front of him.

Certainly couldn't fill out any forms, or inform the nurses of his private health details.

'Would you mind?' they said, handing me a clipboard. He'd just been moved to a hospital room and was sleeping most of the day.

It would've been embarrassing to admit that I didn't know about his private health – that we didn't share those things with each other. Married, together for a decade, and the man still insisted on keeping it all separate. It had been the source of many arguments, over the years.

'Of course.'

And I thought, *I'm just going to do it this one time.* I'm just going to dig once, even though I knew it was wrong. That if I waited long enough, he'd be awake and lucid and able to input the details himself.

But something still didn't feel right, and I couldn't help but think this moment was giving me something I'd never get again. A chance to understand him even better than I thought I already did.

So, I dug.

Drove home and rifled through his paperwork. His work computer. Read through his insurance information and his income statements. Even found his high school graduation certificate, which I was surprised he'd kept.

Found his bank details.

Found his bank statements.

Logged online and read through everything – went back twelve months, looking at every line in those accounts.

And I saw the payments. Found them pretty easily. Thousands of dollars out of his account every second month. A regular payment, but something I couldn't decipher. Who on earth was he paying? And why?

I waited to confront him. Waited two days, because I wanted him to be conscious and alert.

That day, when he was rested in his bed, he reached out with his good hand and gave mine a squeeze. 'I love you.'

I pulled out the bank statements – printed, stapled – and rested them atop his blanket-covered leg. On the first page, I'd circled one of the payments in black marker.

His face grew pale. 'You went through my things?'

'We're married.'

'I wanted to keep this—'

'Separate, I know.'

And then he did something I wasn't expecting: he relaxed. Smiled. Let out a strained breath – even chuckled. 'Oh, it's a relief,' he said, hand to chest. 'I wasn't expecting that. I feel *relieved*, Charlie.' He looked down at his injured hand. 'This doesn't feel like such a big deal anymore. And I'm not even mad you went through my things.'

'I went through your things because you hide so much. You're transferring thousands of dollars a month to . . .' I looked down at the statements. 'I don't even know where.'

He was still completely at ease, and sighed. 'It's child support.'

'Sorry?'

'Child support.' He let his head tip back onto the pillow. 'I have to pay it until the kid turns eighteen.'

Of all the scenarios I was imagining in my head – gambling

addiction, loan shark, hush money, affair – a *child* was not one of them.

'Wow,' he said, hand back on his chest. 'You have no idea how good it feels to finally tell you.'

'You have a child?'

He nodded. 'Brief fling a few years before I met you. It's a bit of a long story.'

The room was silent, and I think what annoyed me most was not the truth of it all – although that *infuriated* me – it was how content Dave looked. Like a huge weight had lifted off his shoulders. How dare he be happy?

And then he grabbed my hand, like nothing had changed. Looked at me like we hadn't just had that conversation.

I flicked his hand away, recoiling. He felt like filth to me.

He clocked my expression. 'What? Only a couple more years and I won't have to pay it.'

'A couple more years and we can forget you have a kid. Great.' I stood. 'Do you see them?'

'Who? The mother or the girl?'

'A girl,' I said. 'It's a girl.'

'No, I don't see them. Why would I do that?'

I looked at his face. His beautiful, beautiful face, and thought, *You are the ugliest person I know.* I could've curled over and emptied my stomach onto the floor. Who *was* this man I married?

'I was young,' he said, sitting up. Pleading. He'd realised my reaction was not in his favour and his expression resembled fear.

'How young?'

He paused. 'Twenty-four.'

'An *adult*, Dave. You were an adult. Oh my god.' I press my fingers to my forehead. 'You have a kid. A *kid*.' I let out a laugh. 'What a perfectly normal thing to find out on a Tuesday.'

'They're fine without me,' he insisted. 'I pay extra. She's married now, and the girl probably thinks that's her real dad. And it doesn't bother me at all. I don't think about her. It's okay.'

My *god*. 'I'm not thinking about *you* right now. Who cares about *you* in this scenario?' Then I turned away. 'Can't even look at you. You never told your parents? Josie? The others?'

He shook his head.

'A *child*, Dave. Are you kidding me? A child you pretend doesn't exist.' I ran a hand through my hair. 'You haven't seen her? Never?'

And in that moment, I think he knew I was never going to be on his side. That we might not come back from this. Because my face was almost melting, I was that horrified. Distraught for that poor girl out there, completely abandoned by her own father.

'She *could* know,' I said. 'She could know that's not her real dad. Have you thought about that? She has a father she's never seen – do you know what that could do to a person?'

Realisation dawned. 'Oh. You're not mad about the money.'

'I would do anything to see my father again. *Anything*.'

I'd pay all the money in the world. I'd say whatever needed to be said. I'd drive across the country, or fly across the world. If my dad was out there, somewhere, I'd find him. And that girl out there had a father and he wanted nothing to do with her.

I was disgusted.

'It's not the same,' Dave said, trying to justify his choices. 'I'm not your dad.'

'You are not half the man he was,' I said. 'He would never have done this.'

Dave avoided eye contact. His eyebrows drawn, his lips trembling ever so slightly. He was frightened of me.

'I want kids, I do. Just, not that one. I want one with *you*. Maybe when I'm better, we'll try? And we can pretend you never found out. We were so happy. *Are* so happy. This doesn't need to change anything, does it?'

Except it did change everything. Confirmed what I'd been trying *so* hard to pretend wasn't true.

I know this man. And I do not love him.

PART THREE

One week later

CHAPTER FORTY-TWO

'Well, here we are.'

Dave wheels me inside his apartment. Extends a hand as if showing me the place for the first time. As if I didn't live here for years. 'I've got the spare bedroom set up for you.'

Then, for the third time this afternoon, he looks down at my plastered body. One broken arm and one broken leg. Very grim. Would not recommend. On the same side too, which somehow makes it worse. I'm still reeling from it all – the fall, the hospital, having to move back in with Dave.

He closes the door behind me, then clocks a lone shoe on the ground near my chair. He hastily tosses it into a nearby cupboard, and I take a moment to assess the apartment.

The whole place is different. Alarmingly different.

The cream couch has been replaced by something violet and stiff. Utterly foul. The white, circular coffee table is gone and there's a floor lamp against the wall. One of those tall ones with a beige rattan top. I can't see the terrace because Dave has the blinds half-closed, but I'm wondering if the plush furniture out there is gone, too. And then my mind wanders to the master bedroom, which we painted a dusty blue. And now the colour feels ruined for me, like if I see that misty tone again, I'd instantly think of Dave.

I wonder if the neighbours are still here – that Italian woman across the hall who baked through the night to manage her insomnia, and the young family down near the fire exit who rode their bikes together on Sunday mornings. Shortly before I left, a man named Louis moved in next door and I often heard him speaking fluent French to family on the phone – it reminded me of my father, bringing a surprising amount of comfort in the days leading up to the separation.

'I'm glad to be out of that hospital bed,' I say, even though I'm completely mortified by this whole situation. Not only do I take a torrid tumble down an escalator and find myself in a wheelchair for the next five weeks, but I'm in my ex-husband's apartment because he was the only person I thought to call who I knew would turn up. Isn't that just horrific?

'When did you move back?' I ask.

Dave walks towards the kitchen, and I'm relieved to see it's been kept the same. The kitchen table, round and ribbed, is still there, as is the striped rug underneath it. Dave hasn't yet rid himself of *everything* we lived with.

'Couple of weeks,' he says, leaning against the marble countertop. He scratches his cheek, then runs a hand through his ashy brown hair, which is fluffy from a wash and, in my opinion, a bit too long. 'I think Dad was getting sick of me, to be honest.'

'He'd never.'

There's a small smile. After meeting him at a work event, Ivan once described Dave as looking like unbuttered bread – pale, with a thin mouth and a bland expression. I'd scolded him at the time, because what a rude and foul thing to say about my husband, but now that I've had some distance from Dave, I can see it.

He totally looks like unbuttered bread.

Dave says, 'I haven't told him yet. About us.'

Beat. 'Really?'

'Really.'

'Oh, Dave, no.' I'm astounded. We've been separated for over half a year. 'He didn't wonder why you moved home for months?'

He looks ashamed. 'I told him it was to help take care of the vineyard. Told him I was worried about him.'

Silence, for a few moments. Then, I mutter, 'How is he? Your dad?'

'Do you care about my dad? Or are you just trying to find something to talk about?'

I'm trying to find something to talk about. 'I care about your Dad.'

'Then he's fine,' he says, fiddling with the gold watch on his right wrist. His hand is healed now, although some of his movements are slow and jolty. 'Considering retirement.'

'Been considering it for twelve years,' I say. 'I'll believe it when I see it.'

He smiles, then clears his throat. 'I assume you've told Penelope? And Naya?'

'I told them straight away.'

He smiles, nods. 'How are you feeling?' he asks, then touches his earlobe (seemingly for something to do).

I've got no idea why he said yes to all this; it must be terribly uncomfortable for him as well.

'I'm okay,' I say. 'I don't need babysitting. I'll just . . .' Then look around the apartment. 'Amuse myself.'

A moment of silence passes, and then Dave meets my eye.

'I'm sorry you fell down an escalator,' he says. It's a moment or two before I realise he's being genuine, and not intending to be funny. 'You could've been seriously injured.'

'I am seriously injured.'

'Yeah, but, injured even wors— You know what I mean.'

One week in a hospital bed and now five weeks in this apartment before these casts can come off. I'm not exaggerating when I say I didn't have anyone else I could call. Quinn would've been my next guess, but honestly, it's all a little too soon. She'd think I'm coming on too strong if I were to ring her from a hospital telling her I need help because I've broken some bones and I need a place to live for a few weeks. But every time I remember that Dave was the only person I felt I could call, a small piece of me chips away.

When he met me at the hospital, he didn't look nearly as dishevelled as I was expecting. No unkempt hair, wrinkled clothing, slender frame, bags under the eyes. I thought I'd turn up to the hospital and the ambulance door would open to reveal an absolute shell of a man. And I'd work my hardest not to feel sorry for him, because he did this to himself. I'd lay there and think, *You're to blame here.*

But he looked, well, good. Put together. Ironed jeans – black, potentially a recent purchase – with a buttoned-up, pastel linen shirt. Not sure I'd seen it before. No fugly khaki pants in sight. There was a scent of sandalwood in the air: his cologne.

I felt thrown. Last time I'd seen him, he was clawing at his hair as he begged me to stay, cradling a crushed hand. Telling me we could fix us. That he'd do anything to keep me. But when I saw him, in that ambulance bay, he looked composed.

Dave goes to fix me a cup of tea, and a bite to eat.

'I can do that,' I say.

He raises an eyebrow. 'Can you?'

I look down at my wheelchair, and remember I can't. Not yet. I'm still working out how to get around, let alone make a beverage.

Fuck. I'll be forced to rely on Dave for so much – food, movement, water, getting into bed. This is going to be awkward for the both of us.

'I'm glad you called. I was feeling awful about everything.' Pause. 'I was being a solid arsehole. Can't believe how many times I texted you about the ring.' He glances at me. 'But it's been nice to see you, this past week.'

He's usually not this funny. *I'm glad you called.* As if I rang him casually one morning, not the paramedic on the way to the hospital. *It's been nice to see you.* Broken limbs and all, helping tend to me in hospital.

Perhaps what he's trying to tell me is that he misses me. That even with me in a hospital bed, dazed and doped up on painkillers, he's enjoyed my company.

'I'm actually quite furious with myself,' I say. 'Who falls down an escalator?'

He hides a smile.

A little later that afternoon, when my phone rings, he fishes it out of my bag and hands it to me on the sofa.

It's Genevieve.

'You're not going to answer that?' he says. 'She's been ringing you every day.'

Decline call. I'm still fuming about the whole situation. She told Dave I was planning to leave. You'd think broken bones would give me perspective, maybe encourage me to let the smaller things go, but this is still a massive thing in my mind. I intend on being bitter and angry until the end of time.

'Can't believe she told you.'

'Can't believe you were planning on leaving me.'

'I did leave you.'

He shifts. 'Well, yeah, eventually,' he replies. 'I wish you'd told me earlier that you were unhappy.' He sits down beside me.

'Not my fault you didn't notice.'

'My mother was dying.'

'So was I!' Okay, too much. Very inappropriate. 'Sorry.'

His mouth twists, ashamed. He stares at my phone, nestled in my lap. 'You're not going to tell her? About the fall.'

'Don't know,' I say, opening the scores of messages I've received from her over the past fortnight. She knows something is wrong, but she doesn't understand what it is.

'And your family? Are you—'

'Dave, come on.'

He raises his arms. 'I just think they'd all want to know. Your Mum, especially. And Naya.'

'Turns out my sister doesn't like me very much.'

I think of you as dead. I've never heard such venom come from her mouth – I feel like I've been poisoned, and it's seeped through every crevice of my body, unable to be extracted.

'Your sister loves you a dumb amount. She once told me she holds a great deal of respect for you, chasing your dreams.'

I realise he's being serious. 'How do you get so many people to tell you things? Genevieve, Naya.'

He smirks. 'For one, they might like a distraction from Leonard's injuries.' He sinks into the sofa. 'How are they?'

'Mum bought a slow cooker.'

Oh, and Naya is angry with me. And I've neglected my family. And the reason Leonard is injured is because he's always helping Mum, and perhaps I shouldn't have found his feeble body so amusing all these years. And my family lied about the anniversary celebration just so they could see me.

'I loved her cooking,' he says, then smiles. As if reminiscing.

It's a little absurd. How easily we fall back into our old rhythms. How nice it is to speak with him, without all the anger and the tension.

It's not that I've missed Dave. I haven't. Not as my husband, anyway. Not in any way that makes me want him back. But as one of my best friends? Oh, yes, I've missed that. I miss him in the way I wear a lot of dark grey clothing, because he once pointed out that it suits me and contrasts well with my blonde hair. I miss him in the way I complete a crossword before bed every night, because he introduced me to the app years earlier. I miss him in the way I still buy the same brand of washing powder we used to use.

I miss him in the way he changed my life, in all the littlest ways.

'Why did you help me?' I ask. 'All those days at the hospital. Setting up the spare bedroom.'

'Couldn't say no, could I? What kind of person would that make me?'

'I would've understood if you told me to fuck off.'

He grins. 'Sometimes I do think about telling you to fuck off. Then I remember that I ruined everything.'

He's quiet when he speaks next. 'Was it ever really about the girl?' he asks, voice quiet. 'Or was that just an excuse to leave—'

There's a knock on the door – a few loud bangs, but so forceful it feels like the whole apartment is shaking.

And then Dave's face falls. Instantly, it's white. And he's looking at me like he's terrified, and he's sorry, and then he's running a hand across his forehead. 'Oh god, I'm so sorry. I completely forgot.'

'Forgot what?'

He rises and starts turning in all different directions, like he doesn't quite know what to do first. Open the door? Explain to me what's going on? He runs a hand down his T-shirt, as if realising it's an inappropriate thing to be wearing. Then he looks at me, wearing trackpants and an unwashed jumper, and winces.

'I'm hosting a dinner party tonight. With everything that's happened, I forgot to cancel.'

'A dinner party?' I say, straightening. 'With who?'

And then, from the other side of the apartment door, I hear a familiar voice. 'Dave, open the door. We've got alcohol and we want to drink it.'

Josie.

'Oh god,' I say, running a hand through my tangled hair. Looking down at what I'm wearing, which is horribly basic and far too casual for a dinner party with the group. I've got a broken arm and a broken leg, for Christ's sake! My body is filled to the brim with pain relief medicine.

Another bang on the door, and then two voices.

'Come on, Dave, hurry up.' Cinar.

'I need to use your loo.' Emmanuel. 'And Diego's carrying the apple pie and it's burning his fingers.'

I'm frantic at this point. Cannot even move from the lounge because I've not yet mastered the art of transferring myself to and from the wheelchair without Dave's help. And that man is way too frazzled to help with anything right now.

'Tell them to go home.'

'Fuck,' he's saying, over and over and over again. 'Maybe I just don't answer?'

'We can hear you in there.' Cinar, again. 'Who on earth are you talking to?'

In a state of mania, Dave rushes over to help lift me into the wheelchair. Swivels me around so I'm in the corridor. Tells me I can hide in the second bedroom, if I want.

'*Hide?*' I repeat, mortified. 'That's ridiculous. I'm not hiding.' It's a ridiculous notion, and at the very least I'd need some time to manoeuvre the chair around his furniture. Time we do not have.

'What's going on in there?' Josie asks. 'We're coming in.'

And then Dave and I share a look. A trapped kind of look, because we both remember, at the same time, that Josie knows where the spare key is hidden. That right now, she's probably reaching above the hallway light to secure it.

'Last chance to hide,' he says.

I do consider it, for a moment. Because I cannot face them tonight. Simply *cannot* sit here during a dinner party with that group. Not after everything that's happened. Not after the fortieth and the group chat, and that awful discussion with Josie on the street.

I look awful. I feel awful. All I want to do is hide from the world until I'm healed. Until I'm ready.

They *cannot* see me like this.

CHAPTER FORTY-THREE

They see me like this. Absolutely no way to avoid it, them pouring through the door like that. Josie, Shaun, Emmanuel, Diego, Cinar.

Even if I *did* want to hide, there simply wasn't enough time.

'Oh my god,' Josie says, looking at me. Running her eyes down my body and over the wheelchair. She has one hand to her chest, and a white porcelain salad bowl in the other. Then she swings around to face Dave. 'Did you do this?'

He is horrified at the accusation. 'Oh bugger off, of course not.'

'I fell down an escalator,' I say. And then the room grows quiet. Stunned, all of them, halted by the door.

The silence stretches for far too long.

And then Diego cries out. 'Jesus, my fingers.' And darts to the kitchen bench to drop down the apple pie. Even with a tea towel, he isn't able to escape the temperature of that dish. I can see his red, raw fingertips as he raises his hands.

It seems Diego's apple pie isn't enough to draw focus away from my injuries. After a mere second, they're all looking at me again.

'Are you okay?' Shaun asks, stepping forward. 'I'm so sorry.'

'I'm okay, thank you.'

Dave tells them, 'Charlie is staying here until the casts are removed.'

'Right,' Shaun says.

Cinar turns to Emmanuel. 'I thought you needed to use the loo?'

'Urge is gone now,' he says, watching me. 'Something far more pressing has come up.'

I'm aware of what I must look like – unkempt, unwell, my hair tangled into knots – but all this staring has me feeling incredibly uncomfortable.

'It's not a big deal,' I say. 'I fell down an escalator, Dave's been helping me, and I've only got a few weeks until these' – I point to my casts – 'are removed. Would prefer we don't linger on it. Just pretend it hasn't happened, okay?'

Another moment of staring and then the group murmurs in agreement. Josie's gaze lingers on me for a moment and I try and read her expression.

The air between us is so different now, her birthday party seems like a lifetime ago. I feel like the world has shifted twice over since then.

Later, I reminisce at the dining table. It's remarkable how much this dinner feels exactly like it used to. How easily we can fall back into old patterns, sitting here together.

Shaun, who has a habit of sharing shocking things he finds on the internet, shows us all an article about the world's most secure prison – impossible to escape, apparently.

Then Emmanuel, always overreaching, looks at the photos. Mulls it over for a moment, then sits a bit straighter. 'I reckon I could get out.'

Josie throws a napkin at his head, calling him absurd. Even Diego counters him. 'And how would you do that?'

'I don't know,' Emmanuel responds, shrugging. 'But I think I could.'

'Sometimes you struggle to unlock your front door,' Dave says.

'That's different,' Emmanuel says, holding up a finger.

'How is that different?' Cinar asks, one of the first things he's said since we sat down.

Emmanuel's mouth opens, and then he slumps a little. 'I have no idea.'

And they're laughing. Then topping up wine, and finishing off their meals. Every so often someone asks me if I'm feeling okay, but mostly, they all take the opportunity to catch up on what they've missed.

'We're so busy,' Diego says, when Shaun asks him about work.

'Busy running away from Charlie.' Josie lets out a sharp cackle. It's the first sign she's had too much to drink.

There's an awkward silence around the table.

Dave looks down at his plate, and Diego's head goes into his hands. 'I'm so sorry, Charlie,' he says. 'I saw you and panicked.'

It's remarkable how little I care.

Josie lets out another laugh, then realises her glass is empty. She reaches across to grab at the bottle. It's quick, but I see Shaun give her a look. A warning. *Careful*, he's saying. Because we can all tell how close she is to being a hopeless inebriate.

She ignores him and pours herself a glass anyway. 'Charlie, we've all been awful people. *Awful.*' She takes two gulps of wine. 'I feel like I've had to apologise to you every time I've seen you, and I'm ashamed. We behaved terribly.'

'You did,' Dave says, lifting his gaze to meet hers.

The table is silent.

'You all did,' he clarifies. 'The fact she called *me* when she fell is an indication of how you've all treated her.'

At least they have the decency to appear embarrassed, all of them. Diego cannot look me in the eye.

'It's fine,' I say, feeling uncomfortable.

Dave looks at me, pointedly.

'It's not fine,' I correct.

Another moment of silence and then Josie knocks her glass over, fumbling as she tries to put the bottle back into the centre of the table.

Shaun whispers under his breath. 'Jesus, Josie, slow down.'

Josie doesn't know her own volume. '*No*. I'm having more. My mum has the kids tonight and so *this mum*' – she points to herself – 'is drinking whatever she wants.'

Everyone's looking down at their empty plates now, not daring to make eye contact.

It seems that Josie is not done speaking. Leaning forward, she points at Dave's glass of wine. 'Cherish this while it lasts, because *one day* you'll have kids and you'll be sober most of the week. It's horribly boring.'

It feels like someone has sucked the air out of the room. Josie keeps speaking, but I've tuned it out. Instead, Dave and I are looking at each other from across the table.

And I know, without us speaking, that we're both thinking about the same thing. About his daughter. About the support payments I found. About how no one at this table knows and Dave's been hiding this secret for almost eighteen years—

Shaun whispers something to Josie again and she snaps. '*Stop*.' She slaps her husband's upper arm, and no one at the table speaks. 'Stop telling me to slow down. Everyone is having a good time. Aren't we?' She looks around. 'The band's back together. Something to celebrate.'

Two more sips and then she continues with a laugh. 'Well, except for Cinar. Poor guy finally knows what it's like to be dumped—'

'*Stop*,' Shaun shouts, and we all jump in our seats. Retract, like someone's pulled a string. It's the first time any of us have heard Shaun shout, and it's alarming. Didn't realise it'd be quite so booming. 'Just stop speaking.'

Everyone looks at Josie, and then back at Shaun.

Josie tries to laugh it off. '*This* guy, trying to tell me what to do. Right, okay, Shaun. Whatever you say—'

'Can we not?' Shaun says. 'We're having a lovely dinner with our friends.'

Would we say it's lovely? We've heard them bicker, but never like this. Never to this extent. And for a moment, no one knows what to do. Or where to look. I curl my upper body down, trying to make myself as small as possible.

This is nothing like how it used to be. This is nothing like how I *want* it to be. I should've made Dave send them home. Maybe I should've hidden, like he suggested. These people are not my friends. And before, it bothered me, but now it doesn't.

This is the last time I'll spend time with this group, and I'm fine with that. I'm a different person now, and we've outgrown each other. There was once a time I was devastated to have been removed from the group. Now, I'm glad. I'd rather spend time with Ivan and Dora. Or Graham. Or Quinn—

'Sorry,' I say, interrupting the group. Turning to Cinar, I reach out. 'Did she say Quinn broke up with you?'

He looks up at me, and nods. There's pain across his face. 'She told me she couldn't commit,' he says. 'Ironic, right?'

CHAPTER FORTY-FOUR

By the next afternoon, word has got out about my fall.

After the disastrous dinner party, Cinar messaged Quinn, who messaged Cleaver, who told Dora, who messaged Ivan, who messaged just about every single employee at the radio station. And somewhere along the gossip chain, someone messaged Graham. Suddenly, everyone knew the reason behind my extended personal leave.

I get an onslaught of calls, as a result. People checking in, asking how I am. Colleagues I barely know, sending their well wishes and their get well soons.

There are now so many bundles of flowers at Dave's apartment he struggles to find enough space for them without resorting to the floor. When Graham sends a delivery of sixty-four frozen dinners, Dave grumbles as he tries to cram them all into the freezer.

'He knows you've only got casts on for five weeks, right?' he says. 'And that you're living with me? I am perfectly capable of buying you food.'

I'm on the sofa, resting. My leg is aching, my arm is itching underneath the plaster, and I'm feeling incredibly frustrated by the whole thing. I've become so reliant on Dave and it's irritating me to the point of tears. Last night, after everyone left, he had to help me undress and then place me on the shower chair. Had to stand there and watch as I washed myself, in case I fell. He saw me naked all the time when we were together, but for some reason this was different. Intimate, uncomfortable. I squirm at the memory.

'Right, well,' Dave says, clapping his hands together. 'I'm off.'

He's visiting his dad this evening. 'You *sure* you're okay by yourself?' he says, standing at the edge of the sofa, hands clasped together, doubt clouding his expression.

'Will you stop asking me that?'

'How will you go to the toilet?'

'I'll use my other arm. Or I'll hobble on one foot. Maybe I'll crawl, just for something different.'

He doesn't look convinced, and maybe deep down I'm doubting myself, but I cannot keep Dave confined here for five weeks.

'If I call your mum, she'd be here tomorrow to help you.'

I gesture to my plastered arm. 'And I'd smack you with this if you did.'

He rolls his eyes, exhausted. He does not owe me anything; he can leave whenever he'd like. But even now, after we've separated, he's still making sure I'm okay.

'I'll be fine,' I repeat.

After he departs, I last all of twenty minutes before I call Quinn. Not because I need to, but because I want to.

When she arrives, using the spare key to let herself in, she breezes through with groceries in hand. Looks down at me for a moment, asks if I'm okay, then carries on as if nothing were different. As if *I* were no different. I could've kissed her.

'Mushroom ravioli, as requested.' My mother's latest recipe. 'Do you need anything?'

'Yes,' I say, sitting up on the sofa. 'Tell me what happened with Cinar.'

She lets out a dramatic sigh. 'Oh god, he was all over me,' she says, unpacking her grocery bags in the kitchen. 'And I wasn't expecting it.'

She washes her hands, then returns to the conversation. 'To be honest, I think I dated him because I knew it'd be fleeting. I thought, "Oh, this guy won't want me for long, it'll be fun." And then he suggested we holiday overseas and I thought, *fuck*, he might just fall in love with me.' Beat. 'I just knew he'd never leave me, if things kept on. He should never have told me what he thought about divorce. Made me realise he'd cling to my body long after I was dead, you know?' She pauses, then shifts her stance. 'I remember loving Perry so much I wanted to be with him all day. Would've followed that man to his rural eggplant farm if he'd asked me.'

'And Cinar?'

'He did this thing where he'd walk two steps ahead and then call to me. "Come on," he'd say, but in this high-pitched voice like one might summon their dog. And he'd reach out and wiggle his fingers.'

She reenacts it, then continues. 'And whenever someone asked him how we met, he'd describe me as the black-haired woman with two rums who he met at the art gallery bar. Can't believe how often he narrowed me down to a hair colour. I don't even like rum – I ordered them by mistake. But I do think there is a plus in all this,' she says, slicing mushrooms. 'He told me, on multiple occasions, how nice it was to be with someone who had *lived*.'

'Lived?'

'*Lived*,' she repeats, and we both laugh. 'No doubt a comment on my age, which I'll remind you is only one year younger than him. So, I can't be certain, but I think he'll stop dating women in their early twenties now. He's got a taste for women his own age and now he's got an entirely new pool of people to meet.'

'Maybe that's why he dated the youth,' I say. 'Because they liked being smothered.'

'Or maybe they were doing the smothering, and that's why he got bored. Either way, I think Cinar will be just fine.'

This is the most I've heard about their relationship since they started dating. If this were Genevieve, I would've had daily updates. Weekly debrief sessions over a wine (or four). I would've known the breakup was coming.

'You could've told me,' I say. 'Any of this, or all of it. You could've told me.'

She counters. 'And you could've called me. When you had your fall.'

I hold her stare. 'I was worried I'd be a burden.'

She tips her head. 'Why would you think that?'

Because we haven't been friends for very long? Because I'd be uprooting your life? Or, perhaps, because I didn't know I could?

It still feels premature, to lean on her like that, but maybe I wasn't giving her enough credit. Looking at her as she cooks me dinner, and then glancing around at all the flowers and gift baskets, I realise that maybe Dave wasn't the only person in my life who would've helped me.

She returns to the kitchen and before long is searing chicken on a frying pan. 'When do you go back to work?'

'Not sure yet. I've taken a few weeks of personal leave.'

'Miss it?'

Graham's replacement was announced last week. Mid-forties, female, former journalist. Ivan and Dora, who met her briefly, learnt that she once broke a leg skiing and thus told me we'll have something to discuss – and bond over – when I return to the station.

'I do, actually.'

'Tell me more about Josie being drunk last night,' Quinn says. 'I've imagined it many times, but have yet to see it.'

'I've seen her drunk before, but this was different.'

She winces. 'Was it tragic?'

'More like someone who proposed in public but got a *no*. You just wish you weren't a witness She's usually so measured, but when she's been drinking it's like the crown topples off. Her mask comes down and behind it all she's just like us.'

Quinn tips her head back. 'This is going to sound mean—'

'Go on.'

She laughs. 'Before I met Josie, Cinar described her as if she were this long-haired, poised goddess. Calm and collected, you know?'

'And you don't agree?'

'I don't think I do. When I met her, it looked like someone had used a big spoon to gong her head. She's got this surprised look all the time. Confused. You know?'

There's a pause for a moment and then we're cackling.

'Is that mean?' she says, between laughs.

'Yes,' I reply. 'But you're not wrong. And now I can't unsee it.'

The sun has long set and the apartment grows dim. When Quinn turns on the light, she asks, 'Where will you live?' And I know, without her saying it, that she's talking about after I have my casts removed. When I no longer need help from Dave. 'Because I've got a spare room. Don't usually have anyone in it, but I could clear it out if you wanted it.'

'Oh.'

Quinn surprises me a lot. I'm never sure exactly what she's going to say, or how she might respond. I often wonder if she's bored with me, if I'm too predictable for her, and then she offers me a place to live and all my expectations are thrown.

I'd been trying so hard to replace Genevieve that it took me a while to realise Genevieve is not replaceable. And perhaps it's insulting to try and fit Quinn into that box. Quinn, who used to dress like a hobbit and doesn't feel one ounce of shame about it. Who coats her body in tattoos, who gives her opinion freely without worrying how it might affect my feelings. Who avoids commitment. Who ends a relationship, unbothered, with someone who might just be in love for the first time in his life.

I look at her, as she's preparing a meal for me, taking care of me, and I think, *You are nothing like Genevieve. You are your own person. And I think, in time, I could come to love you just as much as I love her.*

Later, after we've eaten and she's cleaned the kitchen, Quinn waits for Dave to come home before she departs. And when there's a quick rap at the door, we assume it's him. Perhaps he's forgotten his key, or his hands are full and he can't reach it. Perhaps he's just being lazy and knows that Quinn can open the door for him.

And so, neither of us is quite prepared to see Genevieve at the door, thirty-one weeks pregnant and furious.

'*You,*' she says, pointing. Charging forward, one hand under her bump. Behind her, I see Bruce, looking sheepish. 'You injure yourself like this and you don't tell me? I've been calling you for *weeks.*'

CHAPTER FORTY-FIVE

Two minutes of Genevieve yelling at me and Quinn decides to flee. 'Best I'm not here for this, I think. Call you tomorrow, Charlie,' she says, slipping out the door.

Her exit does not deter Genevieve. 'Look at you,' she says, which is meant to show sympathy but makes it sound like I'm dirty. 'I cannot believe this.'

She's in absolute disarray, from the top of her head right down to her toes. Her hair, now much longer, is yanked up into a bun – messy, big and a wee bit greasy. She's wearing an oversized, buttoned-up shirt, flared leggings, and sandals on her feet. Her ankles are swollen.

'Christ,' I say, because I'm afraid of her in this moment. Might be the most alarmed I've ever seen her. And even though I'm still *so* mad at her, my body is completely overtaken by guilt.

Bruce went to the bathroom almost as soon as they arrived and hasn't been seen since; I suspect he'd like to flee too.

'I knew something was wrong,' Genevieve says, folding her arms. 'I *knew* it. I cannot believe you didn't tell me about this.' Then she exhales, as if she's finally got it out of her system. She can relax, now she's reprimanded me for long enough. 'I need to sit.'

She searches the room. Up until now, she was just so furious with me, I think she forgot about her surroundings. 'Oh my god. What is *that*?'

She's seen Dave's purple couch. 'I know.'
'It's hideous.'
'I know.'
'What was he thinking?'
Then she looks at me, smiles, and we both say, 'He wasn't.'
Oh god, I've missed you. 'You want something to eat?' I ask. 'There's leftover mushroom ravioli in the fridge.'

She gags a little, hand to her mouth. 'I should, but I actually can't.' And then she plops down on Dave's couch. Exhausted, her head tips back and she closes her eyes for a moment. Removes the hair tie from around her red hair and lets it fan out over the purple material.

'How are you feeling?' I ask, wheeling myself towards her.

'Rough. I give pregnancy zero stars.' She then waves a hand in front of her face. 'You should hear me at night when I'm trying to sleep. I sound like a pug.'

'You look great.'

She opens one eye. 'Liar.' Then, both eyes open, she straightens. Sympathy crosses her face. 'I'm still angry with you.'

'I know.'

'How are you? Dave was vague on the details.'

'He called you? What a snake.'

She shrugs. 'I think he figured, well, you can't leave him *twice*.' Then she calls out to her husband. 'Bruce, stop hiding.'

Bruce walks out of the bathroom, hair at odd angles and bags under his eyes. Looking like he hasn't slept in days. 'Hey, Charlie.'

'You look terrible.'

He doesn't rebut me.

'How did you guys get here?' I ask, then nod towards Genevieve. Because we both know her doctor advised her not to fly after thirty weeks, and I know Bruce wouldn't let her defy that.

Genevieve and Bruce catch eyes, then he squirms and I put two and two together.

'Oh my god, did you *drive?*'

Silence.

'*Genevieve!*' I exclaim. 'That's like, sixteen hours.'

Bruce holds up a finger, smug. 'Did it in fifteen.'

'Speeding is not a flex,' Genevieve says. 'Go have a sleep. You look like shit.'

Bruce does not need to be told twice. He yawns, then disappears into the second bedroom.

I turn back towards Genevieve. 'You drove here? In one day?' I'm aghast, frozen in my chair.

'Not in one day.' Then holds up two fingers.

'You *drove* here, though.'

She is instantly defensive. 'You weren't answering my calls, or my text messages. I got worried. You're not supposed to stress out pregnant women, Charlie.'

And for the first time, I realise how that silence would've made her feel. Would've affected her. How selfish I was being. 'God, you're right. I'm sorry.'

She appears satisfied, running a hand over her belly. 'Look at you,' she says, running an eye over my body. 'I'm so sorry.'

'I fell down an escalator.'

She winces.

'I'm so embarrassed,' I say.

'Oh no, Charlie, don't be embarrassed.' She readjusts her position on the sofa. 'Are you in pain?'

'Sometimes,' I say. 'Mainly I'm just frustrated.' I'm so reliant on others, and for the first time in perhaps my whole life, I'm starting to crave being alone.

'Let me get you a glass of water,' I say, as I make my way over to the kitchen. It's a strain on my unplastered arm, and then one of the wheels gets stuck on the rug under the coffee table. It's a moment or two before I'm clear.

Genevieve quickly stands. 'Let me.'

'No, let me try.' After my accident, Dave moved an assortment of kitchenware – plates, mugs, cups, cutlery – and placed them all in the lower cupboard by the sink, so I could reach. I fish out a glass then stretch over to place it in the sink, turn on the tap and fill it.

Genevieve is beside me the entire time, as if waiting for me to make an error. 'I told you,' I say. 'Let me try. Go sit down.'

But she doesn't. Instead, she leans against the bench, looking down at me, arms folded across her chest. Glass of water forgotten.

'Are you going to tell me why you were avoiding me?'

I run a hand through my hair. 'Dave called to tell you about my fall but didn't tell you why I was ignoring you?'

'No.'

My hands turn into fists. 'That is classic Dave.'

But Genevieve doesn't care. There she is, looking at me expectantly.

'You told him I was planning to leave him.'

Recognition dawns, and her mouth forms an O. Uncomfortable, she looks away. Reaches up and touches her unbound hair. Then, visibly frustrated, she says, 'God, he *is* a snake, isn't he?' Sigh. 'Charlie, I'm so sorry.'

'When?'

She glances away, smacks her lips together. 'It was a while after you told me. I wasn't going to, of course. And I'm sorry I did. But that man was ruining a good thing.' She reaches across to squeeze my hand. 'I could see how much you were struggling and I thought it could be fixed.'

'I wasn't struggling.'

'You *were* struggling,' she reiterates. 'Most of the time you pretended everything was fine. But you'd make these snide comments, and I knew you weren't happy.'

I didn't realise I was doing that. I think of Josie and how she speaks about Shaun. Maybe we weren't so different after all, and that's why we're no longer able to be friends. We suited each other for a brief period in our lives, and now we're just too different.

'If it helps, he was distraught,' Genevieve says. 'Started crying. Didn't want to lose you. Realised he was being unfair.'

Oh. That doesn't make me feel better. Not at all.

'And then he proposed,' she says. 'And things seemed better.'

'For a while.'

'You never should've married him. I'm sorry.' She makes a strained face – chin tugged down, mouth wonky.

'I never should've moved here with him.'

She's alarmed, instantly. 'No, that's not it. Don't regret moving here. Your dreams were too big. And Dave was good for you, for a time. Got you out of your hometown, helped you settle here. But then—'

'We never should've got married.'

'No.' Guilt crosses her face. 'I'm sorry, Charlie, I never should've told him. If I didn't, he might not have proposed and maybe things would've been different.'

'Nothing would've been different,' I say. 'If I could go back in time, I'd end it long before then, but I didn't know, did I? Needed to live it, I think.'

We're silent after that. Me, contemplating everything. Genevieve taking deep breaths and indeed sounding like a pug.

Our eyes meet. 'I tried to replace you,' I admit.

'Oh.'

I grab at her hand. 'It's not the same.'

We say nothing further. Don't need to. We just stay together in silence – me, injured, and Genevieve pregnant – and know that even with other people in our lives, we need to make sure we have each other. In whatever format we can.

ISN'T IT NICE WE BOTH HATE THE SAME THINGS

My phone *pings* with a message from Naya. It's the first time I've heard from her since my visit home. Since she told me I'm dead to her. My first thought is Dave. Did that sneaky fucker call her too? But no, that's not it.

> Charlie, I'm in town in a few weeks for a wedding.
> Can I see you?

CHAPTER FORTY-SIX

One day later and I'm still flooded with alarm. 'Maybe there is no wedding and she's just coming here to yell at me.'

Genevieve frowns. 'That seems like a lot of effort, even for her.'

We've come to a local park for fresh air and some lunch – just the two of us. It's a bright, clear day. Warm, but not muggy. Everything is green after an evening of heavy rain, and there are scores of families here, setting up rugs for a picnic.

'She really told you that she thinks you *dead*.' Genevieve says it like a statement, not a question. I've filled her in on the anniversary and she's not stopped talking about it for the past ten minutes. 'What an awful thing to say.'

She walks slowly, guiding my chair. In my lap rests an insulated lunchbox packed with juice and sandwiches. She and Bruce are in a hotel nearby, even though I've insisted, many times, that I don't need them here. That they don't need to take care of me.

'I provoked her,' I say. 'I couldn't help it. Saw a button and I pushed it.'

Genevieve is still disturbed. 'I don't think that matters.'

Now out of breath and in need of a rest, she gestures to a nearby bench and sits, pulling everything out of the lunchbox and handing me a bottle of water. It takes a moment or two for her to find a position on the bench that is comfortable, and she groans as she goes through the endeavour. Presses a gentle hand to the side of her bump.

'Are you okay?'

She smiles. 'All part of it,' she says, then scratches. And scratches. And scratches. 'But the itchiness is killing me.'

'Itchiness?'

'Everyone experiences it,' she replies, as if she knows hundreds of pregnant women personally. 'Carpal tunnel, too.'

'Nine weeks to go,' I say, mostly to myself. 'I feel like I only just found out and now here you are, two months from birth.'

Her response is lethal. 'Well, I'm glad it's going fast for *you* – I want her out.' She looks down. 'Did you hear me? If you're one day over forty weeks, I'm going to reach in and pull you out myself.'

I admire the bossiness. 'You're going to be a great mum.'

'I know,' she says, leaning back on the bench.

'Have you finished the nursery?' I ask, because the last time we spoke about it, all they'd done is paint the walls. And I want to know if she's bought everything, or if she's still holding back.

'Almost,' she says. Then, assessing my stare, I can tell she knows what I've been thinking. 'I'm still terrified.'

'I'd be surprised if you weren't.'

She runs a hand over her stomach. 'I want her out, but I also want her healthy. If something happens—'

'Nothing is going to happen,' I say, cutting her off before she can tear up.

'I'm sorry.'

'Stop apologising.'

'No, not about the baby. About *you*. And Dave.' She reaches out and grabs at my hand. 'I never should've told him.'

I am silent, and bite into my sandwich – turkey, cranberry sauce, lettuce. Take a sip of my water.

'I thought I was helping. I wanted you to be happy. And at the time, I thought *he* could make you happy, but now I know you don't need anyone to make you happy.'

I'm slowly learning this too. I've been relying on others for a long time – years – and now I'm learning balance. Learning what it's like to be around the *right* people but also experiencing what it's like to survive on my own. If there's anything this year has taught me, it's that.

'I thought I could move away and things would still stay the same with us,' she says.

'They can't. But that's not a bad thing. It's just, different.'

'When you weren't returning my calls, I went a bit mad.'

'Oh god, I'm sorry.' I reach for her. 'I was being selfish, only thinking about myself. I didn't even realise what it would be doing to you.'

She nods, then points at me. 'I'm putting in a new rule. We speak at least three times a week on the phone. And we text.'

'Always.'

'And you don't ignore me again,' she says.

'That depends,' I joke. 'What else did you tell Dave?'

She looks unimpressed.

'I don't ignore you again. I promise.'

CHAPTER FORTY-SEVEN

A week passes – another seven days of healing and hurting and learning to be independent again – during which I'm confronted with reality: Dave is getting on my nerves.

At first, we were fine. Cordial. He felt sorry for me, I felt sorry for him, and we knew this was only temporary. But I'm now considering a coma, just for a break. Not sure how I managed to leave my husband just to live with him again.

(Obviously grateful he's looking after me and working very hard not to provoke him too much, else he wheels me out into the corridor, shuts the door, and forces me to fend for myself.)

'Can you turn your phone on silent?' he says, in the living room after it *pings* loudly with a text message. 'Haven't missed *that* since you left.'

It's his favourite new saying. *Haven't missed* that *since you left*.

'Haven't missed your frustrated snark,' I reply. We hold each other's gaze and enter a stalemate. I'm confident, without even asking, that he's just as annoyed as I am by this situation. He's been stomping around the place for days, snipping at me.

'I can move in with Quinn if I'm bothering you so much.'

'Don't be ridiculous, her building doesn't have an elevator. And you barely know her.'

'Funny,' I say. 'Sometimes I feel that way about you.'

Four more weeks until I'm cast-free, and I can move out.

Move on. Away from Dave, but also this overwhelming attention from others. I love my friends, I do, but Genevieve, Bruce and Quinn have been popping around almost every day and it's driving me a bit mad. Sometimes all I want to do is lie down in silence. I think of Graham's mansion and feel that would've been a great place to recover, if he hadn't sold it.

My phone beeps again – another text message from Graham checking in on me – and he groans loudly. 'Seriously.' Looking at me, he says, 'We might need some rules. No phones on loud.'

I add, 'Well then, no more complaining about visitors.'

'No more saying "Aaaaaahhhhhhh" after every sip of your coffee.'

'No more mumbling.'

He frowns, and suddenly, things accelerate.

I continue. 'No more eating with your mouth open and letting food fall onto the plate.'

'No more fake British accent when you're trying to be funny.'

'You told me you liked that!'

He looks pleased. 'Yeah, well, I lied.'

'No more lying.'

That one gags him for a moment, and guilt crosses his face. Then he recovers. 'No more pretending your family doesn't exist. And no more pretending you can do everything instead of asking for help.'

'Oh, come *on*, that one is valid. If I need other people to do everything for me, I might explode,' I say. 'And I don't forget that my family exist, I just . . .' I cannot seem to finish my sentence.

'I know.' Then he runs a hand through his hair, before meeting my eye again. 'How was it? The anniversary.'

Pause. 'You're not the only one who thinks I've forgotten my family.'

'Naya still taking care of your mother?'

'Every day.'

'Is that the reason you haven't told them about the accident?'

I nod. 'She'll turn up and take care of me. And I don't think that's very fair.'

'She's an adult – it's her choice.'

I shake my head. 'It's not a choice – she can't help it. My mother is perfectly capable of taking care of herself, she's just too nice to tell Naya that.'

He's silent for a moment, and without even asking, I know he's thinking about his mother. That downcast expression, that silence. It was a companion in our relationship for so many years.

He catches me watching him. 'I'm fine.'

'I hate it when you say that.'

'When I say that I'm fine?'

'When you *pretend* you're fine,' I say, letting out a frustrated groan. 'Do you have any idea what it was like for me, living with you? Trying to help you? It was killing me, Dave. *You* were killing me.'

He looks like he's been slapped.

'Genevieve tells you I'm thinking of leaving and you don't think to ask *why*?'

'I know why,' he says.

'No, you don't,' I say. 'You *don't*. I was going crazy. And I tried talking to you about it, but your mum was sick and you'd completely shut down and I realised we were *so* different and we barely spoke to each other. I had no one.'

'You didn't have no one.'

'I had you. I had Genevieve. That was it. Everything else was yours, not mine. And I didn't realise it until we split.'

He looks around, confused. 'So I'm the bad guy for letting you into my life? Introducing you to my friends? My parents? If it weren't for me, you'd still be stuck at that corner store.'

'I wouldn't,' I say, pointing at him, finger trembling. Making sure he knows how much I believe this. 'I would've left. Might've taken some time, might not have happened straight away, but I would've left.'

'Right. Okay.'

'God, I hate it when you say that. *Right. Okay.*'

He's about to combust. 'Jesus, what do you expect me to say?' he splutters.

'How about, sorry? Sorry, Charlie, that I shut you out. Sorry, Charlie, that I made you unhappy. Sorry, Charlie, that I wasted all that time you stayed with me because you felt too guilty to leave. And then when you *did* leave, sorry that I pestered you about an engagement ring you don't even have, because you lost it and I was too self-obsessed to even notice.'

He narrows his eyes. 'What?' His voice sounds guttural, sharp.

'The ring,' I say, slapping my hand onto my thigh. 'I lost it, eight months before we split.'

I couldn't do it. That afternoon with Quinn, I couldn't buy a replacement just to accelerate the separation. Couldn't justify the money, couldn't stand in front of Dave and pretend it was the same ring. Couldn't end our marriage on a lie. So, I'm doing what I should've done weeks ago – I'm telling him the truth and bracing for impact.

He pushes off from the sofa, steps closer to me. Affection gone. Smile gone. 'You lost it?' he asks, then looks down at my finger, as if needing to prove it's not there. 'Charlie, we had lawyers working on that settlement for months, waiting for that ring. You told me you had it.'

'No, I didn't.'

'You said you had it.' He's ferocious, fingers tense.

'You assumed I had it.'

He pauses, realises his error. Runs a hand through his hair in frustration. 'What a *complete* waste of everyone's time.'

'You're not going to ask me how I lost it?'

'Fine. How did you lose it?'

'It fell into the harbour.'

'Jesus Christ.' He rubs a hand over his chin. 'You lost it.'

'And you never noticed.'

That stops him where he stands, though there's still a fury in his face that he's doing his best to contain. 'You should have told me.'

I pick at my fingernails. 'I was trying to work out what to do. What to say to you.'

'The truth?' he says, hands on hips. 'How about that?'

'I was still so mad, in the beginning. Mad about her.'

He groans. 'At some point you're going to have to get over that. It's got nothing to do with you.'

'I will never get over it. *Never*. You have a *child*, Dave. A living, breathing child. And you treat her like she's nothing. The second I found out, there was no going back. Sometimes I wish it was an affair. I wish it was a woman and that you slept with someone else. I'd still hate you, but I wouldn't be so disgusted by you.'

He looks away.

'You kept that secret from me for years, and you had no right. Maybe I would've understood, if you told me from the beginning. *Maybe*. But you didn't give me the chance. Now you can tell your lawyer this is done. All of this is done. There's no ring, no possibility of a ring. After I move out, we move on. Live our lives.'

He points at me. 'Both of us are responsible here. *Both* of us. You were going to leave me.'

'I was *thinking* of leaving you.'

He scoffs. 'You never wanted to marry me. You never wanted *this*.' He gestures between us. 'You wasted my time.'

'*You* wasted *my* time.'

He is defiant. 'Both of us ended this marriage. *Both*.'

'I'm not accepting that,' I say. 'This is not *my* fault. I was there for you, the entire time. When your mum was sick, when you weren't speaking to anyone, when you weren't leaving the bed. I stayed with you.'

He stills, looking at me. Grave, haunted. 'You make it sound like it was a chore.'

Maybe it was, now that I think on it. 'You didn't try to save this until I was gone. You were surprised when I left, but you knew it was coming. You *knew* I was unhappy, and you didn't do anything about it.'

He wasn't expecting me to challenge him on it. I've stumped him for a moment, then he nods, as if accepting the retort. Holds up his hands. 'Okay, fine, yes. I didn't do anything about it. I can accept that.'

I press my fingers into my forehead, overwhelmed by where this argument went.

Dave is, evidently, not quite finished. 'God, this is so done, isn't it? We're so done.'

'We would've split eventually,' I say. 'If it wasn't me, it would've been you. This wouldn't have lasted forever. You know that, right?'

He doesn't answer me. Simply blinks, swallows, looks down, and then steps back. Straightened and stoic. Finally, he says, 'You're insufferable.'

'You haven't even told your dad we've split. It's been months.'

'I know how long it's been,' he snaps. He rests a hand on one hip, balls the other into a fist. 'I fucking loved you, you know. Why do you think I'm here? Looking after you. Do you know how many times I watched that video of Graham falling over, just so I could see you? You looked good. I hate that.'

The room grows silent, and neither of us quite know what to do. Dave starts wiping down the kitchen bench, which doesn't need wiping, and I pick at the frayed ends of my arm cast.

'Do you regret moving here with me?' he asks, finally. 'Do you wish you stayed?'

Those are two different questions, and I'm not sure if they have the same answer. Not that I need to give an answer, because he's already rattling off another one.

'Was I really killing you?'

And I'm certain of that one. Know exactly how I feel about that question. *Yes, you were. Slowly, piece by piece, you were killing us both.*

And I let you.

CHAPTER FORTY-EIGHT

Over the next few days, I become rather inventive around the apartment.

I loop a hair tie around the head of a water bottle so it can be carried more easily; I fasten a sponge to a pair of tongs for the shower; I clip a lanyard to my phone so it hangs around my neck and frees up my hands; I position the hat rack beside the bed so I can stand more easily. I start using a backpack for what might be the first time since school, and I buy one of those grabber toys so I can reach things on the floor like laundry and towels. Four times a day, I exit the apartment, ride the elevator down to the ground floor, circle around the block, and then return.

Slowly, day by day, I am regaining my independence.

Dave has been keeping his distance. Cooking, cleaning, helping me when I need it (and *only* when I ask for it), but largely leaving me alone. I don't even know where he is right now. He was gone when I woke, bleary-eyed as I tried to remember what day it was. Saturday? Monday? No, it's Friday. Definitely Friday.

Good lord, has Dave been working at all since I had my accident? I've been so wrapped up in myself, and then so furious with him, I never thought to ask.

*

During a moment of unearned confidence, I decide I'm going to cook some breakfast – an omelette.

I've grabbed a bulky, fluffed pillow from Dave's hideous lounge and slipped it underneath me as a booster. I'm grabbing plates and a spatula and a small frying pan from the lower cupboards. A small task but I feel triumphant.

Then I take one look at the stove and realise that even with a booster pillow – even with a second one – I can't see the omelette cooking unless I stand and balance on one leg. And sure, I can do that, but only for so long. I've barely used my muscles in weeks. I've got a minute, if that, before I have to sit back down.

And so it's a cycle of standing, checking and flipping the omelette, then lowering myself back down. And all the movement pains my limbs, and I'm sweating and I'm aching and a large part of me wants to cry because I feel I may have been too eager here. Maybe I'm not ready after all.

But I'm just so sick of relying on people. Every time someone offers to help me with something, I think of Naya. It's inevitable, and shame bleeds through my chest. I *still* have not told my family, and there's only so long I can hold off. She's going to be here soon and there'll be no hiding it then—

I flop back down onto the chair. My leg is quivering. The omelette isn't cooked through yet but I'm considering eating it anyway. How much longer is this going to take?

Up again. Flip.

Back down.

Up again. Flip.

Back down.

I fear I'm going to need a day-long nap after this. One meal and I'm done for. Up, down, up, down, up, down. Then, a minute or so later, I'm satisfied. I think the omelette is done. It certainly looks cooked. And if it's not, I'll inhale it anyway, because I'm starving and I'm tired and I'm ready to go back to bed.

But as I grab the pan handle and swivel my chair, I misjudge my grip and the whole thing slips out of my hand. It's like slow motion: I watch the pan drop to the floor, clatter and bounce, and my omelette splatters all over the tiles.

My resolve disintegrates along with it. 'Motherf—'

'*Charlie.*'

I turn, and realise Dave is standing at the threshold of the apartment, a plastic chair in his left hand and his wallet and keys in the other. His face looks stricken.

'Jesus, Charlie, what are you doing?' He drops his things and darts forward to the kitchen. Turns off the stove, picks up the pan and throws it into the sink, then grabs a cloth and swipes up all the scattered omelette from the floor. 'Are you okay?'

'I just wanted to cook myself breakfast.' I move away. 'This is so *frustrating.*'

'You still have three more weeks.'

'Yes, Dave, I know that. Thank you.'

He lets out an exhausted sigh, tosses the cloth in the bin. Then, hands on hips, looks me in the eye. 'I thought we agreed. You call Genevieve if you need something – she's around the corner.'

'I *want* to do things myself.'

'Well then, maybe start with some toast next time. Not an omelette.' He's laughing.

'I was doing so well.'

'You burnt the shit out of it,' he says, amused. Picks up the bin from the counter and angles it so I can see the remnants of the omelette inside – charred.

'Damn it.' I sigh.

Sympathy crosses his face. Lines etched across his forehead, sagging shoulders, his mouth a thin line. 'I'm sorry.'

'For my burnt omelette?'

'For everything.' He leans against the counter. Then, finding the words, he says, 'I pestered you for that engagement ring because I was angry at you for leaving.'

'You didn't even notice I lost it.'

He is morose. 'In my mind, we were fine. Before you found out about everything, we were fine. But we weren't doing well, were we?'

'No, Dave, we weren't.'

He nods, straightening. Grabbing the frying pan and placing it in the dishwasher.

'Where were you? I woke up and you were gone.'

'Oh. I just . . .' He gestures to the front door, where he'd dumped the plastic chair. 'Bought you a new one for the shower. Noticed the old one was uneven in the legs.'

'Right.' I'm a real arse.

'But, you know, I'll toss it if you don't want the help. If that's something you'd prefer to buy yourself.' He smiles, genuine, and I am reminded of his best trait – selflessness. And so maybe it isn't guilt that has him helping me. Maybe he's helping me because he wants to. Because he knows it's the right thing to do.

CHAPTER FORTY-NINE

Ivan and Dora arrive Sunday evening to take me out of the apartment for a couple of hours – it's like day release, for prisoners. Ivan, wearing a new pair of trousers, refers to it as a rescue mission.

'Blink twice if you'd like us to arrange a hit,' he says, about Dave, as we exit the apartment building. 'We'll take him to a farm and shoot him, like a cow.'

'We're okay now, I think.'

Together, they bring me to a nearby pub. An old-town English sort of pub, with earthy wooden walls and cobblestone steps, mismatched tables, a jukebox, and a warm glow in the windows as light beacons from inside.

We secure a table out the front, and they help me park my wheelchair. Once we're settled, Dora says 'Right then' and orders us all dinner, nibbles and a round of drinks.

Once she's back, a bowl of fries now on the table, Ivan catches my attention. 'Do I look slimmer?' he asks. 'Since you last saw me?'

No.

'Yes.'

'Knew it.' He's chuffed.

'He's on a new diet,' Dora says, rubbing her brow.

'Instead of snacking,' Ivan starts, 'I just . . . don't eat.'

'Right,' I say.

Dora then turns to me, placing a hand over mine. 'How *are* you?'

'Oh, we don't need to talk about me. I'd love it if we don't.' I shake my head in Ivan's direction. 'Let's go back to talking about Ivan.'

'Great,' he says. 'I love talking about me.'

Dora chuckles. 'Wait until he tells you about the conversation with his aunt this morning.'

Ivan's face stills, darkening. He's been betrayed.

'Why?' I ask. 'What happened with your aunt?'

Ivan eventually relents, extracting his phone from his pocket. Opens his text messages, then slides the phone across the table. 'She got engaged over the weekend, so I messaged her.'

> Congratulations on your engagement! So exciting.

> Aw, thank you! Your mum tells me you've been to two warehouse sales this month, how amazing!

'Oh no.' That's all I can manage, I'm afraid, because I'm completely taken by laughter. Deep, guttural belly laughs that have me curled over, hand to face.

Dora is in fits, small tears pooling in the corners of her eyes, her cheeks reddening.

'Mortifying,' Ivan says, hands flat on the table. 'I'm *mortified*. I will not be replying.'

Dora leans forward. 'I've thought about nothing else all morning.'

Another laugh, and I'm reminded of how things used to be. Before the fall. Before Graham left. How much time I spent with these two – how much I enjoyed being with them.

'I want to know everything,' I say, sipping my drink.

And so, they rattle through all the updates from the past few weeks, like items from a catalogue.

'Wedding planning is almost done. Just need the dress tailored.'

'Landlord refused to do anything about the mould, so I've found a new apartment.'

'Cleaver's got the flu, the poor thing.'

'I've actually been to *three* warehouse sales this month.'

Then, finally, Dora says, 'And we're loving the new host.' The conversation stills. I sit straighter, look between Ivan and Dora. Dora, unable to meet my eye. Ivan, wincing.

God.

In all the commotion of my recovery, I'd completely forgotten that this was her first week on air. I haven't been listening at all, have no idea how she's going.

'Oh,' I say. 'So, she's good then, is she?'

'Dora's exaggerating,' Ivan says, and I see him kick her under the table. 'She's clunky, still finding her feet.'

'She's not *clunky*,' Dora says. 'You're making that up.'

'I'm trying to make Charlie feel better,' he says, gesturing to me. 'Grandpa was her favourite.'

'Stop calling him grandpa,' Dora says.

'Five-time divorcée.'

'That's worse.'

'Bald.'

'*Ivan.*'

'Empty nester.'

'His housekeeper lived there,' Dora counters.

'No, she didn't,' I interject. 'I was crashing there, for a while.'

Ivan drops his fries. 'What?'

'I lived with him. Those last few months before he left.'

'You secretive bitch! Why didn't you invite us round?'

'I thought you'd gossip.'

'You're damn right I would've gossiped.' Ivan is aghast. 'Tell me everything.'

'Not much to tell, really. It was a house.'

'A house? That's it? That's all we get?' he asks, dismayed. 'Did you rotate through all the bathrooms? Use a different toilet every time? I would've pissed in all his pools.'

'There were only two.'

'*Only?*'

Dora adds, 'Quickly, tell us the best and worst part of it all.'

'Best part, the space. Worst part, the space.'

'Oh, it must be very hard living in a mansion,' Ivan says, rolling his eyes.

'It *was*. Much lonelier than I would've thought. I didn't always see him. It's a bit big, for two people.'

They're quiet, pensive.

'I still can't believe he's gone,' I say. 'If they'd given us more time. Another year, or even six months, we could've turned it around. I'm sure of it.'

Ivan looks away. Dora gives me an encouraging smile. 'I know.'

'But she's good?'

Dora and Ivan look at each other. 'We think so,' Dora says. 'She's got some great ideas. And she's funny. And she's—'

'Young?' I ask.

Dora shakes her head. 'She's *different*, Charlie. Quirky. Energetic. Eager. And I hate to say it, but she's current. Sometimes I felt like Graham was just going through the motions, doing the same thing he'd been doing for years.'

Yes, but that's what so many people loved about him. That's what *I* loved about him. He was familiar, he was confident. He was a comfort.

'There must be *something* you don't like about her.'

Ivan is quick. 'She's got orange hair.'

'Stop,' Dora says, horrified. 'She doesn't have orange hair. It's brown.'

'It's a dark orange,' he says.

Dora laughs. 'It's *brown*. Regular brown hair.'

Ivan shrugs, disinterested. 'She did wear a nasty pink sweater one day,' he says. 'It wasn't serving.'

'I swear, you'd rather die than be positive about anything,' Dora adds.

Ivan flips her off, then grins.

Dora, ignoring him, checks to make sure I'm okay. Leans towards me, smiles. 'Brown hair or not, she said she's looking forward to meeting you. And we're all excited to have you back soon.'

Straightening, I continue. 'Do you think people blame me? For what happened to Graham?'

Dora's head tips. 'Why would people blame you?'

'I oversee the show. I craft the segments—'

'It's not your fault,' Ivan says, sincere. 'And it's not Graham's fault, either. I think people were just ready for a change. Someone different.'

'And you can't say you didn't try,' Dora says. 'You never left the station. You were far too obsessed with building an amazing show. With saving him.'

My mouth twists. 'I think part of that was me hiding from Dave, too.'

'Knew it.' Ivan snaps his fingers. '*Knew* that's why you stayed back. Never came drinking with us until you left him.' He looks at Dora. 'Don't you remember? I said to you, there's no *way* she's happy with that brand of vanilla if she's staying *here* all the time.'

That reminds me. 'I see what you mean now,' I say to Ivan. 'He definitely looks like unbuttered bread.'

Ivan reaches out and grabs my hand. 'You've escaped, that's the main thing.'

CHAPTER FIFTY

'Do you need me to get you anything? Some water? Coffee? Maybe a pillow for your back?'

Genevieve has overstayed her welcome. She's not even living here and she's overstayed it.

'I'm okay, honestly.'

She's been faffing about the apartment at all hours of the day. Vacuuming, cooking, cleaning, scrubbing the toilet, wiping down the cupboards, steam-cleaning the lounge. She orders Dave around like he's my servant and I can tell he feels uncomfortable. It seems to be this unspoken competition between the two of them – who can tend to me the most.

But at least Dave lives here! If anyone should be scrubbing a toilet, it's him.

'Genevieve,' I say, holding out a hand as she darts into the spare bedroom to strip the bedsheets. 'You don't need to do any of that. I'm getting pretty good at it.'

She walks back out, horrified. 'You've been washing your own bedsheets? With a broken arm and a broken leg? *Dave* is making you do that?'

Dave, who is in the apartment and sitting over at the dining table, is offended at the allegation. 'Excuse me. She insists on doing it. Any time I've attempted to help, she's squealed at the top of her lungs like a dog.'

We catch eyes, and laugh.

I turn back to Genevieve. 'Please stop.'

'Okay, okay.' She raises her hands, surrendering. 'No bedsheets. I'll get started on the meal prep.'

'You're thirty-four weeks pregnant.'

'And?' Hand on hip, she looks murderous. Then, when I don't reply, she stomps into the kitchen and starts pulling out groceries and pans to cook.

Honest to god, I need to get rid of her. One, it's wildly unnecessary and bordering on slave labour. Two, she's on maternity leave and should be resting. And three, she's reminding me of Naya right now, in the years after Dad died. I love her, I really do, but this cannot continue.

'Genevieve, stop.'

Dave nods. 'Yes, Genevieve, please stop.'

'Dave, I cannot *believe* you let her wash her own sheets.'

'Genevieve, go home, please,' I say.

She shakes her head, and her hair flutters around her face. 'Not yet. I'll just do this and then head back there.'

'I don't mean your hotel,' I say. 'I mean your real home.'

She stops, then, turning to me. 'What?'

'Go home.'

She splutters, 'But I'm here to help.'

'I don't need it.'

Dave catches my eye, whispers, 'Thank you,' and puts his hands together as if in prayer. Then he scurries off to his bedroom. He never did like being around Genevieve when she was in a mood.

'I get my casts off in ten days,' I say. 'And I've survived a month already. I'm *fine*.'

She struggles to comprehend that she is not needed. Turns around in a circle, as if looking for some kind of task. 'There must be something I can do.'

'Yes, there is.' I rub a hand along my jaw. 'You can go home and rest.'

She rolls her eyes, then walks over to me. Perches herself on the edge of the lounge, her belly protruding and her hands resting atop it. 'I don't want to leave you.'

'I'll be fine.'

'I know you'll be fine,' she says. 'But if I leave, I won't get to see you every day anymore.'

'Oh.' I shuffle closer to her.

'And I'm worried I won't hear from you again,' she says. 'I'll be waiting by the phone like I was before.'

I sigh. Jesus, I really hurt her. 'I promise I'm not going to do that again. I'll be calling, and messaging. I was mad before, and I was only thinking about myself. And I'm *sorry*.'

'I blame Dave,' she says, raising her voice. 'What a snitch.'

From the bedroom, he calls out, 'I've missed you too, Genevieve.'

She turns to me. 'If I get even the slightest whiff that something is wrong, I'm forcing Bruce to drive me back down here.'

'You're a good friend.'

'I know.'

CHAPTER FIFTY-ONE

Dave finds me lying atop the spare bed on Thursday evening. 'Are you all right?'

'Genevieve is gone. They left a couple of hours ago.' And I needed a moment, I want to say. Because I've just had to experience her leaving, again. Because the next time I'll see her, in a mere few weeks, she'll be a mother, and it feels like we're about to arrive at something monumental and I want a moment to acknowledge it.

He walks further into the room and lies down next to me. Shuffles a little and rests his hands – clasped together – over his belly. He's been to see his dad today, and the drive home appears to have tired him. Under his eyes, the skin is a little sunken. His hair's been tugged in all sorts of places.

Together, we stare at the ceiling – white, tinged with yellow, faint hairline fractures in the centre. In the corner, an old water stain has returned – dark, the size of my torso.

'Look,' I say, pointing at it.

And he groans, frustrated. 'Damn it.'

'You should get someone back out to check—'

'All right, all right,' he says, silencing me. He did always hate it when I had to remind him of things. Even when I was right.

He raises his left hand, turns it over and then back the other way. 'I told my dad,' he says. 'About us.'

'Oh.'

'He said he's going to miss you.' Then, there's the hint of a smile. 'And that he suspected it.'

'Six months, Dave, of course he suspected it.'

Dave looks back at the ceiling. Mulling it over.

'Why didn't you tell him before?'

He turns to look at me, with a stricken expression. Eyes, heavy. Brow, furrowed. And I just *know*.

For me, this relationship was over a long time ago. But for him, it's only just happened. It wasn't me leaving him, or me moving out. It wasn't the separation agreement or the shattering of our mutual friendships. I can sense, just by looking at him, that telling his father was Dave's way of acknowledging that this marriage was completely severed, unsalvageable.

'I'm sorry,' he says. 'That I was slowly killing you. I didn't realise. If I could go back, I'd change so many things.' He shifts, rolling over to face me. Head rested in a hand, propped up by an elbow. 'I would've told you about her at the start.'

He draws circles into the patterned mauve bedcover as he speaks. 'I would've handled things better when my mum was sick.'

It's comforting to hear that he acknowledges his behaviour – I like hearing it.

'She wasn't supposed to die like that,' he says. 'Everything in her body shutting down, slowly. Sometimes I felt like you were lucky. Your dad wasn't in any pain.'

I stiffen. 'I don't think either situation is ideal.'

He's nodding before I've even finished my sentence. 'I know, I know. I just mean—'

'I know what you mean.' Because I can remember what she was like as we progressed towards the end. How her body started to fail her, and she couldn't walk. Or use her arms. Needed assistance to breathe, and Dave was making sure the machine was serviced every few months. The infections, and the swallowing difficulties. His mother was dying before his eyes and there was nothing he could do about it.

'It's only been three years, and I think about her every day. One day it'll be twenty years,' he says. 'I don't know how you handle that. He's been gone from your life longer than he was in it.'

That's the first time I've realised that, and it hollows me out. All these years I've been robbed of him. Robbed of conversation, of his cooking. Robbed of him walking me down the aisle. Robbed of his advice and his perspective. Robbed of the happiness he gave those around him – robbed of seeing Mum light up when he was near.

I brush away tears.

Dave goes to comfort me, almost out of instinct, but stops himself. Instead, he murmurs, 'You never spoke about him. In the beginning, I wondered if you were estranged, and then I realised that was just your way of dealing with it.'

I smile, grim. 'I should've handled things differently too. I couldn't even tell you what his favourite film was.'

I can't decide what's worse – that Dave is still mourning his mother, and that he cannot forget her, or that I tried too hard to forget my father. And because of that, I barely remember anything about him.

'If I didn't think about him, I could forget how devastated I was that he was gone,' I say. 'I think that was my strategy.'

He holds my gaze.

'I was so mad that I missed his final moments. *So* mad. And it's stupid, I know. But I wish I was there when it happened. I felt so alone, when I found out how he'd died. And I never wanted to feel that again.'

This time, when he reaches for me, he doesn't stop himself. And I let him squeeze my hand.

'When I met you, I think I was looking for an even greater way to forget him,' I say. 'And moving away did that.'

He nods and bites his lower lip. And I let myself think on that for a beat longer. *When I met you, I think I was looking for an even greater way to forget him. And moving away did that.*

The guilt is all-consuming. Maybe, after all that, Dave was right. Maybe he wasn't the only one responsible for the downfall of our marriage.

CHAPTER FIFTY-TWO

Ivan and Dora have joined me at an apartment inspection, as I prepare for my casts to be removed next week.

'Well, it's no work of art,' Ivan says, hands on hips, face tipped upwards as he looks around the place. 'But at least Dave doesn't live in this one.'

Two bedrooms, oak floorboards, high egg-white ceilings. The apartment has been staged with furniture, and I run my hand over the gas-lift bar stools as we pass them. There's a paved courtyard downstairs, which feels a bit flash. Long and thin, and no in-built wardrobes, the whole place can be toured in under five minutes.

'You could afford bigger,' Dora says, as we move through the kitchen.

Dora's done a test run of her wedding glam – her skin fake-tanned golden brown, hair curled into a low bun with extensions for volume, a thin layer of make-up with smoky eye – and I'm afraid I barely recognised her when she arrived. Ivan was so taken aback by her new look he was stunned into silence for a good ten seconds.

'Not sure I need bigger,' I say. Because I've had that, in Graham's house, and I don't crave it. Don't feel at home in such a big place. What would I even do with more bedrooms? More space to self-loathe, I guess. How morose!

Ivan does not share the same opinion. 'Can't believe you never told us you lived with him.' He shakes his head, disappointed in me.

'It wasn't all that great,' I say again, assessing the bathroom from the threshold. The doorway is far too narrow for the chair, and I fear I'll get trapped inside if I proceed. But I stretch forward and scan what I can from here – the black-and-white titles, the shower over the bath, the mirror cabinet.

'Right, okay, sure,' Ivan says from behind me. He's now collapsed on the sofa and is flicking through his phone. 'Grandpa had his own *housekeeper*.'

His own housekeeper, cleaning team, pool cleaner and groundskeeper. But I don't tell them that, of course. Need to keep *some* level of mystery (and I fear Ivan's poor heart would seize).

I capture a brief video of the place and send it to Genevieve, and she responds straight away.

Cute!

The speed in which she replies to my messages always feels like a personal attack – a reminder that she fears I'm going to hurt her again. I miss having her nearby, but I know how happy she is to be home.

'Oh god,' Dora exclaims, as she walks into the bathroom and sees herself in the mirror. She turns her head – one way, then the other – and winces. 'The lighting in here is a lot harsher. Do I look okay?'

Ivan catches my eye.

'Too much fake tan?' she says, stretching out her arms, borderline panicky.

Ivan and I say nothing, for a moment. She looks swish, but she doesn't resemble herself. She's usually so pale, and fair skinned. Hair short, thin and flat. Fingernails, unpainted. Ears, bare. Eyebrows, unsculptured and certainly not as dark as they are today.

'You look good,' I say. And Ivan nods, although he cannot look at her directly.

'Not too orange?'

I consider being honest. Then, instead, say, 'You look fancy.'

'Is that a good thing?'

'Fancy is good,' Ivan says, and then he ducks off into the bedroom. I fear if he stays any longer, he'll start being honest and then we're all in trouble.

'What about my make-up?' she says, fingers pressing gently on her cheeks.

'It looks nice.'

'Just nice?'

I don't know what I'm supposed to say. She looks lovely. But she looked lovely before.

'This is the first time I've had acrylic nails,' she says, extending out her hands. 'Maybe they're too long—'

'Right then,' Ivan says, re-entering the room. 'Shall we head?' He's jittering, bored. Never can sit still for too long.

All talk of Dora's new look ceases, and we tell the real estate agent, who until now has been hovering near the door, we're ready to leave. 'Thank you,' we all chime, and he nods. It's remarkable how well-dressed all the agents are – primed and sleek.

Angling towards Dora and Ivan, I say, 'Thank you for coming.'

'Of course we came,' Dora replies. 'We're friends.'

It's the first time she's said that about me – *friends*. And it makes me smile, makes me giddy. *Friends*. How juvenile, for me to hold onto that word. But how lovely it is to hear someone say it for the first time.

Before we exit the apartment, I grab her hand and hold her back. 'Your wedding photos,' I say. 'Your parents will frame them and put them all around their house. They'll live on your social media, and every year, on your anniversary, you'll see them as a reminder. It's inevitable. So, you need to be happy with how you're going to look on the day because if you *don't*, you'll wish you could go back in time to this moment' – I point at the ground – 'and tell yourself to change it.'

She is rooted to the floor for a moment, looking down. Then, she quickly ducks into the bathroom again. Takes one brief look at herself and loses the plot. 'Cleaver's going to think he's at the wrong wedding. I look like my great aunt Cynthia.'

Ivan hides a laugh.

She is still horrified. 'I'm going to tell them to strip it back. This isn't me.'

'I think that's a good idea.'

I laugh, and Ivan steps forward. Places a hand in front of him, as he delicately chooses the right words. 'Does this mean I have permission to make fun of you now? Because your skin is the colour of clay.'

Dora howls with laughter, hands straight to her face in shame.

CHAPTER FIFTY-THREE

I tell Naya to meet me at a café for brunch, and then I make a disastrous attempt at hiding my injuries. I don't want her to see me and worry. I don't want her to be struck by *another* injured family member. Don't want her to think I've turned into Leonard. Don't want her to know I did this because I was trying to message her and apologise (which I now realise I never ended up doing).

I cover my arm with a shawl even though it's far too warm. Angle the chair so the table somewhat hides my leg. Position my body so I don't look too rigid. Put a smile on my face so my anxiety is not immediately obvious.

It takes Naya less than one second to see through the charade.

'Oh god,' she says, reaching forward and grabbing at the shawl. Looking at my plastered leg and arm, jaw open. 'What has happened?'

It's been years since I've seen her without the children. And she looks *good*. Handbag over one shoulder, she's had her nails done, painted shellac and deep red in colour. Her hair recently trimmed and skin smooth and moisturised. She's wearing her nice clothes – ironed, that's how I know – and I suspect she's plucked her eyebrows.

'I fell down an escalator.'

'Who falls down an escalator?' Then immediately catches herself. 'God, sorry, my brain thought you were Leonard and just went straight to frustration.'

'I'm fine, really,' I say, holding up my good arm to reassure her. 'Pain is mostly gone and the casts come off later this week.'

She stumbles a little, after that. 'When?' Hands in the air. 'How?' Hands through her hair. Tries to get more words out. Fails.

Then she straightens, looks around at the café. Glances back outside to the road. 'How did you get here?'

And then I point behind me, at the table in the corner. Dave is seated with a latte, toasted banana bread, and his laptop. Working through inventory for his dad. 'I've been staying with him while I recover.'

That stuns her so much, she's forced to sit to collect herself.

'I know,' I say, reading her expression.

Then Dave sees her looking and holds up a hand. Waves and smiles (he always did like her). Naya returns it. 'Is it weird he's over there by himself? Should he join us?'

'No, best pretend you don't see him.'

Then Naya holds up both hands, her head snapping back. 'I have so many questions, but . . .' She trails off, rising again. Turns towards the counter. 'I need something for this.'

I think she's going to come back with coffee, but she returns with a bottle of wine.

Later, once I've filled her in, she tells me she needs a moment to process it all. Just cannot seem to understand how I managed to fall.

'I wasn't paying attention,' I say. 'I was distracted.'

'With what?' she asks, and I'm not sure how to respond. Because I don't want to lie to her, but I don't want her feeling guilty.

'Oh.' She sits back. Perhaps does the maths in her head, with the timing. 'After we fought.' She looks away. 'I've been wanting to apologise. I can't believe how I sounded. I heard it, you know? That night, I was thinking about it and thought, *That's not me.*'

She reaches out and grabs my hand. 'I don't want you feeling guilty for leaving.'

Looking down, I realise I've drained my first glass of wine already. 'Thank you. But you were right about Mum. You and Leonard have been doing everything.'

She smiles, as if appreciative. As if thankful for the acknowledgement. Then tucks her hair behind her ears and I'm reminded of her appearance.

'Whose wedding is tomorrow?'

'Juliet and Bruno.'

'Who?'

'You know, Juliet and Bruno.' She clocks my dubious expression and huffs. 'I went to school with Juliet.'

'And you're invited to their wedding? How long has it been since you saw them?'

She bites her lip. 'I was a bit surprised by the invitation but thought it'd be nice to go. See them.'

'And you wanted a break from the kids.'

She folds immediately. 'Of course I wanted a break from the kids. I've got enough children to start a band. You know, if they had any talent.'

After a moment, she looks over my injuries again – my leg, first, then my arm. Pushes her wine glass away, for a moment. 'Why didn't you call? You ring Dave, of all people. You don't tell us? You don't tell *me*?'

'I didn't want to worry you.'

She narrows her eyes. 'You were calling me every second day until you came home for the anniversary. And then, nothing.'

'I thought you didn't want to speak to me.'

'I didn't. But, come on Charlie, this is big.'

I pour a second glass of wine. 'You have four kids, Naya. I didn't want to inconvenience you—'

'Bullshit.'

And so the excuses continue. Because I don't want to hurt her feelings.

'I wanted to get better first.'

'Bullshit.'

'I wanted to find out how bad my injuries were before I called.'

'Bullshit.'

I look away, ashamed. I crack a couple of knuckles. 'You've spent years taking care of other people. And I knew that if I called, you'd both be here taking care of me. You, especially. And I didn't want to put you in that position.'

She is silent for a few moments. 'I've been trying this new thing where I let Mum do things by herself. It's been very freeing – should've started sooner. I've told Leonard he shouldn't fix her place anymore. If something is broken, we'll get someone in.'

'*We'll?*'

She realises her mistake. Smiles. '*Mum* will get someone in.'

'You were treating her like she's a relic.'

'And you were treating her like she didn't exist.'

Silence.

'I'll call her when these casts are off. Tell her what's happened.' Then, I point at Naya. 'Don't tell her before I get the chance. I know you're itching to do it.'

'You're going to visit home more often, right?' she asks.

And suddenly, I'm thinking about Mum. About the anniversary and the fight, and the fact that Raphael didn't recognise me. About Dad, and how I can no longer remember what he smelt like – how he sounded.

'My biggest regret is that I wasn't there when he died. Which seems odd, because you *were* there and it affected you as well. But I just wish I could've been there for his final hours, and every time someone brings him up, I feel that again.' I roll my shoulders back.

'I feel Dad in every room of that house, and I felt like Mum was just waiting for an opportunity to bring him up in conversation. When Mum said she was organising something for the twentieth anniversary, I felt like I couldn't breathe.'

Naya doesn't argue. 'I'd be lying if I said I wasn't jealous when you left home.'

'You could've left, if you wanted to.'

'I couldn't,' she says. 'You know I couldn't. If you'd seen Mum. If you'd heard her that day, you wouldn't ever have left.'

I nod. 'Dad's death forced your hand, and that's not fair on you. I'm going to visit more, I promise.'

'Thank you.'

I do my best to keep the next question delicate. 'What were you like, before his death? Mum mentioned it, and you wouldn't tell me. About how you changed when he died.'

'We all changed.'

'I know,' I say. 'I moved across the country with someone I didn't really know because of that day. And we know how Dad's death affected Mum. But you? Maybe I was too young.'

'Or you just forgot,' Naya says. 'It's been a long time – I wouldn't expect you to remember who I was before his death.'

I nod again, tucking a piece of hair behind my ear.

Finally, after a moment of silence, Naya leans in. 'I didn't want children,' she whispers, almost like she doesn't want anyone to hear.

'What?'

'I didn't want children,' she repeats. 'And I know I was sixteen, so I could've just been thinking that because I *was* a child, but I remember being adamant that I was never going to be the kind of person who settled down young. I wanted to travel. Explore. Work. I never saw myself getting married before thirty. I certainly didn't see myself with four kids.'

She straightens and continues. 'But then Dad died, and things changed. I had a mother who couldn't get out of bed and a sister who needed to go to school. Suddenly I felt much older. I felt this heightened level of responsibility. And all the things I thought I wanted? I think I realised it might be a lonely life,' she says. 'Something about being around Mum after it happened, and taking care of you. What I'd hoped to be doing when I got older just didn't seem to matter anymore.' She shrugs. 'I guess my priorities changed.'

She takes one final sip of her wine. 'I couldn't imagine anything different now, to be honest. Sometimes when it's quiet, late at night or perhaps in the morning when the kids haven't yet woken, I think of Mum. Her face when I ran into their bedroom. The sounds that came out of her mouth – it was more horrifying than seeing Dad's body next to her. And I guess, since then, I've felt this great need to keep people close to me. Like perhaps they could disappear at any moment, and so I can't possibly leave them.'

I reach forward and clasp Naya's hand, because she's crying again, and I want to reassure her. This is the best – and one of the only ways – that I know how.

Naya offers a smile. 'I've spent most of my life taking care of other people. And it was necessary at first, but then it wasn't and I kept going. I never learnt to stop.'

Then, she catches eyes with Dave. 'Am I really supposed to pretend I don't see him? It's weird.'

I lower my voice. 'He's got a daughter, almost eighteen. I found the paperwork when he hurt his hand.'

'Oh.' Naya sits back. 'Well, fuck.'

'And he doesn't see her.'

'*Ever?*'

I shake my head. 'Has never met her.'

Her eyes widen, and then she picks at her fingers. 'That's why you left?'

'One of the reasons.'

She nods. Then smiles. 'What about how he eats his food?'

'That was another.' And together, we glance behind us at Dave. Watch as he eats his banana bread. Watch as some of it falls out of his open mouth as he chews. Naya laughs.

'This is all your fault, if you think about it. You kept telling me I barely knew him and I wanted to prove you wrong.'

She is horrified. Juts a finger into the table. 'You *didn't* know him. The man has secret offspring.'

And then we're laughing again.

CHAPTER FIFTY-FOUR

One thing I've always found remarkable about Dave is how easily he forgets juicy information. He could be with the boys all day, come home, say it was fine but then later that night, on the verge of falling asleep, he'll say, 'Did I tell you Emmanuel is considering plastic surgery on his biceps? Did I tell you Cinar wants to trek to Everest Base Camp? Did I tell you Shaun's got a troubling mole on his elbow and Josie's nicknamed it Molar Bear?'

And so, when we're in the doctor's office waiting for my cast removal and Dave tells me he has *news*, and that he only found out five minutes earlier in a text message from Josie, I know it's going to be good. And when he says it's shocked him, and that he cannot believe it, I know it's going to be *really* good.

'They've split.'

'Who?'

'Josie and Shaun,' he says, staring down at his phone. Complete shock written across his face. 'They've split.'

'Holy—'

'I know.'

'What happened?'

'I don't know.'

'Did Shaun leave her?'

'I don't know.'

'Has one of them moved out?'

'I don't know.'

I point at his phone. 'Well, find out. What do you mean you don't know?'

'She *just* texted me.'

'Have you replied?'

'Not yet. It feels personal,' he says. 'It *is* personal.' Then looks at me as if to say, *You remember, don't you?*

'Call her after this. Check she's okay.'

'Yeah all right.' Then he nudges me, grabs my attention. 'What makes you think Shaun left? Josie could have left.'

'Josie's the one who messaged,' I say. State it like it's a fact. An easily understandable piece of information.

'And?'

'When I left you, how did the group find out?'

Dave sits back. 'Ah.' Because he messaged them all. Because he was devastated, and shocked, and needed comfort from his friends.

'We should go see Josie,' he says. 'I'll call her, find out where she is. And then we should go see her.'

'And Shaun,' I add.

He looks at me and frowns, as if the thought hadn't occurred to him.

'And Shaun,' I repeat. And then, when he says nothing, I continue. 'Why do we do that? Pick sides.'

'I'm not picking a side.'

'You're picking a side.'

He splutters a little, lost. 'I'm no— I don—' Then he straightens. 'I've been friends with Josie since high school.'

'And she's been with Shaun for six years.'

He extends his hands, as if grabbing at air. 'Am I *not* supposed to go see her?'

'You're not supposed to forget about Shaun.'

'Who says I was?'

'You did. Just now,' I say. 'I've seen this before. At Josie's birthday, and our coffee date. In those group messages, and Diego running away from me at the mechanic. The little fuck.'

Dave chuckles. 'That was a bit funny.'

'I was heartbroken. I considered keying his car.'

'His car is trash. Keying it would've improved it.'

Outside the doctor's office, we hear staff making an almighty fuss about a crashed IT system. Someone pops their head in to tell us it won't be long, and then we're alone again.

'Promise me you'll go see Shaun—'

He groans, running his hands down his thighs. 'Will you drop this if I promise?'

'Yes.'

'Then I promise I'll go see Shaun. I'll call him. And I won't run away from him if I see him outside the mechanic.' He throws me a look – salty and frustrated. *Are you happy now?*

'I don't believe you.'

'Christ.'

'You're going to cut that poor man out. All of you.'

He looks at his watch. 'How much longer is this going to take?' he says, then reads Josie's text again. 'If I knew this was going to be such a trigger for you, I wouldn't have said anything.'

And then both our phones light up with an alert. A new group chat has been created, by Emmanuel, titled *Have you heard?* There are five of us in it – Emmanuel, myself, Dave, Cinar, Diego.

Emmanuel: holy shit

Cinar: Cannot believe it

Emmanuel: saw it coming

Diego: You did not

> **Cinar**: Do we know what happened?
>
> **Emmanuel**: she's not answering her phone
>
> **Emmanuel**: we should see her

I turn to Dave. 'See? Picking sides.'

He rolls his eyes. 'We're not picking sides.' He punches out a message into the group.

> **David**: We should go see Shaun too. Has anyone heard from him?
>
> **Diego**: I wonder if Josie will keep the house
>
> **Emmanuel**: no way she's letting him stay there if he's left
>
> **Cinar**: How do we know he left
>
> **Emmanuel**: you don't remember the dinner party?

'Funny,' I say, leaning over Dave's phone. 'It almost looks like ... they've ignored you?'

He appears ashamed, not meeting my eye, his jaw hardening.

> **Cinar**: Still no answer from Josie. Hope she's okay
>
> **Diego**: Should we send something?
>
> **Emmanuel**: anyone got those recipes from when we cooked for dave?
>
> **Emmanuel**: sorry for the reminder, dave
>
> **Dave**: your cooking is shit, don't make that stuff for Josie

> **Emmanuel**: you cook then. now that your beard is gone and you're washing your clothes again

Dave is silent beside me, then puts his phone away. Group chat gone, all communication ceased. Too close to home, being reminded of that time. He might be in a better place – we might be communicating again – but it's still incredibly raw for both of us.

'They cooked for you?'

A moment's pause, and then Dave nods. 'Yeah.'

'But they're—'

'Terrible at it. I know.' He straightens, smiling. 'But I enjoyed the company. You?'

'I got nothing from them. No messages, no meals. Just an awful conversation at Josie's birthday, a string of accidental messages, and a coffee date where she tried to find out how things ended.'

He smiles. 'They tried with me too.'

'You didn't tell them about your daughter?'

He stills. 'No.'

'You ever will?'

He doesn't answer.

In my hand, the group chat continues to *ping*. Message after message, exchanging theories and stories. Talking about Josie like she's been attacked. Talking about Shaun like he's the suspect.

'You think they did this when we split?'

'Absolutely.'

I do not say anything in the group chat. Do not make a comment about Josie and Shaun, do not indulge them with an opinion on the split. Do not want anything to do with them and their nasty thoughts, their back and forth guesswork about the end of a marriage.

These people are not good people.

'We'll visit both,' Dave says, looking at me. 'But Josie first.'

'Okay,' I reply. 'Josie first.'

CHAPTER FIFTY-FIVE

Fuck Josie: I visit Shaun.

One week after my cast removal, still a little unsteady on my feet, I catch an Uber over to his new rental apartment, late morning, with a six-pack of beer.

Opening the door, his posture is stooped – shoulders sagging under his own weight – and his face etched with lines. His hair, short and blond and once neatly combed, is now streaked with grey. Face unshaven.

'Charlie.' He visibly relaxes, a weary smile breaking.

'Shaun.'

We come together in a hug, and the tension eases from his upper body.

'How are you?' he says, gesturing to my leg. Then, my arm.

I'm still regaining my strength, but I'm healing and the aches are subsiding and the itching long gone – it fills me with glee. 'It's like remembering how to walk again.' I kick out my right leg and jiggle my foot, as if showing him that everything is operational. Bit wobbly, but functional. 'You?'

He shrugs, arms slapping down against his sides. 'Oh, you know, surviving.' Then he opens the door wider. 'Come inside.'

Boxes are piled in the corner of the living room and paperwork is strewn across benchtops. It's a three-bedroom, two-bathroom rental on the ground floor, with a small concrete courtyard out the back. The place feels stripped bare, has that 'just moved in' vibe. No artwork, no photos, not even a cushion on the stock standard three-seater grey sofa.

He thanks me for coming. 'Didn't expect to hear from anyone.'

'You haven't heard from the others?'

'Just you,' he says. 'And Dave.'

'I'm sorry.'

He shrugs, gives me a *What are you gonna do?* look. 'I knew it'd happen.'

'Did you? I didn't.'

He smiles. 'I know,' he says. 'Thought you had balls, coming to Josie's fortieth.'

'She was my friend.'

With a double take, he looks at me when I say *was*, his expression unreadable.

'The kids?' I ask, looking around. There is evidence of them having been here – toys scattered, tiny shoes in the hallway, packet snacks on the kitchen counter.

'Josie picked them up this morning. We're trying to work out a roster.'

I drop my bag onto the kitchen table, pull out a stack of papers. Printed this morning, and stapled. I hand them to him.

He flicks through the pages, frowns.

'Recipes,' I explain. 'Ones my mother has sent me every day since she found out about me and Dave. They were a huge help. Thought I'd pass them on.'

Couldn't think of anything else, I want to say. *Wanted to help, but also knew you'd be fine on your own, in the end.*

There's a silence in the room, while he reads a few of them. Runs a finger down the ingredients. And as I take another glance around the room, I feel foolish. Shaun has two young children;

he knows how to take care of himself. He doesn't need my mother's recipes. He will think me an idiot.

'Thank you,' he says, and I realise he's teared up. His cheeks puffed, his lips a firm line, as he tries to hold in emotion. Like he's trying to make himself as small – as unnoticeable – as possible. 'You have no idea.'

He holds those pages with such a delicate touch, I feel compelled to tell him that I can forward them over email too.

A few minutes later, each of us nursing a beer, we're outside in his courtyard. Have sunk into a couple of durable, steel-framed black chairs. Shaun's legs are crossed, a hand resting on the cushion. He looks out over the courtyard, and then turns to me. 'Josie thought it would be contagious, you know.'

'When you left Dave,' he continues, 'she was acting like it was some kind of disease. "Don't stand too close." She wanted to find out what went wrong. Didn't want it happening to us.'

'She told you this?'

'Didn't need to.' He sips. 'Saw it on her face. In how she acted.'

'You know that's ridiculous, though, right? I'm not contagious.'

And suddenly, he's chuckling, head tipped back. Such a stark contrast to how he usually acts, it feels foreign to see it. It's been such a long time since I've witnessed him like this. A laugh that colourful, hidden.

'You should've seen her,' he says. 'These past few months. It was like we'd just met. She was pretending to be happy. She had this whole ruse going.'

But I'm not thinking of the ruse. Or how in love she wanted them to seem. I'm thinking of all the times she dismissed him, and how she spoke of his uselessness. How drunk she got at the dinner party. How easily she snapped at him.

'She was awful to you.'

He points at me, to correct. 'Only when she couldn't contain it.'

'Still not a good thing, Shaun.'

And he curls that finger back, tucks it behind a thumb, and retreats. Looks away, embarrassed.

'Are you okay?' I ask, and he nods.

'Don't you worry about me.'

'I think it's been a while since someone worried about you, Shaun.'

'I'm fine.'

'*Are you?*'

And he looks at me, and it's the most assured I've seen him since I arrived. 'I really, really am. I knew what would happen, when this ended. When *I* ended it.'

How did you know, and I didn't? I want to ask.

'I drove home from work last week,' he starts. 'And I parked outside the house. The house we'd worked *so* hard to buy. We'd spent years saving, and months looking. It was everything we both wanted. And I could hear the kids inside, these high-pitched screeches they do when they play. And I sat in my car. Just sat there, for almost twenty minutes. Because I didn't want to go inside. And I just knew.'

It sounds achingly familiar.

'That I needed to leave her.'

'Oh.'

'And I sat there for another fifteen minutes, and I just let myself enjoy what normality I had left, before I blew everything up. Looked at that house, and my wife's car in the driveway. Listened to my kids. Even ran a hand over that hedge out the front before I walked into the house. Last time, you know?'

'Right.'

'And then, later that night, after the kids were asleep, I drank half a bottle of wine and told Josie I didn't want to be married anymore.'

He sips, not meeting my eye. 'So, yeah, I'm fine. I knew what I was doing. I knew what was going to happen.'

He puts his beer down on the ground beside his feet, then extends a hand to me. Raises an eyebrow. *Your turn*, he's saying. And I realise I'm expected to share.

'I had no idea what was going to happen. I was an idiot.'

'You're not an idiot.'

'I was an idiot,' I repeat. 'Walked into that fortieth thinking everything would be the same.'

'Josie made me wear white pants that night.'

'I know,' I say. 'They didn't suit you.'

'They're in the bin now.'

'Where they should remain.'

He chuckles, and silence ensues. I *could* tell him about Dave's daughter. About what I found when he was in hospital. But telling someone that was the reason we split would be a lie. To him, and to myself.

Dave's daughter was my getaway car out of that relationship. Just like Dave was my getaway car out of my hometown.

'I fell out of love with him,' I say, and he looks at me. 'That's it, really. We weren't right for each other, and it took a long time to figure that out. And an even longer amount of time to do something about it.'

He nods, satisfied. And then takes a deep breath in, looking out at that courtyard again. And smiles.

I realise he's right. He's going to be perfectly fine.

'Do you need company? I'm seeing Quinn this weekend. You should come.'

He hides another smile. 'You starting a club for divorced people?'

'Why? You want to join?'

'I've got the kids this weekend, but thank you.' Then, checking the time, he makes a hissing noise. 'Christ, lunch time already.

You hungry?'

'I could cook? Let me see what Mum's sent today.'

But then I check my emails, and I scroll and I scroll and I scroll. Past the lawyer's emails and the spam emails. Past the sales alerts and the appointment reminders.

But there is nothing from my mother.

For the first time in almost six months, my mother has forgotten to send through a recipe.

CHAPTER FIFTY-SIX

Later that afternoon, just as I'm about to phone her, Mum rings. Very spooky, the timing. It's as if she knew. As if she had a sixth sense that I needed to speak with her.

Immediately, her voice booms through the phone. 'I've just spoken with Naya, and I'm very upset with you.'

'I'm upset with *you*.'

'You didn't tell me you were injured, Charlie.'

Immediately, I counter. 'And you didn't send through a recipe.' I'm back at Dave's, now, tidying the apartment. Collecting my things, getting ready to move out. And while I *should* be telling her about my fall, I feel the missing recipe is far more pressing.

'When?' Her voice softens, her anger halted.

'This morning. I've checked three times.'

'Well, that's not right,' she responds, confused. 'I scheduled it. There must be an error. I'll check it now and resend.'

'No, don't. I don't need it.' *I don't need it.* And with that, every ounce of my body that was helping hold in my emotions starts to splinter. In one, tumultuous, dramatic moment, everything completely breaks apart. I do not *need* my mother anymore, at least not in the same way. I feel healed, like everything that has been weighing me down has been shed from my body and I can finally move on. It is both freeing and terrifying.

'Are you crying? Oh no, Charlie. You're crying. Is it the recipe?'

'No.' Then, a moment later, 'Yes.' Walking into the spare bedroom, I sit down on the edge of the bed. Let my forehead rest in my hand.

'You want the recipe?'

'I don't need the recipe.'

'Oh. Okay.'

'I'm good. I'm okay without it. I gave them away today to someone who needed them and it felt good and then I saw there wasn't a new one and now I'm crying and I feel stupid. Just, pretend I'm not crying.'

'Okay.'

I hiccup, blink through a few tears. 'Tell me about him. Please.'

'About who?'

'Dad. Tell me about him. I don't remember what he sounded like. What he smelt like. I don't remember what his favourite movie was, or his most annoying habits. I've forgotten so many things about him.'

'Oh, Charlie.'

'He was a good person, right? I didn't just think that because I was young?'

'He was a *great* person.'

'He was happy?'

'*So* happy.' Clearing her throat, she continues. 'He loved making focaccia and pushing his fingers into the dough. When it rained, he'd stare out the window with a coffee and close his eyes, because he said it was one of his favourite sounds. The first time he heard you laugh, he cried. The first time he heard you cry, he smiled, because it meant you were healthy. And if you'd asked him, he would've said he didn't have a favourite movie. Because it changed every week, depending on his mood.' She pauses, for a moment. 'Charlie, I have *so* many of these. All you have to do is ask.'

'Okay,' I manage.

'And Charlie,' she starts.

'Yeah?'

'When we went to bed that night, he said he was a proud man.'

'A proud man?'

'Proud of you. And Naya. Proud of me. Happy, you know?'

'Oh, that's good. That's really good. I like hearing that.' I feel I might be glowing. I'm warm, and buzzy.

'You're going to be fine, Charlie.'

'I fell down an escalator.'

'I know.'

'Raphi didn't recognise me.'

'Raphi eats chalk.'

I laugh. Wipe my nose with the back of my hand. 'I miss you.'

'That just means you need to come home more often. This place isn't big enough for you, Charlie.'

I spent so many years avoiding home, and I'm *exhausted* by it all. I barely know my own family, and it disgusts me. Maybe I tried so hard to forget them because I felt guilty for leaving – for forging a career – or maybe it was guilt from not being home the night Dad died. There is so much there to unravel, and I feel I'm only at the beginning.

'I'll be home more.' And this time, when I say that, I actually mean it. 'I'm good at surviving,' I add.

'You are,' Mum says. 'You know why?'

'Because I get on with it?'

I am confident, in this moment, that she is smiling. 'Yes, exactly. Because you get on with it.'

CHAPTER FIFTY-SEVEN

On my final day in the apartment, Graham calls me from Morocco. His reception is patchy, and background noise loud – a collection of wind, beeping cars, distant chatter and birds squawking.

'I wanted to hear your voice,' he says. 'Wanted to check you're all right.'

'Did you get your hair transplant?'

'That's not an answer.' Pause. 'And no. Decided I don't need it.'

'Decided you couldn't be twenty-nine again?'

He laughs, inhales. 'No. Decided I'm fine without it. I'm old, and I look it.'

'Right.'

Muffled, he thanks someone. 'Just out for a drink. Will send you a picture.'

'Please don't.' I straighten. 'I'm packing right now. Wearing baggy slacks and an oversized shirt, and I'm arms deep in tape and flatpack boxes. You'll make me jealous.'

He is silent for a moment, and I worry he's dropped out. 'Hello?'

'I'm here.' He sips, says *ah*. Then continues. 'You told me I was running away.'

'What?'

'When I said I was leaving, you told me I was running away,' he replies. 'It was in the middle of your big speech about how I was being a whingey sook and needed to get over myself. Remember now?'

Ah. 'I do,' I say, sitting down on Dave's lilac couch, discarding the tape and the scissors on the coffee table. 'And?'

'And I'm in a tiny little city where everything is blue, and no one knows who I am and no one has seen that video and the weather is mild but crisp and I'm drinking mint tea, and I realised you were absolutely right. I've run away.'

'Sounds like a nice place to run away to.'

'Charlie, if you could see this place . . .'

'Are you coming home?' I ask. 'Is that what you've called to tell me?'

'No, I've called because I miss you,' he says. 'And to tell you that you were right.'

'I like being told I'm right.'

He chuckles. 'My body clock still has me waking at three, and I've got all this time to myself. Sometimes, at four o'clock in the morning, I imagine you're with me. I imagine we're in the kitchen and we're making a pot of coffee and we're talking about our lives.'

'Graham—'

'You're not blaming yourself, are you?'

The ratings. My stomach lurches.

'Because you shouldn't. I'm happy, Charlie. And when you go back to work tomorrow, you remember that.'

Tomorrow. My first shift back since the fall. New host, new ratings quarter. 'I will.'

'Good.'

'Are you going to listen? To the show?'

He laughs. 'Of course not.'

'But you'll be coming back, right?'

'At some point,' he says. 'Someone once told me my career isn't over, and I think they might be right.'

I smile.

'So, you're moving out,' he says. 'You found a place?'

'I did. Rental apartment across town.'

'With who?'

I look at the boxes and shake my head. 'No one. I'll be living alone.'

'Good for you.'

CHAPTER FIFTY-EIGHT

'You know, this is the second time you've packed up and left this apartment.'

Dave says it like it is genuinely the first time he's realised. As if, seeing the taped boxes at my feet, he's the only one here to join the dots. Like he's pointing out something funny that I haven't yet noticed.

'Far less of it this time,' I say, looking down at it all. A few boxes and two bags of toiletries. Some medications. Leftover food he's not going to eat.

'Still,' he says. 'I'm getting déjà vu.' His smile is forced, and he cannot look me in the eye.

Moments like this, I feel genuinely sad about everything that's occurred. Something that could've been great – that could've lasted – has crumbled and we're off now. On our own. Ten years, and we're saying goodbye once again. It takes a lot to push that down, cast it aside. To tell myself, *Hey, you did nothing wrong.*

'Maybe you'll roll an ankle or sprain your wrist,' he says, musing. 'And you'll call me again.'

'Do you want me to call you?'

'No, that would be strange. I don't really know what I'm saying.'

His incoherence is quite the challenge this morning, but I sympathise with the jumble in his mind. All that time with someone, gone. 'I had to update my emergency contact on some forms this morning, and it was a strange feeling.'

And then he laughs. An open-mouth chuckle, kind of dopey. 'I should apologise for something before you leave, actually.'

'Oh?'

'I lied to you, before. I already knew you lost the engagement ring.' Shuffles his feet along the ground. 'Didn't know *how* you lost it, but knew it was gone.'

I baulk. Step closer. 'For how long?'

'Like, the whole time.'

'*The whole time?*'

'Yeah.' Then he puts one hand on his hip. 'Were you ever going to tell me you lost it?'

'No.'

'Really?' His eyes widen, his chin lowering. 'Shit.'

Remembering all of his text messages, and all the emails from my lawyer, I frown. His anger, just a few weeks ago, when I told him and he acted shocked. 'You *knew*, this whole time.'

He attempts to explain. 'I realise how cruel I was being, and I'm not proud of it. After you lost it, I waited ages for you to tell me what happened, but you never did.' He leans against the wall, one leg tucked behind the other. 'Figured you were embarrassed, so I never said anything. And then when you left, I was so upset I asked about it just to make you feel guilty. Told the lawyers I wanted it back just to reach a settlement. I wanted to see what you'd do.'

'I thought you just wanted to see me again.'

'No, I was angry at you.' He looks away. 'You left me because of something that happened before we were even together.'

'I left you because I didn't love you anymore.'

And suddenly, the apartment is painfully silent.

'Oh.'

'Sometimes there doesn't have to be a reason,' I say. 'We were good together, and then we weren't.'

'But you made it about the girl.'

'Your daughter.'

Pause, and then he exhales. 'Yeah, my daughter.'

The way he's looking at me tells me he's expecting some kind of explanation.

'I could never do what you did.'

He bites his bottom lip. 'Good to know, thanks.' And then, folding his arms across his chest, he meets my eye. 'How long had you fallen out of love with me?'

I choose to ignore the question. 'You seriously knew I'd lost the ring? I tormented myself for months over that! You should've said something. Sometimes I think I've seen the worst in you and then you somehow top it.'

A flash of guilt crosses his face, and then he steps closer. His chin tilts an inch to the right. 'Charlie, how long had you fallen out of love with me?'

I let out an exhausted sigh. 'A while.'

'Before the wedding?'

'I don't know.' But I do know. *Yes, before the wedding, and I married you because I didn't know how to walk away. Because I thought we'd be fine, and we weren't.*

He's in pain, I think, but he's also accepting it. All these months and he seems to understand now that we did the best we could do. We are both at fault here, and I cannot continue blaming Dave when I am equally responsible.

He's quite the aggressive nodder when he's coming to terms with something.

'Right, well, okay. Shit, I guess.' He lets an arm fall down by his side. The other, running through his hair. 'When you told me about the ring, you asked if I thought we would've split eventually. Said if it weren't for the girl, that it would've ended on its own.'

'And?'

'You're probably right. As much as it pains me to admit.' He looks up at me. 'But it would've been you. Leaving. It always would've been you. I could never.'

When we hear a truck horn downstairs, we know my removalist has arrived. That we're parting, now. Him, off to see Josie, Cinar, Emmanuel and Diego. Me, moving into my new rental, then dinner with Quinn.

'Thank you,' I say. Wave my hands around the apartment. 'For all this.'

He says nothing, but his lips pinch upwards into a smile.

'You're the only one who—'

'I'm not,' he says. 'I'm not the only one. You've got Quinn. And Genevieve. Graham, and your work friends. And my friends, if you'd have them back.'

'I wouldn't,' I say. 'But I get what you mean.'

He smiles, looks down.

'Your friends aren't very good friends.'

From my front pocket, I pull out Dave's spare key. Drop it into his open palm. Watch as his fingers close over it, fastened firmly in his grasp.

He shrugs. 'I know. But what can I say? I love them.'

EPILOGUE

Bruce, nestling a takeaway coffee in his hands and looking tired in the eyes, meets me outside the hospital room. 'Charlie, you made it.'

Even out here, he's whispering. And it's clear he's a mix of both exhausted and happy, so when he starts tearing up, I'm not sure if I'm meant to console or congratulate.

'I'm a *dad*, Charlie.'

'Oh, Bruce.' Juggling flowers and gifts, I pull him in for a hug. On my shoulder rests an overnight bag and I let it *plonk* down on the tiled corridor floor. 'You're a dad.'

'I can't tell if she's tiny or I'm just big.'

'Both.'

When he chuckles, my body vibrates. I pull away and brush aside a piece of hair from in front of my eyes. 'How is she? How are they both?'

'Good, they're good.' He nods. 'Genevieve's going to be so excited to see you. Maybe more excited than when she met our daughter.' Immediately, he corrects himself. 'That was a joke. You've definitely been knocked down to the second spot. Sorry.'

'Third.' I hold out my hand to mark the hierarchy. 'Baby, Bruce, then me.'

'Oh, Charlie,' he says, laughing. 'You've always been above me. I could only *dream* of her loving me more than you.'

And now we're both crying.

'Genevieve is a *mum*,' I say. 'Holy shit.'

'I know.'

I was finally cleared to fly and it's coincided with Genevieve giving birth. Someone, somewhere, is looking out for us. And we're making up for lost time, like we promised. Regular messages, phone calls during the week. But also, being happy for each other. Accepting that our lives have diverged, will continue to diverge, but knowing we'll make time for one another. I spent so much time trying to replace her when I really just needed to understand how I could keep her in my life, in a different way. That she could never be replaced.

'You want to head in?' he asks. 'I'll grab your bag.'

Crouching, he grabs at the handle and throws the duffel over his shoulder. Gestures to the hospital door, signalling he'll follow.

'Thank you.'

Inside, their hospital room is already filled with scores of flowers, boxes of chocolates and sweets, congratulatory cards and balloons.

Angling around the corner, we lock eyes. Genevieve and me. She's wired, I can tell, and maybe a little strung out. Hair brushed but greasy and pulled back into a low bun. Face pale. But she's looking at me like she's been waiting for me. For this moment. Expectant and thrilled, with a huge grin.

We share a smile, and then she looks down at the bundle in her arms and raises it a little. Rotates so I can see the face. A tiny, plump, sleeping face. She's beautiful.

Bruce takes everything from my hands – the gifts, the flowers, my handbag – without me even asking. Suddenly, I'm not carrying anything. Suddenly, I'm by Genevieve's side. Looking down at this pink-nosed, sleeping baby. Watching as her chest rises and falls.

'She's actually here,' Genevieve says, and then she's crying. Well, crying but trying not to cry because she's trying not to wake the baby. 'She's here. And she's alive.'

'She's gorgeous.' I look back at Bruce, who is smiling, and whisper to both of them. 'Congratulations.'

'How are you?' she asks.

'Who cares about me – I'm fine.' Better than fine. Like weight has been removed from my shoulders, like I've cast aside everything that's plagued me from the past twenty years and stepped forward towards something healthier.

I live alone and I'm happy. And it's still a surprise to reflect on that, because I feel like I'd conditioned my body to wince and cringe at the idea of being alone. For so long my brain thought there was something impossible about all that. How utterly ridiculous, now that I'm out the other side.

Genevieve grabs my hand. Squeezes. 'Charlie, she's *here*. She made it.' Then, laughing, she adds, 'I'm still so terrified.'

'You're going to be *great*.'

Genevieve rotates the baby once more, tucks her inside her arm so she's facing me. She's still asleep, but I reach out and grab her tiny hand. Let her whole hand close around my index finger.

'Charlie,' Genevieve says, looking down at my goddaughter. 'Meet—'

ACKNOWLEDGEMENTS

Once again, I owe an immense thank you to an enormous number of people who helped me along this journey.

Second book syndrome is very real and I'm not sure this book would have been published if it weren't for the following people. I stumbled more times than I can count. When I set out to write my second novel, I knew I wanted to explore adult friendships – how important they are, yes, but also how difficult they can be to make and maintain. It took many false starts to finesse the plot and the characters, and many months of writing (and re-writing) between the first draft and the last.

Firstly, as always, to my agent Caitlan Cooper-Trent at Curtis Brown Australia, who has always been my biggest supporter and cheerleader, and a fantastic sounding board. I will be forever grateful that you plucked me from the slush pile in 2022.

To Penguin Random House Australia – publisher Ali Watts, editors Shané Oosthuizen and Jodie Ramodien, Tanaya Lowden and Grace Howe in marketing and publicity, and the rest of the team – thank you for the endless support. Your guidance, expertise, incredible attention to detail and unwavering dedication to the book means the world to me. To the sales reps and the booksellers, and to Nikki Townsend for another beautiful cover, thank you.

In 2023, I was fortunate to spend one week working on the first draft of this book at Varuna, The National Writers' House in the

Blue Mountains. A huge thank you to Varuna for granting me the much-needed solitude to power through the manuscript.

There's nothing quite like the encouragement of other writers to keep you on task, so a huge thank you to fellow members of the Very Tired Writers group – Alli Parker, Genevieve Novak, Clare Fletcher, Jess Kirkness, Ash Goldberg, Ross Healy and Kait Newell – for your feedback, your guidance, your industry gossip and your company. I adore all of you. Our fortnightly calls have been one of the highlights of my publishing journey.

Thank you to Claire Houston for the sensitivity read of part three – your feedback and insight was invaluable to ensure authenticity in the story.

To all the writers who provided lovely endorsement quotes for the novel – Amy Lovat, Natalie Murray, Clare Fletcher, Michelle Upton, Karina May and Bridget Hustwaite: your support means the world. To the readers, far and wide, who were so encouraging and delightful about *Perfect-ish* and who said such lovely things about my writing: thank you for the messages, the reviews and the recommendations. I hope you love this one just as much.

To my family, for the support, the encouragement and the pre-orders. As always, any similarities between you and these characters are purely coincidental.

For Tim, who might just be the most patient man I know. And supportive. And encouraging. And selfless. I love you. And for Boof, who might be older and wiser but still just as needy. He couldn't care less that I'm an author unless it interferes with dinner time, but he's been a best friend to Tim and me for the past seven years, and a loyal, loving companion.

And finally, my friends, particularly those I've been lucky to meet since my move to Sydney. An interstate move is, at times, a very lonely experience, and I can never express how grateful I am for all of you. You know who you are, and what can I say – I love you.

© Hugh Stewart

Born and raised in Brisbane, Jessica Seaborn lives in Sydney and works as a television and film publicist at Stan. Prior to this, she worked at SBS, Allen & Unwin and HarperCollins. Her writing has been published in the *Sydney Morning Herald*, *Sunday Life*, the *Daily Telegraph* and *Body & Soul*. In 2020, she was accepted into Curtis Brown Creative where she completed the first draft of her debut novel, *Perfect-ish*, which was published by Penguin Random House Australia in 2023. She lives in Western Sydney with her partner and a 50 kg bull mastiff named Boof. *Isn't It Nice We Both Hate the Same Things* is her second novel.

A smart, funny and heartfelt anti-romcom by a bright new voice in Australian fiction.

Prue is about to turn thirty and feels like everyone else is living their best life. Her friends are posting online about their amazing relationships, exciting travel plans and newborn babies. Prue, on the other hand, has been dumped by her fiancé, she's dropped out of uni, and her job counselling lonely people only makes her feel more alone.

With the help of her best friend, Delia, Prue sets three goals to turn her life around before her milestone birthday: ditch the job, move out of her brother's house, and find love.

But when Delia's perfect marriage begins to crack, and a secret threatens to shatter their friendship, Prue realises there's a difference between seeming to have a perfect life and finding your own perfect-ish life. And maybe being far from picture perfect is perfectly okay.

'Fans of Emily Henry and Genevieve Novak will enjoy this fast-paced and funny Australian debut about ignoring society's expectations and finding your own kind of perfect.'
—*Readings*

'Crisp, funny and fast-paced, *Perfect-ish* is an all-too-familiar portrait of a woman in crisis. Jess Seaborn's writing is a warm hug from the first page to the last.'
—Genevieve Novak

Powered by Penguin

Looking for more great reads, exclusive content and book giveaways?

Subscribe to our weekly newsletter.

Scan the QR code or visit penguin.com.au/signup